THE

HELL ON EARTH

ROBERT T.C. ROONEY

GOOD VS EVIL

www.facebook.com/GoodVsEvil2059

This paperback edition 2020

First published in Great Britain by Amazon Publishing in 2020

ISBN: 9798669130480

Foreword

Thank you for purchasing this book. If you have previously read my original scripts:

"Good Vs Evil: The Complete Collection"

You will have a great idea what this story is about. If you haven't, strap in.

This is going to be one hell of a story and I invite you to join me on this adventure.

Michael Hartnell slowly became an idea over the course of 2009, my first year whilst I trained to become an actor. By the end of that year, I had written three short stories for the character.

Originally, I believed this would be the conclusion for Michael. I didn't think that I would ever write for him again. How wrong I was!

I am glad I kept on writing for him and these extraordinary characters. I ended up writing twenty short stories and had planned to write more.

The original collection was written in script form and I soon realised not a lot of readers know how scripts work. So these new ideas for short stories became the foundations for what you now hold in your hands.

This is my first stab at a novel. I know I am not the greatest writer ever and chances are, I probably never will be. Apologies in advance for grammar mistakes.

Follow Michael Hartnell throughout this incredible story.

I may not be the best writer to ever live but what I can promise you is this.

This will be the story of a lifetime!

Robert T.C. Rooney

For Thomas,

My DaRooney

One of the greatest men I ever knew

PROLOGUE

The Angel Nejuma

The sun shone ever so bright. It was a warm and beautiful day. The angel, Nejuma seized a moment to himself to take in this day as he began his ascent up the mountain.

The young angel knew his journey could be over swiftly if he used his wings and flew to the top of the mountain.

Despite this and time of the essence, he enjoyed walking the winding paths which reached the peak of this enormous mountain.

Nejuma had been summoned by his father, the creator, God Almighty.

The angel stared with content from the mountain path over most of his home. A magnificent valley stretching for miles in every direction. He liked the trees and rivers flowing all the way to the ocean and the beach.

Nejuma couldn't see the city where all the angels and human spirits called home. His home is a paradise for this is Heaven.

Nejuma always knew his home would one day become the afterlife for all life on the Earth. The scenery of his father's creation still amazed him, he never tired of its marvel.

He feared this may be the last time he ever laid eyes upon his home.

No angel had been summoned or even seen God since "The Fall".

A terrible day, all angels prayed they could rip the memories from their minds and at the same time, the memory served as a reminder of their father's justice.

Nejuma continued his journey on foot to God's temple, the extraordinary building was at the very peak of the mountain. This was the creator's domain and Nejuma best not keep him waiting.

Nejuma appreciated the breeze on his face from the heat of the warm sunny day. He had removed his silver armour and went before his father dressed in a smart brown pinstriped suit with a brown trench coat.

He briefly stopped further up the path to stare at the sun in amazement. Nejuma truly was in awe of his father's creations.

God had created Heaven's sun so bright and powerful, its light shone upon his creations on the planet Earth.

Nejuma resumed his walk. He began to wonder what his father needed of him. No angel had set foot on the Earth for decades.

The thought of going to Earth filled Nejuma with a fear, he dared not speak of, or wish to show any sign of in the presence of God.

After several hours, Nejuma reached the temple. Very few angels had ever looked upon the temple with their own eyes.

It was enormous and beautiful. Nejuma stared at its beauty and as he did, the angel noticed the white colour of its exterior change in the sunlight.

Those few who had ever seen the temple often spoke of how it was similar to a structure on Earth called the Taj Mahal.

Nejuma's eye caught sight of a figure standing at the edge of the mountain, the figure stood gazing upon all of Heaven.

This was not his father. In the absence of God Almighty, he was to be treated as though he were.

Nejuma approached the lord. He was difficult to look upon as the blinding sunlight covered him from view.

Nejuma bowed to the figure and addressed him as "My lord".

The sun lit figure turned and faced the angel.

"Rise" he spoke to Nejuma.

Nejuma rose to his feet. He was having difficulty to look his lord in the face from the intensity of the sun glares. Nejuma felt his eyes squint as he stared at his lord.

"Our Father is currently occupied and has tasked myself with bestowing to you the position of Guardian." The lord spoke in a celebratory tone.

Nejuma is taken aback by the honour of the position and feels overwhelmed by this. He also began to feel concerned in the same moment. This position wasn't given out to any angel.

God had something which he believed only Nejuma could accomplish.

2

"My lord, I am grateful... I do not wish to challenge the decisions of our father... But... is it wise for I, to become a guardian angel? Especially with the role I played in...

Nejuma was interrupted as the figure spoke across him.

"Who you were. Need not matter. For God's will, is for who you have become" The lord reassured Nejuma.

Nejuma calmed himself, knowing his father's wisdom was just.

"Whose guardian am I to be?" Nejuma asked his lord.

"A young boy in Glasgow in the year 2009" his lord replied.

Nejuma felt any concern leave his body as soon he heard the knowledge of when he would meet the boy.

"Do you accept the position, God, our father has bestowed upon you, Brother Nejuma?" The lord asked for Nejuma's agreement.

"I swear upon my life, Heaven and God to fulfil the responsibilities of Guardian from this day forth. I will protect the boy even at the cost of my own life. I swear to God." Nejuma swore his oath to the lord.

"You are now a guardian angel, Brother Nejuma" his lord addressed him.

Nejuma knew the honour of holding the rank of Guardian, very few angels held it and he was responsible for the safety of this young boy from 2009. Should the young man wish to have descendants, Nejuma would also be their guardian.

This is one of the highest honours to be bestowed upon an angel. The highest being: Archangel.

Nejuma addressed his lord who was still hidden in the blinding sunlight.

"My lord, with your permission. I will begin my duties with immediate effect. I will travel back through time to meet the boy".

"You will not be travelling to 2009, Brother Nejuma" his lord calmly responded.

Nejuma became filled with worry and dreaded the answer to his next question.

"If not 2009? Where and when is the boy?"

Nejuma trembled with fear and attempted to conceal his shaking from the lord.

The moment Nejuma had spoken, his lord would surely have heard the concern in his voice.

"You will travel to Glasgow, December 22nd 2059" his lord informed him.

Nejuma could no longer contain his fear and spoke his mind to the lord.

"My lord, no angel has gone there… They fear even to speak of it. For he is…"

The lord interrupts Nejuma.

"We are all aware of what is happening in 2059. God's plan involves you and this boy's role will bring an end to everything Heaven fears… He will come for the boy and he will need protecting until he is ready."

Nejuma was surprised, he would be a liar if he claimed to not be scared. He had complete faith in his lord and their father, God.

"What is the boy's name?" Nejuma asked.

The figure cloaked in sunlight, stepped forward out of the blinding glares. Nejuma saw his lord fully.

He was tall with long brown hair and beard, dressed in white robes.

This was The Son of God.

"Michael Hartnell" spoke The Lord Jesus Christ.

CHAPTER ONE

MICHAEL HARTNELL
APARTMENT 3B
CROWWOOD STREET
GLASGOW

DECEMBER 22ND 2009

9:43pm

Christmas. Michael always loved Christmas, a time to be grateful for all you possessed and be with loved ones.

This year would be different, it was the first year without his parents as they had decided to go abroad for the holidays.

It was also the first year he was celebrating as a husband. He married his childhood sweetheart in the summer. Michael loves his wife, Sarah more than life itself. It was a small wedding with family and a few friends. They decided not to go anywhere for a honeymoon. They wished to focus on their studies before returning to university.

Michael was nineteen years old and Sarah, a year older.

Three days before Christmas. They spent the day Christmas shopping. They had only been home for half an hour. It was time to do the one thing Michael loathed with a vengeance: wrapping presents!

"I still don't see why we must wrap everything tonight!" Michael complained with boredom.

He was bored out of his skull.

"It gets them done and out of the way. Giving us something to look forward to. Stop being a Grinch!" Sarah replied with amusement.

"Grinch?! I love Christmas. I only prefer to sort everything the night before!" Michael wasn't kidding. He always left everything to the last minute.

"If I allowed that. You would be running about the shops on Christmas Eve with all the other panic merchants!" Sarah scoffed in disbelief at the thought.

Michael laughs at his wife's comment.

"It's my tradition. Dad and I do it every year. We find good bargains… Oh, and a free black eye!" Michael joked.

Sarah smiles at her husband's attempt at humour. She momentarily stops wrapping up a present and leans over to give Michael, a loving kiss.

"I love you, Michael Hartnell." She told him with a smile and eyes filled with love.

Michael knew she did. He felt exactly the same way about her.

"I know. I love you too… How did I ever get so lucky?" Michael asked her.

Sarah giggled like a nervous high school girl.

"Could ask you the same. It was meant to be. God is good to our family." Sarah responded with happiness.

Michael and Sarah continued to wrap gifts for family members for another hour before becoming tired. They spent the rest of their evening, devouring sweets and watching a Christmas film on the TV.

Michael felt content with his life, he knew everything God did was good. He was grateful for his wife, family, home, even his university course.

The course was stressful at the best of times, he knew God would be there to guide him through it. Michael had been a Christian all the days of his life, his parents had raised him with their beliefs.

That was how he and Sarah met. They were only children.

Boyfriend and girlfriend since they were six years old.

Sarah's friends had often mentioned how they thought it was sweet.

Michael's friends were completely different. He always chalked it up to be a guy thing. Most had commented on their relationship. One of Michael's friends had always jokingly said "I'm surprised you're not sick of each other!".

It always made Michael laugh.

He would never be sick of Sarah, his beautiful bride, the love of his life and one day soon, the mother of his children.

Michael always appreciated everything he had and felt at peace knowing God was planning exciting times for their future.

A few years, Michael and Sarah will graduate from university and be in their dream professions.

Hopefully soon after, they will be ready to extend their family.

Life is good and nothing was going to get in the way.

The night flew away from them, tiredness hit them suddenly.

All the excitement of Christmas had taken its toll on them.

Michael and Sarah loved this time of the year. It was an awful lot of work for one day. Michael wondered how his parents had coped all these years.

He laughed at the thought of his parents organising Christmas day for the last eighteen years.

He knew he was the grown-up. He thought how old he was and at the same time, how young he and Sarah were.

Michael prepared himself for bed, he brushed his teeth in his bathroom, Sarah by his side, doing the same.

He dribbled toothpaste all over his chin and was oblivious to having done so. Sarah noticed and gently used a damp face cloth to lovingly wipe his face.

Michael always loved Sarah's smile. She had a great one. Beautiful white teeth. He always wanted to kiss her.

They shared a kiss before leaving the bathroom and heading to bed.

Michael sorted his pyjamas. Proper pyjamas, he always thought of sleeping in only his underwear as a pet hate.

Sarah always called them his "Harry Potter" pyjamas. They were old fashioned. Michael joked Sarah was a tomboy. She always slept wearing a t-shirt, usually one of his, a pair of pyjama trousers and in the rare occasions when it was colder outside, she wore a hoodie to bed.

They enjoyed cracking jokes about each other.

The bedroom was lit by one of the bedside lamps on Michael's side of the bed, it was resting upon a bedside cabinet.

7

Half the room was filled with cardboard boxes, full of their belongings which they were yet to sort. They were still taking their time moving in and would finally have time to deal with everything over the holidays.

Michael gave Sarah a goodnight kiss once he climbed into bed beside her. Michael reached for the lamp on the cabinet and switched it off, the room was engulfed in darkness.

Michael cuddled Sarah in bed.

Within in minutes, he was dead to the world, fast asleep, dreaming of his future with Sarah and his family.

He felt older, Michael knew he was older in his dream. Not that he realised this was a dream. No-one ever does in the moment, seeing Sarah holding a child in her arms, her red hair was longer than he had ever seen it in a long time.

He felt proud and unworthy of the beautiful woman who was his wife.

His dream turned. He could hear dogs barking somewhere. They had to be big dogs with barks so loud.

It was a rather unusual bark, it was not like anything he had heard before. The sound filled him with terror as he realised, he had been dreaming and it was transforming into a nightmare.

His pyjamas began to stick to his skin from sweat pouring from him. Michael screwed his eyes shut, he dared not open them.

Michael couldn't remember the last time he experienced a night terror. He struggled to remember how to calm down.

A blood-curdling scream finally awoken him. Michael bolted upright, covered from head to toe in sweat, panting in terror. He was fully awake and something was horribly wrong.

Michael was outside. He was no longer in bed beside Sarah.

He was sitting in an empty street in the middle of the night, the houses all along this street were in ruin, smashed windows and collapsed roofs.

Michael believed he was still dreaming. The sound of vicious dogs nearby kept him alert. It was so dark, he couldn't see where the dogs were. He prayed they didn't see him.

Michael came to the terrifying conclusion, he wasn't sleeping. As he looked upon the ruined houses, he realised, the street was also in ruin. Broken glass, rubbish and burnt out cars were everywhere.

Michael slowly got to his feet, avoiding stepping on any broken glass.

He inadvertently stepped on something. His bare foot slipped on something causing him to fall flat onto his back.

He landed on something which felt soft, he hadn't fell straight onto concrete. Whatever it was, it had broken his fall. What was it? Whatever was, it did not smell very pleasant.

It wasn't until he had gotten to his feet that he actually saw what it was.

Michael's stomach couldn't contain what his eyes seen. It disturbed him.

He vomited at the sight of dozens of decaying mangled corpses littering the street behind him.

Michael felt his heart beating in his chest, it was so fast, he thought his chest might explode.

In the distance, his eyes caught sight of the city of Glasgow, his home.

It was in ruin and several buildings were on fire.

Michael collapsed to his knees in horror.

CHAPTER TWO

MICHAEL HARTNELL
RUINED STREET
GLASGOW

Michael stood in his pyjamas, barefoot, staring in horror at the sight before him.

A Glasgow street in ruin, littered with dead bodies.

Michael couldn't believe this. What had happened to these poor people? Who would do this? The thought of who filled Michael with fear. His heart raced so hard, he felt his pulse in the back of his throat.

He called out as he knew there had to be someone nearby. Someone who was every bit as terrified if not more than he was.

"Hello! Is anybody out there?! Hello! HELLO!" Michael called out, he heard and felt the panic in his voice as he called out.

Dogs barking nearby scared him. Michael jumped with fright when he heard the same human scream from his dream.

Michael began to wonder. Could he still be dreaming?

He screwed his eyes shut. His eyelids were closed so tight it hurt. Michael pictured waking up in his bed beside Sarah before the thought of opening his eyes occurred.

For what felt like an eternity, upon opening his eyes, Michael saw the ruined street he was on and broke down, sobbing hysterically in the middle of the road, dead bodies only inches away from him.

He caught sight of the sky above him, it was cloudy, not a star to be seen. Michael briefly thought it may rain, it did and not in the way he was accustomed to, no water fell from the sky.

It was raining fire.

Michael narrowly missed fire landing on his clothing. He stared at the sky in confusion. His mind could not make sense of this. A terrible thought crossed his mind, he had died in his sleep and this was Hell!

He sobbed so much more, Michael didn't understand how or why he could have died. He was nineteen years old, a Christian all his life and never committed any sins, not so much as a white lie. How was he in Hell?

Sarah… She would be devastated. A widow at twenty years old! The thought of never laying eyes on her for eternity, filled Michael with a sadness he never knew he could feel.

Michael refused to accept his fate, he wiped the tears from his face, sat himself upright. Michael put his hands together and closed his eyes to begin a prayer.

"Father God, I pray to you for forgiveness for I do not understand my being here, in Hell of all places. I pray for forgiveness for any sins I may have committed in my life, I seek your mercy, I will do anything to be free of here and return to Sarah… I am so sorry… I will do anything… Amen."

Michael sobbed hysterically at the prospect of never seeing Sarah again. He closed his eyes for the briefest of moments as he cried.

"You are not in Hell." A voice from behind Michael spoke.

On impulse, Michael launched himself up on to his feet to see who was speaking to him. Michael stared at the man, he felt the man looked out of place. The man wore smart clothes, he looked like a businessman. He was wearing a brown pinstriped suit and trousers, black leather shoes and a brown trench coat, the jacket was unbuttoned.

Michael was baffled by this man, where had he come from? Was this God? Had he come to answer Michael's prayer personally? Don't be ridiculous, Michael told himself.

"Who are you?" Michael asked, the fear still lingered on every word he spoke.

The man in the suit answered him.

"My name is Nejuma. I am an angel of the lord."

Michael sniggered upon hearing this. Despite his beliefs, he knew this had to a wild dream. This could not be real.

"This is a dream! Wake up, Michael! Wake up!" Michael spoke out loud, nothing happened. He still stood in a destroyed street with a man who claimed to be an angel.

"Who are you?! What is this?!" Michael asked. He didn't like not knowing and wasn't sure if he really wanted to.

"The future." Nejuma responded in a calm manner.

Michael laughed at hearing this. It was far-fetched.

"The future? It's 2009... Time travel is... It's impossible!" Michael couldn't wrap his mind around what he was being told. This wasn't true. It couldn't be.

"You were not brought here by any form of science created by your people. Something else has brought you here. God has sent me to return you to your own time period. This is not 2009." Nejuma answered Michael in his calm tone, he didn't seem fazed by the situation.

It was at this point, Michael recognised, Nejuma spoke with a Scottish accent.

Despite being a Christian, Michael knew to ask for proof instead of having faith went against what he believed. This tested his beliefs, he needed to know the truth.

"I don't believe you. You've got a Scottish accent! If you're an angel! Prove it!" Michael demanded of the stranger.

Nejuma, without speaking or a second's hesitation, removed his trench coat, letting it fall to the concrete of the road in a heap. Michael gasped as he stared in shock at Nejuma's wings, enormous in size and covered in white feathers.

The angel extended his wings out fully to allow Michael to witness the beauty and magnificence of his angelic form.

Without blinking, Michael stared at Nejuma's wings in amazement and with fear.

"Michael, I am your guardian angel. This is not 2009. This is December 22nd 2059. This world is extremely dangerous. Most angels fear to come here. You must return with me to 2009. You have no clue as to the dangers lurking..." Nejuma ceased speaking, blood sprayed from his mouth.

Michael was taken aback by this until he saw the edge of a knife emerge from Nejuma's chest.

The angel had been stabbed from behind with such ferocity, the blade plunged through his entire body.

Michael screamed in terror as the knife was removed from Nejuma, his lifeless body slumped to the road.

He was unable to see who had killed Nejuma. In the darkness, Michael saw something which made him feel sick, whatever it was, he had never seen the like before. It was bony and skeletal.

Suddenly, what looked like two red eyes, lit up in the darkness several feet from where Michael stood.

This filled Michael with a fear he had never experienced before and it was enough to kick in his instincts, forcing him to flee the street.

His heart was beating faster than ever, he ran barefoot through the destruction of the street, cutting his soles on broken glass and whatever else was sharp enough to pierce the skin of his feet.

It hardly mattered for the man with red eyes was a good reason to forget any pain he would endure to escape his clutches. Michael's head filled with questions despite running to save himself.

Who was this man? How could he kill an angel with a knife? Michael's fear kept his senses sharp, he had gotten a good head start of the killer.

Michael saw an alleyway leading off the street, it was in between two ruined houses, Michael swiftly looked over his shoulder.

There was no sign of "Red Eyes". Michael took advantage of the opportunity and sped towards to the alley. It was wet and muddy. He instantly felt the cold bite his feet and work its way up his legs as his pyjama trousers were soaked from puddles which had filled potholes from the road in the alley.

Michael couldn't see a thing. It was so dark without streetlights or fires from the streets to light his way. Michael struggled to breathe, he had sprinted faster than he'd ever done before. Michael slumped against a wall in the alley, he was far down it. He looked back at the street, he could only just make it out.

Michael struggled to catch his breath from all the running and the terror of what he witnessed. Michael had never seen anyone die before let alone murdered!

What could kill an angel? As he tried to catch his breath, Michael began to question not what could kill an angel, but who and why?

As the thought ran through his mind, he instantly stopped his breathing. At the end of the alley, on the street he escaped from was the killer, his red eyes glanced up the alley.

Michael with all his strength, became as a still as statue and as silent as a ghost.

Red Eyes turned his attention away from the alley, he muttered something to himself. The killer appeared to be cleaning his knife.

The knife had been used to murder the angel, Nejuma.

Michael kept his focus on Red Eyes, preparing to run if he needed to.

Red Eyes suddenly burst into flames, Michael was confused as to what was going on. The fires died in an instant and Red Eyes was nowhere to be seen.

Where did he go? Had Red Eyes spontaneously combusted? Michael wondered why he cared, Michael understood, Red Eyes was gone. Michael was safer than he had been.

Michael had a bit of time to himself to reflect on what had occurred. He was seated on the ground, leaning against a wall in the alley, breathless.

He decided to try and rest up, restore his energy before considering what to do next.

Michael's peace was shattered the second he decided to rest.

He wasn't alone.

There was someone or something… Behind him!

He couldn't bring himself to turn his head and find out.

Whatever it was, it was growling. It didn't sound like any animal he knew. Michael heard footsteps behind him, getting closer and closer. Was it human?

Frozen in horror, Michael couldn't move as he realised the person was directly behind him. Every hair on the back of his neck stood erect. He felt someone's breath.

Michael slowly turned his head, what he saw, got his heart racing, he felt his pulse throughout his entire body and thought he was about to have a heart attack.

The face was human, whiter than any he had seen in his life. Blood was gushing from the man's mouth as he smiled at Michael in a way which made him feel uneasy.

The man let out a blood-curdling scream as Michael looked upon his face. This was the scream he had heard.

He didn't wait to find out what was to happen next. He sprinted out of the alley, back onto the street. The man was charging after Michael.

"Hurry up! I've found a norm!" Shouted the man.

Michael continued to escape along the damaged street.

Who was the man shouting to and what was a "norm"? Michael had no desire to discover the answer to either. He continued to run the length of the street, the man was still in pursuit of Michael.

"Hurry up, you fucking wasters! He's getting away!" The man called out as he was closer to Michael.

Michael could no longer help himself, he was turning his head, every second, men with white faces and blood-soaked mouths were running alongside the man from the alley. He watched in terror as several charged out of some of the ruined houses on the street.

All of them were being led by the alley man. Michael knew they outnumbered him. There were at least a dozen. He was not about to stop and find out why they were after him.

Michael suddenly lost his footing and tripped. He collided with the road, faster than he realised. His hands and knees stung from the force of the fall. Before he was able to get back on his feet, the man from the alley grabbed Michael and flipped him onto his back.

The man screamed in Michael's face whilst he lay defenceless on the road. The white face freaked him out, the blood-filled smile made his skin crawl.

"Hurry up, lads! I've got him!" called out the alley man.

"Please… what do you want?" Michael begged.

The alley man leaned down to get closer to where Michael lay cowering in fear. He opened his mouth and prepared to bite Michael.

Michael could see other white-faced men arrive and ready to join in. Michael stared at the alley man's white face in horror, blood running from his mouth, not one drop made contact with Michael. He knew this was the end and didn't want to die. He closed his eyes, knowing there was no way out of this… He whispered to himself.

"Sarah… I'm sorry."

Suddenly an unseen force made the alley man's body jerk backwards. He fell back onto the road, Michael saw a wound in the middle of the alley man's head… He had been shot!

How had Michael not heard the gunshot and who killed the man?

The other white-faced men growled at something behind Michael. He mustered up the energy to crawl away from them, keeping his eyes on them as he hid himself behind a burnt-out car on the ruined street.

The men were ready to run headfirst toward something, when all of them suddenly fell to the ground, they too had all been swiftly and silently shot in the same manner as their leader, the alley man.

"You can come out from behind the car." Spoke a voice in the darkness. It was man's voice with a Scottish accent, Glaswegian to be precise. Michael remained silent, frozen with fear. Hoping and praying the man would disappear if he kept quiet.

"I understand. You're scared. I would be too if I were you. They're all dead. You have nothing to fear from me." Spoke the man, whoever he was, he wasn't going to leave Michael alone. He believed the man to be speaking the truth, after all, if he truly wanted to kill him, he could have easily shot Michael first and he would have been none the wiser. Despite this, Michael wished to be left alone.

"Go away! Leave me alone! I haven't done anything!" Michael shouted from his hiding place behind the car. The metal of the car door where he was leaning against was surprisingly cold. It made Michael shiver, his feet were soaked in blood, not all of it was his. How could this be? The white-faced men didn't bleed on him. He remembered the alley and the deep puddles… were they puddles of blood?

Blood water? He thought of the fire raining from the sky. What had happened to the world? What was still going on? Nejuma, the angel told Michael this was the future. Not any future. He told Michael the date, December 22nd 2059.

It was fifty year in Michael's future.

What could do all this?

The man called out to Michael regardless of his wish to be on his own.

"It's okay. You're alright… My name is Tom. What is yours?" Tom asked Michael.

Michael hesitated for a brief moment before replying to Tom.

"My… My name is Michael… Please… Please go way… Leave me alone" Michael was becoming fed up. Why was this stranger still attempting to help him? Michael didn't seek his help.

"Michael, did they bite you? Those men, did they bite you anywhere?" Tom asked, he sounded concerned.

Michael stayed out of sight, still wary and unsure of the stranger, Tom. Despite his saving Michael from the white-face men.

"No!" Michael called back.

"Did they make you ingest their blood?" Tom asked.

What sort of question was this? Why would anyone in their right mind do that?

"No!" Michael responded. He was appalled by the thought of such a disgusting act.

"They didn't get their blood into any open wounds?" Tom asked Michael.

"What in God's name…" Michael was interrupted before he continued

"Answer the question!" Tom demanded.

"No!" Michael angrily replied.

"That's good, Michael. You're not infected. You have nothing to fear from me. Come out from behind the car. I can help you. Believe me, you do not want to be out here… My grandfather and I have killed many of these sons of bitches to help people like you." Tom's words gave Michael the strength to get up on his feet and move out from behind the burnt-out car that sheltered him for the last few minutes.

Michael saw Tom, he was not much older than Michael, he was a young man with short brown hair, dressed entirely in black. It was almost impossible to see him except for his face. He was paler than most people Michael had encountered. Nowhere near as pale as the white-faced men, Michael thought.

His black clothes were like a soldier's combat outfit. Tom had a bit of a beard, he'd obviously not shaven for several days. Michael's attention was brought to the gun in Tom's hand.

Michael never saw a gun before. It frightened him to think of the damage it could do.

"You see. Nothing to worry about." Tom stated as he slid his handgun into a holster on his right hip.

"Come with me. We need to get out of here." Tom stated as he half-turned to walk away.

"I can't come with you." Michael said. He sounded fearful of everything. He was terrified. Tom turned his attention back to look at Michael with confusion, he was bewildered by Michael.

"What? Are you stupid?! The streets are crawling with infected! Demons! Hell hounds and not to mention... Lucifer! Hurry up!" Tom ordered. He shook his head in disbelief at Michael.

Michael was confused. What was Tom talking about?!

"What do you mean? Demons? Lucifer?! What is going on?!" Michael asked. He was confused and scared from the very mention of Lucifer... The Devil.

"Where've you been living?! Under a fucking rock?!" Michael saw from Tom's strong reaction he had the answers Michael was looking for.

"What is going on? Who were those men?" Michael shivered from the cold. He felt it in his bones and heard it in his own voice. He was scared, more scared than before he encountered Nejuma. Millions of questions were racing through his mind.

"You really don't know?! Do you?!" Tom was surprised or at least Michael thought so. Surely there must be others who didn't know what was happening in Glasgow!

" No... I don't." Michael responded. He sounded like a naïve child.

Tom let out a sigh.

"Those men, we call them the infected. They were once normal people. A virus in their blood alters their minds, turning them into slaves to do Lucifer's bidding. One bite from them, their blood mixes with yours... You become like them in seconds, sometimes minutes. Depends on the person."

Michael understood all of Tom's earlier questions. If these men were infected with a virus, capable of affecting their brains... Michael was correct. The white-faced men, the infected, were not in their right mind.

Michael still had questions.

Lucifer... The Devil. If it were true. He was not only real but out there at this very moment.

Michael wanted to know for definite. He dreaded Tom's knowledge.

"What about Lucifer? How did all this happen?"

Tom was about to speak, a scream in the distance halted his response.

Michael knew these were the screams of the infected.

"I'll explain on the way. We need to get going before more of these fucks show up!" Tom said as he gestured Michael to follow him.

"Tom, I don't... I'm not... Do you believe in time travel?" Michael asked. He wasn't sure he believed it himself. Tom's faced reacted to this as if Michael had asked the strangest question in the world.

"Not really. I'm willing to listen on the way." Tom responded. He was anxious as the infected screams began to sound close by.

"On the way where?" Michael asked with caution.

"The safe house. Hurry up!" Tom demanded.

CHAPTER THREE

THE LORD OF THE EARTH

GLASGOW

DECEMBER 22nd 2059

6:30pm

The Lord of the Earth, ruler of humanity is seated on a chair by a mahogany desk. There is a large bookcase filled with books from top to bottom behind him. His study is lit with candles.

He enjoyed sitting in the dark, the breeze from the open balcony door causes the flames atop the candles to flicker. Almost extinguishing their light.

With a motion of his hand, the balcony door slammed shut on their own as if by magic.

The lord continued to sit by his desk, he is cleaning his knife. A beautiful dagger, razor sharp. The hilt was in the shape of an angel's wing and had been crafted to feature feathers. Blood stained every inch of the blade.

The cloth he was using to clean the knife was slowly becoming stained. He accidently allowed his hold on hilt to slip, catching his fingertip as he finished cleaning. The lord winced in pain before smiling at the blood on his finger.

He thought it strange. He had not seen his own blood in what felt like an eternity. The blade was the only thing on this entire planet capable of harming him. The lord smiled as he watched his finger heal before his eyes.

His rapid healing was truly magnificent. No scar, his skin completely healed like he hadn't cut himself. He was slightly surprised. Most other injuries which harmed him had left their marks.

His face endured the worst, pale skinned, black haired and so thin, he was almost skeletal. He grew a goatee, his attempt to improve how he felt towards his appearance. The lord remembered the times when his face was filled with flesh. When his hair was longer and lighter in colour.

Most importantly, he thought of his wings. They were beautiful. Every angel in Heaven had stood in awe of their magnificence. Each wing was six feet in length and covered in large white feathers… No more.

The feathers burned on a day he remembered and would never forget.

The day he was cast into Hell for what was meant to be eternity.

Hell left its mark and earned him new names and titles. The lord went by many of these names, but he always preferred the name bestowed to him at birth… Lucifer.

He was the ruler of Earth, Hell and one day, he would seize control of Heaven and rule over all of creation, he smiled at the thought of his new dominion.

In three days, he will have ruled this little rock for fifty years.

Lucifer smiled at all he had accomplished in his rule of Earth. Humans were in hiding, close to extinction… The way he liked it. Lucifer would like it better when there were no humans left… not even one.

Slippy creatures, always surviving and pissing him off. He needed to be rid of them. Especially if Heaven had suddenly decided to poke their nose into his business. Why now? He wondered. Why after all this time?

It had been decades since any angel set foot on his world.

Lucifer's attention was drawn to the door of his study. The door opened and he smiled as his son entered. Lucifer stood up from his chair to greet him, he walked round his desk, placing the dagger in the inner pocked of his suit jacket.

Despite the flaws of humanity, he loved their Italian silks and bespoke suits and always wore a different one every day. He preferred the darker colours.

"Mammon, how goes the hunt?" Lucifer hugged his son with opened arms. As he pulled away from the hug, he rested his left hand upon Mammon's shoulder. He enjoyed hearing Mammon's tales of human hunts.

Mammon blended in well, he dressed like them especially with his worn-out black hoody and dirty denim jeans. Mammon is younger in appearance than Lucifer, he looked human. Lucifer rested easy knowing his son was nothing like them or his whore human mother who birthed him.

He was the son of Lucifer, every bit as powerful. He was eager to hear all about his son's day of hunting.

"A few less humans out there, father. Unfortunately, none spoke of where they came from. Do not worry, my demons will find the rats nest they call the "safe house"... We did keep some for you." Lucifer caught Mammon's drift as a sinister smile stretched across his son's face.

Lucifer went quiet and Mammon, like any good son, realised there was something wrong.

Lucifer's face was a sight no-one had ever seen and lived. His face was filled with fear.

"Father... What's wrong?" Mammon asked with concern for his father and lord.

"I felt something... A presence I have not felt for a long time... I sensed an angel in the city." Lucifer allowed the knowledge to sink in. Mammon was clearly distressed.

"An angel... Here?! How many?!"

Lucifer felt and heard the fear in Mammon's voice and felt it best to ease his mind.

"Only one." Lucifer responded with a calm and firm tone.

Lucifer's words calmed his son. He saw his body relax upon hearing it.

"One angel?!" Mammon asked. He sounded baffled by his own question.

"Only one." Lucifer confirmed with confidence.

"Where is the filthy bastard?!" Mammon asked with a thirst for blood.

"Dead." Lucifer responded in a matter of fact manner. Proud of his justice.

"You killed him?!" Mammon asked Lucifer. Momentarily, Lucifer thought Mammon had concern for the angel before realising, Mammon would have wanted some playtime with the angel.

"Sorry to deprive you a torture. I wasn't prepared to risk everything. There was a strong possibility he could have been an archangel. It wasn't until he lay dead at my feet, I knew he wasn't." Lucifer explained.

"You knew him?!" Mammon asked with curiosity.

"I knew all of them from before" Lucifer did not speak the day's name.

"Before the fall?" Mammon asked. He was young and curious. Lucifer couldn't be mad at that. He didn't enjoy talking about his fall from grace and proceeded to change the conversation.

"It hardly matters. He was a sorry excuse of an angel. They won't be bothering us." Lucifer said, sounding confident.

"Why one angel? Why not a hundred or all of Heaven? Doesn't it bother you?!" Lucifer felt the fear behind his son's questions.

"I find it more curious than bothering. For one angel to travel here when I am at the height of my power... I am stronger than him! He knows it well. Hence why he has yet to face me... Hell" Lucifer chuckled before continuing to explain his thoughts.

"All the archangels could have battled me today and God would still fail to show his face. No angel has set foot on this world for decades. I do find it strange for one angel and not a very good one at that to come here. If this is Heaven's attempt to retake the world from me. It's a sloppy job! All they achieved today was put my guard up." Lucifer knew he was right, Mammon trusted his advice. He had never been wrong.

"I wouldn't let this worry you, son. Three days' time, I will have ruled over the Earth for fifty years. God can't stop us now and he never will."

Lucifer places his hand on Mammon's shoulders and looks him in the eye.

"I'll be heading out for my own hunt. Have at your survivors till I return" Lucifer prepared to leave the study on foot until Mammon spoke to him.

"Where are you going?" He asked his father.

Lucifer turned and faced him.

"When I killed my brother, Nejuma... He was talking with someone... A boy. I intend to find him and kill him." An evil smile stretched across Lucifer's face, he relished in the killing of humans.

"Who was the boy?" Mammon asked.

"I don't know. I can't help shake the feeling I know him. There was something familiar about him. He reminded of..." Lucifer didn't finish his sentence, he laughed as if what he intended to speak had been ridiculous.

"Forget it. I will not be long." Lucifer shrugged off his silly idea.

"Happy hunting, father." Mammon wished him luck. Not that he needed it. Lucifer made his own luck.

Lucifer smiled like the Cheshire cat, his eyes glowed red as his whole body burst into flames and in the blink of an eye, Lucifer disappeared from the study

CHAPTER FOUR

MICHAEL HARTNELL

GLASGOW

SCOTLAND

DECEMBER 22ND 2059

ONE HOUR LATER

The journey to Tom's safe house felt long. Michael shivered from being cold, the damp clothes he was wearing were no doubt the cause. The heating in Tom's car was barely putting a dent in Michael's cold body. He was struggling to feel warm. Tom's car was a Ford, it looked like it was centuries old. Michael was amazed how Tom was capable of driving without any lights.

Michael jumped out of his skin with fright several times throughout the journey. Many infected people had attempted to bring the car off the road, one had even jumped on top of the roof and pressed its face against the car window on Michael's side.

Tom wasn't stupid, he never engaged with the infected. He did however run one of them over, Tom done so without batting an eyelid. He was unfazed at the terror of the situation. Michael wondered how someone could ever get used to such violence. He soon realised this was probably all Tom ever knew, this was his life, every single second of it was about killing or be killed.

Tom explained to Michael, the journey to the safe house was always random to prevent a pattern forming as many infected monitored your location. These infected would report back to a demon or Lucifer personally.

Tom was silent for a part of the journey till he spoke to Michael.

"Time travel?" he asked Michael, straight to the point and patiently waiting.

Michael was still taken aback by it all, he stammered as he answered.

"I barely believe it myself."

"How in the name of God did you get here?" Tom asked in astonishment.

"I don't really know... One minute... I'm in my bed... in 2009. Then I'm on a street talking to an angel called Nejuma..." Michael launched forward against his seatbelt. Tom had slammed the brakes to stop the car. Michael's chest hurt from the sudden stop.

Michael looked at Tom. His face was serious.

"An angel?" he asked.

"Yes... he said he was an angel." Michael responded.

Tom let out a sigh and sat staring into space, looking straight ahead of him with his head against the headrest of the driver's seat. The disbelief in his faced showed in an instant.

"You don't believe me?" Michael asked. He was worried. Who would believe him? Michael barely believed himself.

"I've never seen one... I do believe you. I was brought up as a Christian... Where is Nejuma? I would like to talk to him." Tom sounded desperate.

"He's dead." Michael broke the news to Tom.

Tom sighed heavily before he faced Michael.

"Michael, as strange as what you are saying sounds, I believe you... You clearly have no clue what's going on here. When in 2009 are you from?" Tom asked.

"What does it matter?" Michael asked. He didn't see the relevance.

"It matters. Trust me. What was the date?" Tom was eager to know. Michael didn't understand why Tom was so interested in one particular date.

"December 22nd." Michael responded.

"Before... You're from before everything started?! My Grandfather lived in the times before all this. He was probably ages with you at the time... I don't know where it began. I do know when... December 25th 2009. Lucifer, he escaped or was freed from Hell. Grandfather never really spoke of it, I always knew the date... I lost him, my grandfather... We got separated a few weeks ago..." Tom exhaled. Michael knew whatever Tom was about to say was difficult and personal.

"He… We were on route to kill Lucifer… I couldn't hold it together… Didn't have the balls to see it through… I let him go alone to try and kill him… He told me the angels fought alongside us for a while before they disappeared and abandoned us! Some angels spoke of a weapon, a knife. Said it could kill anything… I have never met an angel before. It was a story… A story adults told their children… I never once believed it was real. A year ago, we found it. We planned to use it on Lucifer… I don't know where my grandfather is… I don't know if he's even alive!"

Michael is struck with the sudden realisation, he may have seen the knife which Tom spoke of.

"I think… I think I saw this knife." Michael's words got Tom's full attention. Tom looked eager to know everything. It was as if his life depended on hearing it all in the next few seconds.

"Michael, where did you see this knife?" Tom asked with desperation.

Michael was close to tears from fear as he recalled the memory. It was the freshest memory in his mind. He was still processing the horror, he doubted he would ever forget it.

"He… He killed Nejuma…" Michael replied. His voice trembled.

"Who killed Nejuma?" Did you see the killer?" Tom spoke fast. What was he looking for?

"It was dark, I saw… I think… There were wings… But the wings were horrible… His eyes lit up in the dark." Michael explained. He cried. Michael could no longer contain his emotions.

"Were his eyes red?" Tom asked. He already knew they were before Michael stopped sobbing and nodded his in agreement. Who was Red Eyes? Did Tom know?

"You're very lucky to be alive, Michael." Tom said. He was amazed to hear it as if what Michael said was not something likely to happen. For all he knew, it probably wasn't normal even for this world.

Who was the man with red eyes?

"Who is he?" Michael asked. He was terrified at the prospect. He wanted to know and didn't at the same time.

"I'll explain later. We're not safe here. We need to get back to the safe house."

Tom resumed the drive through the deserted and war-torn streets of Glasgow. The streets were treacherous. The destruction of the city. Buildings had collapsed, burnt-out cars and military vehicles, tanks made the road almost impassable. Tom clearly knew the ways around everything.

Tom probably knew these roads like the back of his hand. He could no doubt do it blindfolded.

They were nearly out of the city centre. Tom drove the car down a very long street. Some of the ruined buildings around them still stood tall, he passed the destruction of his home city, if this were truly December 22nd 2059? What happened to his city? The military vehicles, tanks and fighter jets lying destroyed in the streets! What was the government doing to stop Lucifer?

Surely it couldn't be a handful of rebels in a resistance against The Devil?!

This was horrible, things couldn't be as bad to think Tom and his people were on their own?

Continuing down the street, Michael caught a glimpse of something in the ruins of a building, it was a man dressed in black, holding a gun. Michael panicked and began to swiftly turn his attention to other buildings. There were men in many more buildings along the street. Each one of them, dressed in black and carrying a gun.

Michael realised the guns they possessed were rifles. These men were snipers.

Michael looked at Tom, who suddenly turned a switch beside the steering wheel. Before Michael could warn him of the snipers, the car's high beam lights flashed, not once or twice but three times!

"Tom, there are snipers!" Michael shouted in a state of blind panic.

"Relax, Michael! They're the sentries to the safe house. No demon, infected or hell hound makes it down this street. Nothing gets anywhere near this building." Tom had obviously signalled the sentries with his light.

"You're entering the safest place in Glasgow. You can relax. Lucifer doesn't know the location. He never has and we intend to keep it so. We have safeguards in place." Tom explained as the car slowly drove down the street, avoiding the debris.

"We're here." Tom said.

Michael's attention turned to what was in front of him, through the windscreen, he saw the safe house, it was an enormous building, snipers were on the roof.

Sentries, Michael thought. The windows had bars on them and were boarded up. There were many vehicles stationed outside this building. There was a main entrance with two guards present. One for each side of the doorway.

This building was a fortress, Michael noticed as they pulled into a small road beside the entrance to the safe house there were strange symbols spray painted all over the building. He'd never seen anything like them before.

Tom parked the car in front of the entrance.

"Welcome to the safe house, Michael." Tom said whilst getting out of the car. Michael hesitated before mustering up the courage to bring himself out of the car.

Michael stood on the street outside the safe house, he stared at this building and the sentries guarding it. There was a sense of familiarity, but he couldn't understand where from. He looked to Tom, Michael was unsure of Tom's sanctuary.

"How safe is it here, Tom?" Michael asked. Fear was always in his voice. He believed this was his voice forever, he was unable to speak without showing his terror of every little thing.

"Safest place in the city, we have holy oil around the entire building. No infected can cross the circle of oil. Some demons are immune. We have safeguards in place to gain entry." Tom explained to a frightened Michael.

One of the guards at the entrance hands Tom a flask, it was clear plastic flask containing water. The other sentry had a gun aimed at Tom as he attempted to enter the safe house.

Tom seemed annoyed by this.

"Sorry, Tom. Rules are rules. You need to drink. No exceptions." The guard demanded with his gun held high.

"I'm aware. My grandfather made the rules." Tom stated before taking a swig of the water in the flask. Tom holds it out for Michael to take.

"What is it?" a suspicious Michael asked.

"It's holy water. It's a safeguard. No-one gains entry without drinking it." Tom told Michael.

Michael put his lips to the flask and ended up gulping the entire flask. He only intended to drink a sip of water. As soon as the water touched his lips, he had forgotten how thirsty he was.

Tom and the two sentries find this amusing and laugh.

"Well, I guess you're not a demon. Come on in." Tom gestured Michael inside as the doors opened from the inside. Tom, Michael and one of the guards enter the safe house, the sentries like the ones in the buildings were covered in black clothing from head to toe. Unlike Tom, they wore heavy body armour.

It wasn't until the door closed, Michael realised a man inside had opened the front doors. Michael looked all around him, the room is massive, the ceiling was high. The only lights in the place were coming from candles. Dozens of people who looked like they had been through hell and back had beds in rows, all up and down the room.

In the far corner, there was a table with people serving a queue of survivors, it looked like soup and it smelt good, Michael thought. He heard laughter, there were children running around playing games with each other.

Michael hadn't thought about children in this world. Yet now he was. He wondered why anyone would bring a child into this world of horrors. At the back of the room, Michael saw a young woman with blonde hair, she wore a white coat. It was similar to a doctor's medical coat and she was tending to a man's bandage. Was she a doctor?

She couldn't have been much older than Michael, she was in her early twenties, she wasn't as pale skinned as Tom or most of the survivors around him. Michael's attention was drawn back to Tom as the sentry spoke with him.

"Found another survivor?" The sentry asked Tom with a smile on his face.

"You know me, John. I can't stay away." Tom joked before introducing Michael to John.

"Michael, this is John. He's my head of security." Tom stated as John extended his hand out to shake Michael's.

"Welcome, Michael. A majestic name you've got. It's the same as Tom's grandfather. May the man rest in peace." John sounded upset when he spoke of Tom's grandfather.

His choice of words did not sit well with Tom, who became annoyed by what was spoken.

"How many times does it need saying? The man is alive! I know it! Till we find his body, we treat him like he is still breathing!" Tom said in a defensive tone. It was probably to hide his true feelings, Michael suspected.

"It's been three weeks, Tom. Don't you think…" Tom instantly cut across whatever John intended on saying with a rapid response.

"I think nothing. He will be back." Tom interrupted.

Michael noticed parts of the building where walls had once stood, someone had obviously knocked them down in order to create more space by the looks of it. Michael knew where he recognised this building from… He had been here before.

"Tom, what was this place? From before?" Michael asked, he was curious to know if he was right.

"Originally, it was built as a bank, whatever that was. After that, in 2009, it became a church, a group called Genesis owned it. I was told they hadn't long moved in when Lucifer took control of the world, my grandfather founded the safe house here on the first day of the apocalypse. He hoped to create more. Sadly, this is one of only two locations still standing. He anointed the building with holy ceremonies and ritualistic symbols. It prevents any demon from entering." Tom explained.

"Why a church?" Michael didn't understand the significance.

"It's hallowed ground. Best form of defence against demons." Tom replied. This cleared everything up for Michael and he realised where he was.

"I came here every Sunday… I barely recognised it." Michael said out loud without fully realising what he said. John's face was puzzled by Michael's statement. Michael understood that what he allowed to slip out of his mouth would be strange to someone like John.

Michael looked over at Tom for reassurance to further explain his meaning. Tom gave a nod of his head.

"Please continue. We speak our minds here." Tom responded.

Michael took a second to gather his thoughts carefully without sounding like a raving mad man.

"Where I'm from, this is my local church… in 2009." Michael saw the look on John's face which said it all. He must have thought Michael were insane.

"I'm sorry. Did you say 2009? As in the year 2009?!" John asked in disbelief.

"Yes, he did." Tom answered faster than Michael. He was taken aback by Tom's belief in his story.

"For fuck sake, Tom! You can't really tell me you believe this nutter?!" John sounded concerned as he spoke to Tom.

What was difficult to believe about time travel? Surely Michael wasn't the first person to appear in the future? He was hit with a terrifying thought. Was he the first? Had no-one before him ever appeared in 2059 with no explanation?

The thought filled him with dread. John's own fear of Michael didn't help matters.

"To answer your question. I do believe him and he's not crazy." Tom spoke to John. He was trying to nip this argument in the bud.

"You can't let him stay here with such talk!" John exclaimed.

Tom turned and faced John. Up until now, Tom had spoken in a calm manner. Michael feared Tom was going to go ballistic at John. He was clearly undermining Tom's position. Michael knew without being told that Tom was the leader of this community.

Tom momentarily closes his eyes before responding. Whatever he was about to say was no doubt going to settle this dispute, whether John liked it or not.

"My grandfather and I brought you here? Correct me if I am wrong?" Tom asked without raising his voice. What he said, changed John's attitude in a split second as he hesitated to reply.

"Eh… yes." John stammered.

"In the absence of my grandfather, the leader of the resistance, I am his heir. I lead this safe house and I make the rules. We will be taking record of Michael living with us, like we do with every other survivor we encounter. Michael has vital information, which could lead to me finding my grandfather." Tom responded. It effectively ended John's disagreement.

"My apologies, Tom. I meant no offence. I'll resume my post." John said with sincerity. John proceeded to return to his sentry shift and headed towards the front doors which they came through.

"I'm sorry about his behaviour. It's not every day we meet a time-traveller." Tom apologised to Michael. This was all bizarre, Michael still had a good deal to learn about the culture of this community.

"Come this way." Tom gestured Michael to follow his lead.

"Lindsay, do you have a minute for medical assistance and registration?" Tom called over to the woman in the white medical jacket. She was bandaging up a sentry's hand. The sentry is seated on a bed. Lindsay, the young doctor, responded to Tom without taking her attention away from the task before her.

"As soon as I am finished tending to my patients here. Take him along to my office, I'll get him there." Lindsay stated as she continued to deal with the sentry's bandage. Michael was surprised by Lindsay's accent. Everyone he encountered from Tom to Nejuma. Even the infected alley man, all of them spoke with a Scottish accent. Lindsay had an American accent. Michael couldn't quite place which American accent. She was definitely from the United States.

Questions upon questions, Michael thought.

"You heard the doc." Tom spoke to Michael.

"Follow me." Tom said, leading Michael out of the large bedroom and canteen down a long corridor. Michael's mind was racing. How many people lived here? How safe is it? Is Lindsay a doctor or simply the next best thing to a real one? If the world had truly been this way for fifty years, the chances were nobody had any real medical experience or university education. They would have learned to become a doctor by doing it through trial and error.

Michael realised whilst he had been inside the safe house's main room that all the men and women were young. A mixture of people in their twenties and a small few in their thirties. Children too. Michael still couldn't wrap his mind around.

Why were there no older people or even middle aged? Tom led Michael to a small room, Tom switched the lights on to reveal a makeshift medical surgery. It had power, electrical lighting. There was an operating table and other medical equipment.

Michael noticed a refrigerator. It was being used to store medicine vials. Tom's safe house was well stocked, Michael thought.

There was also a small table with two chairs. It has lots of paperwork rested on the surface. Michael knew this room would be the difference between life and death for most people living here. Tom turns and faces Michael inside the medical room.

"This is sick bay. You're in good hands with Lindsay. She will give you the once over. It's standard procedure. She's very good and doesn't bite... Much!" Tom laughs at his own joke. Michael's sense of humour was gone. It was no wonder, considering after everything he endured. Humour was the last thing on his mind. Tom obviously recognised this.

"Wow. Tough crowd. She'll set you up and register you with us. After that, get some rest and we'll try and make sense of everything later. Sit tight and she'll be along in a moment".

CHAPTER FIVE

DOCTOR LINDSAY JONES

THE SAFE HOUSE
GLASGOW
DECEMBER 22nd 2059

A FEW MINUTES LATER

A healer's work is never done. Without Lindsay, the people living in the safe house would struggle to survive.

Things were a lot different with Tom's grandfather being missing. Lindsay believed he was still alive. His Grandfather Michael had been in worse situations before and always found his way back. This was not of the norm as he usually, at the best of times been missing for a few hours or days. He had never been missing for weeks without a sign he was still out there.

Lindsay did not believe in God. She believed in Michael, Tom's grandfather, sixty-nine years of age and full of life and fight. It was exactly what Lucifer hated. Lindsay made her way along the corridor to her office in sick bay.

The young man who Tom found was waiting, he appeared to be looking at her sick bay which Lindsay recognised as admiration. Lindsay respected Tom always finding survivors, the way this one was examining her operating room, equipment, and medicines, she wondered if he knew what it was all for.

Did he have medical knowledge? She would soon find out. He could be useful if he were experienced. The young man realised she was standing in the doorway and reacted as if he'd been caught in the act.

"Apologies… I couldn't help… Your surgery is incredible." He said as he continued to look around the room in astonishment.

"Thanks. I try my best. I always send Tom with a list for medicines when he goes out. Sorry I kept you waiting. My name is Lindsay, I'm the safe house doctor." Lindsay introduced herself and extended her hand out to the young man. He shook her hand as he introduced himself.

"My name is Michael." He responded.

"Michael?" Lindsay was surprised by his name.

"Yes. Tom mentioned his grandfather's name is Michael too." Michael said with curiosity.

"He is an extraordinary man... Sorry, I'm keeping you back. You must be exhausted." Lindsay noticed Michael was wearing pyjamas, they appeared to be in much better condition than most clothing she came across. They looked almost new. Michael's feet were stained in blood. They would need to be sterilised and bandaged if needed.

"I'm going to sterilise your feet and ask you some questions as part of our registration. Are you okay for me to do this, Michael?" Lindsay always got her patient's consent. Nothing was done until an agreement had been reached.

"Of course." Michael responded.

"Please take a seat on the operating table." Lindsay gestured for Michael to sit.

Lindsay pressed a dispenser on the wall and caught a sterilising agent which fell from the bottom. Lindsay rubbed her hands together to cleanse them before putting on a fresh pair of latex gloves.

Michael sat on the operating table, his feet dangled over the edge, he wasn't tall enough to reach the floor. Lindsay prepared sterile wipes before applying them to Michael's feet. He winced in pain at the touch.

"Sorry. Does it sting?" Lindsay asked sincerely. Nothing worse than hurting a patient, she thought.

"No, it's cold." He responded.

Lindsay continued to wipe the blood from Michael's feet. The more she cleaned, she noticed there were small scrapes on the soles of his feet, not enough to justify the amount of blood she had already cleaned away.

"Michael, is this your blood?" she asked him. She was concerned as to why there was so much blood.

"No... it was a puddle... I stepped in... in an alley." Michael told her. Lindsay felt he didn't understand what he was telling her. Surely he must have seen blood rain at some point in his life!

"I see." Lindsay said as she finished cleaning his feet. Unsure of whether Michael had told the truth about the blood.

"All done, Michael. I'm going to get the registration book from my desk. We'll fill it out then I'll show you to your bedding area. Is that okay?" Lindsay explained the procedures of the safe house.

"No problem." Michael replied. He sounded exhausted. A good night's sleep would do him the world of good.

"Please take a seat at my desk" Lindsay asked Michael to be seated. He brought himself down off the operating table and walked over to her desk. She sat on the opposite side of the desk. Lindsay removes a sheet of paper from the book on the desk and slides it across to Michael.

"This is our registration form. We keep a record of everyone living with us. I mostly only require your full name... Sorry, I naturally assume everyone has a surname. I understand if you don't. It's tough out there." Lindsay apologised to him. She hated how she naturally jumped to conclusions.

The majority of people living rough in the city would be fortunate to have a first name, let alone a surname.

"I do... Sign here?" Michael asked Lindsay. He pointed to the registration form. Lindsay felt he seemed surprised by what she was telling him. Something did not sit right with her. His facial expressions to how he reacted to certain things was intriguing and his clothes were strange. Everything about Michael did not add up.

Her suspicions would be questions for another time. His registration and questionnaire were the priority. Lindsay wasn't fully paying attention to what Michael was writing. Lindsay only realised not that Michael was currently writing but that he knew how to.

The more he wrote, the more her interest in him became. Who are you, Michael? Lindsay thought.

"Who taught you to read and write?" Lindsay asked Michael. She was curious about Michael. He seemed flustered when she inquired into his past to the extent, he hesitated before replying.

"My parents." He responded. Michael sounded unsure of his answer. Almost as if he feared he may have said something wrong. Was he lying? Lindsay thought it strange but was willing to let it slide for the moment.

"I know it is hard to keep track of the date. Do you know today's date and your date of birth? It's no issue if you don't." Lindsay asked as she explained the issue of knowing what day it was. Most weren't aware of the year and many did not know their own birthday.

"I do… Tom told me the date and I've always known my own date of birth." Michael replied. He was confident. He wasn't lying as far as Lindsay could tell.

"I need today's date on the form. That will be your date of arrival and your date of birth for medical purposes. Do you mind if I ask a little about your medical history? Have you ever been seen by anyone with medical experience?" Lindsay asked. She felt she asked him well, chosen her words wisely. Her father would be proud, she thought.

"Yes, I have medical history. What do you need to know?" Michael asked. He was ready to help her with whatever she required.

Lindsay believed Michael understood as to why she was inquiring into his history. She found it interesting in a bizarre way. She couldn't understand why something wasn't sitting right with Michael. He was being very helpful, most residents didn't have surnames, couldn't read, or write and either they didn't know if they had medical history or none at all.

"Okay. Do you know your blood type? Blood transfusions are quite common in the safe house and it helps to know." Lindsay explained to Michael.

"Yes, I am universal donor." He answered. Lindsay is taken aback by this. Michael knew medical terms as well as his type. Her jaw must have dropped from shock. She was stunned by his response.

"I beg your pardon?" she asked, wondering if she heard him properly.

"I'm O Negative." He calmly told her.

"I know what it means… I'm surprised you know the term… Are you trained in medicine or healing?" Lindsay was certain Michael must have some sort of expertise. This would be a great asset to the safe house.

"A little… not as much as you from the looks of things. I thought maybe one day… I don't think so now." He told her. Michael was saddened by what he was saying. Lindsay tried her best to reassure him.

"My father taught me… I was a lot younger than you and I thought I knew everything until I met Michael, Tom's grandfather. He taught me skills I never knew existed… Sorry, I'm rattling on." Lindsay apologised. She was passionate about her profession. She proceeds with her questions.

"Are you allergic to any medicines? Any specific antibiotics? I only ask as you have seen, we have access to medicines." Lindsay explains her reason behind her question. He appeared tired. Lindsay only had one last question for Michael. Afterward he would be free to enjoy a well-earned good night's rest.

"None I'm aware of." He responded in his polite and helpful manner. His medical experience would definitely help Lindsay further down the line. She would need to ascertain the extent of his knowledge at a later date. Michael was tired and he was little use to anyone tired and sleep deprived.

"Thank you. One last question before I show you to your bedding area. I apologise, it is very personal. Do you have any sexually transmitted diseases? Public lice in particular? As you have seen all bedding areas are in close proximity. You can imagine. Lice have been a problem in the past." Lindsay put the needs of the safe house first. She knew it was personal. It didn't faze her as she could easily treat it and everything he said, would remain confidential between them.

"I am a Christian. I don't have multiple partners." Michael responded in such a straightforward way. There was a pride in his voice, Lindsay wondered why.

"Christian?" she asked with curiosity. It wasn't every day she encountered a survivor with religious beliefs.

"All my life. My parents are… were too" Michael responded, he changed his choice of words, mid-sentence and seemed saddened by it. Lindsay thought best not to press on it, survivors would share their stories when the time was right for them and not before.

"That's remarkable. Considering all that is going on… Tom and his grandfather are Christian too. My father believes in God, he isn't Christian, but he believes. Not a lot of survivors do. That's largely down to Lucifer as you are no doubt aware of… I can't say I believe in any God, not when there is so much evil outside this safe house." Lindsay was enjoying her conversation with Michael, he fascinated her, and she would enjoy getting to know him better. She told him the truth.

Doctor Lindsay Jones did not believe in God. She often found herself wondering, if there were a God, why had he allowed Lucifer to rule the world for all these years? Lindsay believed if there was a God, he simply did not care about this world.

"You've seen horrors, I know. I also know you must have seen good. This place and the people. What you are doing here is good. To me, you are all doing God's work." Michael said to Lindsay.

His words had great meaning. Lindsay took them as everyone should look out for each other. It had nothing to do with God's will as Michael was attempting to explain to her.

"I see where you are coming from and I respect your beliefs. You would have liked Tom's grandfather, he speaks the same way… You must be tired. Thank you for taking the time in registering with us. I'll show you to your bedding area." Lindsay stepped up from her chair. Michael slowly got to his feet and handed her his registration form.

Lindsay held the form without reading it. The form had been attached to a clipboard and Lindsay placed it under her arm. She would read it in better detail later on before filing it away.

"If you would like to follow me upstairs." Lindsay stated leading Michael out of her medical surgery. Lindsay and Michael headed down the long corridor outside of sick bay and headed further down the corridor, away from the main entrance. The walls needed a good paint job, the mould was the worst. Lindsay felt Tom should have someone deal with the mould at the very least.

His grandfather would have. She felt the safe house was struggling without him. She led Michael to a stairwell at the end of the corridor, they climbed up the stairs in silence to the second floor of the safe house. The corridor on the second floor was nowhere near as bad as the ground floor. It had recently been maintained, the walls had a new paint job and were free of mould.

Lindsay stopped in a doorway further down the corridor.

"Sorry about the climb. This is your bedding area in here. The bed over by the window is yours." She explained to the tired Michael.

Michael momentarily had a look inside the bedding area. He seemed unsure, the windows were barred like every other room in the building and many people were sleeping in their own beds. A few candles were still lit for him to find his way to the bed.

Michael faced Lindsay. He was very timid. Michael had suffered by the way he reacted.

"How secure is the safe house?" Michael asked her. He was scared. He struggled to accept he was safe here.

"You are perfectly safe. The sentries are outside twenty-four hours and no demon has ever seen the safe house. Get some sleep and when you wake up, I'd would enjoy getting to know about your medical expertise." Lindsay said in an attempt to take his mind off any uncertainties he was feeling.

"Okay… I will. Thank you." Michael said.

"Sweet dreams, Michael." Lindsay said as she attempted to depart the second floor. Michael asked her something as she made her move to leave.

"Your accent. It's American, isn't it?" Michael asked with curiosity.

"Yes, it is." Lindsay replied in surprise. Her accent usually threw people off, most Scots always guessed her to be Irish or Canadian. There weren't very many Americans around these days.

"Where in The States are you from?" Michael asked.

"The States?!" Lindsay was baffled. How could he not know about America?

"Yes, The United States of America?" He asked with that same uncertainty. Almost as if he knew he was asking something which sounded silly or strange.

"We'll talk more tomorrow. Rest, Michael." Lindsay said. If he knew the continent of America was once a country of fifty united states, how could he not have any knowledge about what happened? He was a bizarre young man.

"Good night." Michael responded as he entered the bedding area. Lindsay exhaled and began to walk back to the stairwell. Michael was not her usual survivor. He knew things not a lot of people would know and asked questions no-one else considered to ask. Who on earth are you, Michael? She thought to herself.

As Lindsay reached the stairwell entrance at the end of the second floor corridor, Lindsay took hold of the clipboard under her arm. Curiosity got the better of her. She stopped to examine what Michael wrote. She instantly lost her grip on the clipboard in a split second from what she read.

Michael wrote his date of arrival as "December 22nd 2059". There was nothing out of the ordinary there. It was his date of birth which made her head sizzle, "October 5th 1990". His name was the most shocking, "Michael Hartnell". Lindsay stared back along the corridor, frozen in place by his words. Tom needed to know at once.

Lindsay stared back along the corridor toward the door which led into the bedding area where the survivor, Michael was currently sleeping. She feared the unknown and this was not normal in any way.

She spoke her thoughts out loud in disbelief. It couldn't be true.

"That's not possible!"

CHAPTER SIX

TOM

SICK BAY

THE SAFE HOUSE
GLASGOW
DECEMBER 23rd 2059

04:30am

Tom entered the sick bay. He had been in the middle of receiving an update from the rooftop sentries when word reached him. Lindsay urgently required his attention. Tom figured it would no doubt be regarding medical supplies from his time outside the safe house. He was in no mood for her demanding, bossy attitude and was prepared to take none of her bullshit.

He would tell her the truth. He didn't find any and she'll get them as soon as he acquires any. Upon entering sick bay, he half expected her to be in her usual mood with him for not acquiring any supplies. This time she looked different.

This was out of character for the doctor. She wasn't sat behind her desk like normal. Lindsay was pacing up and down the surgery. Tom knew she was concerned about something. This was more than not finding new medical supplies. What was so bad to worry her?

"Thank you for coming… I really don't know what to do?!" Lindsay exclaimed. She spoke fast and Tom felt her stress from listening to her voice.

"Calm down. What's wrong?" Tom asked with concern for Lindsay. What was going on would be serious. He never saw her like this before.

"Michael…" Lindsay stopped speaking. Her breathing was rapid. She was terrified. Tom wondered what she was trying to tell him.

"What about him?" Tom asked her with the need to understand her.

"Where did he come from?" Lindsay asked in a state of fear.

"What does it matter?" Tom stated. He was beginning to feel annoyed. Why was Lindsay so concerned about a young guy in pyjamas. He felt like she was wasting his time.

"Tell me, Tom!" Lindsay said. She was nearly shouting at him.

'Keep your voice down! I found him on the south side" Tom responded in a slightly agitated tone.

"I didn't ask where you found him. Where does he come from? Something is not right with him. Did he say anything to you?" Tom felt like Lindsay was interrogating him.

"What did he say? Has he hurt you?" Tom asked her.

"No, of course not. As far as talking to me, he has… Something doesn't add up! He is well spoken, clearly educated and asks the strangest questions." Lindsay stated to Tom in panic.

He felt like she was blowing all of this out of proportion.

"Like what?" He asked. Tom knew his sarcasm was showing. He didn't really care. The last six years he endured all kinds of verbal abuse in sick bay from Doctor Jones.

"If you must know he's universal donor!" She stated. Tom knew he hit a nerve as she was becoming defensive, the smugness in her voice told him. He also had no clue what she meant. Lindsay often enjoyed using medical terminology to make him feel small or stupid.

"Universal donor?" he asked with the hope that Lindsay might elaborate on the matter.

"His blood type is O Negative. Do I need to remind you what that means?!" Sarcasm didn't suit Lindsay, thought Tom. He hated her cheek and often felt he needed to keep Lindsay in line. His grandfather was the leader of the safe house. She never dared challenge his authority in front of anyone and doubted she ever did when alone with him.

"I know what it means. Good news, we can draw blood from him tomorrow." Tom responded sarcastically. She was boring him now. There were other urgent matters which required his attention.

"Then he asked me about America!" Lindsay said with the same stress filled voice she had upon Tom's arrival to sick bay.

42

"What about America?" Tom asked Lindsay. He wondered what the hell any of it mattered to Lindsay or Michael.

"Before Lucifer, what was America?" Lindsay asked Tom. He was beginning to lose patience with her.

"I don't have time for a history lesson. Cut to the chase!" Tom impatiently responded.

"Michael asked me where in the states I was from. He referred to America as the United States of America… How many people even know of America, let alone what it was called before Lucifer rose to power?!" Lindsay was scared but Tom didn't feel the same way, if she knew what he knew, this conversation wouldn't be happening.

"I didn't even know it was called by such a name… Like you said, he's well educated. There are still books around the city…" Lindsay interrupted Tom before he continued to speak in Michael's defence.

"Come off it, Tom! He is asking questions he should know answers to. Why would he ask about America?! Has he been living under a rock?!" Lindsay was confused and Tom knew for certain what was happening and laughed.

"Why are you laughing?" Lindsay asked. She sounded insulted. Tom immediately stopped laughing.

"He didn't tell you?" Tom asked Lindsay. Michael no doubt kept quiet about everything. Maybe even lied after John's reaction to his story.

"Tell me what?" Lindsay demanded.

"He claims to have travelled through time. He says he is from the year 2009." Tom replied, knowing full well how crazy it made him sound.

Lindsay was silenced for a moment.

"And you believe him?!" She asked in shock.

"I rescued him from a gang of infected. When he was safe, he demanded I leave him alone… Nobody has ever once asked me to leave them alone in the dark. Every survivor I have encountered has always been grateful to be free of the never ending darkness and demon infested streets… He asked me questions, I initially thought he was soft in the head until I came to realise. He truly had no clue about anything. It was at that point, I knew Michael was different. So, yes. I do believe him… Hell, I've seen stranger." Tom explained to Lindsay. He prayed this was the end of it. Tom was too tired to keep up his defence.

Lindsay then handed him a clipboard without saying a word.

"What's this?" Tom asked as he grasped the clipboard. There was registration form attached.

"It's Michael's form. I've highlighted what he wrote. Look at his date of birth and surname." Lindsay said. Her arms folded in front of her chest. She was on edge. Tom saw that much from her body language.

"Date of birth. October 5th 1990, like I told you, he claims to be from 2009... Surname..." Tom stares at Michael's surname in a state of disbelief. It felt like hours before he next spoke. Only seconds had passed. His brain tried to make sense of what his eyes read.

"How is this possible?" Tom asked. He tried his best to hide his own concern. It obviously showed, how could it not?

"I don't know... If Michael is from the past as he claims and is who he says is. You know what that could mean." Lindsay said. She was trying to explain the ramifications. Tom was well aware of its meaning.

"There is another possibility. He is lying to you. Why? I do not know." Lindsay was in the dark as much as he. Tom knew they both had to be certain.

"Michael wrote down my grandfather's surname and his date of birth... How the hell could he know that?!" Tom was baffled by this. Could it be true? If not, he feared the endless possible alternatives.

"It's possible he's undercover... For Lucifer." Lindsay suggested. Tom noticed how much she was shaking from fear.

"No way! No-one in their right mind would be a minion for Lucifer. Humans haven't worked for Lucifer for years! He's got demons doing his dirty work." Tom stated in an attempt to disprove the theory.

"Did Michael go through the security checks, holy water?" Lindsay asked with suspicion.

"I may have been born at night. It wasn't last night! He drank the water like everyone else. No exceptions! He's not a demon. He bloody downed the flask in one go!" Tom laughed nervously as he thought of the memory.

"Lucifer may know our location... He may have decided to change his strategy. Get a human to come here, integrate into our way of life and kill us all!" Lindsay was talking like a crazy lady, Tom needed to calm her down.

"Lindsay, calm yourself. I think you're jumping the gun a little too far. If that cunt knew our location, he would come here himself. He's been searching for it for fifty years. Lucifer would be here in the blink of an eye. That circle around this building, keeps out most demons… It has zero effect on an angel!" Tom exhaled. Stressed beyond belief. Getting worried when he didn't need to.

"Lucifer does not know our location and if we keep doing what we have always done, he never will." Tom hoped this was it. Lindsay allowed paranoia to tell another story.

"Tom, who's to say Michael isn't Lucifer… We all know Lucifer can shape-shift, transform into any form he desires!"

Paranoia was dangerous in the safe house. What was said, could not leave the sick bay.

"He's not Lucifer." Tom responded. His gut feeling had never failed him.

"How can you be so sure?" Lindsay was terrified. She allowed fear to take control of her.

"If he were… We wouldn't be having this conversation. We'd already be dead… Michael is sleeping as we speak. When he awakens, I will speak with him and get the whole truth. Till then, what has been said. Does not leave this room. We keep this between us. I don't want a panic on our hands. This stays with us. Can you keep it a secret?" Tom pleaded with her. The last thing he needed was for fear to spread like wildfire throughout the safe house.

"I can, and I will, Tom." Lindsay's word was her bond. She would not break her promise. Tom's mind raced. If Michael was truly his grandfather and had time-travelled from the past.

What could it all mean for the future?

CHAPTER SEVEN

MICHAEL HARTNELL

THE SAFE HOUSE

SECOND FLOOR BEDDING AREA

GLASGOW

DECEMBER 23RD 2059

10:30am

Michael Hartnell had fallen asleep sooner than he expected. He couldn't recall being awake for long. He must have been exhausted. As he woke, Michael lay in his bed. His mouth was dry, he was gasping for a drink of water. Michael turned his head to look out the window.

Steel bars were on every single window. They were old and rusted. Still as strong as ever by the looks of it and had been there for years from the level of deterioration on the bars.

Michael recalled seeing bars on every window from outside the safe house. There must be four floors, the building was wide and covered in strange symbols, like glyphs and Tom explained what they were.

He only just noticed it was still dark outside. The sun had not come up yet. He felt as though he slept all night. Maybe he hadn't. Michael thought he possibly slept till the following night. He was embarrassed by the thought.

Michael never done that before. Not even at home, he thought of himself as a guest in Tom's safe house and felt the need to apologise for sleeping the day away. Surely he had not sleep for as long as he believed.

Michael sat himself up in the bed. It had surprisingly been very comfortable. The beds had been recycled from a hospital. All the beds were on wheels and were secured to prevent them rolling out of place and had white steel headboards. All beds were immaculate, not a bit of rust or filth to be seen. The bedding areas and Lindsay's medical surgery were the cleanest rooms in the safe house.

The corridors required a bit of attention. They hadn't been attended to for a while by the appearance of downstairs. Michael thought of Lindsay and the registration form. She was cagey when speaking of her homeland. Michael hadn't stop to think about what had happened in Scotland, could have happened to the world. What condition was the United States of America in? Was it even still called that? He wondered.

A lot had happened in fifty years and he wanted to know about the future. Lindsay probably thought he was a simpleton with all his questions. When he was in her surgery, he considered levelling with her. Tell her the truth, he woke up in a street fifty years in the future.

It probably didn't matter by now. She would have read his form and seen the date of birth he signed. Michael knew eventually if there was no way back to 2009, this would become his home and soon everybody will know his story. He was a time-traveller.

Michael worked out what nineteen years previously would have been. It would be the year 2040. Freaky, he thought. A date in his future but it was the past in this time period. Time travel was complicated and head hurting.

He thought it best not to lie about when he was born. So instead of claiming to have been born in 2040 to fit his own age, he wrote his real date of birth on the form. October 5th 1990, as strange as that would be for Lindsay, it was the truth. Before he went to sleep, Michael prayed to God. He prayed to return home to Sarah and for all of this to have been a terrible nightmare.

No joy. He was still stuck here in 2059 at the end of the world. Michael had no dreams as he slept during the night. He often referred to this as black sleep. No dreams, only sleep. When he adjusted comfortably in a sitting up position, Michael saw there were two people awake on the other side of the room.

A young woman and a man, they were ages with Michael. They were talking to each other, the young woman smiled at the man. They were a couple, Michael thought. The man was one of the sentries from the front entrance, he had been standing with John when Michael arrived at the safe house.

He was still wearing his black uniform and body armour with a gun in a hip holster. He must be off duty, Michael thought.

"You're awake!" The young woman exclaimed as she spotted Michael sitting upright. She and the young sentry headed over to his bedside. The sentry stood at the edge of Michael's bed and the woman sat down on Michael's bed beside him.

She wore ragged old pink pyjamas, she had either been sleeping or was preparing to go to sleep when she became aware of Michael.

"Hi, I'm Karen. Are you thirsty? Have some of our water." Karen said as she handed Michael, a steel flask.

His throat was raw, dry as a bone. He swallowed a large gulp of water and did not drink more than one gulp for the fear he may finish Karen's water. He didn't know whether water was in short supply. He politely handed Karen her flask back without having another drink. He didn't wish to be rude.

"Thank you… I'm Michael. Sorry, I didn't realise how thirsty I was." He apologised for the quantity of water he drunk to quench his thirst. Karen was a cheery person, always smiling and appearing to be full of life. She could hardly focus on Michael as she continued to stare at the young sentry who was standing at the bottom of Michael's bed.

"Don't worry about the water. We get plenty of it. Tom picks it all up direct from the site where they produce it… This is my boyfriend, Peter" Karen introduced the sentry to Michael. She was so happy to introduce him to Michael. He predicted right. They are a couple.

Michael found it pleasant to meet them and wondered what Karen meant by water being "produced". Surely with conditions as bad as they were, no-one had made the scientific discovery to create water?! Michael remembered this was the future. Despite the oppression these people lived under, someone, somewhere would still be practising sciences. What an achievement if it were true!

"It's a good thing Tom found you. How long were you out there?" Peter asked Michael. He realised Peter was merely curious and Michael wasn't exactly sure how people would react to his unexplained journey through time. He wanted to keep the conversation going, it was nice to talk. He knew he needed to say something. The last thing he wanted was to make their heads spin at the thought of time travel.

Michael always liked people and enjoyed talking. Speaking to Karen and Peter helped take his mind off everything he encountered.

"Longer than I care to remember." Michael lied. He never wanted to witness the things he saw, the infected, watching an angel be brutally murdered, the killer was a monster, hidden in the darkness. He thought of the glowing red eyes. They were enough to give anyone nightmares. Michael wished he could forget it all.

"Did you have anyone out there with you? I'm pretty sure if you tell Tom, he will go out and look for them." Karen said. She was very thoughtful of Michael. Michael couldn't begin to comprehend how people survived, families and friends getting separated and lost to the extent they would be unable to find each other due to circumstances changing in the blink of an eye from the horrors on the streets. Michael imagined that was the only life anyone could be living here in 2059. A cruel and terrible world, where every day held the strong possibility it may be your last day on earth.

"No, it was only me." Michael lied in an attempt to change the subject.

"Did you lose anyone out there?" Peter asked Michael. He felt it was asked with such casualness, Peter may have well asked Michael, "what's your favourite colour?". Michael understood these types of questions were no doubt considered normal for this time period. The streets are a war zone. Survivors would only be focusing on living. They'd hardly be reading books or going to football matches, watching films in cinemas, attending weddings like people living in Michael's present day.

"Peter, don't be rude! He's been through a lot." Karen scolded her boyfriend for his curiosity.

The reality struck Michael like an express train. He had been mysteriously transported to the future, fifty years from his home time period. There was no trace to explain how he came to be here. If Michael could not find a way to return to 2009, he would not only need to stay at the safe house on a permanent basis.

Michael Hartnell would never see his wife again. He would never see his parents or any one he knew. He came to a shocking realisation. He had lost everything he ever held dear.

"It's okay, Karen. He's only curious... I lost my whole world." Michael broke down in tears. It was true, all of his loved ones were in 2009. If they somehow managed to survive the day Lucifer was freed from Hell, they may not have been lucky further down the line. Michael was being realistic. They were dead. He would never see Sarah again for as long as he lived. He would never be able tell her how much he loved her. He sobbed uncontrollably at the thought. As he cried, Michael experienced and felt emotions he never wanted to feel. His cries sounded like someone else's as he made sounds he never heard before. He was grieving.

"You poor thing. You'll be alright." Karen calmly spoke to Michael with such a caring and soothing voice. She wrapped her arms around Michael. He couldn't help but hug her back and cry into her shoulder.

"Sorry I asked, Michael." Peter said to him with genuine sincerity. Tom entered the bedding area from the hallway. He instantly grasped that Michael was upset.

"Apologies… I'll come back later." Tom said as he prepared to leave the bedding area.

Michael wiped the tears from his eyes and face to find out what Tom had come to tell him.

"It's okay, Tom." He said as he found the strength to leave his bed. Michael looked at Tom and understood something was important. Why else would he come to the bedding area in the dark of night?

"Is everything alright?" Michael asked him.

"Do you mind if we have a quick word in private?" Tom asked Michael. He was standing in the doorway to the corridor, gesturing Michael to lead the way.

"Of course." Michael responded, wondering what Tom needed of him.

CHAPTER EIGHT

TOM HARTNELL

THE SAFE HOUSE

SECOND FLOOR CORRIDOR

GLASGOW

DECEMBER 23RD 2059

10:35am

Tom leads Michael out of the bedding area. He needed to know once and for all. Michael followed Tom into the corridor. Tom briefly looked him up and down. He couldn't bring himself to believe this man to be his grandfather from the past. Michael strangely looked familiar. Tom barely remembered his own father but what he did, he remembered his face and how Michael seemed to possess similar facial features to David Hartnell, Tom's father.

Michael did remind Tom of his father but not his grandfather. Old man Hartnell was a tough as nails, sixty-nine-year-old who refused to take shit from any man, demon, or Lucifer. He never once could have imagined that man as this scared boy. Michael said, he somehow travelled through time from December 22nd 2009.

If this were true. It would mean this young man was yet to witness the very beginning of the apocalypse. The day Lucifer destroyed the world. It would only be three days in his time period till it would all happen. Tom struggled to believe it. The thought of time travel made his head hurt.

Surely this was an elaborate cover to enter the safe house. What Tom didn't understand was, whoever this young man is. Why pretend to be a younger Michael Hartnell? Especially by registering under that name! None of it made any sense.

It would in a matter of minutes. Tom knew the best place to ask was in his grandfather's office. It was out of the sight of curious eyes. As they made their way along the corridor to the office, Tom spoke with Michael to lull him into a false sense of security.

He didn't want to let Michael know he was onto him in the event he was a mole for Lucifer.

"How are you coping, Michael?" Tom asked. Hoping Michael or whoever he was would slip up somewhere and add more fuel to the fire which was Tom's fury. Tom surprised himself as to how well he hid his rage.

"I won't lie. It's been tough… I think about home… It's hard. But I pray I will somehow get back." Michael said. Tom thought if he were a spy. He definitely had the Christian act down to a tee. Tom required more from Michael. He needed him to keep up the story he was selling. Tom knew exactly which button to press next.

"Must be difficult being a time-traveller?" He asked Michael. He patiently waited to see his reaction. Tom Hartnell believed a lot of things, but he couldn't accept that the young man walking beside him was a younger version of his grandfather.

"Difficult isn't how I would describe it. I struggle to understand it, never mind explaining it." Michael responded. Tom surprisingly thought that was well answered. Michael wasn't boasting about time travel like it was an achievement and he wasn't telling Tom what he wanted to hear. Whoever Michael is, Tom had to find out.

He himself was praying for this to be true. He wanted it to be so. The more he wanted it, he realised it was likely going to turn out to be one of Lucifer's mind games.

Tom continued to keep up the pretence to avoid any suspicion from Michael. "My apologies for not being able to provide you with fresh clothing. We're in short supply of lots of things." Tom said with the hope if Michael is a spy, he would attempt to inquire into the safe house's weapons.

Instead he merely responded with something Tom knew all too well.

"I thank you. I am happy with my pyjamas than nothing at all. I'm always grateful for what I have." Michael responded with his Christian ideology to the extent, Tom instantly knew where this phrase came from.

"You make do with what you have. My grandfather says something similar." Tom said with a slight chuckle. He was beginning to believe this guy actually sounded like his grandfather. There were only two possibilities, Michael was telling the truth and one day would live to become Tom's grandfather or he wasn't and all Michael had been doing was a performance, played a little too well for Tom's liking. It made him mad to think he was being manipulated.

Tom Hartnell would show this young man no mercy if he were to be discovered a liar.

"What time is it, Tom?" Michael asked him with concern.

"It's twenty to eleven in the morning." Tom responded. He wondered why he cared. Michael was newly arrived at the safe house, he had yet to be assigned any duties. Unless, he is a spy, the time could be something he required. But for what? A trap of some kind? Tom worried at the thought of the unknown.

"When does the sun come up?" Michael asked Tom with bizarre curiosity. Was he for real? Tom thought.

Tom decided it be best to continue playing "Michael's" game and tell the alleged time-traveller the truth and judge Michael's reactions to throw off his suspicions of him.

"There is no daylight. Not anymore. I'll explain more in the office." Tom said as they arrived at a door close to the stairwell. This was his grandfather's office and room. Tom opened the door and welcome Michael in. The room was as his grandfather left it, bookcases filled with books, a desk where he read. His bed was in the middle of the room. The bed had been neatly tucked in. No-one had slept in here for three weeks.

His grandfather always made his bed, every morning. He always said, "If you're not prepared to make your bed in the morning. How can you expect to do anything with your life?" Tom momentarily smiled at the memory before coming back to reality. His grandfather was always full of old sayings, he often always claimed that wise men in the days before the apocalypse had spoken them. Tom always thought he secretly invented them and passed it off as though others had created them.

As soon as the imposter crossed the threshold from the corridor into the office, Tom knew he needed to act fast and get the truth from him.

"What is it you want to talk about, Tom?" Michael asked. Before the door slammed shut. Tom was faster than a heartbeat, he seized hold of Michael by his upper arms and thrust him against the office wall. Michael looked taken by surprise and scared as Tom used one arm to hold Michael's arms against the wall. Tom needed to restrict Michael's movement. Arms were always the best to hold back and then with his free arm, Tom jammed his arm underneath Michael's chin and began to lean against his throat. He knew he had Michael's complete attention.

"Do you take me for an idiot?" Tom asked. The truth would come now or Michael would drop to his knees, gasping for air. Tom loosened his grip to allow Michael the chance to speak.

"Tom… What are you doing?" Michael said. He was scared and surprised by Tom's sudden actions which bound him.

"Do you take me for a fucking idiot?!" Tom shouted in Michael's face. He flinched at Tom's shouting.

"No!" Michael cried. Tom knew he'd put the fear of God into him.

"That was a sick and twisted cover story you told to get in here. What I don't understand is why you would pretend to be my grandfather." Tom quietly told him with a tone filled with fury, he was testing Michael's reaction. He looked as if Tom spoke something which made no sense. He either didn't know or he was an extremely good actor.

"I don't know what you mean." Michael responded. He looked puzzled.

"You know! You wrote my grandfather's surname and his date of birth! That's low! I almost believed you were a time-traveller. Now I see, it was the story he told you to spin. Where is he? Where is Lucifer?! You tell me where the son of a bitch is!" Tom demanded. He was taking no prisoners.

"Tom… I don't know where The Devil is… I am from the year 2009!" Michael stammered with terror. Tom no longer believed a word he spoke.

"Don't lie to me!" Tom shouted. He let his grip on Michael go and reached for the gun from his hip holster and pointed the pistol in Michael's tear-filled face.

"Tom… Please… I am telling you the truth… I was born on the 5th of October 1990, in Rottenrow Hospital… My parents are Georgina and Robert Hartnell… My wife's name is Sarah…" Michael pleaded with Tom.

Tom's anger passed like a speeding bullet and all he felt was guilt. Stronger than any he ever felt in his entire life. Michael spoke of things which only his grandfather knew.

"Sarah?" Tom asked. He was amazed by Michael's revelation.

"Yes. My wife's name is Sarah!" Michael began to shout through his tears.

Tom immediately holstered his weapon for he believed Michael to be truthful. He wasn't an undercover spy for Lucifer. Michael was exactly who he claimed to be. He is Tom's grandfather from the distant past.

"I believe you... I am sorry... Forgive me... Michael, do you know my surname?" Tom knew who Michael was and he needed Michael to see it for himself.

"No... I don't... Please let me go... I don't... I don't want to be here." Michael cried. Tom knew his approach was wrong. It had been necessary to uncover spies. Unfortunately, Michael had been truthful and scared half to death.

"My name is Thomas Hartnell... You really are from before? From before the apocalypse?" Tom asked with fascination and fear in the same moment.

"Yes." Michael replied. His throat sounded different from the crying.

"Sarah Rooney Hartnell. That is your wife's name. Isn't it?" Tom asked him. Michael's crying seized and he stared right into Tom's eyes. Tom knew Michael wondered how he knew the name.

"How do you know her name?" Michael asked in astonishment.

Tom exhaled before taking a deep breath. He was still trying to wrap his mind around their current situation.

"Five years after Lucifer escaped from Hell, you and Sarah have a son. That boy grew up and became my father... I was born twenty years ago... Michael... I am your grandson." Tom said. It felt and sounded strange as he told Michael.

Tom saw in Michael's face. He had already arrived at the same conclusion as both men stood and knew the truth. They are family. However strange and impossible it was, Tom and Michael stood in silence for a moment.

They were still adjusting to the idea. Tom didn't fully understand time travel and knew he probably never would. He was certain of one thing.

"I can't begin to understand it... You are him. I see it now. Meaning... Shit! You must find a way. I don't know how but you are my grandfather... If you don't get home, my dad will never be born and neither will I! The fact we stand here, having this conversation is proof. You must get back to 2009... I promise..." Tom is interrupted by Michael who suddenly begins to freak out with Tom.

"Get away! Leave me alone!" Michael shouted. It was overwhelming to hear everything. Tom desperately tried to calm Michael before he pushed Tom out of his way.

Tom did not anticipate Michael's reaction and fell on his backside from the force of Michael's thrust against his chest. Tom swiftly jumped to his feet as Michael stormed out of the office. He was running and Tom knew he needed to catch Michael before he done something stupid. Michael was not thinking clearly.

By the time, Tom entered the corridor, Michael reached the stairwell. Tom sprinted along the corridor in pursuit of Michael. When he reached the stairwell, he caught a glimpse of Michael's head as he ran downstairs. Tom knew he was attempting to leave the safe house. Tom couldn't let it happen. It will not happen. He thought as he jumped down the stairs to pick up the pace and catch up with Michael.

Michael was on the ground floor, pushing past anyone who was in his way. Tom was behind him as they both ran into the main entrance, the people in the bedding area stared and wondered what all the commotion was.

"Michael!" Tom shouted as Michael tackled past the sentries at the door. Michael opened the front door and ran out of the safe house. Tom made it to the entrance and immediately stopped. The sentries on the rooftop of the safe house and the buildings across the street, began firing warning shots at Michael's feet.

"HOLD YOUR FIRE!!!" Tom shouted to the sentries. He completely forgot about them and their orders to shoot any unauthorised departures from the safe house. Tom dreaded to think what could have happened if the sentries had shot and killed Michael.

Tom saw Michael in the middle of the street. He looked terrified and stood frozen with fear as he took in all his surroundings.

"Michael, come back!" Tom pleaded with Michael. He was scared for him. Michael briefly stared back at him before running away. Tom's heart sank as Michael ran in the one direction no-one would ever go. Michael ran into an area which the survivors had come to know as: The Forbidden Zone.

Tom watched in horror as his pyjama wearing time-travelling grandfather ran barefoot, disappearing in the darkness into the devil's nest. Tom knew Michael would find no safety in the north of the city. It belonged to Lucifer and his demons.

Michael was a long way from becoming the man who Tom knew as his grandfather. He would be defenceless and would suffer a fate worse than death if he were to fall into Lucifer's clutches. He feared what would happen if Lucifer discovered who Michael is destined to become.

Lindsay and John rushed to Tom's side as he stood in the doorway of the safe house.

"Tom, what the hell is going on?" John asked in confusion.

"Michael's ran off!" Tom stated as he came back inside the safe house.

"What happened? Is he okay?" Lindsay asked with her doctor's concern. Tom knew other than himself and John, she was the only other person who knew the truth about Michael.

"He's overwhelmed… He won't be okay if we don't get out there and find him. Michael ran north." Tom was filled with dread.

"Shit!" John exclaimed. Everyone knew how dangerous the north is.

"You mean towards…" Lindsay didn't finish her sentence. Most were frightened to even speak his name.

"Stupid bastard! I told you he was crazy, Tom!" John shouted at Tom.

He was in no mood for his nonsense.

"Shut your mouth! He was telling the truth." Tom said to stop this escalating out of control.

"How can you be so sure? You only met him a few hours ago!" John said to Tom. He didn't like John's attitude and knew what he was going to say next would not only silence John but make his head spin to try and understand it.

"Michael is my grandfather… From fifty years ago."

CHAPTER NINE

MICHAEL HARTNELL

THE FORBIDDEN ZONE
GLASGOW
DECEMBER 23RD 2059
TWO HOURS LATER

This is crazy, Michael thought. He knew it was true. Tom is his grandson, fifty years in his own future. Michael's head hurt thinking about the complexities of time travel, his mind struggled to think of a solution to return home and get back to Sarah.

He cried, wandering the streets of a ruined and war-torn Glasgow. Michael shivered from the cold. It bit at his skin through his pyjamas like a million invisible creatures, every inch of his body was freezing. He had never been so cold.

Michael knew now, running away had not been the wisest decision he ever made. All he really wanted was peace to process everything he discovered. He would have found none at the safe house. Tom would have been in his face, in search of answers to questions which Michael could not tell him.

There was no peace out here in the darkness despite the streets being deserted and quiet. Michael did not know whether this was a good thing or bad. He prayed he would never find out, the fear of the unknown scared him beyond any worst nightmare.

This was no nightmare. The apocalypse is here and Lucifer, The Devil had ruled his world for fifty years. Yet somehow, Michael's future self, endured all of this, he became the leader of the safe house. He and Sarah at some stage in his future had a child.

What kind of people would bring a child into this mess?

He thought of Sarah and more so about the way in which Tom had spoken of her. It was past tense, like a memory. Had Sarah been killed during the apocalypse?

Michael shook his head in disbelief and frustration. It couldn't happen, it will not happen, he promised himself. He refused to believe it as the truth.

His teeth chatter as the cold continues to bite his skin, his breath had been visible in the air. It was winter, but nowhere near as cold as the winter's he was accustomed to in his own time period. His head filled with questions. Tom had said, there was no daylight anymore. How could that be possible?

Michael looked at the sky. There were no stars to be seen. What had Lucifer done to the world? How had anyone ever survived with him walking the Earth and no sun to warm them?

Michael walked barefoot, his feet were sore and cold from the distance he had travelled. He walked for what felt like days. It was hard to tell with no daylight. He held onto his arms in a futile attempt to warm himself. As he continued to wander the deserted street, he realised he did not recognise the area and he lived in Glasgow all his life. It was the same as every street he had encountered since his arrival in the future. Another question he desperately needed answering. The most important as it could potentially hold the key on how to go back in time.

Houses were in ruin and vehicles were damaged. All the cars were alongside the pavements outside of properties. Only a handful were stuck in the middle of the road.

It was at this moment, it hit Michael. Why hadn't he noticed before? There were no bodies. Corpses had littered every street but since fleeing Tom's safe house, he hadn't seen any.

He wondered if it meant something sinister. Michael tried to think of better thoughts. This area may have been evacuated in time, maybe no-one in this area had perished at the very beginning. He prayed to be right. Michael could not bear any more horror.

A scream somewhere further down the street brought Michael to a halt. It was an infected.

Michael's breathing became rapid, his heartbeat was so hard, his entire body was pulsing.

The screams grew louder. There was more than one and the infected were nearby. Michael searched in every direction for any sign of them, his instincts had kicked in and he was determined to never encounter an infected ever again.

He leaned against a burnt-out car as he continued to observe the street for any sign of life, praying he wouldn't see them. Further along the street, he saw them become visible, a white face emerged from the darkness, charging in his direction.

Michael on instinct, launched himself through a broken window of the burnt-out car he had been standing beside. He landed face first on the car's backseat, it was filthy and uncomfortable, his only means of survival. He needed to turn himself around and lie on his back if he stood any hope of living. He lay on his back, making himself as small as he possible could to avoid detection.

The infected sprinted past the ruined car without giving it a second glance. They had not seen Michael and he was glad of it.

For what felt like an eternity, Michael lay there in the backseat, frightened to move, he had not heard the infected screams for some time. Michael had no clue as to how long he lay there. Had it been half an hour, an hour or two? He did not know.

What he knew was, he was becoming colder with each passing minute. The lack of movement made him shiver. Michael needed to get up and move, praying the whole time the infected were a good distance away from him.

Michael plucked up the courage, he thought of finding a way back to Sarah. She would be enough for him to brave whatever may be outside the car. He grabbed hold of the driver's seat headrest to pull himself up. His stomach rumbled. He hadn't eaten for what felt like forever. How could he be hungry at a time like this? He thought. Get your priorities right, he said to himself as he climbed outside the car to stand on the road next to the car.

He thought of Sarah, she was the strongest person he ever met. He knew she would have survived this world. Michael needed to discover where she is now. In order to do so, he needed to go back to where he last saw her.

The apartment they lived in together.

It was only a day ago when he last saw her. It would be fifty years for Sarah.

The complexities of time travel would drive anyone mad. He thought back to Tom's words. Tom is Michael's grandson. How could he return to the year 2009? If there were a way, Michael would find it. Not for himself but for Sarah, his wife.

With no better idea in mind. Michael committed himself to head for his apartment. First, Michael required his bearings. Where was he currently? Then he needed to figure out the best route to the flat on foot. Michael looked all up and down the street for anything to give him an indication to his location.

There were no street signs to give him a name. He continued to look as he stood in the middle of the road and at the same time, he kept his eyes peeled for the infected. Michael would be a sitting duck if they decided to return to the area.

The sound of footsteps got all of Michael's attention. At the end of the street, there was a man, he was searching for something, he had a rucksack over his shoulders. Michael watched with curious eyes as the man collected things from inside a car further down the street.

Michael realised the man was human and he was foraging for supplies to survive. Michael initially thought it best to leave the man be. It would be hard for any human alive to distinguish a friend from a foe.

The man might think Michael would want whatever he found, things could escalate into something ugly real fast. Michael knew the chances were the man could tell him where he is. If Michael could ensure the man he did not want his supplies, he might be able to help him on his journey. Michael only required the man to point him in the right direction and he would be on his way.

Michael knew the risk and needed to get a hold of the man's attention without scaring him away. Here goes nothing, Michael thought.

"Hello!" Michael called out to the man. The man looked as though he had jumped from fright. Michael realised the man probably had not expected to hear a voice call out in the darkness.

The man looked up the street, Michael seen the stranger had registered he was there and not only did he appear to not be afraid, he was welcoming, he waved his hand to Michael before walking along the street towards him.

As he reached Michael, he was able to see the man was indeed, human. The man couldn't have been much older than Michael. He wore a ragged black suit. It was old and dirty. The man had the same pale complexion as every person Michael had encountered. The man's hair is black and greasy, it had grown down to his neck.

Michael felt sorry for him. The man had obviously been living rough.

"Hello, my goodness. Can't remember the last time I seen a friendly face... Apologies, my name is Lu."

Lu said to Michael as he extended his hand out to shake Michael's.

Michael shook Lu's hand.

"My name is Michael." He responded. Michael heard the cold in his own voice.

"It's very nice to meet you, Michael. You been out here long?" Lu asked Michael.

He sounded concerned for Michael.

"Not long… Can you tell me where I am please?" Michael asked.

"The north of the city." Lu answered.

"Where in the north of the city?" Michael asked with desperation. He needed to know his location.

"It's just the north… You look like you've been to hell and back… Tell you what. I've got a place nearby. Get a change of clothes, something to eat and I'll help you get where you are going." Lu said to Michael in an offer of hospitality.

Michael was unsure, he did want to eat and a change of clothes. But he needed to try and find his apartment.

And hopefully find an answer to returning home.

"Thank you… I do appreciate your offer. I am looking for Crowwood Street. If you know where it is. Can you point me in the right direction?" Michael asked Lu.

He was grateful at Lu's offer, he only had one thing on his mind: Sarah.

"Out here? On your own? No, come with me, Michael." Lu seemed horrified at the thought of Michael wandering the streets of Glasgow by himself.

"It's alright… I think… I'll be fine alone." Michael responded through chattering teeth. The cold was the worst.

"You don't sound sure. Here's an idea. Come along and see my place. If it's not for you and you're still set on going. I'll point you in the right direction. I vaguely have a clue where you mean." Lu responded with the same hospitality. His manners were incredible for someone who had nothing, Michael thought.

"I really need to get where I am going." Michael stated in the hope Lu would understand why it was so urgent.

"Come to think of it. I do have some old maps from before. Might be of use." Lu told Michael.

Michael is amazed to hear Lu possesses maps from before the apocalypse. He could figure out where they are and find Crowwood street in a matter of minutes.

"Brilliant. Can I see them?" Michael asked. One step closer to home, he thought.

"I don't have them with me. They're back at my place. Come with me, get yourself freshened up, I'll look out the maps and you'll be on your way." Lu's words struck Michael. It was only now he wondered why Lu was being so generous to him.

"Why are you doing this?" Michael asked with curiosity and suspicion.

"Doing what?" Lu asked. He didn't understand what Michael meant.

"Why help me? You don't know me." Michael said. He wondered why Lu was prepared to give Michael, a complete stranger: Everything.

"There are so few of us left. We can't afford to not help each other." Lu responded with tears in his eyes.

Michael knew how bad things were. Humans would have to band together in order to survive. The world lost so much. The last thing they could lose was each other. Michael knew Lu probably was his only chance at finding any clue to Sarah's whereabouts and hopefully, a way home.

Michael felt he had no other option but to go wherever Lu called home.

"Okay... I'll come with you." Michael replied. Fully accepting whatever hospitality Lu had to offer.

"Fantastic! It's not far from here. You'll fit right in... I believe the old saying is, we'll get on like a house of fire." Lu chuckled at his own humour.

Michael smiled. Lu is very well spoken. Michael let a little laugh out too. He couldn't believe this young Scottish man was quoting Glaswegian sayings. They were still being spoken at the end of days. For a moment, Michael had almost forgotten his surroundings.

A spine-tingling scream from a distant infected brought both men back to reality.

"We best be moving. If there's one. There are usually more. Follow me." Lu gestured as he began walking back down the street. Michael quickly followed Lu into the darkness to put as much distance between them and the infected. He wanted the distant infected to stay distant.

Lu walked at a brisk pace. Michael understood why. Lu didn't appear to possess any sort of weapons. Michael didn't think he would fare well against a group of infected unarmed. No one would.

Michael caught up with Lu and walked side by side with him. They could barely hear the screams. Too far away to do any harm. Michael felt at peace with the knowledge.

"Tell me about yourself, Michael." Lu asked as he continued his brisk walk along the street.

This street didn't appear to be as bad, less buildings and no burnt-out cars.

"You'd think I were insane if I told you." Michael responded. Not everyone would understand being from another time.

"Insane?" Lu asked with puzzlement.

Michael realised Lu probably didn't understand the word. No-one would have received a formal education in the apocalypse. What Lu knew he learnt from doing.

"I mean crazy. Sorry." Michael apologised for confusing Lu.

"No, I know what you mean. Why would you think yourself insane?" Lu asked with genuine concern for Michael.

"It's a long story, Lu." Michael responded to avoid getting into all the details of travelling through time with no explanation.

"Well, I very much look forward to hearing all about it." Lu said to Michael in the hope of encouraging it out of him.

"Later perhaps. How much farther is it?" Michael anxiously asked.

"Not far." Lu answered with a smile across his face. His teeth were rotten, Michael felt sick at his smile. He felt awful to react in such a manner. Lu is helping him and Michael knew whatever kind of life Lu had endured. It would have been tough. Michael, without having to ask, knew Lu would have witnessed things, no human should ever see and lost things he could never understand.

He felt sympathy for Lu and was not prepared to share it with him. People are difficult enough in his own time. What were they like in 2059? Lu may take offence at his sympathy.

Michael kept his thoughts to himself as they walked for a little while longer. They definitely were somewhere Michael had never been before. There were mansions all along the street, each one of them in ruin. All the mansions had enormous front gardens, the trees were leafless and dead. Every mansion overlooked what Michael thought was a loch. Where is Lu's place? Michael thought.

Something was different. Lights shone further down the street. What was it? Lu was leading Michael straight toward the light. They became brighter as both of them began their approach.

Michael became unsure of where Lu was leading him. Any light would be a good target.

The infected would be sure to see it and then there was Lucifer. Michael prayed he would never cross paths with him. Michael finally saw what the lights are. They were security lights for an enormous mansion.

This was Lu's place.

The mansion is immaculate, cleaner than anything Michael had seen in 2059. The house had been painted white. Michael knew the colour was impossible to keep clean. Yet, this house was in pristine condition.. Untouched, despite the world surrounding it. Michael thought it strange.

Suddenly Michael acknowledged the lights which lit up the building. They weren't candles. They were flood lights. Lu's place had electricity. He thought of Tom's safe house in the city centre. The entire building had been illuminated by candlelight. How did Lu possess power?

Lu stopped outside the mansion, he opened a gate and gestured Michael to walk up a stoned path leading to the entrance of the mansion.

"Here it is. Home sweet home! A slice of paradise, hidden from the rest of the world." Lu said with a grin. Michael felt like Lu was showing off. But why? How did he have all of this? Michael registered from a quick glance of the garden, the rooftops, and the entrance of the house.

There were no guards.

Something did not add up about this picture.

"Where are your guards, Lu?" Michael asked. He prayed he didn't need to be suspicious of Lu's home.

'I have no need of guards." Lu calmly responded without a care in the world.

"Why not?" Michael asked. This did not make him feel at ease. His mother's words were going through his mind. "If it looks too good to be true. It probably is."

He thought of them in the second before Lu explained why.

"No-one knows this place exists. Except for a few... Demons and humans stick to the city. There is nothing of interest out here... I should have mentioned we have electricity. We have a generator. We only put the lights on to lead me back. I've been out here for days, searching for supplies...

I understand if you want to go. You are free to leave. If you do, you go without our maps. My people need them to navigate from here. We cannot afford to lose them. You understand, right?" Lu explained the operations of his household.

Michael believed Lu. He sounded honest and genuine. There was a group, living in a mansion at the end of the world. He really needed those maps. The risk of losing his only hope of getting back to Sarah, was not worth being suspicious.

"Yes, I do… I accept your hospitality." Michael thanked Lu.

"Follow me." Lu said as he led Michael through the gate and onto the stone path. Lu reached the front door before Michael. The doors opened inward on their own. Lu strolled through the door, like he owned the place. Suppose he did, Michael realised.

Michael stood outside the front door, he stared inside the mansion. It is beautiful, white marbled floors, the walls painted white with portraits and paintings hanging on either side of what Michael took for a large hallway. Lu is standing in the middle of the room on a white marble staircase with beautiful banisters. The marble banisters and pillars led all the way upstairs.

Michael couldn't see anything else. He caught a better look at the portraits on the walls. There is something sinister about them. The lights, shining in Michael's eyes, hurt. He'd grown accustomed to the darkness.

Despite Lu's explanation, Michael could not shake off the bad feeling he had. Something is wrong.

"Come on, Michael. I'll give you the tour." Lu offered as he waved his hand, gesturing for Michael to enter.

Michael stepped over the threshold, his faith would protect him, he thought. In the same second, Michael is suddenly seized from both sides by two unseen assailants and dragged further inside the house. He is forced onto his knees at the staircase in front of Lu. He was standing only a few steps up from where Michael is kneeling. Lu smiled with a wicked grin.

Michael's panic returned with a vengeance. He was terrified out of his wits.

"Lu, what is going on…" Michael shouted with fear for his own life. Why was this happening?

Michael caught a glimpse of the two men who had grabbed him and were holding him down. They were dressed from head to toe in black. Their clothes were like rags and Michael let out a gasp. The sight of their faces.

They were paler than any human in 2059. Their eyes were the worst.

The pupils of their eyes looked like… They looked like the eyes you would expect to see on a corpse.

Dead!

The iris was a glowing green colour almost like an animal when light strikes it in the darkness.

These men were not human.

"What are you?!" Michael asked in a blind state of panic.

"Demons." Lu responded on their behalf.

Michael's attention turned back to Lu. In the blink of an eye, Lu's appearance transformed.

Lu was older, he must have been in his mid-fifties, Michael thought. His skin is paler than the demons, his black hair became shorter and was no longer greasy. It looked clean and as if he had run a comb through his hair. His ruined suit was pristine and flawless. It was black and brand new. Michael looked upon Lu's face. He had a goatee beard and his whole face is so thin, he was almost skeletal. He'd became taller too.

"Who are you?" Michael asked. Knowing full well, he was not going to like the response. How stupid had Michael been to be tricked by a demon?!

Lu and the rag-wearing demons laughed at Michael.

"Humans. So very typical! I can't believe you fell for my performance I put on out there." Lu said with such a sinister tone.

His accent had also changed. Lu was no longer Scottish. The accent sounded like a southern one, an American southern state accent. Michael couldn't quite place the state it reminded him of. It sounded like he had a hiss in his speech like a serpent. Lu appeared to be enjoying this power he held over Michael.

"Who am I? I go by many names. You will address me by my proper title… I am Lucifer."

Michael nearly fainted upon hearing this. Lu is Lucifer, The Devil and he played his role, a wolf in sheep's clothing.

Michael would not allow Lucifer to smell his fear. God would protect him as he done all the days of his life.

Michael Hartnell had never feared The Devil before. He was determined not to start today.

"Satan!" Michael shouted before he spat in Lucifer's face.

Lucifer slowly removed a handkerchief from inside his suit jacket and wiped the spit from his face. He took a moment to inspect it before viciously striking Michael across the face with the back of his hand.

It hurt more than any hit to the face from any bully. Michael's face stung, his lip burst open, he spat his blood onto the white marble floor. He tasted the metal of his own blood as he lifted his head to stare at Lucifer in defiance.

"Never address me by such a vile name, ever!" Lucifer slowly spoke to Michael with a fury in his tone. Michael had pissed him off.

"That's who you are! You are The Devil! I do not fear you!" Michael continued to stare him out before Lucifer and the demons burst into a fit of hysterical laughter.

"Fear me?! You would be a fool not to! I am The Lord of The Earth. If I wished it, I could incinerate you from the inside out by a mere snap of my fingers. You should be terrified! You ought to show me some bloody respect, you filthy norm!" Lucifer coldly spoke to Michael, he was holding back the full extent of his rage, Michael felt.

Lucifer's words had no effect on Michael, he would not allow the fallen archangel to intimidate him. As a Christian, Michael felt it was his duty to show evil, it had no place here or anywhere.

"Respect needs to be earned, Satan! I do not fear you. God will defeat you." Michael defiantly declared.

Lucifer laughed harder at Michael's argument against him. The demons also found it funny. They laughed hysterically alongside their lord. Lucifer attempted to maintain himself. He let out a couple of sniggers, he was trying his best not to continue laughing.

"God?! That fucking asshole! Do not make me laugh! I have ruled your world for nearly fifty years, the governments and armies collapsed in a day, Heaven and its angels abandoned you all. God, if he could stop me, he would have already done it. Face it, Michael! God does not care about any of you. I am the one who rules your world. God lost the battle between Heaven and Hell, the day I walked free... I am God! Kneel and pledge your allegiance to Lucifer or die!"

Michael stared at Lucifer's disgusting face in silence for a moment. Lucifer's grin turned his stomach, Michael watched as Lucifer's eyes glowed red. Lucifer was the one who killed Nejuma.

"Burn in hell!" Michael shouted in one last act of defiance. He knew it in his heart, Lucifer would surely kill him.

Lucifer laughed from the shock of Michael's response before swiftly knocking Michael out cold with his fist.

CHAPTER TEN

TOM HARTNELL

THE SAFE HOUSE

GLASGOW

DECEMBER 23rd 2059

11:25pm

Tom stands with Lindsay at the entrance to the safe house in the assembly area of the main bedding area. He is there to address the residents living in the sanctuary.

"I am going to need some volunteers. This morning, a friend of mine, a new resident ran from here. He's alone and scared. Making it our job to go out and bring him home. Who's with me?" Tom patiently waits to see who would step forward. Everyone began to talk amongst themselves.

John stepped forward.

"You can count on me, Tom. Now and always."

"Never doubted you, John. Anymore volunteers?" Tom asked as he slowly began to lose his patience.

Tom noticed that Peter Carlisle stepped forward. He is one of Tom's oldest friends. He had known Peter for as long as he could remember.

"I'm coming too." Peter declared as he volunteered.

"Thanks. Anyone else. This is your last chance to volunteer." Tom waited for one last time, if no-one else came forward, it would mean his three-man team would be Michael's only hope for a rescue.

A young man stepped forward. Tom didn't really know him too well. His name is Kyle and Tom thought he wasn't the sharpest tool in the shed. Another volunteer stepped forward, Robert, his name is. Tom remembered his Grandfather Michael, had suspended him from a sentry post for being a panic merchant with a trigger-happy finger.

Considering where they were destined, Tom may need someone with lightning fast reflexes to sudden movements.

Kyle is silent as he approaches Tom. Both he and Robert are dressed all in black, their clothes are ragged. He had spare body armour for them to go under their black sweaters. They would be well hidden in the darkness of the forbidden zone and they needed to protect themselves from the chances of an ambush. There is a reason the north was called the forbidden zone. Not very many ever returned from it.

Robert spoke to Tom as he approached him.

"I know your grandfather benched me. I hope I can make it up to you and him, Tom."

Tom put his hand on Robert's shoulder and nodded his head.

"You will. There is no room for error. You come with us. You may not come back." Tom explained. He is ensuring Robert knows the risk of what he is signing up to.

"I know… I want to make things right." Robert responded in agreement.

"Make him proud." Tom said.

A young woman stepped forward. Rachel or Raquel as everyone had nicknamed her for a laugh. As far as Tom was aware, she hated the Raquel nickname. Tom had witnessed first-hand. She is an excellent shot from above. He had yet to see her experience on the ground. He prayed his team would be enough.

"Thanks. Everyone else. Go about your business. We will be back soon." Tom declared to the residents. Everyone departed the assembly to resume their daily business and resume their routines.

Tom felt surprised by the behaviour of the residents. Things had not been right for the last few weeks. It all began after his grandfather's disappearance. He felt saddened and understood in the same moment.

Tom faced his team at the safe house entrance. Two armoured sentries stood at the barred entrance. Lindsay is standing with the team. It's only now, Tom registered that Lindsay is not wearing her medical coat. She is dressed from top to bottom in black and has body armour on underneath her black jumper. She was planning to come along with the team.

No way in hell was Tom about to authorise this.

"You're not coming." Tom informed Lindsay.

She is struck by surprise. He could read it off her facial expressions. She is pissed off about not being included. Tom knew she was preparing to back chat him.

"Why? Michael is out there! I am more qualified to go out there than most." Lindsay argued, she attempted to persuade Tom to alter his decision. She should know by now how stubborn he is once his mind is made. He always stuck with it.

"Michael ran north into the forbidden zone. It's too dangerous! If we don't come back. I will need you here. Anything happens to you. This place loses its only doctor." Tom knew Lindsay would put the needs of the many before the few. It is her duty as a doctor to preserve life.

John spoke up. Tom knew he was beginning to get anxious for time.

"Tom, we better get a move on. He's been out there a while. Fuck knows what is happening to him."

John was right, they needed to proceed with their mission.

"Take the others outside. I'll join you in a moment." Tom explained.

John nodded his head in agreement as he turned and led Kyle, Robert, Peter, and Rachel outside. They walked up to the large barred doors. The sentries removed the wooden barricade from its holder to allow the doors to open and let the team exit the safe house.

Tom overhears John radioing the rooftop sentries to alert them of their departure.

Lindsay continued to plead with Tom.

"I am coming with you, Tom. Michael may require medical assistance. If he is seriously injured, he could die... You said he is your grandfather. A version of him from the past. If he were to die before your father was born. You could cease to exist."

Tom went silent at the thought. Could that happen? If Michael died. Would Tom just vanish into thin air?

"I can't begin to comprehend the complexities of time travel paradoxes. And to be honest, I don't think it is worth the risk to find out. I am coming." Lindsay's words made Tom's head hurt and he needed a moment to think.

If Michael were to die here and now at the age of nineteen. It would change everything.

72

All the lives Michael will save in his future, would perish, the safe house would never be established. Would the remains of humanity stand a chance against Lucifer without Michael Hartnell, the leader of the resistance? The thoughts of an alternate time filled with endless horrors was not worth lingering over and changed Tom's decision on Lindsay accompanying the team.

"You make a convincing argument." Tom needed no more justifications as to why Lindsay needed to be included in the search mission. He agreed with the doctor.

They made their way out of the safe house. Tom nodded his head as he passed the sentries, indicating to them he wished for the barricade to put back up and seal the doors. Tom and Lindsay joined the others on the street. Peter noticed that Lindsay is accompanying them.

"Why is she coming?" Peter blurted out in surprise. He sounded pissed off and no doubt thought Lindsay would prove to be a liability.

"My decision. That's all you need to know." Tom shut it down instantly.

"What's the plan of attack?" John asked Tom. He patiently awaited instructions from his leader like a good soldier.

It felt strange being in charge of the resistance. It had always been Tom's grandfather. He grew up knowing the day would eventually arrive. He hadn't expected it to be now.

"We'll be on foot. We can't risk a car inside the forbidden zone. We'll be searching every street from top to bottom. The streets are crawling with infected. Hold a tight formation. Anyone running off into the darkness can easily be mistaken for an infected. Does anyone have any questions?" Tom asked with the hope for silence.

"What about Lucifer?" Peter asked without any sign of fear. Tom found this surprising. Most people feared to mention his name.

"What about him?" Tom responded without a care in the world.

"What do we do if he decides to show himself? It is his territory!" Peter responded. Tom knew Peter had yet to encounter Lucifer in the flesh. None of them with the exception of himself and John had.

Any man or woman who crossed paths with Lucifer and lived to tell the tale would have been extremely lucky in Tom's eyes. He had encountered Lucifer more times than he cared to remember and nothing about Lucifer was pleasant. He is rotten to the core.

"Run like fuck. Nothing we possess can harm him. If by some misfortune our paths cross. Run! Save yourself. If Lucifer doesn't kill you right there and then. He will give you a fate worse than death."

Tom saw his words had an effect on everyone present. Everyone except for John and Lindsay could barely look him in the eye.

"Anything else?" Tom asked. Knowing full well no-one would dare ask anything else after listening to what he told them.

Silent as a graveyard. No-one said a thing.

"Follow my lead." Tom instructed as he walked past the group. He is followed by Lindsay then John with Peter, Robert, Kyle, and Rachel following closely behind them as they begin their walk away from the security of the safe house and towards the darkness and unknown terrors of the forbidden zone in search of Michael.

The forbidden zone is only a couple of miles away. No sentry had found Michael anywhere nearby. The only place he could be was north. The Devil's playground. They kept a tight formation with guns at the ready.

Tom handed Lindsay her own pistol. She took a hold of it and looked surprised by his offering it to her.

"Just in case." Tom said.

"I've never fired a gun before, Tom." Lindsay said with worry.

"It's ready to go. All you have to do is aim, point, then blast whatever is coming at you. You don't stop till its dead. Send them straight to hell."

Lindsay had barely left the safe house since her arrival, six years previously. The only time she ever left was in search of medical supplies with an armed guard. The forbidden zone is a completely different game. No gun, no survival.

Everyone stayed close as they continued walking through the dark streets. Tom could only just make out an old road sign "You are now leaving Glasgow". This is it.

The beginning of Lucifer's domain. There was no going back. Crossing the line into enemy territory is risky alone but with a group. Tom feared whatever was about to play out.

He and his grandfather, Michael's future self, had crossed this perimeter a great many times. They always made it back alive.

The last time was three weeks ago, when he and his grandfather had the knife. The only thing capable of killing Lucifer.

That was the last time Tom ever saw his grandfather. He felt awful and sick. He knew the guilt would eat away at him for the rest of his life. Tom Hartnell would remember that day. He would never forget it. He thought about how he would die. If he were lucky, he could live till the same age as his grandfather. Tom knew that reality was a dream.

The truth is, someone or something would get him in the end. An infected or demon, maybe even Lucifer himself. Tom knew he would sooner put a bullet in his skull than suffer whatever cruel ideas Lucifer no doubt had in mind.

Tom's face must have shown a lot. Lindsay spoke to him.

"Are you okay, Tom?" She asked him with concern.

His expressions said it all.

"I'm fine. Staying focused." Tom responded in an attempt to shrug off everything he thought.

"You look like a man with deep thoughts." Lindsay stated. She was like a mind reader, Tom thought, shaking his head and letting out a small chuckle.

"I must be like an open book. It's all so much to take in." Tom told her. Too much was happening at once. Always something going on, but this was different. In times of struggle he would look to his grandfather for advice and now he couldn't.

"Time travel would be hard enough for anyone. But when it's your grandfather…"

Tom immediately interrupted Lindsay.

"Keep your voice down." Tom said. For a couple of reasons, to not draw attention to their location and to ensure the others didn't find out Michael's true identity. A quick glance back at their faces suggested they hadn't heard a thing. All of them were too busy, keeping their focus on what is in front of them with a gun at the ready. Praying nothing would lunge at them from the darkness.

Tom turned his attention back to Lindsay as they continued their search in the wasteland streets of the forbidden zone. Nothing in these streets to scavenge, no bodies littering the roads like any other in the city centre and surrounding areas.

Lucifer liked his territory clean, not very many survivors ever seen where he resided.

Only once before had Tom ever seen Lucifer's mansion and he'd no intention of ever setting foot there again. The forbidden zone stretched for miles, there were ways around it but there isn't much further north that anyone would have any need of travelling up there.

"I don't know how the others will handle it. It's not that I find time travel hard to grasp. I know he is my grandfather. It's..." Tom spoke to her at a quieter level. He didn't know how to speak what he was feeling.

"What are you thinking, Tom?" Lindsay sounded concerned for his mental state. A good doctor, he thought.

"It doesn't matter." Tom shrugged off her question to avoid explaining how he really felt.

Bad thoughts out in the city could get you killed. He didn't want to dwell on it in Lucifer's territory.

"Tell me." Lindsay asked in her usual doctor/patient way of speaking.

"It's ever since he went missing..." Tom held back tears. He knew what he was preparing to say would make it real. He took a deep breath.

"My grandfather... He's dead." Tom admitted.

"You don't know for sure." Lindsay tried to keep Tom's faith alive.

He thought her kind for doing so. Unfortunately, it was time to look at the facts and accept the truth.

"Lindsay, he's dead. If he were still breathing, he would have found a way back. Had he failed to kill Lucifer... He would have come home... Lucifer killed him. There's no other explanation to why he has been missing for three weeks... His luck ran out... The residents know it too. Did you see how they reacted when I asked for volunteers?"

She of all people must have been aware and noticed the attitude changes among the survivors living in the safe house.

"They're scared, Tom. No-one can honestly admit to wanting to set foot in the forbidden zone."

Lindsay was trying to defend them. Tom respected her for not taking a side.

"I can't help feeling like they've all lost hope. Had my grandfather asked for volunteers. Every man, woman and child would have stepped forward for him... I am not the man he was... I will never be as great a man as him. How does one compete with his legacy?"

Tom doubted his own leadership.

"You are a great man. Do you honestly think it all happened overnight for him? Not very many people get the opportunity to meet a relative from before. You have seen what he would have been like at the beginning. How do you think the frightened young man, the same one you are looking for did the great things you speak of?" Lindsay was trying to get him to understand something. But what?

"What are you saying?" Tom asked her.

"He got on with it. Doing whatever needed done to survive. Exactly what you are doing. Rome was not built in a day." She's right, Tom realised.

Michael, his grandfather would not have been born into a resistance leader. His knowledge, skills and respect were hard earned. Michael would have adapted to the world around him. Tom knew it would take time to come to terms with his grandfather's death for everyone.

He thought of this as a chance to redeem himself, save the younger version of the man who would become his grandfather, the fearless warrior who stared Lucifer in the face and told him "No".

The man who would lead a resistance for humanity's right to live.

Michael is out there somewhere.

Tom knew he would find him even if it cost him his life.

CHAPTER ELEVEN

MICHAEL HARTNELL

LUCIFER'S MANSION

THE FORBIDDEN ZONE

GLASGOW

DECEMBER 24th 2059

06:30am

Michael awoke. He felt groggy. His head pounded. Michael's throat was dry. Had he been asleep? How did he get here? He remembered. The stranger who introduced himself as Lu. He lured Michael into a trap before revealing his true identity: Lucifer.

Michael put all the pieces back together as he came to. He remembered everything that occurred. He had defied Lucifer's demands and paid for it with a fist to the face.

His eyes stung. He dreaded to open them. He was unable to move. He immediately discovered why upon opening his eyes. Michael struggled to free himself. Someone had bound his wrists and ankles to a chair in a dark room. He gagged at the smell inside the room.

There were bodies close by. Despite the darkness, Michael saw the mutilated corpses across from him. They had no doubt suffered a fate worse than death before dying. What was left of them was barely recognisable as human. They had been tortured to death.

The room he is in. It is a torture chamber.

He attempted to rock the chair from side to side. His effort was futile. The chair had been bolted to the floor. He only just realised. He was stripped to his underwear.

Michael let out a whimper. He knew there was no chance of escape. He would die in this room. Lucifer would be his torturer before he departed this life.

"Ah! You're awake!" Lucifer's southern accent spoke from behind Michael. He flinched upon hearing The Devil's spine-tingling voice. Michael felt his skin crawl at the thought of Lucifer's touch.

The pale skeletal face emerged from out of the darkness. Lucifer stared Michael dead in the eye. Michael dug deep for the courage to face Lucifer. He was not going to give him the opportunity to relish in his fear.

"I trust you slept well. Thought you were never going to wake up. I like my patients to be awake when I perform. It's more fun that way. My last one, he stayed with me for thirty-six hours! Can you imagine that? Humans are different. I've tortured demons and angels for less the time. Don't worry, my friend. I'll be sure to keep you alive for the grand finale."

Lucifer chuckled before leaning in closer to whisper in Michael's ear.

"I hope to break the record." A slimy smile spread across Lucifer's pale face. Michael barely reacted to Lucifer's words. He was praying in his mind to endure whatever Lucifer planned for him.

Lucifer began walking circles around the chair. Michael dreaded to think what twisted thoughts ran through Lucifer's mind. What did the mind of the original evil think of? Michael knew his own thoughts too well. He figured there was nothing left to lose. There was only one way this was going to end.

Michael knew there no was no chance of a happy ending for him. He had questions and Lucifer had answers. Michael prepared himself to ask the question. The same one he had when Lu, who was actually Lucifer had found him.

The question that had been running through his mind with every waking second from his mysterious arrival in the future.

"I take it you were the one who brought me here?" Michael asked knowing full well it had to be Lucifer. How else could he have travelled through time to 2059?

Lucifer walked around him, muttering his name in a mocking manner.

"Michael, Michael, Michael!" Lucifer muttered before he stopped circling him to look the young man in the eye.

"I hope my hitting your head hasn't affect your memory. I know how fragile you humans can be. Of course, I brought you here. We walked through the front door." Lucifer was mocking him. Michael knew he was avoiding the question with this ridiculous charm act that Lucifer thought he played well.

Michael shook his head. He found himself laughing ever so slightly at Lucifer's denial. Whether it be from his nerves or simply because Michael thought it pathetic. He did not know.

"Cut the performance! You know what I am asking." Michael shouted at Lucifer.

For a moment, Michael wondered where his sudden bravery had come from. He had shouted at The Devil! Michael then thought. Only a stupid idiot would have done so. But he needed to know the truth.

Lucifer leaned in closer and stopped his face directly in front of Michael's.

His fear slowly returned as he realised all he done was piss off Lucifer.

Lucifer's face is the stuff of nightmares. The eyes were the worst. They were red. He is the red-eyed man who killed Nejuma.

Michael hid his terror. He was not prepared to show his fear.

"Know what?" Lucifer asked whilst he made some sort of sucking noise behind his teeth before sinisterly licking his lips. What went on in that head? Michael thought. Did he really want to know?

"You brought me to the future." Michael stated.

Lucifer paused and stared at Michael in silence for a brief moment before laughing hysterically.

"I don't think so, Michael. I am a fallen archangel. There were many a miracle I could perform before I was cast out. I never did get to sample time-travel. Must be a new thing for my brother and sister angels." Lucifer responded.

He was lying. He had to be.

"You are lying!" Michael said to Lucifer. He did not believe him.

"Afraid not." Lucifer responded. He was no longer speaking to Michael with his mocking tone which Michael had become acquainted with. Was Lucifer telling the truth?

"You're telling the truth?!" Michael was stunned by this. The Devil telling the truth. He couldn't believe it. Lucifer had no witty or smart-arse remarks about Michael. Everything he spoke was all about himself and Heaven.

"Honest to Dad!" Lucifer responded with his right hand up to God. Lucifer mocked God. Despite that, he was telling the truth.

Lucifer is not responsible for Michael's arrival in the future.

If it hadn't been him. Who? Who else could transport someone from the safety of his present day to the horrors of the apocalypse?

"How did I get here if it wasn't you?" Michael asked his thought out loud.

Lucifer stared at Michael. He thought Lucifer was thinking about how to torture him.

Michael realised it wasn't that. He was curious about Michael. What he said to Lucifer had intrigued him.

"A few weeks ago, I killed someone... Time travel? What is your surname? I imagine you would have one with a first name like yours." Lucifer spoke calmly. His voice was quite soothing considering the situation.

Lucifer must have known something which Michael did not. If it had any potential to help him, Michael was not about to speak his name. Michael knew he would suffer whatever torture Lucifer planned to inflict upon his body and bear the affect it would have on his mental state.

"What is it to you?" Michael demanded in a hope to get an insight into Lucifer's thoughts.

"You look awfully familiar. Have we met before?" Lucifer asked. He stared at Michael's face with puzzlement.

"Do you think I would be here if we had?" Michael responded with a typical Glaswegian's sarcasm. It was his turn to withhold information. Michael knew little about his future-self with the exception that he had lived until this year as the leader of the resistance.

Lucifer surely knew the name "Michael Hartnell".

What would Lucifer do if he knew his name? Kill him? Lucifer would with a doubt kill him. He was the biggest threat to his reign.

Tom's grandfather, the leader of the resistance against Lucifer. To speak the name, Hartnell. It could have disastrous consequences not only for those still alive at the safe house. Michael had no clue what affect his death could have on the past. He thought of the timeline in his head and what would cease to exist.

The leader of the resistance would never have existed. Michael feared his death could mean the resistance itself would never have even been established. It would be like killing Hitler in his cot. History would change only this time, it would not be for the better of mankind. Every victory of the resistance would become a defeat at the hands of Lucifer.

For Michael to die here, it would change everything in both time periods. He will not allow this to happen.

"What is your name?" Lucifer demanded. Michael felt the anger in his voice.

"Do your worst." Michael responded. He prayed for the strength to hold on and not give in to whatever pain was coming. Lucifer's face filled with fury before he struck Michael across the face with the back of his hand.

"Wrong answer! We can do this the easy way or we can do it my way! Your surname or I'll hit your head till it is mush!" Lucifer said with such coldness. He enjoyed this.

Michael coughed up blood. The taste of blood filled his mouth. He spat it on the floor. Some of his blood had accidentally landed on Lucifer's leather shoes.

Lucifer, of course did not see this as an accident.

The fury of the fallen archangel was coming.

"Is that the best you can do? My gran in Cranhill hits harder than you!" Michael took full advantage. He would never permit Lucifer to know his full name. Every time Lucifer hit him. Michael would insult him.

Lucifer chuckled at Michael's defiance. He slowly unveiled the dagger, the blade he used to kill Nejuma.

The knife, the only thing capable of killing an angel. Tom told Michael about how he and Michael's future-self had intended to use the blade on Lucifer.

They had failed. The knife was in Lucifer's possession. It stood out from everything else. The blade was a magnificent piece of craftmanship. Michael couldn't read the carved writing on the dagger. It was a language he had never seen before. As Lucifer took a good firm grip of the handle, Michael caught a glimpse of it. The handle was shaped like a large feather. An angel wing, he thought.

Ironic, he thought. A knife capable of killing angels would look the way it did.

"Boy, you are going to tell me your name or I will use this on you." Lucifer's Cheshire cat smile stretched across his pale thin face.

"You talk some amount of shite!" Michael laughed at Lucifer's interrogation tactics. Michael felt he endured worse from playground bullies until Lucifer's back hand struck his face for a second time.

"That wasn't a very nice thing to say, Michael." Lucifer chuckled at Michael's pain.

"I know what that knife is and what it can do!" Michael responded through a mouthful of blood.

Lucifer stood in silence, a smile of admiration stretched across his vile face. Michael knew that got Lucifer's attention away from his surname for a moment.

"Oh, really?! And what do you know of this dagger?" Lucifer held the dagger near Michael's face to show it off with pride.

"It can kill you… I'm Glaswegian. You think this is the first time I have seen a knife?! If you are going to use it. You better do it right. Make a cunt of it! I will not hesitate to use it on you!"

Lucifer grinned at Michael's promise. He laughed in his face.

"I'd like to see you try." Lucifer said to him with such vile hatred before cutting Michael's bare arm. He winced in pain. He would not bring himself to scream. Lucifer would enjoy it if he did. Michael prepared himself to deprive the nourishment of Lucifer's sick minded entertainment.

Before Michael attempted to hit out with some form of insult, Lucifer ran the blade across his bare skin again. He did so swiftly, Michael had not expected it. The pain was worse than the first time. He let out a whimper and knew this was the end.

Michael would die here despite learning about his own future. He would never be reunited with Sarah. That was worse than anything Lucifer could inflict upon him.

"TELL ME!!!" Lucifer's fury vibrated through the darkness of the torture room. He was furious. His voice and anger that came with it reminded Michael who Lucifer truly is. He was The Devil and he would never be able to hide it. No matter what act he played.

"Go to hell, Satan!" Michael spat his words in distaste at Lucifer's childish temper tantrum.

Lucifer, faster than a heartbeat, slashed the blade across Michael's arm.

Michael let out a whimper of pain. He could not hide how painful it truly was. His arm is a mess. Lucifer had slashed across the same wound. Michael's blood ran like a river from the wound, dripping onto the floor, pooling at his feet, mixing with the dried blood stains of Lucifer's previous torture victims.

"I have all eternity. The question is, how far do I need to go for you to talk?" Lucifer enjoyed this and at the same time he was desperate to know.

"Okay… I will tell you." Michael responded.

Lucifer chuckled at Michael. He was terrified. Michael would have to be stupid to not be scared. Lucifer put his hand to his ear and leaned his head towards Michael in the manner of a spoilt brat with such a sarcastic attitude.

"They always talk. Tell me what I want to hear." Lucifer stood up straight and patiently waited to hear Michael's name.

"You're not all I expected to be… Pretty shit really… Disappointing! Where's your forked tail or horns?" Michael laughed. He no longer cared what Lucifer done to him. He was not going to be responsible for the deaths of innocent men, women and children.

Lucifer's eyes lit up, red with fury and glowing.

"Wrong answer!" Lucifer stabbed the knife through the back of Michael's hand, through and through, pinning his hand to the arm rest of the wooden chair.

Michael's scream filled the room, he couldn't hide how painful it felt. Lucifer licked his teeth, relishing in Michael's suffering. He swiftly extracted the knife out of Michael's hand. It felt every bit as agony as being stabbed.

Michael's breathing became rapid. He struggled to catch a breath after experiencing such a sharp and sudden pain. Lucifer pointed the knife in front of his right eye.

"Please… No more." Michael begged Lucifer. He wasn't about to give Lucifer the name he was so desperate to hear. Michael only wanted it to stop. He could endure no more torture.

"Tell me or I stab out your eye then feed it to you!" Lucifer pretended to shiver at the thought of it. He secretly enjoyed the idea. Michael winced in pain and breathed heavily, desperately trying to overcome his pain with rapid exhales and inhales.

Lucifer stretched his arm back with the angel blade in his grip. Ready to plunge the knife into Michael's eye socket.

"NO! I'll tell you!" Michael shouted with all the strength he could muster. It had been too much. He could no longer handle the pain. Lucifer laughed at Michael's surrender before placing the knife inside his suit jacket pocket. Lucifer had cleaned the blade on a handkerchief before doing so.

"You lasted longer than I anticipated. Tell me your name." Lucifer waited in suspense. Michael let out a sigh and closed his eyes for a moment before speaking his name.

"It's Hartnell! Michael Hartnell." Michael saw the look on Lucifer's face. He was surprised. The Devil looked as though he had seen a ghost. He briefly walked away and turned his back on Michael in silence.

The surname had a shocking effect on Lucifer's way of thinking. Michael knew a spanner had been flung into the works. He was clearly struggling to process it. Michael immediately became hit with guilt. He was no scientist or a geek. If Lucifer were to murder him here. It would be the end of everything he was ever meant to do.

An entire future would be wiped out in a single second.

Lucifer turned and faced Michael. He looked him up and down. A smile on his face not a sinister one. He looked genuinely amazed at Michael and let out a laugh. It wasn't laughter of his sick amusement or sarcasm. It was almost as if he were laughing because he realised something he never knew. But should have.

"It all makes sense... Michael Hartnell! A time-traveller! When are you from?" Lucifer asked Michael with fascination. He showed an interest in the possibility of time-travel.

"2009." Michael replied. His throat was raw from all the shouting and screaming. His voice sounded hoarse. Michael was in a lot of pain, his hand still bleeding, he lost a lot of blood. Michael felt the difference in his body as he became dizzy, like his head became lighter.

"When in 2009? What was the date?" Lucifer became anxious to know. He too was astonished at the extraordinary revelation that he was face to face with an enemy from fifty years before the time of the apocalypse.

"December 22nd 2009." Michael responded weakly. He needed a hospital, his chances of survival without medical assistance were next to impossible from what was done to him.

"Incredible... So, we haven't officially met yet? Why did I never see it? I knew you looked familiar. FYI, you get really old! How did you do it? How are you here now?" Lucifer became puzzled by Michael's presence. Michael wished he had the answer. It was the only question on his mind.

"If I knew. I wouldn't be here. That's the truth. Torture me all you want for how I time-travelled… I cannot answer what I do not know. You had a hunch I was Michael Hartnell. Why not ask me if you knew? Why was it worth torturing me? You're a monster!" Michael spat the blood from his mouth, his jaw was in agony. He knew fine well why Lucifer had tortured him. He had done it for the sheer pleasure.

"Monster, Satan and Devil! Humans really misunderstand me." Lucifer stated with disgust at Michael's choice of words to best describe him.

"What's to not get? You are The Devil!" Michael half expected a slap across the face for addressing Lucifer as such. Instead, he stood there in a moment of silence. Lucifer looked saddened. What was he playing at? Michael wondered. What game was he playing to manipulate him?

"The Bible is a lie, Michael." Lucifer spoke with emphasis. He hated the very mention of God's word. Michael could see as much. Lucifer's words were poisonous.

"Don't speak of God's word like that!" Michael shouted with all his strength. He was raised a Christian for all nineteen years of his life. Michael Hartnell was not about to let Lucifer's false words control everything he believed.

"That's exactly my point. You defended that dusty old book because I told you the truth. You've been manipulated, Michael. You and every other good Christian before you." Lucifer words were toxic. Not one word of it was the truth.

"The truth?! You are incapable of it. The Prince of Lies is one of your names. Save the manipulation for someone else. I know who you are and what you truly are!" Michael's disgust for Lucifer grew by the second.

"The Bible only tells one side of the story. What if I told you, it was wrong? It makes me out to be a villain. What if I told you, I am not the bad guy?" Lucifer's voice was calm. There was no anger or fury. He wasn't trying to frighten Michael, he thought. This was Lucifer, simply talking to him. Michael felt this was an attempt to trick him into a false sense of security. He would not be seduced by Lucifer's lies.

"Get away! You've had the entire world at its knees for fifty years! You are the villain!" Michael responded with disgust.

"When you look at it in that manner. I suppose it does…. When my father, God made the first humans. Every angel was curious. Why had he created life outside of Heaven? And not just any life. He created mortals in his image. He gathered us and demanded we love humans more than him. When I told my father, "I can't". He sentenced me to eternity in the fiery pits of Hell…Tell me, Michael. Does that sound fair to you? A father sending his son to Hell for saying he couldn't love anything more than him?"

Michael was in silence. He didn't expect this. Lucifer spoke with such a calm tone. He felt the sadness that the fallen archangel tried to conceal.

"When I was freed from Hell. I was furious with my father. I thought "You want The Devil. I'll be the fucking Devil!" and began the apocalypse… I thought the moment this world fell, God would return, stop me and tell me I was wrong… Anything! He never showed. If God were as good, graceful or vengeful as the old book claims him to be. Where is he? Why has he not lifted a finger to save his favourites? The answer is simple… He doesn't give a shit!" Lucifer spat his last words with vile disgust. His hatred for God showed and Michael was ready with a snidey remark.

Michael stopped himself from responding when he saw something extraordinary. Something impossible. Lucifer had tears running down his face and Michael felt sorry for him.

He felt sympathy for The Devil.

Lucifer wiped his tears from his eyes. He slowly walked closer to Michael and raised his hand out towards Michael's head. He flinched at the thought of Lucifer touching him.

"Don't be frightened." Lucifer's voice was soothing.

Michael was bound to the chair. He didn't exactly have a say in what Lucifer did next. He placed his hands upon Michael's head, the palms of Lucifer's hands lit up. The light shone from Lucifer's hands and brightened up the entire room. Michael felt like he was experiencing an adrenaline rush. What was happening?

When the light went out. Michael felt like all his energy had been restored. Lucifer, with the snap of his fingers, released Michael from the chair. The bonds keeping him tied down, un-did themselves like magic.

As Michael grabbed his wrists to soothe the pain he had felt, he realised the pain was gone. His hand wound where a knife had been only moments ago had healed. The cuts inflicted upon his body were gone. Lucifer healed Michael. He looked upon Lucifer with surprise.

"You healed me?" Michael asked with confusion.

"And they say I am not merciful." Lucifer said to him. He still couldn't quite believe he was healed of all his wounds and pain.

"Now it's time to end this world. Once and for all." Lucifer's words brought Michael back to reality. He launched himself up out of the chair, ready to take on Lucifer.

"No! I won't let you destroy the world!" Michael declared.

"Dear father, Michael! You misunderstand me. I am not going to destroy the world. I am going to end the apocalypse and restore everyone who has died back to life." Lucifer surprised Michael. It couldn't be. It was a trick, he thought.

"What?" a stunned Michael responded.

"Don't look at me like I'm the bad guy. I am rectifying the situation. You want the truth? All of this, my ruling the world. It was an act. I wanted to prove God did not care. At midnight, it will be Christmas day, fifty years since I was freed. Today will be the beginning of a new era. I, Lucifer will change the world, heal it and give its people, a new message." Lucifer preached to Michael.

"What message is that?" Michael was curious what message Lucifer could bestow upon a restored human race.

"I want the world to know, God is a lie. I was wrongly cast out from Heaven. I want to bring peace to the world. After tomorrow, God will be no more. Everyone will look upon me as the new God." Lucifer's words hurt Michael. Had his entire life been a lie? His worship of his lord false? It couldn't be. Michael Hartnell needed to know.

"Does God really not care about any of us?" Michael verged close to tears as he asked.

"No, Michael… He doesn't… Not one bit… If he did. He would be here. Once I have restored humanity and healed the world. Everyone will know the truth. This is where you come in, Michael."

Michael was taken aback. Why did Lucifer need him? What could Michael do that the fallen archangel could not?

"What do you need me for?" Michael asked in astonishment. He was baffled by all Lucifer spoke.

"Three weeks ago, I attempted to restore everything... You... Not you... The future you, he tried to stop me... In the struggle, I killed him... Accidentally! Apologies in advance. I need your help. It can only be you in this moment. You are chosen." Lucifer pleaded with Michael for his assistance.

All Michael could think about was in fifty years' time, he was going to be murdered by Lucifer. The man Tom knew as his grandfather was dead.

"You killed me?" Michael became horrified to know the day of his death.

"I did... I am so sorry. I never wanted it to happen... We have a chance. We can prevent it and change all of this. I require you to come with me to perform a charm. It will restore everyone who has died back to life." Lucifer's words were encouraging. Michael couldn't believe his life was a lie, his religion and everything was a sham!

He still didn't understand where or how he fit into all of this.

"What makes me so special? Why do you need me?" Michael felt overwhelmed by all this. He was confused and frustrated.

"Your blood." Lucifer responded in a tone that was supposed to answer Michael's questions. It had no effect on him. It was questions upon questions. Where did his questions end?

"What is so special about it?" Michael asked. He was puzzled by what his blood was needed for.

"Michael, think about it. One moment, you are safe and sound in 2009. The next, you are running for your life, fifty years in the future. The only thing capable of bringing you here is Heaven. It leaves a trace. The powers of Heaven flow through your veins. I require magic from Heaven to restore life. Your blood will be full of it. I need your consent to perform this charm to work. What do you say, Michael?" Lucifer had given Michael an awful lot to think about. Why would Heaven want Michael in the future? It didn't make any sense. Unless, Michael's mind created crazy theories as to why.

Complicated time-travel theories. Why was he here? Who brought him to the future? This was insane. This was madness!

"I am not saying yes. If I do, if I help you fix the world… Would you be able to return me back to my own time period?" Michael felt desperate to get back home to Sarah.

He would do anything. Michael Hartnell would sell his soul to Lucifer. Anything he asked to hold his wife once more.

"Why would you want to go back in time?" Lucifer was curious by such a request. Michael could tell he didn't understand his reason behind it.

"My wife… Sarah. She is back there." Michael told Lucifer who made a gesture which allowed him to understand and empathise.

"I don't know if I can. I promise if there is a way. I'll find it. I will get you home. Failing to do so. There is another option." Lucifer had all of Michael's attention. What could be the alternative to going home?

"What do you mean?" Michael curiously asked with anticipation about whatever Lucifer had in mind.

"If you help me. We'll restore every human life to have perished in the last fifty years. If she is dead, I could always bring her back to life. I can also make her the way you remember. Perfect in every way. It'll be like you had never disappeared from 2009." Lucifer's offer was out of this world.

Michael felt emotional and was afraid to show his tears.

Tears of joy, the thought of having Sarah back filled him with so much happiness. He couldn't come to comprehend. It was too good an offer to refuse.

Michael brought himself back together and looked Lucifer in the eye. He had patiently waited for Michael's decision.

"I'll do it… I'll help you." Michael nodded his head in agreement.

Lucifer smiled and stretched his hand out to Michael.

"We have a deal?" Lucifer gestured for Michael to shake his hand.

He grabbed hold of Lucifer's pale and bony hand.

Michael and Lucifer shook hands, striking a bargain.

"Yes." Michael declared as he made a deal with The Devil.

CHAPTER TWELVE

DOCTOR LINDSAY JONES

THE FORBIDDEN ZONE
GLASGOW
DECEMBER 24th 2059
07:43pm

The group had been in the forbidden zone for nearly twenty-four hours. Lindsay had advised Tom to allow the group to rest, their food and water had run out. Everyone was becoming restless and if they hadn't stopped to recuperate. They would become reckless.

Tom agreed to stop for an hour. Lindsay knew Tom was itching to continue the search for Michael. They found a piece of Michael's pyjamas. He must have got it snagged on a destroyed car.

Lindsay could see John and Peter had prepared for long periods of time outside the safe house. They were taking the opportunity to rest and were sleeping. Tom had discovered an abandoned house.

Everyone was resting in the house's living room. Tom and Rachel stood near the window as a lookout, he held the fragment of cloth from Michael's pyjamas in his hand. Lindsay knew there was nothing which would stop Tom from finding Michael. He was becoming anxious.

Several infected had run along the street outside at least three times. They would need to be on the move soon. It would only be a matter of time before the infected found them.

Lindsay realised they had searched the majority of Lucifer's territory. There was only one other place to search. The only place on Earth every human feared.

Lucifer's mansion.

Lindsay remembered Tom had only ever seen the mansion from the outside. No-one who had ever set foot inside, came back out. The mansion killed all who entered through its doors. Lucifer allowed none to survive.

Lindsay looked around the room. Kyle was pacing up and down the room. He seemed agitated. Lindsay earlier on attempted to convince him to rest up. He was not for having it. The forbidden zone would be enough to keep anyone awake.

Your worst nightmares wouldn't come close to anything you were to encounter here. It was beyond the stuff of nightmares. No human should ever witness what went down on these streets.

Robert was in the process of cleaning his gun, taking it apart and cleaning it on a small table as he sat on a damaged old couch. His sharp eye had saved them a few hours earlier. He spotted two infected in the darkness and managed to eliminate them within seconds of reaching the group.

Tom made sure the infected bodies were carefully hidden. They wanted their presence in the forbidden zone to remain a secret.

The last thing the group wanted was every infected or demon looking for them. The discovery of the infected bodies would bring all the power of Hell down upon them.

They had hidden them well. The bodies had been put inside what people used to call "wheelie-bins". They would remain hidden for some time. Hopefully enough to find Michael and be back to the safe house before Lucifer caught on to their being in his territory.

A scream from outside alerted the group. John and Peter had woken up from their deep sleep. Kyle stopped dead in his tracks at the sound of the screams getting closer to the house. Robert had finished cleaning his handgun and reassembled it within seconds. He was prepared to gun down any infected should they breach the entrance to the house.

Tom and Rachel stood their ground at the window, guns pointed and aimed for the street in the event of an ambush by the infected.

The infected footsteps could be heard. There was probably a dozen of them. Always travelling in a pack. A sigh of relief came from everyone in the group when the infected ran past the house. They remain undetected by Lucifer and his forces.

"That's the fourth time they've been by here in the space of an hour. We'll give it a few minutes before we head." Tom instructed the group. Lindsay knew he was right. The infected would eventually find them. If not the next time, it would be the time after. They needed to move on. Staying in one place was too dangerous.

"Are we going back to the safe house, Tom?" Kyle asked. His voice was filled with fear. His whole body shook. He was frightened. Only an idiot wouldn't be.

"No. Not yet. There's been a handful of places we haven't searched. Michael must be close by. We can't give up on him." Tom had to find Michael. His very existence depended on Michael's survival.

"Where do we search next, Tom?" John asked him as he awaited Tom's instructions.

"Lucifer's mansion" Tom responded with dread in his tone. He closed his eyes at the mention of the place. The group suddenly became wide awake and ready to protest against Tom's orders. Who could blame them? Lindsay thought.

"What?!" Kyle exclaimed. His breathing became rapid. Lindsay was concerned he may have a panic attack.

"He said we're going to Lucifer's mansion. Keep up or we'll leave you behind, dipshit!" John was in no mood for Kyle. He had zero patience for him.

"No-one gets left behind, John! We've all got each other's backs!" Tom was furious at the very thought of any man or woman being left behind. There was no survival of the fittest in his eyes. It was if a person needs your help, you help them.

"I'm going back. I am not going anywhere near that slaughterhouse!" Rachel exclaimed.

"You can't go walking back on your own, Raquel!" Robert shouted. Lindsay was concerned of their noise levels. It could attract unwanted attention. Tom looked out onto the street, through the window. There was no sign of any infected.

"I've got a gun. I think I can handle myself! Stop fucking calling me, Raquel! My name is Rachel, cunt!" She was furious and scared. Filled with determination to flee for the safety and security of the safe house.

He prepared to strike back at Rachel's defensive attitude. Tom cut in before Robert escalated the argument any further.

"Knock it off! Both of you! I went about with that attitude. Got a gun, I can do anything... Do you know where it got me?" Tom calmly asked them.

Robert and Rachel were silent. Lindsay knew what Tom meant. He was talking about what happened three weeks ago. The night his grandfather went missing.

"I lost my grandfather... He... He wanted to continue on and kill Lucifer... I was scared... Scared to go anywhere near that mansion and see the mission through to its end... Maybe if I had, he would still be here, Lucifer would be dead and this nightmare over." Tom hid his emotions well. His speech hit the team in the right way.

No person alive wanted Lucifer ruling over what remained of humanity.

"Tom, if I know your grandfather. He'll be fine and we will find him." John, the ever-loyal friend did not want to see Tom suffering. He attempted to comfort him. Tom shook his head. Tears were visible in his eyes. Everyone felt the same for his grandfather. He was like a father to them all. Tom exhaled sharply. He looked John in the eye.

"My grandfather is dead... I never wanted to admit it... Now I have a second chance... I have a shot at redemption. Enough talk. We need to get our arses in gear!" Tom headed out of the living room through the doorway leading out to a hall.

The group, one by one followed Tom out into the hallway. The front door had been heavily barricaded with old household furniture to ensure a better chance against an infected pack.

Tom, John and Peter carefully and quietly removed the barricade to allow the necessary room for the front door to be opened. Everyone had their guns aimed at the door. Tom looked back at the group as he held onto the door handle. He held up three fingers and slowly retracted them back into a fist, a countdown for when he was about to open the door.

Tom opened the front door, no sign of infected or demons. Tom and John took the first steps out of the house. They walked through the remains of the house's front garden and out into the street of an area formerly known as Bearsden.

The city was in ruin, the forbidden zone was in a better state than most streets. Lindsay could make out Tom's all clear signal to beckon the team out. One by one, the search group followed Tom and John into the forever darkness of Lucifer's territory to continue their search for Michael. Tom's grandfather from fifty years in the past.

Lucifer's mansion was nearby. Lindsay had never seen it before. Tom and his grandfather were the only two people who had ever been within a hundred yards of his home.

And now, a small assault force of seven were on foot, walking straight to the devil's doorstep. Lindsay's eyes hurt as the sky in the distance was polluted with light. The lights were coming from Lucifer's mansion and they were illuminating the sky of the forever night.

It would take some time to reach the mansion. Tom was leading the group. John and Peter protected the rear of the group. All was quiet on the streets. There were no infected or demons. Nothing!

Silence had fallen and Lindsay couldn't decide whether that was a bad or good thing. She felt uneasy. Something did not sit right with the silence in the street. They weren't much further from the mansion.

Tom stopped dead in the middle of the street. Something was wrong.

"Do you see something, Tom?" John called to Tom.

"I'm going to head on further. Get a good look at the mansion." Tom said so calmly.

"At least take one of us as back-up." John said to Tom with concern for his safety.

"I'll be faster by myself. Need to assess his mansion in terms of demon numbers. Can't risk it. Not with all of us walking up there with no clue what is waiting for us. I'll be a few minutes." Tom explained. He walked off into the darkness to scout out the perimeter of Lucifer's mansion.

Lindsay knew Tom would be back rapidly. He was always a quick scout on missions or so she heard. The group watched every direction, guns at the ready.

"Watch your aim. We don't want to shoot Tom. Be mindful of what is coming out of the darkness." John instructed the team. Lindsay knew John to be right. Tom made himself vulnerable to friendly fire. Lindsay looked around the group, Rachel and Robert kept their guns pointed in the direction Tom had left them.

Kyle watched to the right of the group. He wiped his tears away. The fear of the unknown was too much. Lindsay looked him, up and down. His trousers were soaking. She felt sorry as she concluded Kyle had urinated himself from the fear. John guarded the back of the group in the event of an attack from behind.

Peter aimed to the left of the group until he suddenly lowered his weapon and let out a sigh. He holstered his weapon. Peter turned to face John and spoke to him.

"Something is bugging me about Tom." Peter grabbed John's attention, despite this, John Ralston never lowered his weapon or took his eyes off the area he was covering. He attempted to silence Peter.

"Whatever it is. It can wait, Carlisle!" John responded as he looked down the barrel of his handgun.

"What did Tom mean by redemption? His grandfather is dead. How does saving Michael fix that?" Peter was curious. Lindsay knew the truth. The rest of the group minus herself, Tom and John did not know the whole truth about Michael's identity.

"That's not my place to tell you. We survive this. You can ask Tom yourself. Until then, be quiet and keep watch." John still did not turn his head to speak with Peter, he never so much as looked at him to answer. His sight was focused on the darkness of the street.

"No, John! I will not be quiet. I am not doing a damn thing until you tell me why! I volunteered. We all did. I think we have the right to know why we are coming all this way, for one fucking person who chose to run away!" John sighed, he turned his back on the darkness and looked Peter in the face. He spoke to the group.

"I'm going to level with you all… I cannot promise that it will make sense. Hell! I didn't understand it… But it is true… Michael, the guy we are all out here searching for. He is Tom's grandfather." The group were as silent as ghosts.

Lindsay knew they didn't understand what John revealed to them.

"What are you on about? He's the same age as Tom!" Peter shouting. This concerned Lindsay of the noise level. John was too loud. Lindsay registered that John had a swift glance behind him. They didn't want to attract the attention of any nearby infected or demons. Especially being this close to Lucifer's mansion.

"Keep your voice down. It's complicated… He is not the Michael we know. One day, he will be…" John was cut off by Peter.

"What the fuck are you talking about?!" Peter's voice echoed in the street. It set everyone on edge. There was a moment of silence until they knew for certain that nothing heard Peter's shouts.

Silence. No infected screams. Nothing.

"Michael is Tom's grandfather from the year 2009." John told Peter. He wasn't beating about the bush. He said what Peter needed to hear. Peter scoffed at John's response.

"Time-travel?! Are you mad?!" Peter laughed in disbelief.

John swiftly grabbed Peter by his jacket and stared him in the face. Peter immediately ceased laughing. The group were on edge. Lindsay knew John had to settle this if they were to find Michael and make it safely back home in one piece.

"You listen to me. This is real and it is happening right now. Did you know fifty years ago, there were a lot of people who didn't believe Lucifer existed? Old man Hartnell told me when I was a child. I couldn't understand how people from before didn't believe he was real... Unfortunately for us. We have never had such a luxury... The world we live in belongs to him. To Lucifer. The Devil is real and apparently so is time-travel. Why do you find it so hard to believe?" John asked him.

Peter smirked at him before spitting in John's face.

"You and Tom are fucking crackpots! You have us out here looking for an idiot who claims to be old man Hartnell..." Peter thrust John away from him with both hands, forcing John to the pavement.

"Fuck this. I'm off!" Peter exclaimed before bumping past other members of the group. John climbed to his feet to call out to Peter as he continued walking away from the search party.

"Peter!" John called.

Peter stopped dead in his tracks and turned to face the group. He was a hundred yards away. He smiled with such a smug look and shook his head with disapproval. Peter turned to resume his walk, faster than a heartbeat, a white-faced infected launched itself from out of the darkness in front of him.

Before anyone could react, the infected man grabbed Peter and tore out his throat with his bare teeth. Blood squirted out of Peter's neck as he collapsed to the road. The infected man stood, staring at the group.

Everyone was frozen still at the horror they witnessed. The infected smiled at them with a mouthful of blood.

There was a loud gunshot. The infected was struck in the head and killed before it could take one step closer to the group. Lindsay looked behind her to see where the kill shot had come from. Who shot the infected?

Out of the darkness, Tom Hartnell appeared with a pistol in hand. He returned from his scout and took out the infected.

"Keep your eyes focused! We don't know how many more are out there!" Tom ordered.

"We need to kill Peter before he turns." Robert blurted out in panic.

"I'll do it. John, cover me!" Tom ordered as he approached where Peter lay. Blood flowed from his neck wound like a river. He lay in a puddle of his own blood, clutching at his wound.

"Tom, be careful… His blood will be infected." Lindsay called out to him to stress her concerns as a doctor. They couldn't risk touching Peter's blood.

Tom nodded his head in agreement with her before he reached Peter. He was still alive. He coughed. Lindsay knew there was absolutely nothing to do to heal him even if he hadn't been bitten. There is no cure for the infected virus. Peter was drowning in his own blood.

Tom would need to be quick before Peter turned and became one of the infected. he leaned down close beside him, carefully avoiding the pool of Peter's infected blood. He tried to talk. Whatever he was trying to say, Lindsay was unable to hear a word of it.

"Don't try and talk, Peter" Tom said as he prepared to shoot Peter in the head.

A mercy to be shot in the head than to run around as one of Lucifer's abominations. Peter had tried to tell Tom something. What it was. No-one but Tom heard.

Lindsay in that moment knew Peter had drawn his last breath. He was dead.

Tom had between ten and twenty seconds to ensure Peter would not return as an infected. Tom brought the gun up to aim at Peter's head. Before he got the chance to pull the trigger. Peter turned into an infected and knocked the gun free from Tom's grip.

The gun was flung across the street and lost in the darkness.

Peter jumped to his feet. He was infected.

His face was white and blood dripped from his mouth as he screamed with the infected call.

Rachel screamed at the sight of the infected Peter and in a fight or flight moment. She chose to flee and ran for her life away from the safety of the group. In the horror that was unfolding, she had run in the wrong direction. She ran towards Lucifer's mansion.

"Rachel!" Lindsay called out for her in terror.

The group stood their ground. Tom did not make any sudden movements. Peter was only inches away from him. The whole time, Rachel's screams grew fainter and fainter. She was too far away. Suddenly all anyone heard was silence. Rachel was no longer screaming in terror. She had to have been killed by whatever heard her.

Tom slowly began taking steps away from Peter. He snarled at Tom. Lindsay knew he was attempting to allow the group to acquire a clean shot of Peter. The infected could be killed the same way as any human, a headshot was a guarantee.

Lindsay quickly looked at John. He waited for the right moment to take the shot. Peter was too focused on Tom. He never noticed John getting the right angle for a kill shot.

"Filthy norm!" Peter shouted at Tom. John finally acquired the shot and fired, killing the infected Peter. Lindsay couldn't believe it. She thought of Peter's girlfriend, Karen. She will be devastated to hear of his death.

Tom found his gun which Peter had knocked from his grip. Tom swiftly checked it over and inserted the handgun's magazine inside the compartment. He prepared his gun for shooting as he returned to the group.

"Which way did Rachel go?" He asked.

Lindsay heard the urgency in his voice. He was angry. The infected had killed his friend.

"She ran this way." Lindsay told him. Her heart sank at the thought of which way Rachel had gone.

"Follow my lead." Tom said as he began to run up the street with the others running behind him. Weapons aimed to kill for anything hiding in the darkness. They continued running until they found Rachel's body. They were only a hundred yards from the mansion.

Lindsay felt sick. Her doctor's stomach could handle most but even she could barely look upon Rachel's mutilated corpse. Her blood smeared the street, her body had been torn to shreds with limbs scattered across the road. She was ripped apart.

Lindsay had never seen a death as brutal as Rachel's.

"What did this?" Lindsay spoke her thoughts.

Robert was furious, he looked all around the street and towards Lucifer's mansion, where the only source of light came from.

"I'll tell you what! The infected! You fucking animals!" Robert shouted in the direction of the mansion.

Lindsay and John looked more closely at Rachel's remains. Her flesh looked like something much larger than an infected had bitten her.

"Is that a bite mark?" Lindsay asked. This was nothing she ever encountered before.

"This isn't an infected bite! They wouldn't tear her to shreds. They would let her turn… Tom!" John and Tom obviously knew what they were dealing with.

"Fuck!" Tom rolled his eyes in despair. Lindsay knew Tom already had a horrible idea of what could have done this.

"Hell hounds." Tom stated quietly.

"What?" Robert asked. He had no clue to what they were. Lindsay knew of them. She thought they died out. There had been no sightings of them for a couple of years.

"Dogs from Hell. Shut up and stay focused." John shouted orders to Robert.

Lindsay held her gun high. She knew how dangerous these beasts could be. Tom and John stood their ground, guns held high. Robert and Kyle did the same. They were terrified. Kyle shook with fear. Lindsay knew only an idiot or a madman wouldn't feel fear in this situation.

Fear would hopefully keep them alive.

"What do they look like?" A panicked Robert asked.

"LIKE THAT!!!" Kyle shouted. He scared the living daylights out of everyone and with good reason. Back the way they had come from, in the middle of the street, sat an enormous black rottweiler with glowing red eyes. The hound was the size of a bear. It was a horrific sight.

Hanging out of its mouth was a severed human arm. This was what had killed Rachel.

Out of the darkness, two more vicious hounds emerged and stood beside Rachel's killer. The hell hounds growled at the group. The one that killed Rachel devoured her mangled arm in one enormous and disgusting bite.

"KILL THEM!!! KILL THEM ALL!!!" Tom shouted as the hell hounds charged towards them into a blizzard of bullets which Tom, John, Lindsay, Robert and Kyle unleashed upon the beasts from hell.

The hell hounds were wounded. The shots were not fatal as they continued to run down the street towards the group.

"Kyle, get back!" Tom shouted as the lead hound became dangerously close.

Kyle ran out of bullets and stood frozen in fear as the hell hound pounced upon him. Kyle's scream filled the street. The hell hound ate him alive. Lindsay cried at the horror she saw. She couldn't bring herself to look away. The hound began to shake Kyle's lifeless body like a ragdoll.

A bullet struck the hound's head, killing it. Tom shot the vicious black dog. Kyle was dead. The second hell hound had cut John off from the rest of the team. John fired shots into the sky to get the monster's attention.

"Tom! Find Michael! I'll buy you time!" John shouted to his commander. Tom shook his head in disagreement. John had made the decision. He winked at Tom before staring at the hell hound.

"You want a piece of me? Come and get me, you ugly son of a bitch!" John shouted at the devil dog before firing a shot at the hound's body. It yelped in pain.

Lindsay, Tom and Robert watched in horror. The other hell hound kept them from getting anywhere near John. He was beyond their reach. They helplessly watched as the second hell hound charged at John, chasing him into the darkness.

"JOHN!!!" Lindsay called for him.

The last hell hound snarled at Tom, he had tried to get a clean shot of the beast's head whilst it walked circles around them on the road to the mansion. Tom dropped his gun in pain. He held onto his ears in agony. Lindsay and Robert couldn't help themselves and done the same.

There was a high-pitched whistling sound coming from behind them.

The hell hound instantly calmed and run off towards Lucifer's mansion from where the whistling sound occurred. The hound ran past the group without so much as giving them a second thought.

Tom swiftly got a hold of his weapon.

"Where is it going?" Robert wondered in confusion.

He wasn't the only one who didn't understand what just happened.

"Tom?" Lindsay said his name, hoping he would know what was happening.

Tom remained silent.

"What the hell was that noise?" Robert demanded. The unknown scared him and Lindsay. Tom sighed as he closed his eyes in frustration.

"It's Mammon." Tom responded in a quiet tone. He almost sounded like they had endured a defeat. For they had been. Lindsay knew who Mammon was and what he was capable of.

This was a defeat. They had lost.

"What's Mammon?" Robert asked. He didn't know. Only a few did. Everyone should know of him. Mammon was as every bit as dangerous as Lucifer.

"The Devil's son. The Antichrist." Tom told Robert. He was devastated. To come all this way and be captured.

The hell hound came into view with a chain around its neck. Its master had it on a leash as he emerged from the shadows. Mammon was dressed from head to toe in black. He wore a black leather trench coat with black jeans. His long jacket was filthy from trailing the ground. Mammon also wore a hoodie underneath the jacket with the hood up. His face was almost hidden.

Mammon stood in the centre of the street. Lucifer's mansion was lit up behind him. The hell hound sat at Mammon's side. The dog towered over him. He addressed the survivors.

There was no way to escape this. Their luck had run out.

"Nice to see you again, Tom." Mammon addressed them. His American accent echoed in the silent street. Mammon looked at them with a sinister smile. Robert immediately showed no hesitation and repeatedly fired his gun at Mammon until he ran out of bullets.

Every round he fired, stopped an inch from Mammon's face. Lindsay immediately recognised, Mammon was no doubt using his supernatural abilities to hold the bullets back. Telekinesis was one of Mammon and Lucifer's abilities.

Mammon momentarily stared at the bullets. He admired that Robert, had the audacity to attempt to kill him. He raised his hand and as he done so. All the bullets flew back towards Robert. Several missed him and for a moment, he thought he had been spared until the last round struck him between the eyes.

Lindsay screamed when Robert's lifeless body hit the ground with a deadweight. She clung to Tom for dear life. Everyone was dead.

She mustered up the courage to bring herself to look at Mammon. He laughed at Robert's futile attempt to assassinate him.

"Get it over with already!" Tom shouted at Mammon. Lindsay and he knew, Mammon was toying with them and if it were her time to die. She wanted to die now than endure whatever Mammon desired of them.

Mammon shook his head and smiled menacingly.

"Not yet, my friend. My father would like to see you." Mammon chuckled with amusement.

CHAPTER THIRTEEN

THE MASTER OF HELL

LUCIFER'S MANSION

THE FORBIDDEN ZONE

GLASGOW

DECEMBER 24th 2059

10:57pm

Lucifer stood upstairs in his mansion hallway to overlook the entrance. All the screaming and gunfire had gotten his full attention. The only fools who ever dared come this close to his mansion were the Hartnell's, the foolish idiots, he thought.

Lucifer drank blood, he always enjoyed virgins' blood from his goblet. He designed his chalice to have small human skulls on each side of the goblet. It had indeed been made from human bones and The Master of Earth and Hell was not prepared to let the young time-traveller know what his goblet contained.

He returned Michael's pyjamas. All freshly cleaned and ironed for him, always good to have servants. Pity about his tailor, the only human he truly missed. At this present time, Michael Hartnell was Lucifer's guest and he had special plans for the young Christian. Lucifer watched the front doors to the mansion open on their own accord.

The lord watched from above as he looked down his long staircase to the white stainless marble floor of his hallway. Mammon and one of his hounds brought in the intruders.

Lucifer did not recognise the young woman. He sniggered at the thought of a woman making it this far. His mind wandered to his plans for her. Lucifer hadn't enjoyed a good fuck in weeks. He enjoyed his human virgins. Especially their blood once he had his wicked way with them.

Lucifer almost dropped his goblet at the sight of Tom Hartnell being led in with a hell hound behind him. This was too good, Lucifer thought.

"My father will be with you presently." Mammon said to his prisoners. Lucifer began his decent down the marble staircase towards Tom and the woman.

"Do you think John is still alive?" The woman asked Tom. They were oblivious to Lucifer's descent.

"I don't know. I pray he is." Tom told her before his eyes caught Lucifer at the bottom of the staircase. He stared at Lucifer with a burning fury.

Mammon unleashed his hell hound. The giant dog ran towards its master, Lucifer.

Lucifer began petting the hell hound. The dog enjoyed his hands running through its fur.

"Who's a good dog? How many nasty hoomans did you eat?" Lucifer spoke to the beast before looking up at Tom and the woman. Tom, ever fearless of Lucifer stared him out, fury filled the young resistance leader's face. Lucifer knew Tom hated him and felt nothing but disgust towards him.

Lucifer enjoyed rubbing it in with Tom. He always enjoyed taking the piss out of any Hartnell. Tom was not his grandfather. Old man Hartnell's boots were too big even for him to fill, Lucifer thought. He found it pathetic. He could never match up to the kind of man Michael Hartnell was.

"Mr Hartnell, how lovely to see you. You brought me a girl too. Can't say I have had the pleasure. What is your name, my darling?" Lucifer addressed the woman. She was terrified. Her face was red and so were her eyes. She'd obviously been a crying a lot.

Humans, so frightened of everything.

Lucifer riled Tom, he responded defensively.

"Fuck you!" Tom shouted at Lucifer.

"Disappointing. I only asked her name. I would also like an apology. I believe you killed one of my dogs." Lucifer attempted to get further under Tom's skin and provoke a reaction.

"Sorry... I wished I'd shot the bitch sooner" Tom's defiance was such a typical Hartnell attitude.

Lucifer watched without blinking as his son, Mammon struck the back of Tom's head with his fist. The girl let out a cry as Tom collapsed to his knees, clutching the back of his head in agony. Mammon hit him harder than he needed to.

"Show my father respect. He is the lord of your pathetic little world! Filthy human!" Mammon spat on Tom. Lucifer looked his son in the eye. Mammon took a few steps back. He was being warned and Mammon did not wish to anger his father.

"Enough, Mammon. Mr Hartnell and his little girlfriend are our guests." Lucifer looked her up and down. He licked his lips seductively. The woman closed her eyes at the sight of Lucifer. He laughed as he knew her skin crawled at the thought of his touch. He enjoyed it like that.

"What do you want from us?" The girl addressed him. Lucifer was amazed.

"She speaks!" Lucifer mocked her. He and Mammon had a little laugh between them.

"Well!" She demanded of Lucifer.

"Your attitude is so very similar to that of a Hartnell. Your name?" Lucifer asked her. He hated not knowing who he was speaking with.

"Don't!" Tom told her.

"I don't believe I was speaking to you, Mr Hartnell." Lucifer stared down at Tom.

"My name is Lindsay." The woman introduced herself to the fallen archangel. He only realised she was an American. Not very many of them left, he thought.

"Lindsay what?" Lucifer waited. He was becoming impatient.

"Doctor Lindsay Jones." Lindsay addressed him with hatred in her voice. She despised Lucifer. Not that he cared.

"Oh, a doctor! Well, you know who I am. Nice to make your acquaintance, Doctor Jones." Lucifer mockingly greeted her.

"You haven't answered my question. What do you want with us?" Lindsay's fiery attitude was to Lucifer's liking. He enjoyed seeing a woman all worked up.

"I want to fix the world." Lucifer told the survivors.

Tom started to laugh hysterically at Lucifer.

"You?!" You destroyed the world! What do you think fixing the world means? A world without humans? Whatever game you are playing, I am not buying into it… Where's my grandfather? What have you done with him, you son of a bitch!" Tom shouted at Lucifer.

He wanted to know what happened three weeks ago.

Lucifer leaned down to look Tom, face to face. Tom's eyes never left Lucifer's face.

"Which one?" Lucifer asked. Tom's face was a picture. The lord wished the young fighter could have been able to see it from his perspective. Lucifer felt he was able to read Tom's mind. His face asked "How do you know?".

Lucifer knew Tom couldn't believe that he was aware of Michael's existence. Tom was visibly shaken by Lucifer's revelation. He remained silent, no witty Hartnell comeback.

"Yes, I know about the time-traveller. Unfortunately, the old man you know as your grandfather is dead… He was killed a few weeks ago, son." Lucifer's words lingered. Tom instantly jumped to his feet to strike Lucifer's face with a punch. It had no effect on Lucifer.

No human was capable of inflicting any harm upon his body. Lucifer watched with amusement as Tom clutched his fist in excruciating pain. He may as well have punched a brick wall.

"Tom, you must know you can't harm me." Lucifer mocked him.

"I did… Doesn't mean I won't try." Tom said before revealing, a concealed gun. Tom fired the gun's entire clip upon Lucifer's body. Lucifer didn't flinch. He looked down at his suit and shirt. There were holes in his suit from where bullets had struck him before ricocheting. Lucifer was furious.

"You fucking people! No respect! My tailor died three years ago!" Lucifer shouted in rage. He had lost too many suits because of the Hartnell's over the last fifty years.

Mammon struck Tom over the head in retaliation. Blood ran down the side of Tom's face. He collapsed to the floor. Tom's blood ran onto the white marble floor.

"Take that, filthy human!" Mammon shouted before kicking Tom in the ribs as he lay on the floor.

"Enough, Mammon!" Lucifer's shout vibrated throughout the hall. He forgot how loud he was at times. Mammon backed off. His thirst for blood wasn't been quenched at the moment. Lucifer raised him well but for now, Mammon had to supress his killer instincts. The lord required Tom every bit as much as he needed Michael.

Lucifer couldn't use Tom if he were dead. Mammon needed to be patient until the time was right.

"Where is Michael? What have you done to him, monster?!" Lindsay shouted at Lucifer. He hated it when men called him monster. Surprisingly, he didn't mind women addressing him in such a manner. It was like foreplay to Lucifer.

"Face it, Lindsay. The cunt has killed him." Tom spat his words of defiance at Lucifer. The human mind truly fascinated The Master of hell. How could they be so gullible?

"On the contrary, I haven't. I can't, even if I wanted to. That would be what we call a paradox. I would have thought you'd have understood that, Tom." Lucifer chuckled at Tom's stupidity. He looked back up the staircase.

"Michael, you can come out!" Lucifer called upstairs.

Michael walked out onto the balcony of the mansion's upstairs. He looked refreshed. Clearly Michael took full advantage of Lucifer's generous hospitality. All washed and freshened up with a smooth clean-shaven face. Michael was still happy to wear his pyjamas despite Lucifer's offers of an Italian suit.

Michael slowly approached the hall. He hesitated to come down the marble staircase. Lucifer knew it would be hard to see his friends like this. He felt Michael needed to see how they treated their lord and master.

The young Christian stood beside Lucifer, Lindsay didn't understand why Michael stood, side by side with The Devil. Tom looked up to see Michael with Lucifer. He was horrified to see Michael in the mansion. Lucifer knew they would try to get Michael out of his grip.

"Michael? Get out of here now!" Tom shouted to Michael. He could barely look at Tom or made any attempt to escape Lucifer's clutches. Tom was bewildered as to why Michael was not running for his life, like any sane human would do in this situation.

"Michael! Run! What are you waiting for?" Tom shouted. He didn't understand what was happening.

"Tom, Tom, Tom! Michael is not my prisoner. He is here of his own free will." Lucifer taunted Tom.

"Michael, what is he talking about?" Lindsay asked. She was scared and couldn't contain her emotions. Neither she nor Tom understood Michael's reason for allying with Lucifer. Michael looked to the leader of the fallen for reassurance, almost as if he were silently asking for permission to explain his actions to his friends.

"It's alright, Michael. Tell them. Make your friends understand." Lucifer encouraged him to tell them the truth.

"Lucifer is going to end the apocalypse. We are going to perform a charm to bring everyone who has died back to life." Michael's voice was shaky. Lucifer knew Michael was worried what Tom and Lindsay's responses would be. Human families were complicated, Lucifer almost laughed at the thought. He smiled as Michael's words sank in.

All was going according to his plan.

"Michael, whatever he has told you. He is talking out of his arse! He is evil! He has killed billions of people! Four of my friends died getting here... Peter... You met him. He was killed by an infected, one of HIS creations! He died, begging me to tell Karen how much he loved her... Michael, Lucifer killed my grandfather! He killed your future-self... You are him, Grandfather. Please believe me! I swear to God, it is the truth... You can't trust Lucifer... He'll kill us all!" Tom Hartnell cried. He was desperate.

Lucifer had never seen Tom cry. He never seen him so pathetic before. It felt right to finally see Tom suffer. He finally done it.

Lucifer had turned the Hartnell's against each other.

Michael leaned down to look at Tom. What he said next. Lucifer didn't expect.

"I am very sorry, Tom... My faith in God is gone. I have joined Lucifer." Tom's world was turned upside down, completely shattered.

The young man who would become his grandfather was erased from history. Lucifer hid his excitement, this was incredible. He wondered how long it would take to affect the timeline if at all. Especially after what he planned for Michael. Time would be tricky, he figured. Chances are, after Lucifer's plans were done, the timeline would be kept in line. No alterations. History would remain intact. Pity.

Lucifer had often thought of a million ways to destroy Tom Hartnell. What was happening, he never could have imagined. It was perfection for as long as it lasted. The Lord of The Earth would relish in it for the time being.

"Michael, he is brainwashing you!" Lindsay shouted.

"Shut up!" Michael barked at the young doctor. Lucifer nearly bit his tongue, Michael was savage. Lindsay was taken aback by how Michael snapped at her with such defiance.

Lucifer enjoyed watching this unfold. Michael Hartnell always had veins full of piss and vinegar, he thought. The fury of a Hartnell was like nothing else on this planet.

"Lucifer told me the truth. God, if he truly cared… Where is he?" Michael responded. He was upset. He didn't know why his grandson and his friend were not siding with him.

"Don't worry, Michael. They are small-minded. Incapable of understanding what I intend to do." Lucifer walked behind Michael as he poured his pestilence into his ears. Filling his head with lies.

"I understand you." Tom blurted out. Lucifer wondered what was coming next. It hardly mattered. It would be a feeble and futile attempt to win Michael back.

"What next? Destroy the planet? Take us all to Hell?! What is your plan? You twisted son of a bitch!" Tom shouted. He spat at Lucifer's leather shoes. Lucifer momentarily stared at the saliva on his shoes. He felt a hard kick to Tom's head would remind him of his place in the world.

Lucifer restrained himself in front of Michael. He had killed men for less. If his plan were to work, he needed Michael on his side.

"You see, Michael. People who are supposed to be your friends are not willing to stand by your side, at a time when you need them the most. I haven't mistreated them in any way shape or form. Since their arrival, I have been struck, shot and spat on. If I were as evil as they claim me to be, would I not have retaliated? Would they still be drawing breath?" Lucifer allowed his words to take effect on Michael and manipulate him for as long as he needed him.

The time-traveller was on his side. Michael was in the palm of his hand and would be until Lucifer no longer needed him.

Lucifer's attention turned to the entrance, his hell hounds in the mansion gardens were barking loudly. Gunshots from what was no doubt a shotgun occurred. Lucifer filled with rage. Someone outside was killing his dogs. He watched the front door at the end of the hall, listening to the sound of the beasts howling in pain. Gunfire silenced them.

The door was kicked in and entered none other than, John Ralston.

Lucifer shook his head in disbelief. He found this priceless.

"I should have known. Welcome, Mr Ralston!" Lucifer greeted him. John unload both barrels of the shotgun at Lucifer's chest. Everyone but Lucifer and Mammon ducked to the floor. The bullets bounced off Lucifer's torso and struck various walls in the mansion hallway.

"Shit!" John shouted as he desperately tried to reload his weapon. He never had a chance. Mammon charged him to the floor and viciously beat his face. Lucifer's suit was completely destroyed beyond repair. He looked at his clothing with disappointment. He was ignorant to Mammon beating the life out of John.

Everyone watched in horror as Mammon repeatedly punched John's face. His face slowly no longer resembled his. It was covered with blood.

Mammon stopped hitting John's face and began choking him with both hands around his throat. John struggled to breathe. He couldn't free himself of Mammon's grip. Lucifer knew his son wouldn't stop until John was dead. Normally he would let him finish the deed.

He couldn't afford to do that. Not today.

Lucifer like a flash, crossed the room and pulled Mammon away from John. He coughed on the air when he was finally free of Mammon's grip.

Lucifer thrust his son against a wall. He did it so hard, a statue of "The Whore of Babylon" fell over and smashed into a dozen pieces as it struck the marble floor. Lucifer made sure Michael and his friends could not hear what he was about to tell Mammon.

"We need four. We've got four. Don't fuck this up!" Lucifer whispered to Mammon. He calmed in an instant as Lucifer loosened his hold on his son's trench coat.

Lucifer walked back into the centre of the room. John was half dead. Lucifer knelt beside him. John was in no state to defend himself. His face was a mess. A broken nose, several teeth missing, a detached retina and the markings on his throat. Lucifer placed his hand upon his head. In the blink of an eye, a light emitted from his hand and healed all of John's injuries.

Lucifer made his way towards Tom. He did not welcome Lucifer's hand touching him. Lucifer nodded his head and placed his index finger upon Tom's head and healed his bleeding scalp.

Lucifer walked back to the bottom of the staircase and stood with Michael.

"I apologise for my son's behaviour. It is time for change. Today, I will end this apocalypse. From this day forward, I will be God." Lucifer announced to everyone present.

Michael flinched as three enormous hell hounds made their way down from upstairs behind him. They growled as they walked towards their master. Salivating all over the marble steps.

"Don't be scared, Michael. They're harmless." Lucifer assured him. The hell hounds were loyal to him. They were big pansies until Lucifer ordered them not to be. The three hell hounds passed Michael and Lucifer to surround Tom, Lindsay and John.

The group stared at Lucifer with hatred and defiance. He knew his plan for them would never work without their consent. He used the hounds as a security measure to force them to act out his will.

"My friends, should you try and run. These dogs will drag you back to witness my miracle." Lucifer addressed the survivors. They were his prisoners to do with as he pleased.

"How soon till you can perform this charm?" Michael asked.

Lucifer immediately took Michael's tone for excitement. It was deeper than such an emotion. Michael Hartnell truly believed Lucifer's little piece of fiction, the resurrection of all who had died.

He recognised Michael was anxious and desperate to see his wife.

Lucifer placed his hands upon Michael's shoulder and told him what he wanted to hear.

"As soon as we arrive in The City of The Dead." Lucifer smiled as his plan neared completion.

CHAPTER FOURTEEN

MICHAEL HARTNELL

LUCIFER'S MANSION

THE FORBIDDEN ZONE

GLASGOW

DECEMBER 24th 2059

11:58pm

Two minutes to midnight. Michael had observed as Lucifer and Mammon made preparations for the charm. The charm which was going to resurrect everyone who had died during the apocalypse.

Michael realised in two minutes it would be Christmas day. He concluded it would represent something different after today. If what Lucifer planned to do actually worked. It will change everything forever.

Lucifer and Mammon carefully poured holy oil in a circle around Tom, Lindsay and John who were being guarded by hell hounds. They were vicious and terrifying dogs, they looked like rottweilers with the exception of their gigantic size and blood red eyes. Michael's friends had been silent for the past hour.

Michael did not make any attempt to speak with them. He understood their whole life had been a lie. Lucifer was not the big bad they had believed him to be. Michael only wish he could make them see what he saw. He decided not to try and preach Lucifer's message. He figured it better for them to experience his miracle and witness it first-hand.

As soon as they made it to wherever Lucifer called, "The City of The Dead". They would see for themselves and know the truth which had been supressed from them and the world.

"Finished." Lucifer declared as he and Mammon completed the circle of holy oil. Lucifer discarded the glass bottle which had contained the oil. He threw it across the room without a care in the world. The glass exploded the moment it struck the marble floor.

"What is the oil for, Lucifer?" Michael asked curiously.

Lucifer turned to face Michael with an enormous joyous smile on his face.

"I am creating a portal. It requires holy magic to purify those present. Anyone performing the ritual needs to be cleansed." Lucifer explained his reasons for the circle of holy oil.

"I thought anything holy was… Well, like poison to you?" Michael was careful with his words. He didn't want to anger Lucifer. He was amazed at the power which Lucifer possessed and terrified of what he was capable of.

"Do not be afraid of me, Michael. Speak your mind. To answer your question, any holy objects are dangerous to all demons. It has no effect on me." Lucifer responded without fully explaining to why he is immune to its effects.

"Why doesn't it affect you?" Michael calmly asked The Lord of The Earth.

Lucifer slightly laughed and stared at Michael, he looked flabbergasted.

"I am not a demon… I was an archangel. Still am." Lucifer became emotional, he sniffled as he wiped his tears away with his fingertips.

"I was cast out from Heaven, leader of the archangels, the morning star… I am cut off from my home, never to return. My brothers and sisters who were cast out for my disagreement with… Him!" He couldn't bring himself to say the name. Michael saw the pain of his past. Lucifer continued to speak with him.

"They became demons. Their wings burnt and they lost their heavenly forms making them demons of Hell. I, however… My wings burned, I never lost mine and so, I remained an angel in Hell until I escaped fifty years ago." Lucifer's words affected Michael. They hit him hard.

"Do you still have them… Your wings?" Michael asked with so much sympathy for Lucifer.

Lucifer hesitated. He had a moment with his own thoughts before suddenly unveiling his wings. Lucifer never moved an inch. His wings flew out from the neck of his suit jacket.

Michael stared at Lucifer's wings in horror. They weren't as magnificent as the angel Nejuma's wings. They were giant in size and horribly mangled. There were no feathers, they were skeletal and his flesh was burnt. The fires of Hell damaged them. Michael realised the condition of them meant Lucifer's injuries were permanent.

"I am so sorry." Michael apologised to Lucifer.

He retracted his wings in the blink of an eye.

"Shed no tears for me... After today, it will no longer matter. You may know this little teleportation spell." Lucifer elbowed Michael in a joking manner. Almost similar to a friend having banter with him.

"A what spell?" He asked Lucifer with such confusion. What did Lucifer mean? Why would Michael have any familiarity with spells or teleportation?

"I forget. You haven't performed magic before. The future you, he knew a lot. He would give Harry Potter a run for his money.... I guess that life will never happen. The time is now." Lucifer declared.

"Rise!" He shouted to Tom, Lindsay and John. They were inside the circle of holy oil with the three hell hounds that guarded them. All three of them stood to their feet in silence.

"Hurry up already!" Tom shouted in defiance.

Michael couldn't understand his anger. The whole world was about to be restored to life and healed. The past would no longer matter. John's face was filled with fury. Michael felt unsure if his rage was directed towards Lucifer or himself. He felt like he had betrayed their trust.

From their perspective he had. Michael felt sorry for Lindsay. She had sobbed continuously for the past hour, her eyes looked tired from all her crying.

"The miracle shall begin momentarily." Lucifer declared in a celebratory tone. Mammon stood by his father. Lucifer raised his hands into the air and started to speak in a strange tongue, a language which Michael had never heard before. He initially believed Lucifer may have been speaking Latin. He came to the conclusion it wasn't. The language sounded much older.

The circle of holy oil burst into flames and engulfed the entire area inside it. Michael, on reflexes, raised his hands up to defend his upper body and closed his eyes, believing he was about to be burnt to a crisp. When Michael Hartnell opened his eyes, what he saw, he couldn't wrap his mind around.

They were no longer in the mansion. It was dark and somehow, they had magically appeared outside. The ground they all stood on was a garden. No, it wasn't a garden. Michael understood what Lucifer's spell was.

He transported them somewhere else. Michael knew they were somewhere that was high up on a hill. He looked ahead of him and saw what remained of Glasgow's Royal Infirmary across the hill from where they stood.

The hospital was in ruin and the roofs at several parts of the Victorian building were on fire. The sky was lit up from the fires burning it. Michael's eyes adjusted to the darkness.

Lucifer and Mammon were by Michael's side as they had been in the mansion. Tom, Lindsay and John were still with them, surrounded by the giant beasts from Hell. Michael looked behind him, there were gravestones and monuments as far as the eye could see.

He knew where they were. They were up the hill inside Glasgow's Necropolis in the middle of the city centre.

"Welcome to The City of The Dead!" Lucifer welcomed everyone in such a grand showman style announcement. Michael wondered how the Necropolis would play into Lucifer's plan.

"This is the Necropolis?" Michael asked in confusion. Why were they here?

"It hasn't changed much in fifty years, Michael." Lucifer told him.

"Traitorous little shit! Wait till I get my hands on you!" John shouted at Michael, who took it to heart. How was he a traitor? John had nothing but hatred for Michael. Tom put his hand on John's shoulder to calm him down.

"He is not a traitor. Lucifer is manipulating him." Tom told John before looking directly at Michael.

"Don't listen to him, Michael. He is not your friend… Grandfather, you can walk away from this with us… Please, before it's too late." Tom pleaded with him to see reason.

Michael turned and faced Lucifer. He was already watching him.

"Don't listen to them, Michael. God has corrupted them. In a few minutes, they will be on our side." Lucifer reassured Michael. He still felt guilty. Michael knew if this worked, all will be forgiven. Humanity will be reborn.

"He did all of this, Michael! This horrible world is all his doing! You caused it all. YOU FUCKING MONSTER!!!" Lindsay screamed at Lucifer. Mammon briskly walked towards her and slapped her hard across the face.

116

Michael felt sick, he did not wish to hurt anyone. He didn't particularly like Mammon. He was a loose cannon with a short fuse.

"Don't ever speak to my father with such disrespect!" Mammon shouted at Lindsay. She whimpered with fear. She held her slapped cheek in pain. Mammon's slap must have stung. Tom's face said it all. If looks could kill, Michael thought.

"Enough, Mammon! I am more than capable of speaking for myself." Lucifer was calm, his words reminded Mammon of his place. He stepped away from Lindsay, Tom and John. Tom comforted Lindsay. Michael heard her weep.

"My apologies, Doctor Jones… In a few moments, no-one will ever again call me a monster." Lucifer smiles. He raised his right hand and clicked his fingers. With a snap of his fingers, flames erupted from the dead grass of the hillside graveyard. The fires burned in between Lucifer and where Michael's friends were in the centre of the graveyard.

The flames died in a flash and the surface they all stood on, lay a burnt circle with a five-point star, a pentagram in the centre of the circle. It was enormous in size. At least ten feet in diameter.

"What do you need me to do?" Michael asked Lucifer. He felt uneasy at the sight of the pentagram. Michael grew up believing it to be a symbol of evil. Another lie he had been told, he thought.

"All in good time, my friend." Lucifer chuckled at Michael's anxious attitude. Michael felt impatient, he wanted this to be over, he wanted so badly to see Sarah and for the trust of his friends to be restored.

Lucifer began speaking in Latin, "Protestas inferna mi confirma. Protestas inferna mi confirma." He chanted. Michael knew what the rough translation was in English.

"May the power of Hell strengthen me." Lucifer must be channelling the power of Hell directly through him to perform the charm. The pentagram began to glow. It emitted a bright red light and illuminated the area around them.

Lucifer approached the centre of the pentagram and stopped in the middle to get a better look at everyone present.

"Michael, stand on this point of the star. Mammon, you take this point." Lucifer said as he directed Michael to the top of the star. Mammon stood on the right-hand point opposite him. Michael was ready to begin.

Lucifer turned to face Tom, Lindsay and John.

"You three, take a stand at the last three points." Lucifer asked politely.

"Sure! We'll do that. As soon as you kiss my arse. I will never do what you tell me!" Tom barked with defiance towards Lucifer. He was angry.

Lindsay looked up for the first time, she had kept her eyes on the ground. Frightened to look at Lucifer. She spoke to Tom and John.

"Maybe… Maybe we should do as he says." Lindsay's voice trembled with fear as she considered Lucifer's orders.

"No fucking way!" John shouted.

"Need I remind you. My dogs will drag you onto those points if I give the command… I am trying to do this the nice way." Lucifer nodded his head in the direction of the three hell hounds surrounding them. It was a reminder of their presence and of the alternative to doing the easier option.

Michael hoped it wouldn't come to it. Lindsay looked at both Tom and John before making the decision to stand on the point to Michael's left. She did it out of fear. Nonetheless, she willingly chose to walk over of her own volition as oppose to being dragged over in the jaws of a hellish beast.

"Thank you, Doctor Jones." Lucifer acknowledged her participation.

"How about it, gentlemen? Don't make me use those dogs." Lucifer reminded Tom and John. They took a moment, looked to one another for assurance and without speaking a word, they walked onto their respective points of the pentagram.

They faced Lucifer without blinking, their hatred for him was strong.

"Try anything and I will kill you." Tom threatened Lucifer.

Lucifer put his hand to his face in despair.

"Always the same. Believe me, after this charm is performed. You will have no interest in killing me." Lucifer sounded certain of himself. Michael knew he would be right.

The world and all its people were to be restored. Who in their right mind would want to kill the saviour of the world?

"We'll see." Tom responded with his same temper.

Tom wasn't letting go of his fury any time soon. Lucifer shook his head at Tom's attitude before reaching inside his suit jacket. Lucifer removed the angel blade from his inside pocket. He leaned forward and held out the hilt of the knife for Michael to take hold.

The dagger truly was a thing of beauty. Michael admired it for a split second. The handle was shaped like an angels' wing and on the steel blade itself were words in no language he recognised.

Michael hesitated before reaching out for the handle to receive the blade from Lucifer. The angel blade was the only thing in the world capable of harming or killing The Devil. The level of trust with such a weapon meant only one thing. Everything Lucifer told him was the truth.

Why else would he bestow it upon Michael? He wondered what reason Lucifer had given him this blade. What did he need Michael to do?

"This is where your help comes in, Michael." Lucifer said to Michael. He didn't understand his role in the charm.

"Tell me what to do?" Michael asked. He was ready to do whatever Lucifer required of him.

"The only way you can be standing here is because the powers of Heaven brought you to 2059. Your blood is full of Heaven's divine energy. All I need from you is a drop of your blood. It has to be given willingly." Lucifer instructed Michael.

He knew Lucifer wanted him to cut himself and allow for the blood to be an ingredient in the charm. He hated the sight of his own blood. He knew the slightest nick to his skin was going to be painful. He dreaded the thought of running the magnificent angel blade across the palm of his hand.

A small price to pay in order to heal the world and resurrect its people. To hold Sarah in his arms. Michael prepared to cut the palm of his hand.

"Michael, don't!" Lindsay called out to him just as he was about to cut himself. He looked Lindsay in the eye. She couldn't take her gaze away from what he was about to do.

"I have to… It will end the apocalypse." Michael told her in the hope she would understand his reasons for why he needed to.

"Lucifer is taking you for a ride, Michael. He is lying to you!" Tom shouted to Michael. He was genuinely concerned for him. Michael saw that in the man who would one day be his grandson.

"Michael, you have the knife! Kill him!" John shouted to him in an act of desperation.

Michael couldn't kill anyone. Especially not Lucifer. The thought of killing a living creature filled him with an unspeakable guilt.

"I won't." Michael responded to John with all his will not to show the horror he felt from being asked to commit such a horrible crime.

"Let's change the world, Michael." Lucifer's southern accent calmed him. It was time to claim back everything they had lost. Michael looked at Lucifer then his friends before running the blade across the palm of his right hand. He winced in pain.

Michael did not realise how sharp the blade actually was and cut deeper than he intended. Blood flowed from his hand and dripped onto the burnt grass. The five-point star began to glow with a red light.

Everyone felt the ground beneath their feet rumble as it began to split open. Large cracks appeared across the pentagram. Michael jumped with fright as the sound of thunder drummed and lightning struck monuments in the graveyard. Fires burned and illuminated the entire Necropolis.

"It is done!" Lucifer declared with sheer bliss.

"Is it working?" Michael shouted. Something did not feel right.

The world was turning crazier, he thought.

Lucifer laughed hysterically. If Michael didn't know any better, he would have taken him for being insane.

"Oh, yes! It certainly is, Michael! You broke the seal!" Lucifer responded with joy.

"Father, this is amazing." Mammon said to Lucifer. He was barely able to take his eyes away from the crumbling ground they stood on. Enormous cracks continued to the tear the ground apart.

"The seal?" Michael didn't understand.

"We tricked you, stupid human!" Mammon laughed.

Everything was a lie. Lucifer was not going to end the apocalypse, he wasn't bringing all who had died back to life. He had used Michael to do his dirty work for whatever was unfolding.

A lost and broken Michael looked to his friends. Tom, Lindsay and John still stood on their points of the pentagram. They were not angry with him. He knew that. Michael was tempted by Lucifer.

The Devil used Michael's love for Sarah as a tool to bring about more destruction. He felt guilt in the role he played and dreaded to think of what evil Lucifer made him commit.

"It's alright, Michael." Tom assured him. Lindsay and John nodded their heads in agreement. They held no grudges against Michael. After everything he done, they still had his back.

"I am sorry, Tom... Please forgive me." Michael cried. Tears ran down his face. Michael would never be able to redeem himself for this unspeakable betrayal. He had betrayed everything he knew, his family, his friends and his faith.

"There is nothing to forgive... You are family, Michael." Tom told him. It made Michael feel worse. Tom was his family. He was his future grandson and he betrayed him.

"War, Famine, Conquest and Death! Tom, always the fighter. I can think of no-one better to turn the rest of humanity against each other. You will be War's vessel. Lindsay, a doctor, a healer. The opposite will suit you. To watch the last humans, starve to death. You will be Famine. John, a truth seeker. You will be Conquest, to spread my message to those who survive this day." Lucifer told Michael's friends with such charm.

He loved the sound of his own voice, Michael thought. Lucifer turned his attention to Michael.

"Michael, my old friend. I fooled you once and twice. I have saved the best for you. Your future-self, he was all about preserving life. Now it is time to end lives. You will become Death." Lucifer's smile stretched across his face with a vile delight. He was pure evil.

"You son of a bitch! You made us release The Four Horsemen?!" Tom shouted in fury for using such deception.

"The walls of reality are thin in this location. The seal to the horsemen's prison required both Heaven and Hell's magic in order to free them. I had almost given up hope of ever freeing them... Then Heaven delivered to me, a time-traveller! Not just anyone. They gave me, my mortal enemy!" Lucifer laughed at what he revealed.

He licked his lips with delight and eye-balled Michael with such a sinister smile.

"It's all your fault, Michael." Lucifer taunted him. He and Mammon laughed hysterically as the pentagram split wide open. Michael was finished feeling sorry for himself. He was tired of being the victim. He would no longer take shit from anyone.

Not even The Devil himself would stop him. Michael held onto the angel blade as tight as he could. Before he knew what he was doing, Michael ran towards Lucifer, whilst he was still laughing with his son. Lucifer was surprised as Michael plunged the dagger into his chest.

Lucifer screamed in agony and with rage as the blade pierced his bulletproof flesh and stabbed him in the chest. Blood stained his white shirt as he collapsed from the impact of being stabbed by Michael.

Michael held onto the dagger as Lucifer fell and lay on the grass next to a headstone in the graveyard.

"Burn in Hell!" Michael screamed in anger at Lucifer.

"Been there! Done that!" Lucifer laughed.

Michael never wanted to hear his laugh for as long as he lived. He extracted the blade from Lucifer's chest and in one quick clean blow, Michael Hartnell stabbed Lucifer in the neck.

The fatal blow had silenced Lucifer as he was in mid-laugh.

Lucifer is dead. Michael killed him.

Michael felt horror for his actions. It went against everything he believed. It did not matter that the person he had killed was The Devil. It was still an unforgiveable sin.

Michael Hartnell was a murderer.

Mammon stood apart from the others with the three hell hounds at bay. He seemed unfazed by his father's murder. Michael thought it strange. Mammon had stood by and watched as his father was stabbed to death. Michael half expected to be beaten to death in revenge.

Mammon was not shy when it came to hurting people. Michael committed the worst act anyone could ever commit against his father. He killed Lucifer. Yet, he remained still, staring at Lucifer's lifeless body. Mammon was emotionless.

Tom, Lindsay and John looked like they were over the moon. Almost ready to celebrate. They were happy. The ruthless tyrant who ruled over their world for fifty years was dead. His reign of terror was brought to a bloody end.

Their happiness turned to concern in seconds. Tom stared at the pentagram. It was still glowing with a red light. Thunder was rumbling and lightning struck the ground in multiple locations all over the city and in the distance. As far as the eye could see. The world felt like it was ending.

Michael felt uneasy. What was happening?

"Why hasn't the spell broken? Are those bastards still coming?!" Tom shouted in frustration.

Lucifer was dead. Michael realised the spell must have been connected to Lucifer. He was dead. How could The Four Horsemen still be coming?

"Seriously?! You thought it would be that easy?!" Mammon spoke to them as if they were idiots.

Lucifer's lifeless body jerked upright and to everyone's horror, he gasped for air. He is still alive, he grabbed hold of the gravestone behind him to pull himself up and onto his feet.

Michael was filled with terror as Lucifer stood upright with the angel blade still embedded in his throat. Lucifer grabbed the hilt of the knife and immediately hauled it free. He let out a small whelp. It must have been excruciatingly painful. Lucifer's neck wound healed within seconds. The hole in his neck was gone, like he was never stabbed.

Lucifer held the knife in front of him. Everyone stood frozen in fear and disbelief. Their victory was short-lived. Lucifer smiled like the Cheshire cat as he examined the blooded dagger. He chuckled at the attempt on his life.

Michael knew he was about to be killed. Lucifer was not the forgiving type. He threw the angel blade away. The knife pierced the ground at John's feet. It had just missed him and no more. Michael turned his attention back to Lucifer. He was covered from head to toe in his own blood.

His smile filled Michael with terror. He knew the reason for Lucifer's smile. He was no doubt thinking about all the terrible things he would do to Michael.

"That's the funny thing about the knife. It's an archangel blade. Can kill ordinary angels no problem. But with me... Too bad you only had one and not seven."

Lucifer chuckled as he waved his hand through the air. As if by magic, Michael was flung by an invisible force across the graveyard. Lucifer used his mind to telekinetically strike back at Michael.

He couldn't believe it took seven blades to kill The Devil. Lucifer was immortal and all powerful. Nothing on Earth could defeat him.

Lucifer's hand burst into flames, he held fire in his hand and smiled wickedly as he crossed the graveyard in Michael's direction.

He suddenly stopped as beams of light from the sky above, struck the ground around them. Lucifer was taken aback. This was not his doing. The hell hounds howled in pain. The light caused them to spontaneously combust and burn alive, turning them to ashes in a split second.

Lucifer's attention was drawn to the sky. A bright light illuminated the night's sky. Tom, Lindsay and John held a hand in front of their eyes. It was bright. Darkness still engulfed the sky, the light only shone through so much of the eternal night. Michael caught a glimpse of Lucifer's face.

He was scared and with good reason. The light from above was making a descent towards the Necropolis. Eight figures were inside the beam of light. Seven of these figures were silver armoured wearing angels with enormous white feathered wings. They surrounded a figure hidden in the brightness of the light from the heavens.

The angels were the seven archangels of Heaven.

All eight of them landed inside the Necropolis, Michael couldn't believe what he witnessed as the light extinguished. The seven archangels were guarding a man in white robes, his long brown hair stretched to his shoulders and he was bearded.

Michael wept with joy for the man in white is The Lord Jesus Christ.

Lucifer was horrified at the sight of Christ.

The Son of God had returned.

The second coming is now.

"No! It can't be. IT'S IMPOSSIBLE!!!" Lucifer shouted his words at Christ with disgust.

"This is the day I was born. It shall be the day I return. Not as a child but as a man." Christ addressed the fallen archangel. His words infuriated Lucifer.

124

"Too late, Nazarene! The Horsemen are coming!" Lucifer shouted in defiance against Christ. He was not going to go down without a fight. Lucifer was never going to admit defeat.

Mammon looked lost and confused. He asked his father for clarification.

"Who is he, father?" Mammon asked. It was the first time. Michael had seen the Antichrist scared. He should be, Michael thought. This man is The Messiah. The one who was promised, the true saviour of the world.

"I am Jesus Christ of Nazareth. The Son of God, creator of Heaven and Earth. It is time for your reign to end and a new world to begin. A world without evil." Christ declared as the archangels made their way towards Mammon.

"You said he wasn't real, father. You lied to me!" Mammon shouted at Lucifer.

Mammon attempted to fight them off. But it was futile. They were far superior in strength and seized him, he kicked and screamed as a light from the heavens struck him. When the light disappeared, Mammon was nowhere to be seen. Lucifer's eyes glowed red with rage.

"What did you do to my son, Nazarene?!" Lucifer demanded.

Christ calmly spoke to Lucifer in a peaceful manner.

"The archangels have sent him to a better place. Somewhere he will be loved and cared for… I apologise, I cannot say you will be treated in a similar manner." Christ informed Lucifer as he silently gave the command to the archangels with a nod of his head.

The seven archangels unsheathed their angel blades. They began their approach towards Lucifer. One of the archangels did not hold a dagger. Michael realised this must have been the blade which Lucifer somehow came into possession.

Lucifer laughed and shook his head at the bladeless archangel.

"Typical, Gabriel. Always losing your toys, little brother." He mocked the archangel Gabriel.

"Hey, Lucy!" John called to The Devil.

It grabbed Lucifer's full attention. The smile on his face was wiped away. John was holding the angel blade, he picked it up after Lucifer discarded it. John threw it toward Gabriel, the archangel had caught it without looking from where John had thrown the blade.

"You were saying?" John was smug. He would enjoy watching Lucifer die, Michael thought.

"It's over, Lucifer!" Tom shouted. He too was happy.

The apocalypse was going to end.

Lucifer shook his head and laughed at their comments.

"You think it is over because Christ has returned. It is not over. It has only just begun." Lucifer declared with hysterical laughter as his burnt skeletal angel wings protruded from the neck of his shirt.

He shot up into the sky, faster than a speeding bullet, escaping the justice of Heaven.

"No!" Tom shouted in devastation.

Michael couldn't believe it. This was supposed to be over. The apocalypse was going to end. Lucifer had escaped to fight another day. As long as he evaded Christ, Michael feared of what Lucifer would do.

The Four Horsemen of The Apocalypse were coming.

Tom immediately turned to Christ. Michael and he both realised, their only hope lay in the hands of Jesus Christ.

"You can stop them! You have to stop the them!" Tom begged Christ. He fully believed Jesus would have the power to stop The Four Horsemen.

"I am unable to. The spell is bound to Lucifer's life. So long as he lives. I cannot stop them." Christ apologised to them. Tom couldn't believe it. Neither could Michael.

"Jesus, I am… I am sorry for all I have done… I am not worthy to speak to you, let alone ask… There must be something you can do?" Michael felt like a sinner, he didn't deserve to be in the presence of Jesus Christ.

"There is nothing I can do. God does not blame you for what has happened. You do not need to apologise." Christ told Michael. He didn't feel any better. The guilt ate at his mind. Michael hated himself for believing Lucifer's tall tales.

"If you can't stop it. Shouldn't we get out of here before they are free?" Tom suggested. Michael thought it best. He had no desire to see the monsters he helped to release.

"You have all had a powerful curse cast upon you. The four horsemen were cast out of Heaven without their corporeal forms. Only their souls remain, Lucifer has chosen you four to be the vessels, their bodies in this world. Leaving this place will not prevent them from finding you. They will possess you and control your body. You will witness all the sins they shall commit. You will not be able to do anything to stop them." Christ informed them.

No-one took the news well. The thought of being possessed by one of them sounded like a living hell. One in which you would be unable to escape.

"What do we do?" Lindsay asked Christ. She was freaking out at the thought of possession.

Christ had a moment to himself before telling them what was going to happen next. What he was about to say was hard for him to speak.

"You will become The Four Horsemen of The Apocalypse." Christ told them in a calm manner. Michael saw how much it was killing him to tell them. Michael couldn't believe it to be true. Too much had happened for it to end this way. Tom did not take it well.

"You can't be serious?!" Tom asked with fear. Michael knew it was true and it was his fault. He had killed them all.

"I wish I weren't, Tom." Christ told him. Michael saw Jesus face, he felt pity for them. He did not wish it upon them.

"Michael?" Christ spoke directly to him. He was sorry for what had unfolded and would do whatever it took to rectify the situation.

"Jesus... I am sorry for trusting Lucifer... And... Losing my faith in your father." Michael cried. His emotions were getting the better of him and he could no longer hide his feelings.

"Michael, The Devil is a trickster. God forgives you. He has work for you. This moment, your history says you live until December 1st of 2059. You do not become one of The Four Horsemen. Time is dangerous and delicate. I will return you to your own time period. This will ensure history will remain intact." Christ had thrown far too much information at Michael.

He was overwhelmed to be going home, back to Sarah and to the safety of his present day in the year 2009. Once it sunk in, reality struck him like an express train.

"What about my friends?" Michael asked, he was concerned about their imminent possession.

"Can't you send us all back with Michael? If we are The Horsemen's vessels. Surely, our not being here solves everything?" Tom stated, he was desperate to escape becoming a host for The Horseman of War. Michael thought he was right. It made sense. Without their chosen bodies to possess, they wouldn't be able to commit the horrors which Lucifer freed them for.

"I am afraid it is not so simple, Tom. The Four Horsemen would simply find alternative vessels. The difference would be, whoever they possess, their bodies would not be able to sustain the power of the fallen angels. They would deteriorate and die. The Horsemen would then jump from host to host, killing countless innocent lives." Christ explained to them with sorrow in his voice.

It was a horrendous thought. Michael realised Tom would not allow the alternative to happen. He was not going to sacrifice the lives of strangers so he could be spared.

"What about sending us back as a team to alter history? You said time is delicate. Can the future be changed?" John asked Christ. It was a fantastic question, Michael thought.

"Unfortunately, there are laws of time. None of you were alive in 2009. You cannot interfere with the past. Michael must return on his own." Christ explained. Time-travel sounded complex and unfair. Michael would be returning to his present alone.

"Do it. Send Michael home. His being here armed with the knowledge of tonight. He can warn us before it happens… Tom, he will become your grandfather. That is the past but for Michael, it is still in his personal future. Think of what he could accomplish in the past." John sounded excited at the possibilities.

As crazy as all this was, a heads up fifty years in advance would play to the resistance's advantage.

"John, you heard what Christ said. There are laws of time. We can't mess with the past." Tom snapped at his friend. He was frustrated and angry by all that was happening.

The sky was still filled with electricity, lightning sparked and struck as far as Michael's eyes could see. It was getting worse, he thought. The Four Horsemen must be close to being released. Lindsay spoke her mind.

"Michael isn't from now. His travelling back to before it all started is still in his future. He can prevent the apocalypse from ever happening." Michael felt the weight of the world and six billion lives on his shoulders.

He knew in his heart it was true. His going back to the present day was a second chance. Michael could stop Lucifer from ever being released from Hell.

"Send me back!" Michael pleaded with Christ. He didn't care how desperate he sounded in front of the Son of God. Michael needed to get home and save everyone by making sure this nightmare never came to be.

"Please take me back. If there is a way to change it all. I will find it. How did it begin?" Michael asked Christ. He wanted to know quickly. Michael felt time was running short. The world around them was spiralling into madness with freak lightning storms.

"Heaven was warded. We could not see where he was freed from. What we do know is it happened in this city. The date was December 25th 2009. For Lucifer's followers to hide the location from God and the angels, they would have performed dark rituals. Look out for any sort of sign which may point to the location of his release. I will return you to the exact moment you were extracted from. I will return you to December 22nd 2009." Christ told Michael.

He couldn't wrap his mind around it. It was impossible. Michael couldn't do this, he thought. It was too much for him. He was nobody. Just a young Christian student and a husband from Glasgow.

"Can you send me further back? I... I need more time." Michael asked Christ. He didn't want to mess this up. He had one shot to rectify his mistake, if he failed, Lucifer would be free to walk the Earth.

The world will tremble under his rule and billions will die.

Christ calmly responded to Michael.

"I can't. There cannot be two versions of you in the same moment of time and space. I am sorry, Michael."

There was a loud bang. The ground beneath their feet exploded upward. Everyone was blown off their feet, the hilltop graveyard was a ruin, a crater had appeared where the pentagram had once been. Everyone got to their feet, Michael's ears were ringing from the blast.

His heart sank as he turned to the enormous hole in the ground. Four ghostly figures hovered in the air. These were the cast out angels who had become The Four Horsemen of The Apocalypse.

Each spirit had a different colour in their ghostly appearances. One was a bright red spirit, another was a bright white colour, the third, a figure made entirely of black and the last fallen angel was a pale green ghost.

Each spirit flew towards their vessels, their hosts. Tom, Lindsay and John stood their ground, accepting their fate, if what Michael planned to do worked.

This dreadful night would never come to pass.

The Horsemen of War, Famine and Conquest's ghosts consumed their bodies. All three of them screamed in agonising pain as they became possessed by The Horsemen. Michael stood frozen in terror as he watched his grandson and friends disappear. They were gone.

The pale green spirit flew for Michael. The closer it became, he caught a glimpse of the figure's face, it was a skull under a hood.

This was The Angel of Death. The Fourth Horseman.

Christ grabbed hold of Michael.

"When you wake up. Find Lucifer and when you do, summon me by my name. Our fates rest with you, Michael Hartnell. God be with you." Christ blessed him as a light engulfed everything around Michael. He passed out from its intense powers.

CHAPTER FIFTEEN

MICHAEL HARTNELL

12 CROWWOOD STREET

APARTMENT 3B

GLASGOW

DECEMBER 22nd 2009

11:37pm

Michael jumped in his sleep. He was back in his bed beside his wife, Sarah. Michael was home in his apartment in Crowwood Street near Glasgow City Centre. He couldn't believe it. He felt refreshed as if he had slept for the last few hours. Michael realised it was because he had been sleeping.

It was all a dream. The apocalypse in the year 2059 was nothing more than a night terror.

Michael's full body jerk had woken Sarah. She sat herself up and switched on her bedside lamp across from her. The light engulfed the bedroom, hurting Michael's tired eyes. It felt like he had not seen light for several days.

Despite barely being able to keep his eyes open in the brightness of the bedroom, he saw Sarah, she truly was the most beautiful woman alive. Her long red hair was untied and hung down to her shoulders. He loved her hair, she looked tired, she was always beautiful to Michael.

His eyes adjusted to the light. Sarah looked concerned.

"Are you alright, sweetheart?" She asked him. He had missed the sound of her voice. As daft as his dream had been, it felt like an eternity had passed since he saw her last. Sarah gently placed the palm of her hand on Michael's forehead.

"Good lord, husband. You're warm. You're sweating like crazy. Are you alright?" She asked him with concern.

Michael kissed her lips with passion, like it was the first kiss he shared with her in years. He loved Sarah more than life itself.

"I'm fine... I had a nightmare." He told her.

"Aw, sweetheart. What happened?" Sarah asked him. She lay her head on his chest. He was self-conscious about his sweat. Sarah did not seem to mind, either that or she was being polite. Michael moved his left arm to allow her to get closer to him. Michael ran his left hand through Sarah's hair. He always found it relaxing. He was no stranger to the occasional night terror.

"It doesn't matter. It was only a dream." Michael told his wife in an attempt to dismiss it. Hoping to never speak of what he saw.

"It's okay. Please tell me." Sarah encouraged him.

"It was daft and terrifying at the same time... You'll laugh, I was in the future." Michael shook his head in disbelief. Sarah let out a little giggle.

"A bit too much sci-fi for me. You love your Star Trek. Was it on a star ship?" Sarah joked with him.

"Surprisingly, it had a biblical story to it." Michael told her. It was a strange dream. It felt so real.

"Biblical how?" Sarah asked with curiosity. He knew he got her interest. She wouldn't let him go back to sleep till he told her the full story. She wanted to know everything.

"I saw the end of the world... The year was 2059. Lucifer... The Devil had brought on the apocalypse... It was terrifying and crazy. Do I sound mental?" He jokingly asked Sarah.

"Yeah. I'll get you sectioned tomorrow. First thing!" She laughed with her husband.

"Sorry to have disturbed you, my dear." Michael apologised to his beloved wife.

"It's okay. Let's get back to sleep. Lots of present wrapping to do in the morning." Sarah teased.

"Oh, my favourite." Michael sarcastically responded. Sarah kissed him on the lips. She smiled as she reached for the lamp to switch the light off, sending the room into darkness.

Michael felt Sarah roll onto her side, he wrapped his right arm around her and cuddled his wife from behind. He smiled with content. Michael was filled with happiness to be with Sarah. She held his hand and instantly reacted to it. Michael's hand stung to the touch.

He let out a small sound of pain. His hand was sore. Why? There was something damp in the bed and he felt whatever it was on his hand.

"What is that?!" Sarah exclaimed. The bedside lamp went back on to light the bedroom. To Michael's surprise, he saw the problem. Sarah covered her mouth in shock at the sight.

"Michael, what happened to your hand?" She asked him with worry. Michael's palm had a clean cut straight across it, blood gushed from the open wound. His eyes stared at the wound in absolute horror.

Lucifer's vile southern accent filled his head. Michael remembered.

"All I need from you is a drop of your blood." Lucifer's words ran through his mind in a state of panic at the possibility. It couldn't have been.

"I think you're going to need stitches. What did you do?" Sarah didn't understand how he injured himself so badly.

"It was real…" Michael was unable to speak. His breathing became rapid. He was terrified. Everything he believed to be a nightmare had actually happened. It was all real.

"What was real?" Sarah asked. Michael knew he was confusing her. He wasn't making any sense.

"My dream…" He struggled to tell her. This was madness. It was all going to come true.

In less than three days' time, Lucifer would walk free from Hell to bring on the end of the world.

"Michael, it was only a dream… I think we are going to have to head to the hospital." Sarah couldn't take her eyes off his wound.

Michael didn't care about his hand. There was only one thing on his mind… Lucifer.

"He is coming…" Michael began to cry in terror.

CHAPTER SIXTEEN

BEN ARMSTRONG

SCOTTISH NATIONAL BLOOD TRANSFUSION SERVICE
GARTNAVEL HOSPITAL
GLASGOW
DECEMBER 22ND 2009

09:48am

Ben Armstrong, a tall, dark haired and handsome man to the majority of his female colleagues. He was not interested in relationships despite the many subtle and not so subtle flirtatious advances towards him.

Ben's only passion was for his job. He was a transfusion practitioner for Scotland's blood bank in Glasgow. His work helped save hundreds if not thousands of lives and enabled him to survive in a more humane way.

The rest of his kind were not prepared to assimilate their lifestyle into today's society. They would rather live in the past. The behaviour of a few kept his people hidden from the world. They were still not common knowledge and Ben thought it best to remain that way.

All it would take would be for one crazed incident and people would be sharpening the pitchforks. Ben preferred the winter months, he was able to walk in through the front entrance at work. It was still dark in the mornings and by the time his shift concluded, night would have fallen. No daylight throughout his working day.

This was better than the summer months. Daylight till all hours of the day. He despised using the old tunnels underneath the building. Nobody knew they existed. Capitalism at its best, build an entire building upon old foundations and cutting corners. Must have been cheaper. The tunnels dated back centuries and were of great use for Ben.

The lighter days were a farce for a shift. It was this or risk his life in the sunshine. He would never along his skin to be exposed to direct sunlight. The burns took hours to disappear even with his rapid healing. Ben could never let anyone know the truth. People had died because of his secret. Never again.

Ben blended in well with his colleagues. He wore make-up on his face to give his bloodless skin some colour. His eyes were the worst. He wore contacts with blue pupils to hide the natural colour of his eyes. His eyes are a dark shade of yellow.

He loved his job as it not only allowed him to redeem himself for a lifetime of sins, his life depended on it. Any and all reject blood samples, Ben would log as being destroyed by incineration. In reality, Ben kept these samples for himself, he used the system to allow litres of blood to disappear within the confines of the law. He created fake patient profiles to allow him access to what he required to sustain himself.

Ben Armstrong is a centuries old vampire.

He had no desire to consume blood directly from any human. When the eternals had been alive. They were the first vampires. How they came into existence, Ben did not know. The eternals had strictly outlawed the feeding on humans. Since their downfall, vampires have scattered across the globe, consuming everything in their path. Vampires were like a cancer spreading throughout a body.

Ben was old fashioned. Human blood was sustenance to him and all vampires. He didn't believe humans needed to die in order for him to live. S.N.B.T.S allowed him to feed without ending human lives. Ben only wished the rest of his kind felt like he did.

Today was a busy day. Only a handful days till Christmas. He would spend it alone as the lab would be closed for the day. He was desperate to process all new donor samples and sign them off as "fit for transfusion" or discard, if unfit. He sat in the lab on a stool at his workstation.

Ben stared into a microscope at one of the new samples. For a moment, he thought the sample wasn't fresh or hadn't been preserved to the proper procedures. Until he realised, the blood was degrading. This was something else, he thought. It definitely wasn't anything good.

He looked over to the workstation across from his. A female lab assistant was doing the exact same process as Ben. She was mid-20s with short blonde hair and wore a white lab coat as did Ben and all other scientists and doctors in the building.

"Gillian?" Ben spoke across the desk to her. Gillian looked up from her microscope.

"Yeah?" she responded.

"Have you got a minute?" Ben asked her.

Gillian nodded her head. She brought herself around to Ben's workstation.

"What's up?" Gillian asked Ben.

"I need a second opinion." Ben stated and gestured to his microscope with the degraded blood sample.

Gillian sat herself on Ben's stool, he stepped up to allow her access to his microscope. Gillian looked through the scope. She took a few seconds to focus on the sample.

"Oh, my." She gasped.

"I thought so." Ben said to her. His suspicions were right. Gillian confirmed his findings.

"How old is this sample?" Gillian asked. She sounded horrified.

"It arrived on site about a week ago. No doubt it would have been donated a week before." Ben explained to Gillian. Standard procedure, whatever samples processed this morning would have made their way to the site a week ago and drawn from the donor's arm at one of the donation centres a week before that.

"Is it from a first-time donor?" Gillian inquired. Good question, Gillian always asked the right questions, covering all the basis.

"Unfortunately, patient confidentiality forbids us from knowing. We only get a long number to identify the sample." Ben told her. It was true. Above his paygrade. Head office held the names to go with the designated serial number.

"They must be informed. The person this sample has come from is HIV positive." The donor would be informed, chances were he or she were unaware. Had they known, they wouldn't have donated blood in the first place.

A shame, Ben thought. Someone's world was about to be turned upside down. He couldn't help but think of the waste, the sample was O-Negative blood type. The blood was universal donor. It was rare and the blood transfusion service needed as much as they could get their hands on. Not this time. It was unfit for transfusion.

"They will be. In the meantime, the entire blood donation needs to be disposed of." Ben informed her. The transfusion service's loss was always his gain.

"You're right. I'll take it to the incinerator." Gillian told Ben. He was not prepared for her to be so keen.

Gillian was a fairly new employee and wanted to impress him. Take the workload off him, the boss.

"No. You've got stuff to do. Besides, it is my sample. I'll take it along in a moment. Could you do me favour and file this sample under "destroyed"? Ben politely asked her. Which she was more than happy to oblige.

"No problem. What's the donor number?" Gillian asked. The sample number had to be logged in the file. Ben allowed her time to scribble the serial number down on a notepad.

Ben always made sure the majority of discards appeared random so if there was ever an audit. There wouldn't be multiple destroyed samples in his name. What he was doing was highly illegal. He had done this for the last decade. It was always another lab assistants name to throw off suspicion with the auditors.

Multiple sites always had discards under different names. Ben's cover was secure. No-one would ever need to know the truth. Ten years, he led the team in his own department.

No-one ever looked at him strangely. He may as well have been… Human.

Gillian finished jotting down the sample number. Ben stared at the blood bag as it rested in the palm of his latex gloved hands. His mouth was on edge. Ben hadn't fed for some time and he was beginning to feel its effects as he held onto the blood bag.

"You okay, Dr Armstrong?" Gillian asked him. She recognised he had gone silent.

"Yes… I'm fine. I think I will have an early break today. I'll be back shortly. Page if you need me." Ben told her before beginning to make his way out of the lab. As he did, he walked past several assistants, working away at their stations. Ben had a great team.

He proceeded out of the door to the long corridor outside the lab. Ben always hated the sterile smell of the facility. Vampire senses were stronger than any human. Smell was one of them. Sight was better too. The worst was the hearing which took most vampires time to adjust. The smallest sounds to humans were like explosions to his kind.

Ben continued walking down the corridor. The colours that the walls and floor had been made in were very National Health Service, he thought. Yellow walls and green floors. Vomit in colour, Ben always jokingly thought. He made it to a stairwell at the end of the corridor.

137

It led right down to the basement. No-one ever went down there. It was private for what Ben desperately needed. He was hungry. He climbed down the steps, each one bringing him closer to be able to give himself a little "pick me up" until his shift finished.

With each step, the back of his throat burned, he was desperate for blood. The burning sensation was something all vampires felt, it intensified and could become extremely unpleasant until blood filled his mouth, making contact with his throat.

The only thing he could compare it to was when humans were absolutely gasping for a drink of water. His thirst for blood was a million times worse and it was no exaggeration. Vampires could become so thirsty, their survival instincts kicked in and they needed to feed by any means necessary.

No vampire would allow themselves to ever be in this state. It normally comes with a loss of time, a blackout in which they lose control and memory until their thirst has been quenched. These types of incidents were rare as they risked the exposure of vampire kind's existence to the world.

The last thing any vampire wished was for a war against humanity. It was in their nature to destroy what they did not understand. Ben finally made it downstairs and quickly made his way into the basement. He rapidly swiped the plastic dividers in the doorway to the basement.

It was empty today. No donations were scheduled to arrive this afternoon. Ben took the blood bag and allowed his concealed vampire fangs to emerge from his upper jaw. Vampire fangs are razor sharp. They had to be so. As they were intended to pierce veins.

Veins in any creature were like a wet noodle, his fangs were like two giant syringes when it came to devouring blood. For the last decade, Ben Armstrong had only ever used his fangs for tearing open blood bags. Ben bit into the discarded blood bag, he made a hole large enough for him to drink out of. In an enormous greedy gulp, Ben drank every last drop of the HIV positive blood and exhaled with relief.

The blood satisfied his hunger and cooled the burn in his throat. The entire bag would see him through till the end of the morning, he would need to drink again. The HIV blood would not sustain him. Vampires are immune to all human viruses and are incapable of becoming carriers for the diseases.

HIV had no effect on him. All it did to the blood for him was affect its taste and ability to keep his hunger at bay. HIV infected blood was the vampire equivalent of fast food.

This was how he blended in amongst the humans. Ben knew this couldn't last forever.

Vampires are immortal and eternally youthful. From the moment they are turned, ageing ceases. He used his job not only as a means to survive. He spent the last decade studying blood. Ben Armstrong was searching for a cure. He hadn't always been a vampire.

CHAPTER SEVENTEEN

HIS EXCELLENCY CARLISLE DALTON

LOCATION: CLASSIFIED

DECEMBER 22ND 2009

01:00PM

His Excellency Carlisle Dalton prepared himself. His suit was immaculate. He began his walk to the briefing room to consult with the other members of The High Table. He arrived at the entrance to the briefing room or the vault as many had come to call it.

Two armed guards stood at the entrance and bowed before him.

"Lord Dalton." They addressed him. The large steel doors were opened as Lord Dalton placed his hand on a palm print reader on the wall beside the door. The security to gain access to the vault was strict. He personally ensured its security would be the finest in the world.

They were in no position to allow outsiders inside the vault. The next step in security was a retinal scan, which he stared into, a bright red light scanned every inch of his eyes.

"Welcome, Lord Dalton." A computer voice spoke as the doors opened inward into the briefing room. The vault was built to withstand nuclear attack and also served as a panic room in which one man could survive for six months. Not that any member of The High Table would ever seek to use this room for such a cowardly, ridiculous purpose, he thought.

Carlisle Dalton entered the vault. The room was always in darkness with the only light coming from the candles placed on the table. The table had a wine glass for every member present. The members of The High Table were all in attendance and seated as he entered. Everyone rose to their feet and bowed in unison as he approached the head of the table.

"Lord Dalton." They all acknowledge him with a bow as he seated himself at the enormous black marble table. Each member took their respective seats after he seated himself. Everyone of importance was present.

Carlisle Dalton is the leader of The High Table of The Illuminati.

"Tell me. What news of our agent?" Carlisle addressed The High Table. His thick Yorkshire accent filled the ears of all members. Several of them were uneasy by his question. The High Table only ever met for two reasons. To inform him of The Illuminati influence over current political matters or when there had been a colossal fuck up.

"Our agent failed to complete the mission." A female member stated. Her voice trembled when she informed her lord. This displeased Carlisle. Lucky for her, he did not kill messengers.

"Is the agent still alive?" Carlisle inquired.

"The agent took his cyanide capsule. All his tech was destroyed, leaving no trace to the new world order's movements." She responded. He thought her voice sounded more confident with this news. She shouldn't be so calm. Carlisle was yet to let her off the hook.

She was a fool to think the matter was resolved.

"Damage report? Who do they believe him to be?" Silence fell in the vault. If a pin were to be dropped. Everyone would hear its impact.

"Obviously, our agent's presence will raise questions. If there are no ties to The Illuminati. Then who is he on paper?" Carlisle was becoming annoyed. It was a simple enough question.

"A rogue MI6 agent." She replied. This almost satisfied Carlisle. He needed to know definitively that they remained in the shadows for what was to follow.

"Thank you." He thanked her for finally answering his question. A typical Republican taking a million years to get to the bottom of a straightforward question. Carlisle Dalton turned his attention to the overweight man beside him. A fellow Englishman and the United Kingdom's Prime Minister.

"Have our friends inside six been informed?" Carlisle asked the British Prime Minister. He nodded his head to confirm with Lord Dalton.

"They have been. Six have secured his identity. To them it'll be as if he'd been with them. We reached out to our friends in Thames House. In case anyone wanted to crosscheck their servers." The Prime Minister informed him.

"You are a magician." Carlisle was impressed with this prime minister, an improvement over his predecessor. Carlisle waved his hand in gesture to cup bearers at the sides of the room to serve wine. The two cup bearers emerged from the darkness and worked their way around The High Table to distribute the wine.

141

A glass of red wine was given to each member of the council. Carlisle addressed his followers.

"My friends, with our position secure. I feel the time is right to finally take control of this world. What I propose will be fast and brutal. The end result will be, complete control of the world under a one-government rule." The cup bearers finished pouring the wine.

Carlisle turned his attention to Steven Palmer, a young man in his early thirties, full of ambition. Dalton had not heard of Palmer until he became The Speaker of The House of Representatives in Washington D.C. earlier this year. Second in line of succession to The White House and presidency of The United States of America.

Carlisle Dalton needed to have Steven Palmer on his side.

"Mr Palmer, I trust all is well in the capital?" Carlisle curiously asked him with the intention of being updated of their current assignments.

"Yes, my lord." Palmer replied. He kept things close to the chest. Carlisle loved this guy. He had been a member for the best part of six months. In that time, The Illuminati had seized more control of America than they did in six years without him. Best of all, the man knew his place at The High Table and Carlisle respected him.

"The President? Anything we can use to bring him into the fold?" Carlisle asked. For his plan to succeed, he required The President of The United States.

"I'm afraid not, my lord. The man is, unfortunately, for our case. He is a boy scout. Never had as much as a parking ticket in his life." Palmer replied. Carlisle took his attitude for one of pride. Quite right to be for what Carlisle would tell Palmer next.

"Disappointing. You have the authorisation to replace him." Carlisle knew Palmer would be the best candidate to replace the goody two shoes currently occupying the oval office.

"It will be done, my lord. What shall be done with the Vice President?" Palmer asked. Carlisle liked his style and smiled. The line of succession in America hurt their cause. If The President had to go then so did the Vice President.

"Whatever you please. Make it look like an accident or hell. It's been a while since we had an assassination. I feel like we are overdue." Carlisle joked. It tickled the humour of all present. Everyone laughed including Carlisle.

"Brothers and sister, the time has come for us to initiate our final operation. It will require all our agents in a series of coordinated attacks." Carlisle told them.

Every member leaned closer, patiently anticipating what The Lord of The Illuminati was about to propose.

"It is time to unleash the inferno. I, hereby declare, The Armageddon Protocols." Carlisle's announcement was well received. There was a round of applause from all members with the exception of one. Why was he not surprised? His fellow sister spoke her mind.

"The Armageddon protocols are extremely risky even for The Illuminati. Perhaps, it would be wise not to move ahead with this so soon." Carlisle never fully trusted a republican politician. She was on this council due to his father, the previous lord of The Illuminati. What dear old dad saw in her, Carlisle did not know.

She was very opinionated and had spoken her mind one too many times. To the extent it challenged his position within the council. Many had attempted to dethrone The Lord of The High Table. He felt she was making a play for his seat. She would not be the first and certainly not the last.

Carlisle would kill any man or woman before he relinquished the power he held over The Illuminati.

"I don't think so, woman. I was born into The Illuminati. My father was the lord before, my grandfather before that. The Dalton's have been the head of The High Table for decades. I have been preparing for this day, my entire life. The time has come and you are telling me to stop!" Carlisle was filled with fury as he defended his position.

She was taken aback by how defensive he became.

"My lord... I am not saying... I am not telling you to stop. I am only suggesting you postpone and wait for a better time." She stammered her words and hesitated to speak them.

Carlisle remained silent. He patiently waited to see her embarrass herself further.

"I am only offering you my opinion, my lord." These would be some of the last words, she ever uttered.

"If I wanted to hear your opinion... I would have fucking asked for it." Carlisle sighed. He didn't particularly enjoy what came next.

"A good surgeon knows when to sever a cancerous limb. You shall speak no more from this day forth." Carlisle stood up from his chair and pulled out a hand pistol from his suit jacket's inside pocket.

He preferred this to a computer chip embedded in the brain to kill members remotely, in the event they had forgotten their place. The technology was unreliable, only good when it worked. A bullet to the head always got the result. It was efficient and economical.

"No, my lord!" She pleaded for her worthless life as he aimed the weapon before pulling the trigger. Her head exploded like a balloon full of blood and brain matter. It blasted away from the table, for the sake of the other council members.

Carlisle had always been an excellent shot. Not one drop of blood on the table. Just as well, he thought. It would be a shame to waste good wine at The High Table. Only the best was drunk at this table. He felt a special wine was in order. Carlisle tracked down Chateaux Margaux 1787. An extremely rare and highly valuable wine from New York. It valued at $225,000 for one bottle.

He had been saving it for a special occasion. If today was not a cause to celebrate, he didn't know what would be. Palmer and the other members were unfazed by Carlisle's shooting of the female member. Carlisle couldn't remember the bitch's name. It hardly mattered.

The Prime Minister had yawned as the shooting had occurred. Couldn't blame him, no-one likes a spoilt sport. His High Holiness, The Pope, who had been seated opposite her, barely registered she had been shot in the head. Carlisle stood up from the head of the table.

These wooden chairs with the enormous black back supports were rather uncomfortable. He grabbed hold of his wine glass and looked to every one of the council. The Prime Minister knew what needed to be done upon his return to 10 Downing Street. Carlisle knew the holy father was aware of his purpose on his return to Vatican City. Palmer would be tasked with removing the incompetent fool the Americans elected for a President.

It would be an incredible experience to finally have a U.S. President among the ranks of The Illuminati and the new President would be Steven Palmer.

Carlisle's eyes reached the chair at the bottom of The High Table. Richard Syme was seated there, Carlisle's second in command and his bastard brother. A secret which nobody within The Illuminati could ever know. Only he and Richard were aware of their relationship to each other.

The ancient laws of The Illuminati meant two brothers were forbidden to lead the new world order. It would be a smear upon the name, Dalton. Had Richard been the legitimate son of Lord Julius Dalton, it still wouldn't be acceptable. A bastard son was far worse. Whoever Richard's birth mother was. Carlisle had no concern about her.

Carlisle would face a fate worse than death if the truth were to be discovered. It never would come to pass. He would make sure of it.

"We all know our objectives. I shall contact you all in forty-eight hours. Richard will see you out. Before that, a toast. To what we have been preparing for since the day we were born." Carlisle addressed The High Table, raising his glass for a toast.

All members of the council stood to attention, glass in hand and raised to their lord.

"To the new world order!" Carlisle toast.

"To the new world order!" The High Table chanted in unison. Every man present drunk their glass to celebrate the order that was to come. Richard proceeded to the vault door, leading to the outside world.

Palmer, the Prime Minister and The Pope, all bowed upon finishing their drinks.

"Lord Dalton." All three of them bowed before departing The High Table. Richard already opened the vault door, the light from outside was blinding. Carlisle saw the body of the female member he killed.

Carlisle clicked his fingers and pointed at her corpse to the cupbearers, who immediately without having to hear a single word from their lord, knew what was required. Both men took hold of her blood-soaked body and carried her out of the vault.

Richard stood in the doorway as the two cupbearers removed the stupid bitch's body from the vault.

"Lord Dalton." Richard addressed Carlisle before bowing to him.

"Would that be all, my lord?" Richard asked his brother. The guards outside were still present. Richard knew he needed to keep up the pretence which Carlisle always thought was an Oscar worthy performance. Suppose all members were good actors in order to integrate themselves as an agent within their respective organisation.

145

"No, I would like a word in private, Mr Syme. Close the door behind you and take a seat." Carlisle ordered. Richard secured the doors. Carlisle let out a sigh of relief. The room was sound-proof and no electronics were ever permitted inside the vault.

He could speak freely now all the other council members had fucked off.

"What a fucking farce!" Carlisle declared as Richard seated himself in the chair opposite the high seat.

"Could have gone worse." Richard stated. True, Carlisle thought.

"Time for a real drink." Carlisle revealed a blank and label-less bottle of whisky which he kept hidden throughout the meeting.

"That's not the century old scotch?" Richard seemed surprised.

"Nothing but the best. We are celebrating." Carlisle couldn't believe the time had finally arrived.

"Why did you not bring that out in the meeting?" Richard asked Carlisle. He thought his brother daft for suggesting such an idea.

"You think I would waste this on that shower of bastards!" Carlisle joked. Richard laughed and shook his head from side to side in amusement. He and Richard seated themselves as he poured himself and his brother a glass each.

"Cheers, Richard." Carlisle raised his glass and both men, chinked their glasses together. Carlisle put the glass to his lips and drank the whisky in one swallow. He exhaled. He enjoyed the drink. Well worth the wait.

"That is something else." Carlisle stated.

"Trumps the wine. No contest." Richard joked. Carlisle chuckled, he agreed.

"Certainly tastes better than the shit Aurelius cooked up." Carlisle commented.

"You've been drinking that shit?!" Richard sounded appalled at the mention of Aurelius and his formula.

"You seem surprised?" Carlisle asked. Surely Richard knew. It was not every day, the sorcerer supreme created the fountain of youth.

"How long have you been taking it?" Richard was worried.

"Relax! Aurelius tested it on himself. It exceeded all his expectations. He created eternal life. Has its flaws, I am not invulnerable. I need to consume a pint of it once a week to maintain my youth. That's been a year since I started taking it. It's incredible, Richard. His formula doesn't only keep me young. It is making me younger." Carlisle hardly believed the effects of Aurelius formula. He knew it was the future.

"Making you younger? How?" Richard was confused. Carlisle didn't understand how. All he needed to know was it did as the sorcerer supreme had wanted it to do.

"I don't understand the magic behind it. But I am getting younger. My wrinkles are disappearing. You remember I thought I was losing my hair? Not anymore, my hair is coming back. It's out of this world!" Carlisle couldn't contain his excitement when he spoke.

"Terrifying. Imagine if that solution fell into the wrong hands." Richard didn't see what this formula meant for the new world.

"In our rule, think what we could do with it. Think of the power we will have. Sell it to the highest bidders, a fortune for a single taste and keep our sheep in line." Carlisle smiled before pouring two more glasses of scotch and put the glass to his lips.

"You're an evil genius." Richard joked before drinking his whisky.

"That's why I am the head of The Illuminati. My drinking Aurelius formula, I will be the head of The High Table till the end of time. What do you think about that?" Carlisle asked. He knew Richard was uneasy.

"Better you than I." Richard responded. He was missing the point, Carlisle thought.

"Have you never thought of taking it yourself. You are second in command and the master of the dark arts. We could rule eternally." Carlisle wanted his brother by his side. He couldn't see anyone else in Richard's role.

Richard laughed nervously.

"Aurelius is the sorcerer supreme. He taught me well. I am more concerned about The Armageddon Protocols. That is currently where my head is at." Richard honestly told Carlisle.

Smart man, he thought. Richard's mind lived in the present whereas Carlisle's thoughts were always in the future.

"I appreciate your honesty. We have done everything. We've created disasters, blamed terrorists, global warming, unleashed epidemics upon the world. Our final act will be war! We will end all world governments and out of the ashes, The Illuminati will be the masters of Earth." Carlisle told his brother as he brought the glass to his lips for another taste of his scotch.

"Carlisle…" Richard addressed him. Carlisle nearly choked on his drink.

"Never address me in such a manner. You must always address me by my proper title!" Carlisle was on edge. Had the wrong people heard them, it would be game over for them both.

"We're sealed off in the vault. We're as private as anyone can be. Chill a bit." Richard shrugged it off.

"Doesn't matter. One little slip up and we'll both be biting a bullet." Carlisle couldn't believe Richard was so careless. Was he mental?!

"My apologies, my lord. May I give you my opinion?" Richard asked as he continued to speak to Carlisle, The Leader of The Illuminati.

"Yes, you may." Carlisle responded. At least, Richard asked for permission before speaking his mind unlike the daft cow he executed.

"Are you sure about this?" Richard asked with concern. Carlisle did not understand what Richard was asking him. Sure about what? He thought.

"What are you talking about?" Carlisle frustratingly asked his second in command.

"What if Armageddon backfires?" Richard asked with fear in his voice. Carlisle was astounded he asked such a question. Instantly, he attempted to end this conversation. This was a risk. All it would take would be for someone to come in and catch them unawares.

Armageddon was airtight. Once it commenced. No-one would be able to stop them.

"It won't." Carlisle responded in an attempt to silence this talk. He knew his response as lord would suffice.

"What if it does? You cannot possibly ensure we will succeed?" Richard sounded scared, not a usual reaction for him. The last time Carlisle ever saw Richard emotional like this was when they were children.

"Do you lack faith in The Illuminati?" Carlisle asked Richard, knowing full well, his choice of words would bring Richard back to reality.

"No, of course not, Lord Dalton." Richard stammered. He knew he crossed a line which not very many came back from.

"Keep such comments to the confines of your own mind... For crying out loud, Richard! Had you spoke in such a manner whilst we were in session... I would have been given no other choice but to execute you! Do you understand me?!" Carlisle was furious. Richard had scared him senseless and deep down, he knew and sat in silence until Carlisle was ready to talk.

"You are family... To kill you. It would kill me! There would be no point in ruling this world without you, little brother." Carlisle couldn't face the thought of life without Richard. It was unbearable.

By the ancient laws, it was forbidden to have a brother, let alone a bastard brother from some whore his father had fucked when became bored of his wife.

"I'm sorry..." Richard apologised. He was at a loss for words.

Carlisle was preparing to continue giving Richard a lecture on how dangerous the next forty-eight hours were going to be, but his brother continued to speak with him.

"Will we be able to stop lying?" Richard asked. He sounded unsure and almost frightened of how Carlisle would react. He truly did not know which lie Richard referred to.

"We tell lots of lies. Be more specific." Carlisle asked in a straight to the point manner.

"In the new world... Would we be able to reveal the truth... We are brothers?" Richard asked Carlisle. He saw how it pained Richard, to have a brother and not be able to tell another living soul.

"I am afraid not, Richard." Carlisle informed his brother. It killed him to tell Richard like this. He was disappointed.

"Why?" He asked his brother and lord.

Richard was putting on the performance of a lifetime to the hide the tears building up in his eyes.

"It has been a secret for the last thirty-two years. It shall remain so. Our good work would all be for nothing if the truth came into the light." Carlisle was calm. He hid his emotions far better than Richard.

"You will be The Lord of The Earth! Who gives a dusty fuck if…" Richard was interrupted by Carlisle.

"My word is final." Carlisle ended it before things spiralled out of control.

"Would that be all, Lord Dalton?" Richard asked. Carlisle had upset him. He knew once all came to pass and he ruled over the entire planet. This conversation would be a thing of the past.

"Yes, I wish to be fully updated of the British Prime Minister, our new President and The Pope's statuses in their roles of The Armageddon Protocols." Carlisle informed his second in command.

"It will be done, my lord. Can I ask what part His Holiness will play?" Carlisle smile at Richard's thinking.

"I like how you think. I re-wrote the protocols after father's passing. Felt it needed my own style. By the time the world clicks on to what is happening. The Pope will address his followers. They will initially think it is a message of hope. All it will reveal to everyone living on this planet is that, we are everywhere."

CHAPTER EIGHTEEN

SARAH HARTNELL

12 CROWWOOD STREET

APARTMENT 3B

GLASGOW

DECEMBER 22nd 2009

11:43pm

Sarah didn't understand. There was nothing in the room capable of slicing Michael's hand so deep. He reacted as if he did not care about the state of his hand, her husband's mind appeared to be elsewhere. Michael was scared out of his wits.

"He is coming…" Michael cried out in terror.

"What are you talking about, Michael?" Sarah asked him. She was concerned for his well-being. He wasn't making any sense. Michael suddenly jumped out of bed to Sarah's surprise. He stared around the room. Michael was genuinely scared. He was beginning to scare Sarah. Michael looked her in the eye as she remained in their bed.

"You know I would never lie to you?" Michael asked her. What was going on? Sarah was worried about him. She knew her husband to be the most honest man she ever met. They wouldn't have married had there been no trust between them.

Sarah saw the bed sheet, it was cover in Michael's blood from his hand wound. It was still bleeding.

"My dream wasn't a dream. It was real… He said… He said, he would return me to the exact moment I left." Michael struggled to get his words out. Sarah was confused. He wasn't making any sense.

"Michael, you had a vivid dream. It's over. You really need to get your hand seen to." Sarah wanted Michael to calm down. He looked absolutely terrified and Sarah for the life of her couldn't understand why.

"No, Sarah! You have to believe me! It was real… I know it sounds crazy. I saw Jesus, he has brought me back in time to stop him." Michael was horrified by the mention of "him". Whoever he spoke of, it filled him with so much fear, he was afraid to say the name out loud.

"Stop who? You're scaring me!" Sarah cried.

"Lucifer… I need to go." Michael told her before crossing the bedroom to get to his chest of drawers, he grabbed his wristwatch from the top of the cabinet and put it on his wrist.

"Go where?" Sarah asked with worry. She felt lost by everything Michael was saying. His behaviour was very strange and out of character.

"I don't know yet… I was told to look for any sign indicating to where Lucifer was freed from." Michael responded, he still sounded scared. Was this a well performed prank? Was he trying to wind Sarah up? Michael rummaged through several cardboard boxes.

They had not moved in to the flat for long. There were boxes in pretty much every room. Sarah sat in silence with tears running down her face. What was Michael looking for?

Michael stopped rifling through the boxes. He obviously found what he was searching for. Sarah's eye caught what Michael held in his hands. It was his radio, an old wireless which he listened to as he studied for university. His hand continued to bleed. He left bloody handprints on the boxes he searched in. The radio was soaked with his blood. Michael was unfazed by all the blood.

"Michael, you have had a night terror. Just because it was religious. It doesn't mean it was real!" Sarah had enough. This was madness.

"Lucifer made me cut my hand. If that was a dream. How do you explain my hand?" He asked her whilst displaying the injury to his palm. It proved nothing. He must have had an accident. But how?

"Isn't this enough to show I am telling you the truth?" Michael asked her as he turned his attention back to his radio and switched it on.

"Michael?" Sarah cried.

"Be quiet just now, please." Michael asked her whilst adjusting the volume on his radio. He was listening to the news. There was always someone broadcasting the news at all hours of the day.

152

"The LHC experiment…" An American voice came from the radio before Michael changed the channel.

"A series of earthquakes hit Los…" Michael changed the channel once more. Sarah realised, he was obviously searching for Scottish radio channels.

A Scottish voice came from the radio.

"And swine flu vaccines will be distributed to the elderly in Glasgow within the new year. In other news today, a man was arrest in Glasgow for the murders of six women. The women were brutally murdered, they appear to have been killed as part of some ritual sacrifice. The man in question, drew a pentagram in their blood…" Michael switched the radio off.

He collapsed to the floor and sat with his back to the chest of drawers. He looked horrified, grabbing his hair in frustration.

"That is horrible… Who could do such a thing?" Sarah asked in utter disgust toward the murderer and his victims.

"It must be his followers… It's starting." Michael said quietly

"Whose followers, Michael?! Stop it! You are scaring me! Your hand is badly bleeding. You need a doctor!" She shouted at her husband. He needed to see reason and come back to the real world.

"Lucifer's followers… They must be preparing… Christ said they must have performed rituals to release Lucifer… This must be the start… It must be the same as what he did in the future but on a larger scale." Michael was upsetting Sarah, he finally registered how badly. Sarah began to sob hysterically.

"Michael, stop it! You are terrifying me!" Sarah shouted louder than she ever shouted in her life. The neighbours would be awake from all the noise. It was only now she realised.

Sarah Hartnell had never once shouted at her husband. They never so much as had a lover's spat. Not ever. Something wasn't right. Michael quickly came back over to the bed. He sat down beside Sarah and consoled her in his arms.

"Sarah, I am so sorry… I wish this were some sort of practical joke… It isn't… It's all true… I am sorry to scare you… I never asked for this… I have to stop him." Michael told her as he comforted Sarah. She pulled away from his hug to look him in the face.

"No, you don't! It was a dream!" What was wrong with him, Sarah thought.

"Do you believe in God?" Michael asked her. What sort of question was he asking her? Michael already knew. They were both raised as Christians and were still practising their faith.

"You know I do, Michael." She responded with the uncertainty to why he even asked.

"Why is anything I am saying so hard to accept… I have spent the last three days in the future. The year was 2059. I know that is difficult to grasp. My head spins thinking about it… I am back to try and change the future." Michael told her. He wasn't being reasonable.

"Time-travel is impossible, Michael!" Sarah responded. She wasn't angry. Was Michael having some sort of mental breakdown? Sarah was frightened.

"Maybe the miracles of God are beyond whatever our minds can believe. God is capable of everything. If you don't believe me. Believe God." He told Sarah as he looked at his sliced hand.

"My hand is the least of our problems… I need to go. I have less than three days." Michael said as if that made perfect sense. Michael quickly undressed from his pyjamas, he grabbed his black denims which he left on the bedroom floor before going to sleep, he always did that instead of putting them in the wash basket. A typical man.

He surprisingly always put his shirts in the wash, but he had been lazy last night, Michael picked up his shirt and put it on. Michael never wore the same shirt twice without washing it. Michael finished getting ready, he put on his black leather jacket and his trainers.

Michael was preparing to leave the flat. Sarah couldn't understand what he was doing. A horrible thought crossed her mind. Was this the end of their marriage?

"Michael, please don't leave me! I love you… Please don't leave me!" Sarah sobbed uncontrollably. Michael put his good hand on her cheek and kissed her forehead.

"I am not leaving you. I have a chance to stop everything. I need to take it… I will return… I love you more than you will ever know. Where I am going will not be safe. I need to know you are somewhere safe and that is here. Do not leave till I return." Michael told her, before standing up, he stared at his wife for a moment.

Sarah saw in Michael's eyes. She could tell he truly did not wish to leave. Nonetheless, Michael turned and left the bedroom.

A few seconds later, Sarah heard the front door open and close. Her husband had walked out of their home into the cold dark winter's night in Glasgow's City Centre.

"Michael!" Sarah cried out his name in hysterics.

CHAPTER NINETEEN

MICHAEL HARTNELL

MITCHELL LIBRARY

GLASGOW

DECEMBER 23rd 2009

09:01am

Madness! Michael must have been out of his mind to roam the streets of Glasgow at all hours through the night. He walked all over the city, searching for any sort of clue to indicate where everything was about to happen, where Lucifer would destroy the world.

Before leaving the flat, he grabbed his first aid kit which he left in the hallway for in case of emergencies. Michael had bandaged his hand up, after having a quick peek underneath the bandages, he knew instantly how severe his injury was. It could wait.

He stupidly realised, this was an impossible task. One which he didn't think he could do on his own. What did he really know about Lucifer? He travelled on foot to the Mitchell library to see what could potentially be uncovered from their books.

Time was short, if Michael failed, in two days' time. The Devil will walk free and bring the full power of Hell upon the Earth. His home city of Glasgow would be the first to fall under Lucifer's rule. It wasn't worth dwelling over. Michael would find a way to alter the course of history.

What he witnessed in the future was not written in stone.

Michael's head was in the clouds about everything. He couldn't stop returning to his memory of how badly he hurt Sarah. He had never made her cry. Guilt was eating away at the back of his head. As bad as he felt, Michael needed to put everything else aside to focus on finding Lucifer before he was released.

Michael had sat outside the library for over an hour before being let in at 9 o'clock on the dot.

Michael sat at a computer with several books on devil lore by his side. He was leaving no stone unturned. Books, he never thought he would ever hold, let alone read were in his hands.

Such horrendous images and depictions of Hell and Lucifer were in the pages of the books he was flicking through. Michael had no clue what Hell was like but he knew his imaginations of Lucifer never came anywhere close to the truth.

Michael Hartnell had stood in the presence of pure evil and he had no intention to ever clap eyes on Lucifer ever again for as long as he lived.

Michael plugged in a set of headphones for the computer to enable him to listen to videos online without disturbing anyone in the library. He hardly wanted anyone to overhear the nature of his research.

Michael spent hours watching history videos on satanic rituals, supernatural lore, Scottish folklore. Michael was stressing out. Nothing he found had been helpful. He couldn't find anything relating to Lucifer in Scotland. What did he expect? It was hardly as if Lucifer made regular appearances throughout history.

The world of the future was proof enough and Lucifer had admitted it too. The moment he was freed from Hell, the apocalypse began.

Michael stopped thinking about where Lucifer would rise from and began to let his brain work. The questions of why and how ran through his thoughts. Why was he being freed and how? Lucifer had followers. He wasn't broken out from the inside.

Lucifer also revealed he had been liberated from Hell. He must have had outside help. Suddenly Michael realised, the answer had stared him in the face. Cults! He thought.

Michael quickly searched for Facebook. He had not long created his profile. It was all new. He only created it for university. Michael barely knew how to operate the social media site. Many believed the site was going to be the future. If Lucifer walked free from Hell, social media would be as dead as Latin, among a great many other things, he thought.

Michael couldn't believe his luck. There were some Anti-Christianity group on Facebook. Why would anyone advertise that specific type of worship online for the whole world to know? The group was led by some guy called Connor Sullivan.

He was young, similar ages with Michael. Connor had to be about eighteen or nineteen years old.

Michael couldn't believe the amount of indoctrination posts within the group. It appeared Connor Sullivan was based somewhere in Glasgow. He led a church, a cult, Michael realised.

No true church would worship The Devil.

His cult attended weekly meetings and to Michael's amazement, all of Connor's preaching's were recorded and uploaded to the group. Michael scrolled through all of Connor Sullivan's videos. He discovered the most recent video had been filmed over a week ago.

Michael dragged the computer mouse onto the video. With a click, he loaded the video and began watching Connor's Church of Satan service. There were cheers of joy in a location which Michael did not know. Despite Connor advertising that he was a Satanist for all to see. He kept the location of his gatherings a secret. There was no address on the site for Michael to locate him.

There was not a shred of evidence to indicate where the video had been recorded.

Connor's followers in the audience cheered as he made his way onto a stage. He waved and blew kisses to the crowd. Michael thought of him as nothing more than an attention seeker who enjoyed the love of anyone who bothered to listen to his nonsense.

Michael was half-tempted to close the video down, he didn't think it right, a Christian watching a satanic worship video. He wouldn't stop watching. Michael knew by the end of this, his hands would be filthy. Whatever vile words Connor Sullivan prepared, Michael would listen to every single one.

For all he knew, Connor knew more than he did. It was vital to learn if he could potentially have something to do with Lucifer. It couldn't be a coincidence, a devil cult in the city where Lucifer would be freed in.

Connor had long black hair and was dressed from head to toe in a black cloak, the front of his cloak had a golden pentagram stitched into the material.

"My name is Connor Sullivan." Michael listened to the video. Connor spoke with an Irish accent.

"Most of you know better as, The High Priest of The Fallen God." Connor's title was ludicrous, Michael thought. He continued to listen and held the headphones tight against his ears. Library headphones were never great. The sound quality was ridiculous. It was almost difficult to hear what Connor was saying.

"It is true what many of you have heard." He told his followers, which got the reaction he desired. All who were present, screamed with excitement. Connor smiled at his cult.

"Our God will walk among us. Our God, many know him by a different name. the problem with that is we know the truth. We know all the lies spoken of him. Our God, our master and our father is the one true God. My brothers and sisters, it gives me great pleasure to announce. We will be the ones to set him free!" Connor was ecstatic.

Michael saw the happiness in Connor's delusion. What he was telling his followers had his complete attention. This was it.

"The angel who was wrongly cast out from Heaven will return. He will thank us in ways we cannot begin to comprehend. Now, you might be wondering when this is all going to happen?" Connor addressed his followers and they all responded, "Yes!". Shouting in agreement as a single voice.

"December 25th." Connor responded before cheers filled the room. Michael's heart sank as he watched the video in horror. He felt petrified for he was unable to bring himself away from watching the rest of the video. It was this cult. They would be the ones responsible for unleashing The Devil upon a defenceless and unsuspecting world.

"Our usual service on the 25th will be taking place at a legendary location called The Whangie. The service will start at 6:30pm, precisely. I ask of all you, my brothers and sisters to join me as our God comes to us. Be there to meet him and join him in the new era. All dates before his return will dated as B.L., Before Lucifer and any after will be A.L., After Lucifer. We will make history." Connor shouted which got him a round of applause, cheers and whistles from his followers.

Michael never felt so disturbed in all his life. Humans worshipping The Devil. They had no concept of what they were about to release. They didn't understand. Billions of people will perish if Lucifer were to set foot upon the Earth.

"May the morning star shine upon you." Connor said to his followers. Was he blessing them? Michael wondered. He was disgusted by all of them. How could they be so blind? Michael then understood and remembered how manipulative Lucifer was for him, only several hours ago for him but fifty years in the future.

He felt no different from the members of Connor's cult, Michael had prepared to swear his life to Lucifer before he revealed his true nature, a wolf in sheep clothing.

"May the morning star shine upon you." The cult chanted. Michael could no longer bear to watch a single second more. What he seen was too much for him. He breathed heavily, he thought for a second he was about to have a panic attack. It was too much for all of this not to be connected.

A cult preparing to free Lucifer on the date Michael had been warned about. The day the apocalypse began. Connor's words matched up with what Michael knew about the future in 2059.

Connor was brainwashed. That much was certain. Michael knew there was no-one else who fit the profile. As warped as Connor Sullivan's preaching was, he spoke the truth. Lucifer would return in two days' time.

Michael threw the headphones off his head in frustration. He lay his head down on the desk beside the computer. He was so tired and distraught that all of this, the fate of every living person now and in the next fifty years were in his hands. He needed to protect them. To do that, he would have to track down The High Priest of The Fallen God, Connor Sullivan.

The future of the human race depended upon Michael's ability to locate Connor Sullivan before he began whatever ritual to bring about Lucifer's escape from Hell. He doubted himself. There was too much at stake with so little time left. Michael took a moment to look at his wristwatch. It was 3:13pm. He had been researching for over six hours.

Time was disappearing with every second. Bringing the horrors of the future closer to Michael's present day. He knew there was a little over forty-eight hours to find Connor and convince him out of this madness of freeing Lucifer.

Suddenly, a hand grabbed Michael's shoulder from behind where he was sitting, Michael jumped with fright. He hadn't anticipated anyone touching him in such an unexpected manner. He was surprised by not making a sound from the shock of it.

As he turned his head around to see who touched him, he did it in complete silence. What Michael saw next, completely blew his mind. It defied everything he knew about life and death. It was not possible.

In front of him stood the first person he encountered in 2059. He couldn't be standing in front of Michael. His mind flashed back to the memory of watching this person being murdered.

For the man beside him was no human. He was an angel of Heaven.

"Nejuma?" Michael asked, he was baffled. Were his eyes playing tricks on him? The suit and trench coat wearing angel was alive and well in present day Glasgow.

"Yes, Michael. I am sorry. I did not mean to startle you." Nejuma apologised. Michael didn't understand. How was Nejuma alive and here with him in the present day?

"How... I thought you died... Lucifer killed you!" Michael exclaimed.

"He did." Nejuma replied with such calmness. He spoke quietly.

"How are you..." Michael couldn't bring himself to ask. It was strange, beyond strange. It was a miracle.

"Alive? Good question. How are you back in 2009? Who do we both have in common?" Nejuma made Michael see the truth. Nejuma spoke in riddles than giving a straightforward answer.

"Christ?" Michael asked, he was the reason for his return home. He brought Nejuma back to life. It was incredible. Believing in the supernatural powers of Jesus Christ was one thing. To actually witness them was something else entirely. Nejuma's focus was on Michael's bandaged hand.

Michael thought it weird, considering everything going on, that the angel's concern was to his wounded hand. Nejuma removed the bandaged to reveal Michael's sliced palm. The bandaged was stained with dried blood. The bleeding had stopped. Michael's hand was filthy. He knew if he didn't get it seen to it would become infected.

Before he could react, Nejuma took hold of the palm. Michael winced in pain, what in God's name was Nejuma doing? Light emitted from the angel's hand and flowed into Michael's. The pain he experienced was relieved in the blink of an eye for when the light disappeared.

Michael's hand was not only clean but healed. Nejuma had used his abilities to fix his hand. Nejuma looked all around them. No-one had witnessed the magic he performed. Michael suspected he was concerned people may overhear their conversations.

"Come with me, Michael. It is not safe to speak here." Nejuma informed Michael. Weren't angels supposed to make you feel safe? Michael did not feel secure. What was so dangerous about the Mitchell library?

Nejuma made his way towards the exit, the Mitchell library was enormous. Michael followed and tried to keep at the same pace as Nejuma.

They headed outside onto the streets of Glasgow. It was midday and snow was heavily falling from the winter's sky. Michael shivered from the cold. He hadn't dressed properly for the cold winter's day.

Traffic in the city centre was at a standstill on the motorway across from the library. The weather had seen to that. Scotland was terrible for snow and this winter had been the coldest in a generation.

Nejuma and Michael stood on the steps of the library. Nejuma looked anxious, he looked all around them. What was wrong? Michael felt uneasy. Whatever was capable of getting Nejuma on edge couldn't be good.

"We have not much time, Michael. I have been restored to life to help you find Lucifer. I am your guardian angel." Nejuma was Michael's guardian angel? Why did Michael have his own personal angel? What was so special about him, Michael Hartnell, the nineteen-year-old Christian medical student? The world had gone mad.

"Why me?" Michael asked. This was crazy.

"I am not at liberty to say. Have you uncovered where Lucifer will rise from?" Nejuma asked Michael. He sounded impatient.

"I... I discovered a cult... They are here in Glasgow." Michael was taken aback by all this. He stammered in an attempt to tell Nejuma what he learned.

"The Church of The Fallen God" Nejuma stated, it wasn't a question. He knew them. How did Nejuma know of their existence?

"How did you know?" Michael asked.

"Heaven believes they may have been involved. Unfortunately, the angel warding. We were unable to see." Nejuma explained to Michael.

"Angel warding?" Michael asked in confusion.

"It prevents angels from coming through. It is all around the country. No angel can get in or out." What Nejuma said wasn't logical. He was here and an angel.

"How are you here?" Michael asked. The angel was terrible with explanations.

"I arrived before the rituals began. We are on our own, Michael." Nejuma's words did not sit well with Michael. The powers of Hell were at play and no help from Heaven was coming.

"Where is God? What is he doing about this?" Michael asked. If no angel could break through.

What was God doing? Surely, he was able to strike at the core of Lucifer's followers and prevent the escape from Hell? Nejuma was silent for a moment. Michael thought for a second he offended the angel. He was unsure if he did and to be honest, Michael did not care.

God had to do something!

"I do not know, Michael" Nejuma responded. He felt the devastation in Nejuma's voice. How could he not know? He was an angel!

"What do you mean? How can you not know?!" Michael thought it was ridiculous. There was no way it could have been true.

"No angel knows. God is not in Heaven… He is missing." Nejuma told Michael. How could God be missing? How was something so unimaginable possible? Michael couldn't believe it. Had something happened to The Almighty?

"Did Sullivan mention where he plans to free Lucifer from?" Nejuma waited for Michael's response as he changed the subject. Michael tried to remember where Connor spoke of. It was a funny old name.

"He called it… It was a strange name. The Whangie… I think." Michael said, unsure if he said it correctly. He became more concerned with finding Connor, he almost forgotten the name of the location where Connor and his followers were preparing to gather to release their God.

Nejuma looked horrified at the name of the location. He momentarily walked past Michael. The angel was stunned by what he heard. That much was obvious.

"That's how they did it?" Nejuma muttered to himself. Michael wasn't following. Nejuma needed to level with Michael, explain what The Whangie is and why it is significant.

"Did what?" Michael asked with the hope Nejuma would open up and tell him everything he knew.

"The Whangie is where he will be freed from." Nejuma stated. He sounded confident, almost as if that were enough evidence for him to lead with.

"I read about it. Isn't it a folk story? A legend? The Devil's tail flicked a rock as he flew over it?" Lucifer had no tail, he could fly. Was there truth to an old Scottish myth? Michael was curious and desperately needed to know what Nejuma knew.

"Michael, it is not a story. It is the truth. The story is not completely true. When an angel is cast out from Heaven. After the fall, the angel passes through The Whangie. I believe they will attempt to release him from there."

Nejuma told Michael, who didn't understand how his guardian knew for certain.

"How do you know for sure? If it's not there and we are wrong... He will be freed..." Michael couldn't risk the chance it was wrong. Billions of lives were at stake. They couldn't afford to half know the location. They needed to know beyond all shadow of a doubt.

"Michael, The Whangie is the main portal to Hell. When activated, a portal will open, bridging a gateway between Hell and the Earth. This particular portal has a different name..." Nejuma dared not finish his sentence.

What was so bad he couldn't say its name to Michael?

"What is it called, Nejuma?" Michael asked, his curiosity getting the better of him. As soon as he asked, he knew he was going to regret it.

"The Gates of Hell." Nejuma replied with a heavy voice. The name was the stuff of nightmares to Michael. The thought of Hell being a dimension existing alongside his planet was terrifying. More so that its primary access point was not even thirty miles outside his hometown.

"Oh, God!" Michael exclaimed in shock.

"There have been rituals. Sacrifices all over the city. I do not believe they are finished. I expect we have yet to encounter the worst." Nejuma told Michael.

This was horrendous. Nobody should ever feel what Michael felt. This truly felt like the end of the world. Michael and Nejuma had to put an end to it.

"We need to find Connor..." Before Michael could continue speaking, Nejuma raised his hand to silence Michael. Nejuma was scared. Something spooked him.

"What's wrong?" Michael asked. Nejuma's behaviour was making him feel uneasy and frightened.

"Someone is listening to us. I will draw them away. I will return soon, Michael." Nejuma said and in a split second, the angel vanished into thin air. Michael was perplexed. Where had Nejuma disappeared to?

His heart raced at the thought of an unknown person or persons, listening in on their conversation.

Michael Hartnell was afraid and he was alone.

CHAPTER TWENTY

BRITISH PRIME MINISTER

10 DOWNING STREET

LONDON, ENGLAND

DECEMBER 23rd 2009

04:30pm

The Prime Minister of Great Britain sat at his desk in the office of 10 Downing Street. He was preparing for his departure. He waited for word from the airfield for confirmation, then the path to the new world order would commence.

He sat with a glass of scotch, taking in his surroundings, one last time. He will never again set foot in 10 Downing Street and he would also be the last ever Prime Minister to lead the United Kingdom.

In less than forty-eight hours, His Excellency Lord Carlisle Dalton would ascend to become, The Lord of The Earth with The Illuminati at his side to rule with him.

The Prime Minister's phone rang. It had been resting on his desk in front of him. He sat the glass aside for a moment to pick up his phone, receiving the call from an unknown number.

"Hello." He answered his call. It was Steven Palmer.

"Is this a secure line, Mr Palmer?" He asked, not that it really mattered any longer. Most of the security services were agents of The Illuminati and things were similar across the pond. Palmer certainly seen to that personally. The young politician had the majority of the F.B.I and C.I.A in his pocket.

Nonetheless, Palmer confirmed it was a secured call and inquired into the Prime Minister's departure.

"I am wating for that stupid aide of mine to inform me of the airfield being ready for my departure." He informed Palmer. The young American was calm, he was an intelligent man and knew everything would fall into place, regardless of the Prime Minister's slight delay.

"When has Lord Dalton scheduled the launch for?" The Prime Minister waited for a response from Steven Palmer.

"1800 hours on the 25th... Yes, I will be at the rendezvous point before then. As soon as I know when I am leaving. I will prepare the box... I guess the next time we meet, I will be addressing you as, Mr President." The British Prime Minister laughed with Palmer before hanging up the call.

Everything was falling into place.

There was a knock on the office wooden doors. He presumed it would be his aide. Hopefully with good news.

"Come in." He shouted towards the office door, patiently waiting for the doors to open, his aide entered the office. A young and stupid boy dressed in a suit. He couldn't be older than twenty-five. The Prime Minister thought of him as an idiot, a loyal idiot, desperate to create a good impression with him.

"Good afternoon, Prime Minister.' The aide addressed him when entering the office. The Prime Minister sat in silence, eagerly awaiting whatever news came next for the young aide's sake. It had better be good news, his patience was wearing thin.

"Good news, sir. The airfield has informed me your jet is fuelled and ready for your trip to America." The aide informed the Prime Minister. Finally, some good news. He became sick and tired of sitting, doing nothing whilst the rest of The Illuminati brothers and sisters were preparing for Armageddon.

"Fantastic. I will be out in a moment. Please prepare my car. I shall be brief... Run along!" He told his aide, who quickly stumbled out of the office. Silly boy, had he not been so clumsy, his loyalty could have had potential for the new world order. A pity, he thought as he grabbed hold of his glass, downing the last of his drink in a single gulp.

The Prime Minister stepped away from his chair. The weight of the suit jacket almost took him by surprise. He'd forgotten that he had a firearm inside a specially designed inner pocket. He loved the suits from Savile Row, always happy to meet the needs of the customer and with great discretion.

He opened the top drawer of his desk and lifted out, a black steel box. It was heavier than he remembered, a box small enough to be held in his hands was capable of total destruction. In order to bring in the new, the old needed to be brought down.

This box controlled the United Kingdom's nuclear arsenal, one order from this box could obliterate the entire world. He stared at the box in admiration, it was beautiful to him.

On top, there was a small keypad in the centre of the box with a small screen, it lit up as the Prime Minister rested his right palm on the box. It scanned his handprint.

"Identity confirmed. Welcome, Prime Minister." A computerised female voice came from the black box.

"Please select target or targets." The box's computerised voice requested his target.

He prepared to select The Illuminati target, his aide had unexpectedly returned to the office, unannounced, he simply walked in without knocking on the door.

"Your car is waiting, Prime…" He was stopped dead in his tracks, he knew exactly what he wandered into.

"Prime Minister, that's… That's the nuclear launch control box! What on earth are you doing?" His aide was confused by what he witnessed.

"Let's not play the stupid act. There can be only one reason why I have this on my desk!" The Prime Minister could not believe how careless he had been. The aide was frozen solid with fear, he was clueless to what was about to happen next. If he had even the slightest notion, he would have run like the wind to save his own retched hide.

Pandora's box had been opened and there was no closing it.

"I'm sorry. I really wish you hadn't seen this." The Prime Minister apologised before reaching inside his jacket pocket, he swiftly shoots his aide in the head with a silenced pistol. It was quick, the young aide had not seen it coming. Fast and painless death.

"Please confirm target or targets." The robotic female voice repeated the last option, he had not finished his target selection. As he clicked buttons of the keypad, the screen presented, a map of the world. He selected the United States of America and confirmed his target as Washington D.C. and the surrounding areas of the capital city.

"Target confirmed. Time until nuclear launch: Forty-nine hours and twenty-three minutes." The computer voice confirmed the command. A smile stretched across his face. The Prime Minister's part was over. All he needed to do now was meet with Lord Dalton and Mr Syme at the extraction.

He began to leave his office, he stopped and stared down at the lifeless body of the young man who severed him well ever since he came into office, two years earlier. He felt sorry for him. Loyal idiots were hard to come by.

The Prime Minister removed the gun from his inner pocket, he made time to wipe it down properly to ensure his prints were nowhere to be found, before carefully placing it in the hands of the aide he murdered.

He couldn't have anyone questioning this particular situation. He felt confident that his friends at five would be able to make it look like a suicide, it only needed to last for forty-nine hours then it would no longer matter.

With that in mind, he made his way towards his car.

The last British Prime Minister left 10 Downing Street for the final time, never to return.

CHAPTER TWENTY-ONE

SARAH HARTNELL

12 CROWWOOD STREET

APARTMENT 3B

GLASGOW

DECEMBER 23rd 2009

04:45pm

Sarah Hartnell was seated in the apartment kitchen at her and Michael's dinner table. She was sick with worry and freaking out over Michael's actions. She was physically exhausted from her lack of sleep, crying and the constant fear of not knowing wearing Michael was or whatever he was doing.

She was terrified that something was wrong with her husband. She never seen him like this before, he talked like a raving lunatic. Time-travel and The Devil. Something was wrong with him. She attempted to call his parents. They were on holiday abroad.

Sarah had no such luck of being able to reach her in-laws. They were oblivious to what was happening with their son. The hotel they claimed to be staying in, had no record of guests under their names. It was as if they disappeared from the face of the world. Sarah felt it strange and it did not help her stress levels.

Sarah did manage to get a hold of several of Michael's university friends. Not a single person had seen or heard from him. Sarah stood up from the chair and paced up and down the small kitchen. She had been biting her nails from the stress. They were beginning to sting from the constant biting.

It was always a bad habit of hers when she became anxious. Sarah reached into her jean pocket to pull out her mobile phone. It was nearly out of charge and she only possessed enough credit for two more calls or less.

Sarah scrolled though her contacts to Michael's number and dialled his number for what felt like the millionth time.

The dial tone rung and rung out before going to Michael's voicemail. She decided to leave yet another voicemail on her husband's phone.

"Michael… Sweetheart." Sarah sobbed as she began to record her message for her husband.

"I am so worried about you… Please… Please come home… Call me… Just let me know you are alright… I love you." Sarah ended the call and sobbed hysterically. She couldn't understand why Michael had run out on her.

Where is he? What was he doing? He wasn't thinking clearly. Her mind jumped to all kinds of horrible conclusions. She feared he might be a danger to himself. Sarah brought herself out of the kitchen and headed to the bedroom. The whole apartment was a shambles, cardboard boxes were everywhere.

It really annoyed her but Michael is missing. It put her priorities into perspective. She lay down on Michael's side of the bed. She wanted to feel close to him. She missed him and wanted him home where he was safer.

There was no hope in reaching his friends and to her surprise, his family were nowhere to be found. Sarah knew there was one other person she could seek help from, God.

Sarah wiped the tears from her eyes with a paper handkerchief. She sat upright on the bed.

Sarah Hartnell closed her eyes and clasped her hands together, beginning to pray to God.

"Father God, I pray I hear from Michael. He has scared me beyond anything I ever thought possible. I pray nothing has happened to him… I miss him and don't want to lose him… He is all I have. I pray you deliver him safely home. In the name of Jesus Christ, I pray… Amen." Sarah's faith was strong.

She always sought out God's assistance. She always believed in the power of prayer. Asking of God, fully believing had always been a comfort to Sarah. God had never once let her down, she knew with every fibre of her being, he would not fail her today in her greatest hour of need.

Sarah looked around the room, she didn't know where to start searching for Michael. He could be anywhere. She didn't want to leave the flat on the off chance he returned home whilst she was not here.

Her eyes stopped at Michael's bedside cabinet. Sarah burst into tears when she saw what rested on top of the cabinet next to the beside lamp. It was his mobile phone.

Michael hadn't taken it with him. She sobbed as she seized hold of the mobile. She checked his phone. It was at 50% charge and had been set on silent mode. He was murder for always leaving his phone on silent.

Sarah checked his call log, there were thirty-nine missed calls and voicemails from her phone. She sobbed hysterically.

Michael was out there all alone and she had no means of contacting her husband.

"Where are you, Michael?" Sarah sobbed, clutching onto his mobile like her life depended on it.

CHAPTER TWENTY-TWO

MICHAEL HARTNELL

CITY CENTRE

GLASGOW

DECEMBER 23RD 2009

04:50pm

Michael couldn't believe Nejuma had abandoned him. Who was listening in on them? The terror of the unknown kept his senses sharp. It was a daunting place to be. Every passer-by, Michael couldn't distinguish from a friend or foe.

Somewhere in the city, a cult of satanic worshippers were beginning their ritual to free Lucifer from Hell. It had already begun, he thought. It wasn't by chance a mass murderer had killed six women in cold blood before using their blood to paint a five-point star, the pentagram.

Lucifer's symbol of evil. The mark of his followers.

There had to be something else happening. More than the murders of six women. Whatever was happening around the city, it was powerful enough to keep Heaven from entering the country.

Nejuma told Michael he got through before the angel warding was powered up. It prevented any other angel from entering or leaving the country.

Sirens blared from emergency vehicles all over the city. Police cars sped along the street which Michael was on. What was happening? He'd never seen so many police cars or ambulances out at any time. Something bad had happened. But what?

"Big Issue!" Michael turned and saw a homeless man selling the Big Issue magazine. Michael had always bought one to help feed the homeless in the city and usually always gave the seller, a couple extra quid.

The strange thing was, the homeless knew better than most about the goings-on in the city. Michael wondered if he knew anything as he approached the seller.

"Sorry to bother you. Do you know why all the police are out?" Michael inquired. Word always spread like wildfire in the city. It was like a little network.

"Aye." The homeless man spoke, he'd had a hard time on the streets, Michael thought. His clothes were dirty and damaged. His skin was dirty, the poor man hadn't been washed for some time and he was missing several teeth. Michael felt sorry for him. Whatever he knew was of the upmost importance.

"Some nutcase doacters and nurses up The Royal jumped aff the roof." The homeless man told him. He spoke in Glaswegian slang with a strong Scottish accent. Michael was deeply disturbed by what he was told.

Why would doctors and nurses jump to their deaths from Glasgow's Royal Infirmary? The city was descending into madness.

"Oh, God! That's horrible! Does anyone know why?" Michael continued to speak with the man.

"Naw! Naebody does. Dae ye ken the strangest thing? The wans who jumped aff the roof. When their bodies hit the grund, they made a pentagram!" The Big Issue Seller told the story with a dramatic tone, putting an emphasis on his storytelling like a ghost story.

The sad reality was. This was no story. It was real. Lucifer's followers were still at play in the city.

"Oh, God… It's happening." Michael spoke his thoughts out loud. If he couldn't find and stop Connor Sullivan, Lucifer will be free and what was happening in Glasgow would spread to the rest of the world.

"Am no a religious man. That fucking shite up the hospital has scared the crap oot of me." He told Michael. What was happening was enough to make anyone scared, whether you believed in The Devil or not. Lucifer was worse than any nightmare could conjure up.

"Ye wanting the Big Issue or no, son?" The homeless man asked Michael. Any other day, he would have purchased it. He had been in such a rush. Michael had forgotten his wallet and phone. He didn't even have the key to the apartment.

"No… I'm sorry. I don't have anything on me." Michael apologised.

The friendly nature of the homeless man changed with the beat of a heart.

"Git tae fuck! Ya wee prick!" He cursed at Michael.

173

Charming, Michael thought before proceeding to walk away from the man. Michael couldn't believe what was happening in his city. He walked down an alley to get off the street. He needed a moment alone with his thoughts.

What was he going to do? The whole world was in the dark. No-one on this planet except for himself knew what was coming. Michael slumped against the alley wall and allowed himself to slide to the ground. The snow was deep. It was damp and cold. Not that he cared.

He was more concerned about everyone else's well-being. Should he be shouting everything from the rooftops? People had the right to know. Lucifer was real and he was less than forty-eight hours away from breaking into this world.

Michael would be mad or at least that would be how the last-minute Christmas shoppers would perceive him. He probably wouldn't be the only person on the streets of Glasgow shouting about the end of days. There was many a fruit-loop preaching the end of the world in the city centre.

The only difference with him was, his was the truth. The end was approaching.

Wouldn't it be the right thing to do even if passers-by did indeed think he was insane? The least it could do was warn people. Despite whether they believed it or not.

Michael cried. This was too much for him. It was time. He needed to return home, he knew Sarah would be freaking out. Michael brought himself to his feet and prepared to leave the alley.

"Oi!" A male voice from behind shouted at Michael. He stopped walking to turn and face whoever called out to him. He wished he hadn't for there were three knife-wielding thugs in leather jackets, dressed from head to toe in black. All three of them stood in a line, side by side.

Each had a black woollen hat on their heads, covering their ears. The winters in Scotland were always cold. The men all wore black leather gloves. Each held a knife in their right hand. Michael wasn't afraid. He was pissed off as whatever they wanted from him, it was pointless in the grand scale of things occurring at this very moment.

The longer Michael stayed here, the less time he had to track down Connor Sullivan.

"This is our alley." The man in the middle of the three shouted towards Michael. He was no doubt the leader of this group of thugs.

"I am not wanting any trouble. I'm trying to catch my breath. I will be on my way." Michael politely told them.

All three of them circled around Michael. They were attempting to intimidate him. A few days ago, he would no doubt have felt frightened. He wasn't scared. What Michael Hartnell had encountered in 2059, scared him.

These criminals combined were no match compared to demons or infected. Michael had been personally tortured by The Devil.

"No trouble. So long as you pay the toll." The leader told Michael. The other two thugs laughed. This was fun to them. Whatever use they had for this alley was no doubt illegal and they did not want anyone on their turf, a shake down would see to that with any normal law-abiding citizen who feared for their life.

Michael Hartnell did not fear these men.

"I haven't got anything. Pleasant day to you, gentlemen." Michael politely addressed the gang of thugs. He attempted to walk past them. The leader held Michael back, pressing the palm of his hand against his chest.

"I don't think you understand, friend. When I ask for something. It's called, you give it to us, or we kick fuck out of you. And if you're lucky, worst case scenario. You'll end up at The Royal. I suppose that's not so good today. Especially with the majority of their staff topping themselves." The gang laughed at the leader's dark humoured joke.

These men had no respect for human life. Michael realised men like this would no longer exist if he failed to prevent Lucifer's escape. Their little territorial extortions would be no match for what Lucifer had in store for this city.

"I have nothing. If you're going to me the head-kicking of a lifetime, hurry the fuck up already. I've got somewhere to be." Michael told them in a slightly annoyed tone.

The leader smiled. He couldn't believe the level of cheek Michael was dishing out. The two other thugs remained silent. They too were obviously stunned by Michael's attitude. He guessed not very many men had the audacity to speak like this.

The leader grabbed hold of Michael's leather jacket and thrust him hard against the alley wall. Michael remained silent. This was getting old fast.

"Not so smart now? Are you?" The leader shouted before reaching into Michael's pockets. He was frustrated when he discovered Michael possessed nothing of value.

"Stop fucking me around, cunt!" The leader shouted in his face. He obviously hoped to find a wallet or a mobile in Michael's pockets. He had neither. For not one of them would aid him in his search for Lucifer's rising place.

"Like I have already told you. I have nothing. I'll be…" Michael was thrown into the snow filled ground in anger. Before he had a chance to finish speaking, the gang leader straddled Michael and held a knife to his throat.

"I reckon you have something good and it will be nearby. You take us there, or we will slash your stupid fucking face open!" The leader threatened him. His men were laughing. They obviously felt powerful. Michael saw right through all their threats, he had been shook down and threatened with a beating and now with a knife.

These losers, that's what they were, losers! They were low level street thugs. Incapable of living up to their promises. This was beyond ridiculous. Michael couldn't believe people actually allowed themselves to be scared by these types of idiots. He burst into a fit of hysterical laughter. It was pathetic.

"What's so fucking funny?" The leader shouted in his face, as he made his feeble attempt to hold the blade closer to Michael's jugular.

"You! Does this act really work?" Michael laughed in his face. The thugs were taken aback. This was out of the normal for them.

"I have met someone… He was a real villain. He makes you three look like the Teletubbies! That is real evil. He is older than time itself, he has been to Hell and he… He is coming for all of us!" Michael laughed at the petty criminals. They were nothing compared to Lucifer.

"Who was this guy? The fucking devil or something?" One of the other thugs mocked Michael's comment about Lucifer. They all laughed at Michael. They were not believers. If they were, they would have run for miles.

"Yes." Michael smiled before swiftly kneeing the gang leader between the legs then headbutting him in his moment of pain. Michael wiggled out from under the leader and grabbed his knife, he dropped it from the unexpected retaliation. Michael held the knife in front of him as he launched himself to his feet, preparing to defend himself.

The thug leader held his nose. Michael struck it with his forehead, he felt it crunch upon impact. That nose was definitely broken. The leader had blood all over his face. It flowed between his fingers as he held it.

"Back the fuck away from me!" Michael barked at the thugs. It was over. He was leaving and there was not a lot they could do to keep him in their grip. The gang leader laughed. He was amazed by how well Michael defended himself. He nodded his head to the men.

All three of them reached inside their jackets and drew handguns on Michael. Never bring a knife to a gunfight, Michael thought. There was no way he imagined getting out of this one.

"Scared now?" The leader grinned at Michael being held at gunpoint. The sound of large wings flapping was heard behind the thugs.

"Not when he has a guardian." Nejuma appeared from nowhere behind the criminals. This took them by surprise as much as it did for Michael. They instantly on muscle reaction and criminal instinct, spun around and fired their weapons at Nejuma.

For the briefest moment, Michael worried they had injured Nejuma until he witnessed with his own eyes, the bullets striking Nejuma's chest and ricochet. The trench coat wearing angel's body was bulletproof. Michael understood it must be the same for all angels, Lucifer's body was also impervious to bullets.

The only thing Michael ever seen capable of inflicting any injury upon an angel was the archangel dagger in the future. The only difference between Nejuma and Lucifer, in regard to the dagger were, it would kill Nejuma and Lucifer required an additional six daggers to kill him.

"What the fuck?!" The leader questioned in disbelief. They probably thought their eyes were playing tricks on them. The two thugs ran toward Nejuma, whatever they had planned was futile. Nejuma grabbed both men with his bare hands by their faces and threw them to the ground.

They were not conscious when they collapsed to the snow. Had Nejuma killed them? His enormous angelic white feathered wings emerged from the neck of his coat. His wings stretched out to their full magnificence.

Michael would never become accustomed to the beauty of the divine, for angel wings were not of this world.

"What the fuck are you?" The leader asked Nejuma with absolute terror.

"I am an angel of the lord." Nejuma calmly told him. The Glasgow thug could not wrap his mind around it. He grabbed hold of one of the knives and ran towards Nejuma. He attempted to stab the angel, the knife shattered into dozens of pieces as it struck the invulnerable body.

It was incapable of harming the guardian angel. The leader held the hilt of the knife in shock. Nejuma calmly stood his ground and without any sign of emotion, he placed his index finger upon the man's head.

In a split second, the gang leader collapsed face first into the deep snow. What had Nejuma done to these men?

"Did you kill them?" Michael asked in horror. They were bad guys. Despite their lifestyle, they did not deserve to die. Michael knew so even when he took control of one of their knives. He never would have dared attempted to take any of their lives.

Nejuma shook his head.

"No, Michael. I have only put them to sleep. They will wake in half an hour with a slight headache." Nejuma told Michael. It was a relief the angel had not bloodied his hands on Michael's account.

He did not want anyone to die because of him. He was relieved the gang members were still alive.

"What about you? They will remember what happened? Won't they?" Michael asked. He was concerned what these thugs could do knowing they had attempted to murder an angel.

"They will wake up and believe whatever they choose to." Nejuma told Michael. Michael supposed the angel was right. They would sound crazy if they were to ever breathe a word of the story to anyone and from the strong attitude towards their territory, Michael's hunch was, they would not say a word because if they did. People would find out someone got one over them.

Nejuma reached down into the snow for one of the handguns. He released the gun's magazine to check if the weapon was loaded with bullets.

Michael thought it was strange. Why would an angel need a gun? Nejuma then held the gun out to Michael. He was offering it up for him to take. Why?

"I don't like guns… Why are you giving it to me?" Michael asked him. He hated guns. If it were up to him, they would be outlawed in every country. They cause nothing but death and destruction.

"You will need it. In the event of something happening to me. You will need to defend yourself." Nejuma held the gun out and again gestured for Michael to take hold of the handle.

"Why? What could I possibly want it for?" Michael felt disgusted. Angels were supposed to be good. Nejuma was trying to give him an instrument of death. Michael wanted to know exactly why on earth he should.

"Demons." Nejuma responded with the emotionless tone he seemed to always have.

"Demons?" Michael asked in horror.

"They are all over the city. They were listening to our conversation. I had to catch up and silence them before they could inform their leader. The witch-demon Wormwood. She is orchestrating everything. The hospital staff who ended their lives, she had demons possess them. These deaths are part of a dark ritual. This is the beginning of their attempt to free Lucifer from Hell." Nejuma explained and answered several of Michael's questions.

It filled him with dread. Demons were everywhere and at the heart of their operation was a witch-demon. By the sounds of it, Michael believed her to be every bit as deadly as Lucifer.

"My God!" Michael gasped in horror. Demons all over the city and listening in on his conversation at the library. Michael could not believe this was happening. He would not allow this Wormwood demon to succeed. He had dozens more questions for Nejuma.

How did Wormwood fit in with Connor Sullivan? The only ways to understand how, would be to find Connor Sullivan.

"We need to get a move on and find Connor Sullivan. Before it's too late." Michael said. He desperately wanted this nightmare to be over and for the world of the future to never happen.

"We will, Michael. First, I must ask. Is there anyone important in your life? I believe we need to go to them immediately. The demons I killed, they spoke of killing the one you love." Nejuma's words made Michael ill.

Demons were everywhere and who was the one person he was failing to protect?

"Sarah!" Michael gasped when he realised the grave danger his wife was in.

CHAPTER TWENTY-THREE

SARAH HARTNELL

12 CROWWOOD STREET

APARTMENT 3B

GLASGOW

DECEMBER 23rd 2009

05:04pm

Sarah paced up and down the living room. She felt useless. She tried to get in touch with Michael's parents once more. She had zero success of reaching them. Sarah found this odd. His parents were always available even when they travelled abroad for their annual holiday. Something did not sit right.

Her main concern was Michael. She felt there was no other option in order to locate Michael's whereabouts. She did not really want it to come to this. Sarah held up her mobile phone and dialled "999" for the emergency services.

She knew they were busy, especially with all the horrible incidents happening throughout the city. All she wanted was for Michael to come home.

"Emergency services. Which service do you require?" The operated inquired as to how they could assist Sarah.

"Hi, I need to get in contact with the police." Sarah politely replied.

"Please hold." The operator informed her.

Sarah patiently waited to be connected with the police. She knew Michael needed to have been missing for twenty-four hours before the police could legally declare him a missing person.

Sarah Hartnell couldn't care less that it had been less than a day. If they wanted to charge her with wasting police time, they were welcome to do so. All Sarah wanted was Michael. If that were a bad thing, she would gladly pay whatever fine or serve whatever sentence if it got him home.

"Strathclyde police. What is the nature of the emergency?" The police operator asked Sarah.

"I would like to report a missing person." Sarah told the operator. She resisted the urge to bite her fingernails whilst she held the phone to her ear.

"And who is the person you would like to report as missing?" The operator inquired. Sarah was prepared to give them everything they required.

"It's my husband… His name is Michael Hartnell." She had no other choice. If it were in reverse. She knew without a doubt, Michael would be doing the exact same thing. What else could she do?

"And how long has your husband been missing for, Mrs Hartnell?" The police operator questioned her. Sarah wished she were able to lie. She feared they would not take his disappearance seriously for another eight hours, by then, Michael will have been missing for twenty-four hours. A lot can happen in eight minutes never mind eight hours.

"He got up in the middle of the night. Michael doesn't have his mobile on him. He never goes anywhere without it… I am scared for his well-being." Sarah held back tears. She wanted to be strong for Michael.

"We will do everything we can. I will dispatch an officer to your address. Can you please confirm your place of residence?" The operator asked Sarah. She was taken aback. She did not expect them to treat it so seriously considering he hadn't been missing for twenty-four hours.

"We live in the apartment building on 12 Crowwood Street in Glasgow. It is apartment number 3B." Sarah couldn't believe it. An officer was on route and soon, Michael would be found and hopefully be on his way home. She prayed he would not get in trouble over this. Under the circumstances, she did not think he should be.

"Thank you, Mrs Hartnell. I will forward your information over to the officer. Anything else we can assist you with?" The operator asked Sarah. He had been extremely helpful. Sarah was grateful for his assistance.

"Thank you. How long till the officer gets here?" Sarah was desperate for the police officer to begin the search, sooner than later. She felt bad for sounding so urgent with the police telephone operator.

"The officer is nearby. They should be with you in the next five to ten minutes." Sarah was overjoyed to hear this news.

"Thank you. Thank you for your help. A Merry Christmas when it comes." Sarah thanked the operator.

"Glad I could assist. Merry Christmas." The operator ended the call. Sarah sat down on the living room couch. She was exhausted and felt at ease. She knew the police would be able to track Michael down. Her faith and the power of prayer were strong.

Michael would be home today. She believed it and nobody could convince her otherwise. She nearly drifted off to sleep on the couch. She had only had at best, an hour's sleep. A few minutes sleep was what the doctor ordered. Fear of missing the officer at her front door was an incentive to stay awake. She couldn't afford to let Michael down.

A loud knock on the front door brought Sarah back to her senses. She had not long gotten off the phone with the police. This had to be the nearby officer. She hurried to the front door. She had left the key in the lock. They did not have a peephole on the door. Opening the door was the only way to find out who was there.

Michael had initially worried when they first moved in. Their neighbourhood was relatively safe and the people were kind. Most of them anyway. Sarah opened the apartment door and was taken by surprise. It was not the police officer standing in her doorway.

It was Michael.

"Michael?" Sarah cried with joy and flung her arms around him. She was filled with happiness. He was home safe and sound. It did not matter where he had been or what was going on in his head. He would tell her in time and if Michael required help. Sarah would ensure he received the best and support him through everything.

Michael did not hug her back. Sarah found this bizarre. He did not speak a single word. He entered the apartment as soon as she released him from her tight hug. What was wrong? He was as silent as a mute and a sinister smile stretched across his face.

"I have been worried about you, Michael!" Sarah felt intimidated by his silence.

"And you still should be." Michael spoke. Sarah flinched with fright. His voice was not his own. It sounded feminine. Sarah watched in horror as Michael's face transformed into young woman's face, her hair was black and much longer than Michael's hair.

Her skin was white as milk. Her eyes glowed green. Her clothes also changed, she was no longer wearing Michael's leather jacket, shirt, or denim jeans. She was wearing a black corset and mini skirt. Her arms and chest were covered in tattoos of symbols which Sarah did not recognise.

What was happening? Who was this woman? What happened to Michael?

Sarah couldn't speak, she thought she had lost her voice as well as her sanity from what she witnessed.

"You should still be worried. Because I am not Michael. You'd be amazed by how many of us are in law enforcement. We couldn't believe our luck." The woman laughed. Sarah couldn't believe this. She had to be dreaming. This was a nightmare.

"Who… Who are you? Sarah stammered. She was scared out of her mind.

"Silly human! My name is Wormwood." The witch-demon laughed menacingly.

Sarah's scream filled the apartment as Wormwood, telekinetically slammed the front door shut.

CHAPTER TWENTY-FOUR

MICHAEL HARTNELL

THE ALLEY

CITY CENTRE

GLASGOW

DECEMBER 23rd 2009

05:10pm

Michael couldn't believe how stupid he had been.

"Michael, where is Sarah?" The trench coat wearing angel asked him. Michael was filled with so much dread. He was worried sick at the thought of Sarah on her own. She would be completely in the dark about the true nature of everything going on in the city.

The demons were everywhere. They were spying on him. How long had they been watching him?

"She'll be at home… Worrying about me." Michael told Nejuma. They needed to hurry. Nothing else mattered. Michael had to ensure Sarah was safe.

"Then that is where we will go." Nejuma responded in his calm and emotionless tone.

"I don't understand… Why would they hurt her? What has she ever done?!" Michael didn't know why they needed to hurt her. It was him who they truly wanted to get their hands on. Why not come after him? They couldn't say he hadn't given them plenty of chances.

"I do not know." Nejuma responded. Michael sensed his guardian was trying to spare him pain. He knew why they would want to hurt Sarah.

"Nejuma, tell me. Why would they want to hurt my wife?" Michael demanded.

"They are demons. It is what they do. You are the only person in the world trying to prevent Lucifer's return. Killing Sarah would be a warning from them. They are trying to intimidate you."

Nejuma sucked at comforting Michael. Why was this happening?

Six billion people on this planet. Yet, he was the poor bugger dealt the shit hand of cards. It was too much for Michael. He wanted to know. He had every right to know.

"Why? Why me?! Why would God choose me?" Michael shouted at Nejuma. He felt bad for taking it out on Nejuma, he was just the messenger. But he was the only source of answers.

"You are special. Every angel in Heaven knows you are special." Nejuma responded with a smile. That did nothing for Michael. What did it even mean? It would be question upon question. Michael knew Nejuma wasn't a straight to the point kind of person, he wasn't even a person. He was an angel. They needed to get a head start.

"I don't have time for riddles. We need to get to my wife." Michael couldn't express how urgently they had to back to his apartment.

"Take my hand." Nejuma instructed Michael, holding out his right hand. Michael didn't see how it could help. Nonetheless, he thought it best to obey the angel's instruction and do as he was told. He grabbed hold of Nejuma's hand and in split second. They both stood on Crowwood Street.

They were outside his apartment on the street below. How was this possible? He looked around, amazed. Buses along the main road struggled to drive through the heavy snow lying on the streets of Glasgow.

Michael was puzzled. They hadn't moved anywhere. They had been absolutely still when he gripped Nejuma's hand. They didn't fly, which was no longer far fetched with Nejuma being an angel. Michael swiftly glanced at his wristwatch. It was still the same time as it had been in the alley.

Michael hadn't lost time.

"How... How are we..." Michael struggled to ask what happened.

"Teleportation. All angels possess the ability." Nejuma calmly explained to a bewildered Michael. He would never be able to ever understand the angelic abilities fully. They truly are amazing, far superior to humans in every way, Michael thought.

He was flooded with a surge of emotions as he realised. Sarah was only a few floors away from them.

"Sarah!" Michael exclaimed in panic. Nejuma attempted to grab hold of Michael as he ran towards the apartment building.

"Michael! Wait! You do not know what is in there!" Nejuma shouted as Michael sprinted for the front entrance to the block of flats. He deliberately chose not to hear the angel. All that mattered was Sarah.

They lived on the third floor, as high as up as they could go in the building. He jumped against the door in an attempt to open it with pace. He had no regard for anyone who could have been behind the door. Luckily, the landing was empty.

Michael felt the adrenaline rush through him as he made his way to the stairwell. He sprinted up the stairs, exhaling the entire way. He hated the smell in the landing and stairs. The smell of bleach to mask the stench of urine and cigarettes. He passed the first-floor flats in seconds and continued to run, faster than he had ever run in his entire life up the next set of stairs.

He flew up the stairs as if The Devil were chasing him. He realised it wasn't true. Michael Hartnell ran towards evil. He knew if Sarah were in danger, the spawn of Hell itself would be present. All of this to get him to back off from his mission. If Sarah got hurt. Michael would never forgive himself.

He passed the second-floor flats moments later. This was the quickest he ever climbed these stairs. One step close to Sarah.

Home, he reached the top step and ran towards his own apartment. Michael forgotten to take his key. He repeatedly began pounding his fists against the door, in the hope he reached the flat before the demons did. He wanted Sarah to unlock the door. He needed to know she was safe.

"Sarah?! Open the door! Sarah?! Are you in there?! Sarah?!" He shouted at the top of his lungs. Something was wrong. A terrified scream from inside the apartment delivered the strength Michael required.

He thrust his entire body weight against the front door, he attempted to shoulder the door in. It hurt him. He never done this before and hadn't quite anticipated how strong you needed to be. Sarah was in danger. He would push past any pain to ensure her survival.

The door gave way, the wooden door splintered around the lock. Michael threw himself inside the hallway and in the same action, clawed his way into the living room, grabbing hold of the door frame.

Michael stopped immediately in the middle of the room. He saw Sarah, tears running down her face, behind her stood a pale skinned young woman with long black hair. She was dressed in a mini-skirt and black corset. She wore leather boots and Michael noticed the satanic symbols she had tattooed onto her chest and arms.

She held a knife to Sarah's throat as she stood behind Michael's wife. Holding her hostage.

"Keep your distance or I will slash her throat open!" the black-haired woman shouted at him. Her eyes glowed a bright green colour for a brief second. Michael knew in an instant, she was a demon.

"Let her go now!" Michael demanded of the demon. She could kill him if she so desired. All he wanted was for Sarah to be free.

"I will. As soon as you explain why you are trying to prevent my master's return." The demon asked, holding the blade closer to Sarah's neck. Michael knew who he was dealing with.

This is the demon that Nejuma had warned him about.

"Wormwood, I presume?" Michael stated. It had taken her by surprise. She didn't understand how he knew her name. He read her like an open book. It was all over her face.

"I don't know where you learnt my name…" Wormwood was stunned and looked bewildered.

"How did you even find out about Lucifer? How could you… A disgusting filthy human ever discover that?!" Wormwood was frustrated and repulsed by Michael. She obviously didn't like not knowing.

"I have met him." Michael told her. Sarah was terrified. She didn't take her eyes off him. He would save her. Nothing on Earth or from Hell would get in his way.

Wormwood laughed at Michael. She didn't believe him.

"No, darling. No human has ever clapped eyes on him. Least not in the flesh." Wormwood was right, Michael thought. Technically speaking, he and Lucifer had yet to meet. His first meeting with The Devil had been in the future. It still did not change anything.

Michael Hartnell met Lucifer and knew how dangerous and powerful he was.

"I have met him." Michael calmly responded. He knew Sarah's life depended on his stalling the witch-demon. She would kill Sarah if he didn't keep her talking.

"How?" Wormwood demanded of Michael. He was prepared to tell her everything about the future of the world, fifty years from now. He wanted to tell her that he was going to stop her. Michael wanted to rub the truth in her face. Before he could, Nejuma appeared by his side.

"He had all the might and power of Heaven behind him." Nejuma calmly told Wormwood. She was shaking with fear at the sight of Nejuma. An angel and a demon in the same room. Michael thought of it being no different to a cat and a dog coming across each other. It wouldn't end well.

Michael looked at Wormwood. In this particular situation, she was no doubt the cat. All she wanted to do was flee with her life. Her eyes looked all around the room in panic.

"You little bastard! You brought an angel as your back-up!" Wormwood spat her words at Michael. She wasn't pleased. Nejuma stepped forward.

"STAY BACK!!!" Wormwood shouted in terror, still clutching onto Sarah. She held the knife out at Nejuma. Michael had witnessed the damage knives could inflict upon Nejuma. She would not win this fight.

Michael's fear was Wormwood would attempt to escape, using Sarah as her bargaining chip to freedom. Michael would die before he allowed her to do so.

"Leave now before I turn you to dust." Nejuma's voice filled with fury. Michael hadn't heard the angel speak in such a manner. There was a mutual hatred between the angel and the demon. Michael saw the tension between the sides of Heaven and Hell.

Wormwood dropped the knife quicker than a heartbeat and thrust Sarah free from her hold. Michael reacted and caught his frightened wife in his arms. He held her tight. She was safe. Michael would never again abandon her. He watched as Wormwood burst into flames. She had obviously chosen to run for her life than fight Nejuma.

Wormwood was gone. She used her demonic teleportation to escape being murdered by Michael's guardian angel. He knew Nejuma would have killed her without giving it a second thought.

Michael sought vengeance. He would kill that bitch for what she done to Sarah.

"Sarah, I am so sorry. Are you okay?" Michael asked with tears running down his face. He was concerned for Sarah's well-being.

"Michael, I am... I'm fine... Sorry, I didn't believe you." Sarah cried as she apologised to him. He felt horrible. She had no reason to be sorry. It was his fault all this had happened.

"You have nothing to be sorry for... She's gone. You're safe." Michael told her. Nejuma was standing where Wormwood had been. He was knelt and had his hand raised above where she combusted.

"Nejuma, what are you doing?" He was curious as to what the guardian angel was doing.

"I am trying to track her location. I cannot get a lock on where she went... Her whereabouts are the least of our problems. The demons know an angel is in the city. Their guard is going to be up. We have lost our element of surprise." Nejuma told Michael.

"You're really an angel?" Sarah asked Nejuma. She was fascinated and looked at him in awe. She believed and was very slowly accepting everything.

"Yes." Nejuma responded in his calm manner. Sarah looked back to Michael. He saw how scared she was. Michael understood why. Sarah knew the significance of Nejuma and Wormwood. She cried in fear.

"It's all going to happen... The Devil and the apocalypse?" Sarah asked Michael. It literally was the end of the world. Michael wanted to tell her it wasn't. That would have been a lie.

"I'm afraid so... But, we have a chance. We can still stop it. The three of us can stop it before it ever happens." Michael assured his wife. She had taken it really well with all things considered.

"What do we do?" Sarah asked. Michael knew she was in. Michael had been foolish to think he alone would be capable of stopping Lucifer. He wanted Sarah out of the line of fire. He had forgotten how strong his wife was. Sarah Hartnell was a fighter.

"We need to find a cult leader. His name is Connor Sullivan. He plans to unleash Lucifer upon your world in less than forty-eight hours. It has been two millennia since I last walked the Earth. Are there any means for which we can find out what is occurring throughout your planet at this current moment?" Nejuma inquired into what was available to see the world news.

"I used the radio last night. We could use my computer. It doesn't have the greatest internet connection." Michael informed Nejuma.

The Wi-Fi in the flat was only meant to be temporary. It would have to do in order to track down Connor and see what else was happening around the globe.

"What about the TV?" Sarah asked. Suddenly Michael Hartnell felt stupid.

CHAPTER TWENTY-FIVE

BEN ARMSTRONG

BELLSIDE TAVERN

NORTH LANARKSHIRE

SCOTLAND

NOVEMBER 18th 1813

11:38pm

Ben Armstrong stood at the bar in a tavern. A bit of a shitehole, he thought. The place was filthy and loud with dozens of other drunk miners and navvies. Men were bantering with each other, drinks in one hand and their spare arm wrapped around some tavern wench, who no doubt wished to be anywhere but this dump.

Ben drank his ale. He couldn't be arsed going home, he endured too hard a day in the mines to listen to any of his wife's nonsense. He knew he was about to get a knuckle wrapping regardless of his actions. May as well get a few more ales in him before listening to her shite.

What else was there to life? What did he have to show for himself? Working in the mines since he was a boy, no education, hardly spoke The King's English and did not have two coins to rub together.

Thirty-five years old, he reckoned in a few years he would be dead and buried. There had to be more to life than sixteen hours a day in complete darkness for next to nothing. Winters were an eternity in this country. He longed to feel the sunlight on his skin. Ben gulped his ale, letting out a burp to relief himself.

Ben felt it slowly coming on him. He was becoming drunk. His wife, Penelope, she was going to love that. Bad enough to come home smelling of the public house but to be drunk. His life wouldn't be worth living come the morning. He was better than most husbands. Ben had never once shown his wife the back of his hand, unlike other men he knew.

The thought of striking a woman never brought him any satisfaction or helped him feel powerful. Lesser men hit women.

Ben wanted more from his life. Years ago, he thought about putting some money away, save it till he had enough to buy passage on a ship for Penelope and himself. He wanted to escape from the dull and miserable lifestyle of Scotland towards an exotic adventurous life in the new world of America.

Sad reality, that was a dream. One which he realised deep down would never happen. The dream of a heaven he would never see with his own eyes. Ben prepared to finish his drink when a beautiful young woman approached him.

She was mesmerising, breathtakingly beautiful, long brown hair, a pretty smile, she had all her own teeth, rare for a girl in these parts. She couldn't have been more than twenty years old, twenty-five at the most. Ben could hardly take his eyes off her. He barely looked at her dress, his full attention was on her cleavage. Which was very exposed.

Nothing better than an enormous pair of breasts, no man could resist. He felt lust getting the better of him as she smiled in his direction. Ben noticed she was biting her lower lip. He desired this woman and by the looks of it, she wanted him.

"Buy you a drink, my lady?" Ben slurred his words. He needed to have this woman. She wouldn't be his first harlot and certainly not the last. He committed adultery upon every opportunity. This woman wasn't here by chance, he took her for a lady of the night. Ben didn't mind paying for it. Especially when they were as gorgeous as the woman standing before him.

Ben found her to be peculiar. Her skin was extremely pale, she had an interesting eye colour. They were yellow. Not that Ben cared. He only wanted her for the night.

"Begging your pardon, sir. No, thank you. I have something better in mind." She licked her lips suggestively as she spoke to Ben.

"What might that be?" Ben asked, playing along with her game.

"I want what all women here want. And I choose you." She bit her lip, the woman was driving Ben wild with lust. He wanted her more than he had wanted any other woman. Had Penelope still been this passionate, he wouldn't be fucking whores elsewhere.

"Is that so?" Ben asked, knowing full well she was all his.

"Yes." She responded before grabbing hold of his face. Ben kissed her with a passion he hadn't felt before. He had never been so aroused in his entire life. He caressed her breasts with both hands.

The woman didn't appear to mind. If anything, she kissed him more the longer he felt them. Ben wanted to prepare her for what he desired. He reached his hand up her dress. She held his hand back. Ben was taken by surprise. She had strength of no woman he ever met before.

"Not here." She told him. It didn't change anything. He was going to have sex with her. She wanted him just as much as he wanted her.

"Do you have a room upstairs?" She asked Ben. He shook his head. Was that it? All this for nothing? There was no way he could return to Penelope this aroused and frustrated. He knew he'd have to relief himself somewhere on the walk home after such passion.

"It's been a while since I was fucked outdoors." The woman smiled, grabbing hold of Ben's wrist to lead him away from the bar. They ran past all the drunkards in the tavern, laughing in hysterics as they made their way outside. Before Ben realised where they were going, the young woman dragged Ben by the wrist to head around the back of the tavern, away from prying eyes. It would be the first time he ever been with a whore behind the tavern. It wouldn't be the last, he thought.

It was a freezing cold winter's night. He hid how cold he felt. Ben knew they would be warm soon enough. The back yard was littered with empty wooden barrels. The only ones that were filled with any alcohol were not worth attempting to steal. They were filled with crème de menthe. Disgusting, Ben thought. The robbing bastard who run the shithole had struggled to get the stuff shifted.

Ben was thrust against the wall of the tavern. The woman kissed him. He enjoyed her kisses, open mouth and a bit of tongue. She was a rare whore. One of a kind, he thought. She bit into his lip.

Ben winced in pain and felt to where she had bitten. He looked at his finger, she bit through the skin.

There was blood.

"You bit me?" Ben asked. He wasn't complaining. He felt strange. Almost as if it made him want to fuck her more. Ben prepared to undo his trouser knots. She put her hand on his fingers, stopping him. He looked upon her face. She shook her head to tell him no. What was her problem? Ben wondered.

"What's wrong?" Ben asked her in confusion. Why was she stopping him?

"Nothing. We need to turn you first." She calmly said to him. Her words did not make any sense.

"I beg your pardon?" Ben asked the woman. What did she mean by turn him?

"You have to be one of us." Ben pushed her away from him as he watched a man emerge from the woodlands behind the tavern. He had answered Ben's question. How long had he been watching them?

The man was in his forties, Ben thought. A slight bit of facial hair, he was a Scotsman by the accent. He was very well dressed for someone in these parts. Ben knew he was in some kind of trouble. This had been a con. He felt stupid. He should have known it was all too good to be true.

"Who the hell are you?" Ben demanded of the well-dressed gentleman.

"Not who. The question is. What are we?" The man asked Ben. It was only now he noticed the man was pale skinned and had the same eye colour as the whore who lured him to his mugging.

"Answer me!" Ben shouted at him. He smiled at Ben's defensiveness.

"My name is Nicholas Cowan. You can call me Nick. This is my bride, Anna." Ben instantly turned to face the whore who had been introduced as Anna. He felt scared for his life.

"Hi." Anna mocked him with a wave of her hand and a seductive smile. Whatever urges he felt vanished in an instant. They were laughing. Ben was trapped. It was not worth dying over. He reached into his trouser pocket and threw his coin pouch to the frosty grass at Nick's feet.

All the money Ben had in the world. He was not much of a fighter and he wasn't taking the chance. For all he knew, Nick may have a concealed blade. Anna and Nick laughed hysterically at Ben's surrender of his money.

"I don't want trouble… It's yours. Take it!" Ben said in a panic, hoping they would spare his life. It was all he had. The two pale-faced thieves laughed in absolute hysterics like Ben was a poor excuse for a man.

"Oh, Ben. You have got this all wrong. We don't want your money. Believe me, we have plenty." Ben didn't understand what they wanted of him. He couldn't for the life of himself comprehend how Nick knew his name.

He hardly spoken to Anna. Ben certainly didn't speak his name to her.

"How do you know my name? Have you been watching me?!" Ben shouted. He couldn't help but show his fear. He was terrified. Had they been watching him from afar? And if so, for how long and why? What else did they know about him?

"We are psychic, sweetie." Anna spoke. Ben had almost forgotten she was there. If she wasn't a prostitute and Nick wasn't her handler and neither of them were trying to extort money. What did they want Ben for? He didn't know what Anna meant.

"Psychic?" He asked in confusion, hoping she would elaborate.

"We are telepathic. We hear your thoughts. All of our kind possess this ability. The human mind is an open book." Nick explained to Ben, filling him with terror. They weren't people. They couldn't be... They were devils from the pits of Hell!

"What are you?" Ben asked in a state of absolute terror, he dreaded the response.

"Now he asks!" Nick mocked Ben. He looked around the yard for any possible chance to escape their clutches. Nick and Anna stood side by side. They were smiling at Ben. He felt uncomfortable by their happiness. They were faces of evil and enjoyed his fear.

Ben couldn't bring himself to look away. Nick and Anna had two sharp fangs emerge from their upper jaws, the two-pointed teeth at each side of their jaws were longer than any tooth in their mouths. Ben prepared himself to flee from the captivity of these abominations.

"We are vampires." Anna laughed as her words went in Ben's ears. He didn't stick around for whatever they were planning. Ben sprinted past both of them in an attempt to put as much distance between them and him as his legs could take him. Before he made it to the front of the tavern, Nick was standing in front of Ben, blocking his escape.

How? How had he gotten past Ben without him knowing?

"That's not..." Ben was dumbfounded. It wasn't possible for Nick to have overtaken him without Ben seeing Nick.

"We are faster than humans, Ben." Nick nodded his head to make Ben aware of Anna's presence, she was directly behind Ben. There was no escape.

"Do what you must and be gone, devils!" Ben cursed at Nick and Anna. Ben was seized from behind. Before he could resist, Anna plunged her fangs into Ben's throat. She was drinking his blood, he heard her enjoyment. She made sounds similar to that of a person enjoying a delicious meal.

"That's enough, Anna." Nick casually spoke to her before he bit into his own wrist. Nick's blood dripped from his wrist and ran all the way to the palm of his hand. He walked closer to Ben.

Anna had since let her hold of Ben go. He was in agony and felt fatigued. She obviously consumed a lot of his blood. Ben knew he was a goner. This was where he would die. Anna moved aside from him. Nick knelt beside Ben.

There was a moment of delay. Nick stared at Ben without saying a single word. Ben wanted to know what he was waiting for. Nick looked him up and down with curiosity or was it fascination? Ben wondered as he felt himself slowly slipping out of consciousness.

He tried to fight it by speaking. Ben felt as though he possessed no voice. He was unable to talk. Nick revealed the palm of his hand. It was a dark red. Every inch was covered in blood. Ben didn't understand what Nick was doing.

Nick smeared the blood all over his bite wound, immediately Ben's whole body seized up. He felt himself shake violently and uncontrollably. Ben screamed in pain. It felt like he was on fire and broken glass were under his skin. In his torment, he heard laughter from Nick and Anna.

His whole body convulsed as he lay on the winter ground. Was this death? Was this how it felt to die? What had they done to him? As quickly as it began, Ben found himself free of pain.

Ben found himself being able to jump to his feet with a newfound energy. Ben no longer felt drunk. He was sober for what must have been the first time in a long time.

Nick and Anna were still present. Both of them were smiling. Nick had his hand out to Ben. It was clean of the blood. What was going on? He didn't really expect Ben to shake his hand.

"Welcome. You are one of us now." Nick said to Ben in a celebratory tone. Ben was confused. What happened?

"What the hell have you done to me?!" Ben had every right to know.

"We turned you." Anna butted in.

"You are a vampire." Nick stated, he looked so happy. Ben refused to believe them. This was a nightmare. He tried to convince himself he must have keeled over at the bar from his own drunkenness and all of this was a terrible dream.

Ben felt a burning sensation in the back of his throat. It felt similar to having a cold. Only it was a hundred times more painful.

"My throat… It burns…" Ben said in agonising pain.

"Aw! Baby vampire needs to feed!" Anna mocked Ben. Is that what his throat was telling him?

Ben Armstrong was a vampire in need of nourishment. Vampires devoured one thing, blood. The thought of drinking blood filled Ben with horror and emotionally disturbed him.

Anna laughed in amusement at Ben's pain. Something wasn't right. Ben felt unusual. He couldn't understand what was wrong. He needed to drink blood. The heat at the back of his throat intensified. Ben knew it wasn't the need to consume blood that currently held his attention. It was something different.

Before they turned him, Ben was scared out of his mind. He felt the rush of adrenaline throughout his body. His heart had beaten so hard, every inch of his body pulsed. Ben was still scared beyond his worst nightmares.

That was when he came to understand what was missing. Ben no longer had a heartbeat. He was indeed a vampire, an undead creature, doomed to never feel the sunlight on his skin for eternity whilst drinking the blood of innocent people. He would never allow himself to become like Nick and Anna.

He retaliated against Anna's comment towards his thirst for blood.

"No!" Ben shouted at them. It seemed to surprise the two vampires. Neither of them smiled.

"I will never feed. I am not a vampire! I am nothing like you!" He shouted in disgust before making a hasty retreat. He had planned only to run to the front of the tavern to be free of them. Ben hadn't realised how fast he ran away from Nick and Anna.

Literally, in the blink of an eye, he had sprinted half a mile along the road. He was on a dark country path, fields were on either side of him. Ben halted and stared back at the way he came in total disbelief. How fast had he run? His thoughts returned to what Nick said.

Ben remembered how Nick ran past him without his knowledge.

Nick told Ben about vampires being faster than humans. Were all vampires capable of running faster than a speeding bullet? Ben needed to sit down and have time to process all of this. He had to go home before anything else.

Ben Armstrong had to tell his wife, Penelope.

Dread filled him, he never felt his usual anxious feelings. Ben then again realised his living and beating heart would have been the major factor in the feeling of stress. Despite this, he did not look forward to seeing her. She would be furious with him for spending the majority of his wage in the tavern.

His throat felt as if someone had set it alight. It was becoming unbearable, he knew that there was no chance in hell, he would be able to restrain himself in front of his wife. Ben feared what he could do if he did not feed. What was he to do?

As he pondered on what to do in regard to feeding, he saw a fox in the middle of the country path. It had not seen Ben. Before Ben could stop to admire the sight of the red fox sitting in the middle of nowhere.

On pure muscle reaction, he ran in the blink of an eye, seized the helpless animal and sunk his vampiric fangs into its neck. The fox was dead before he realised. The puncture wounds alone were enough to silence it. Ben had never been so thirsty. He drained the little fox of every last drop of blood.

Ben dropped the lifeless fox to the dirt in horror. He hadn't intended to do any of that. It was as if some form of animal instinct had kicked in, he wasn't in control of his actions. Ben felt sorry for the fox. He admired it, sitting gracefully minding its own business.

Ben was ashamed and sorry for ending its life. Ben wanted to weep for it. He couldn't help how he reacted. His emotions got the better of him. Ben discovered, he wept no tears. What was wrong? Why couldn't he cry? Not one single solitary tear ran down his face.

Being unable to cry was the least of his concerns.

Ben had to see Penelope. It would take him twenty minutes to walk to their little cottage he called home. That would be at a brisk pace. He knew that would be faster and he would likely be on his doorstep before he knew it. He decided to walk slowly. The need to think everything over was on his mind.

Ben wanted time to play all the ways it could go through his mind to prepare himself. A slow walk would take half an hour or a little longer. By then, he would know how to speak with his wife. He began his walk through the darkness.

The burn in his throat was gone. Ben felt sorry for the fox but on his walk in the Scottish countryside he came to the conclusion. It was better he had encountered a fox than a person.

Thoughts of the kind of life he could have raced through his mind. He would never allow himself to harm people. Not like his makers, Nick and Anna. He would learn to live with it. Ben would only drink the blood of animals. He would never kill them.

Ben realised the long winter months meant he would still be able to work in the mines. Summer could become a problem. For now he hardly saw the sun. The last time he seen it was probably August due to the dark winter mornings and long cold nights.

Ben knew he no longer needed to eat or drink, a saving in his wages. They would make it work. He and Penelope could still have a life together. He would help her see that their life together was not at an end. It was only beginning.

His walk had come to an end. He dragged it out longer than necessary to plan how to tell his wife. It still didn't help him feel better. It was a daunting thing. He felt nervous and scared. How would she take it?

Penelope wasn't up waiting for him. There were no candles lit inside the cottage. It was late. She had surely gone to bed. Ben would normally feel her wrath come the next morning, usually when his head was bursting from the previous night's drinking.

He approached the little white stoned cottage as he walked to the door, something strange happened. Ben felt as if some force was preventing him from entering his home. Like an invisible wall stood between him and the inside of the cottage.

It felt weird, Ben decided to knock on the front door. Penelope wouldn't like it. He saw no other way to gain access. His wife would have to open the front door to allow him in. He waited several minutes. She had obviously been woken up. Ben thought of his life. He had always been selfish and committed stupid acts.

He cheated on his marriage at every opportunity. Anna's seduction had played a significant part in his biggest mistake on the worst night of his life.

Had Ben Armstrong been a better husband, he would still be human and not a lapdog of Satan. Cursed to be a vampire, drinking blood, eternal nights and a life which would never end.

The door to his cottage opened slowly. It didn't open all the way. No doubt Penelope wanted to be sure who she was unlocking her door to at this time of night. Penelope recognised it was her husband. She fully opened the door. Ben still continued to be held back by the invisible force, a wall which he could not see prevented him from walking through the doorway.

Penelope was beautiful. Ben was blessed and he always had taken her for granted. Her long blonde hair hung down. She looked exhausted. He had woken her in the middle of the night. She was wearing her white nightgown.

Before Ben could explain the invisible barrier between them, she addressed him and she was not best pleased. He could tell that much. He heard her thoughts inside her head. It was true. Vampires were mind readers.

"Ben, where the hell…" Penelope sniffed the air. Ben knew what was coming next. He didn't need to be psychic to know. The stench of ale and the tart's perfume was a clear indication to his recent whereabouts.

"You were at that tavern! How much of our living have you thrown away this time?!" Penelope spat her words in fury. She had every right to be furious with him.

"Penelope… Yes, I was… I can explain… There is something…" Ben was cut off by his wife's anger.

"Get inside!" She shouted at him. As if an enormous weight had been lifted, he felt free of the invisible force around the entrance to the cottage. It was gone. What had it been? He heard Penelope's thoughts. She had heard all of his pathetic and lame excuses before. What was it going to be this time? His wife wondered.

Ben entered the small cottage. Inside was tiny, only one room, a bed built into the corner of the house. A small fireplace which was still burning away, next to impossible to keep going in order to warm their home in the cold winter nights.

It was a claustrophobic cramped space. Every wall was soaked with condensation, covered with mould and mildew. It was all they had. Ben hoped one day to find somewhere better and have children with Penelope.

Ben hadn't thought about that. Could vampires even have children? He had hundreds of questions about vampires. First, Ben had to tell his wife. She stood in the middle of the room, eagerly awaiting his piss poor excuse for drinking away his earnings.

"Penelope, this is… It's going to be a shock… Let me make you understand." Ben ceased talking as Penelope stared him out with curiosity and worry. She recognised his facial features had changed.

"Your face. It's really pale and your eyes…" Penelope moved closer to better inspect his eye colour.

"They are yellow!" She exclaimed.

Ben did not know this. He had yet to see his reflection in the looking glass.

"How much did you drink?" Penelope asked him. Her fiery temper returned.

"The ale didn't do this. I wish I were drunk. The effect has since worn off…" Ben didn't know how to say it out loud.

"Since what?" Penelope was beginning to lose her patience with him. Her mind raced so fast for Ben to pick up any of her thoughts.

"Since they turned me." Ben said. It was true. The moment his body transformed he no longer felt the effects of alcohol.

"Who? What? Turned you? What are you babbling about?" Penelope was confused. Ben hadn't fully told her. He knew it was better to get it over and done with.

"I am a vampire." He said the truth. Silence fell, the words lingered until Penelope sighed in disbelief. Ben knew she thought of this as the worst excuse yet for his drunken behaviour.

"I am being deadly serious." He assured her whilst she continued to sigh and roll her eyes at his excuse. Ben began to feel a mild burn in the back of his throat. He needed to drink blood. Damned if he would allow himself to lose control.

His upper jaw ached as the vampiric fangs emerged involuntarily. It caused Penelope to throw herself away from Ben, putting as much distance from him as she could. Ben knew she was scared out of her wits.

Penelope sat against the bed, cowering in fear and a hand against her mouth from the shock. Ben told himself to keep it under control and retracted his fangs. He was upset. He never wanted to scare her. He swore a vow to protect her when they married. Ben had failed his wife.

Ben leaned down to calm her. He tried to touch her shoulder. She let out a sound of fear and flinched before he could lay his palm on her. Penelope cried. He knew he would cry too. Except it was the same as it had been with the fox. No matter how emotional he was feeling, no tears came from his eyes.

"I am sorry… I didn't mean to frighten you." Ben calmly spoke to Penelope. She couldn't bring herself to look at his face. Ben thought about the life he envisioned for them and hoped she would see his dream and help to make it a reality. He wanted to let her know they would still have a life together. Ben started to talk to her.

"I never asked for this... It is the last thing I ever wanted... I believe we can still be together. I thought of it long and hard on my walk home. I cou..." Penelope did not allow Ben to finish his sentence. She snapped at him with disgust.

"You are not my husband! Get out of my house, demon!" She was scared and not thinking clearly, Ben knew. It was a lot to come to terms with. He didn't expect her to understand or accept. He had hoped. Hell, he even prayed for all the good it would do. Ben didn't believe in God.

"Penelope, it's me! It doesn't change anything... No matter what they have made me into. I am still me! I am the man you married." He pleaded, desperate to save his marriage.

"So you expect us to live happily ever after? Whilst I go about my day and you, what? Hide during the daylight hours and gorge on human blood?!" She was repulsed at the thought of him. The word "Monster" ran through her mind. Ben heard it as clear as she spoke to him.

The curse of hearing thoughts was enough to drive him mad.

"I cannot help my nature. I will not be able to set foot in the sun ever again. The blood, I will never drink human blood. I can survive on animal blood." Ben hoped she would accept him for what he had become.

"How do you know about animal blood?" She was concerned. Ben knew it better to tell the truth. He would never lie to his wife. He was done with the lies, his human life was filled with lies. If this were to work, there needed to be complete honesty.

"I fed... I killed a fox." Ben told her. It was true. He lost control and fed, the burn in his throat intensified. No more than a sore throat, the little fox had not been enough. Ben required more blood to satisfy his new appetite.

"I never fed until that moment. I lost control and killed it... I know what to do now and I will never allow myself to be a monster." Ben was filled with emotions and he knew Penelope was not for listening. She wanted him gone.

"Get out!" Penelope shouted at the top of her lungs.

"Please!" He pleaded. Ben had nothing without her. Where was he to go? Sure, he made mistakes and was prepared to atone for them in whatever manner his wife saw fit.

"I don't want to see you again." Penelope's tears stained her face. Ben heard her mind.

She wanted her husband back and there was no way he could help her to see it.

They were not getting anywhere tonight, going round in circles of shouting and begging. Ben thought it best to apologise.

"I'm sorry." He meant it, hoping she would see the love he felt for her. It was no help.

"There's nothing to be done that will make me love you." She said with devastation. Ben knew she did love him but couldn't bring or allow herself to let him in to her heart, the way he was. That's when the idea hit him. There was a way to make her understand. It was not right, it was immoral.

Ben was out of options. There was only one way for Penelope to fully understand vampirism. If there is a God, Ben thought. May he have mercy on my soul.

"There is a way... Forgive me." The thought of being alone, doomed to spend eternity in the darkness, consuming blood, watching the centuries fly by and witnessing loved ones grow old and die whilst he remained eternally youthful was a curse.

Ben Armstrong would not be alone. His condition had been forced upon him. He witnessed how it was done to turn a person into a vampire.

Ben and Penelope would be together for eternity… As vampires.

In one rapid move, Ben grabbed hold of Penelope. Before she had even the slightest notion of his intentions, his fangs emerged. He bites into Penelope's neck. She screamed with terror. She was taken by surprise. The blood from the puncture wounds in her neck soothed Ben's burning throat, quenching his thirst.

Had he been human the thought of actually doing this would have made Ben retch.

He enjoyed the taste of her blood. This horrified Ben and he realised he needed to maintain control over himself. He wouldn't allow Penelope to weaken like Anna had done to him earlier tonight. Ben held a tight grip of Penelope, he stared at his right wrist, knowing full well what he had to do next.

It took a few seconds for him to pluck up the courage. He sunk his fangs into his own wrist, half expecting to scream in pain. All he experienced was a slight pinch. Blood smothered his wrist, he couldn't help but be mesmerised as he watched the two small puncture wounds in his wrist heal in the blink of an eye.

Penelope struggled against Ben. She knew not of what he was planning. Nonetheless, she wished to escape his firm grip. In a moment, Penelope would not only know Ben's intentions, but she would be like him, a vampire.

He gently wiped some of the blood from his wrist upon Penelope's neck wound.

"Monster!" She shouted at him, spitting in his face before he released her from his tight hold. For a brief moment he thought it wasn't working or something was wrong in how he did it.

Penelope was stood upright and looked down on Ben with disgust before her whole body shook uncontrollably. His sharp reflexes enabled Ben to see it coming, he held Penelope in his arms. She was in excruciating agony. He rested her on the floor.

Ben stroked her hair as she violently convulsed. No screams came from her mouth. Ben knew too well how painful the transformation was. You couldn't speak, scream or think. At least not about the pain. It was different this time, he saw the blood drain from her face and arms. Her beautiful blue eyes slowly transformed into the yellow eyes which all vampires possessed.

"I am so sorry. It will be over in a minute." Ben apologised. The shaking ceased and Penelope's human life had ended. She was a vampire. Ben smiled at the success of her transformation. He couldn't wait to continue their life together.

"Get away from me!" Penelope thrust Ben off her before standing to her feet. Her turning had been briefer than Ben's. He began pleading with her.

"Don't you see? We can be together... Together, happy and never die... I did this because I love you." Penelope didn't appear to have heard a single word. She stared at her hands in fascination. She let out a gasp as she clutched her throat in pain. Ben knew what she was experiencing.

Penelope needed to feed before she lost control.

Ben could no longer hear Penelope's thoughts. What did that mean? Was it because she was no longer human? Questions for a better time.

"This is incredible!" Penelope exclaimed in sheer delight. Penelope was happy. Ben would feel happier as soon as she fed.

"Is it the same with you? The feeling of such power flowing through you. I feel stronger, faster... I can smell... I smell blood and it is close. Human blood! Christ! It smells so fucking good! Come on, husband. Let's get something to eat." Penelope's fangs emerged. She licked her lips relishing in the anticipation.

Ben had to be firm, rules had to exist for without them, he and his wife were nothing but savages.

"No, we can't drink human blood." Ben stated. He was strict in this regard. Vampire or not, Penelope was still his wife by law, she would do as her husband bloody told her.

"We are vampires, husband. You said it was our nature. We have to feed in order to survive." She responded to his argument. Penelope was right and there was a way to live without harming or killing any living thing.

"We can feed off animal blood. I have done so already." Ben reminded her. Despite the witch trials having been over for nearly a century, the people of these parts were still a superstitious lot. He couldn't allow anyone to get wind of their existence.

All it would take would be a tiny slip up and they would be burning at the stake like the witches of old.

"Fat chance!" She scoffed as if Ben said something completely ridiculous.

"I want a challenge! The power I feel, we should be Gods…There have to be many more vampires who feel the same… Come with me, husband." Ben realised what he done. He created a monster. This was a mistake. She was driven insane by the power and bloodlust.

"I was wrong… I shouldn't have done this to you! Who are you? You are not my wife! You are not my Penny! She would never hurt innocent people for the sheer hell of it!" Ben was disgusted. Penelope stood in silence with a smug expression on her face.

Ben knew that was the face of a woman who did not listen to a single word he said.

"Darling, I am a vampire. It is no longer a wonder why the church fears vampires. We are perfection. We are stronger, faster, eternally youthful with everlasting life. We are better than human. Come with me." Penelope's words were dangerous and deadly.

Ben was not tempted in the slightest at the idea of becoming a monster. He was filled with regret. He knew what must be done. Ben, fasting than a flash of lightning grabbed hold of a wooden chair in the house and with all his strength brought the chair down with a smash against the floor.

He took hold of a sharp piece of wood. The terror on Penelope's face caused her to charge past Ben. She narrowly missed his attempt to plunge the wooden stake into her heart.

Penelope stood in the doorway. She holds her hand to her face to mockingly blow Ben a kiss. He couldn't allow her the opportunity to escape. She was too dangerous.

"See you later, lover!" Penelope smirked before disappearing into the darkness of the winter night. By the time Ben reached the cottage front door, even with extreme speed, Penelope was gone.

Ben looked frantically all over the surrounding area from the doorway and to his devastation.

Penelope was nowhere in sight.

He threw the wooden stake to the frozen grass outside the cottage before collapsing to his knees to scream in a furious rage.

CHAPTER TWENTY-SIX

THE HIGH PRIEST OF THE FALLEN GOD

THE CHURCH OF SATAN

LOCATION: UNKNOWN

GLASGOW

DECEMBER 23rd 2009

07:00pm

Connor Sullivan addressed his followers at one of the regular meetings. He enjoyed these gatherings and the power which came with it. He had never been popular as a child and in less than two days' time, he would become the most important man in the history of the world.

The man who freed Satan from Hell.

He speaks to his followers. Every one of them were present. They would never let him down. Connor appreciated the atmosphere, dark with the exception of candlelight. All of his followers were dressed in black cloaks, they had their hoods up over their heads. It was hard to make out any faces.

Connor knew all eyes were upon him, ready to listen to his preaching of their God, Satan.

"People look to this Jesus abomination or God! They look to these losers for salvation. No-one ever looks to the one who was wrongly cast out from Heaven." Connor saw the cloaked figures nod their heads in agreement.

"If God truly cared. Why would so many people die from incurable illnesses? Why would parts of this world be riddled with poverty? Why would he allow paedophiles who molest children to walk our streets? I will tell you why! It is because it is the other way around. God is the villain. In two days, we are going to show six billion people, the one they all call The Devil, a fallen angel is the planet's salvation!"

The entire cult applauded The High Priest. Connor enjoyed the love of the people. There were cheers of happiness throughout the dark hall.

Connor raised his hands to regain silence in the hall before continuing with his service.

"Thank you. We will meet our God at a place steeped in history and legends. Where, you ask? It is called The Whangie. There is an old folklore story about this location. The legend says Satan was flying over and his tail struck this enormous rock, slicing it in half, creating a pathway. The truth is, this extraordinary rock is The Gates of Hell. This is where our God is imprisoned. The time has come for us to spring him from his prison."

The entire cult applauded and cheered Sullivan's words. He raised his hands to silence the crowd.

"I would not know this story if it wasn't for the beautiful woman in my life. She is here with us tonight to offer us a few words. Give a very warm welcome to my girlfriend, Nicola Woods!" Connor was filled with happiness.

The crowd cheered in excitement as Connor's girlfriend, Nicola approached the stage and began her ascent up the stairs. She too was cloaked in black with a golden pentagram on the front of her cloak. Her feet couldn't be seen as she walked along the stage to join Connor. It was as if she glided towards him.

Nicola removed her hood. Her jet-black hair always drove Connor insane. She was pale skinned with green eyes. Nicola kissed Connor on his lips before she took centre stage to address the Church of Satan. He always liked her in the cloaks, she suited it. Though the cloak always looked better on their bedroom floor, he thought.

Connor felt her lipstick against his own lips. He discreetly wiped it away and caught a glance at the colour. She wore black lipstick. He would enjoy rubbing it off his cock later after they celebrated their lord's return in private. Nicola addressed the gathering.

"My brothers and sisters! Thank you all for having faith in our God, our master and our father! Isn't he spectacular?"

The audience clapped their hands and cheered. Connor knew their love in Satan was greater than anything else in their lives.

"On the 25th of December, the world will see our God walk the Earth. He will transform this world in ways we cannot even begin to comprehend. He will change it for the better. Thank you all for coming this evening. See you at The Whangie." Nicola concluded the service.

The gathering cheered with excitement. The cult slowly began to depart the dark hall. Connor and Nicola watched from the stage as the cult made their exit out from The Church of Satan. He was filled with pride at his achievement. Satan would be free and he was the one to release him.

When they were alone in the hall, Connor felt the lust surge through his body. He grabbed hold of Nicola's waist and pulled her towards him for a kiss. He always enjoyed kissing her. He knew she did too.

"I like it when you speak in service... Turns me on." Connor bit his lip, he wanted Nicola badly. So much that he would be willing to take her here presently on the stage now that they were all alone. Nicola pulled away from his embrace. She was incredibly beautiful.

Nicola's face was filled with happiness, he thought.

"I am an amateur compared to The High Priest." Nicola shrugged off his compliments towards her speaking in the meeting. He felt she was embarrassed by his mentioning it, not her style. It didn't mind. Connor liked her shy embarrassment. She was cute. The happiness on her face returned.

"Not long until he returns. Exciting?" Nicola spoke with delight. Satan's return would change the course of history, science and everything.

Everything the world knew would never be the same. It would be altered forever.

Questions would be answered and maybe answers to questions no-one had ever thought of asking would be told. Exciting didn't even begin to scratch the surface of what Connor Sullivan felt.

"Exciting doesn't even begin to describe my feelings or how all his followers are thinking." Connor stated. He felt disbelief at his dream becoming a reality.

The Devil was returning and nobody would stop it from happening.

"I need to make you aware of a situation. It has to stay between us." Nicola told Connor. She sounded scared as she had a sideways glance to ensure nobody else was present to overhear whatever she was planning to unveil. Connor became concerned. What was she about to confide in him?

"What's wrong?" Connor asked with worry. He held Nicola close to his chest. Nicola was scared. He had never seen her like this before. He felt her tremble with fear whilst he held her.

"What we are doing... It will all be for nothing if that bastard angel discovers the location..." Nicola was close to tears.

"What?!" Connor exclaimed. Did he hear Nicola right? Did she really say "Angel"?

"You heard me. An angel is in the city?" Nicola sounding serious with fury in her voice as she told The High Priest.

Connor didn't understand this. It wasn't possible with the warding the demons had put in place to block Heaven's access to the country. How did Nicola come to learn this and not him first?

"How did you come by this knowledge?" Connor suspiciously inquired.

"I only learnt it before coming on stage… The demons informed me an angel must have slipped through before the warding went up." She stammered. Connor was grateful for her allegiance with the demons. Their intel had never been wrong. If not for them their plan would cease to exist.

Connor had never met any demons. Nicola was the go-between. He knew they were still out making preparations for their lord's return and helping him reach their goal. The presence of an angel was not foreseen or anticipated. Connor wondered how this may affect their plan.

"What… What will we do? What will happen if the angel finds The Whangie?" Connor was running his hands through his hair in frustration. He began biting his index fingernail. He always did so when he was stressed out of his box. Connor had worked too hard for it all to come collapsing down.

"If the angel and his friend, Michael Hartnell find The Whangie…The lord will not return. We have to perform the ritual right with no errors… or…" Nicola did not finish her sentence. She sounded full of fright.

"Or what?" Connor frustratingly demanded to know.

"Heaven will descend upon us." Nicola worriedly told The High Priest.

CHAPTER TWENTY-SEVEN

THE 45TH PRESIDENT OF THE UNITED STATES
STEVEN PALMER

AIR FORCE ONE

LOCATION: CLASSIFIED

DECEMBER 24TH 2009

08:30am

The President of the United States patiently waited for his flight to commence as the plane sat on the runway. He was seated aboard Air Force One, The President's private airplane. He was taken aback at how far he had come in only a year.

Steven Palmer could not wait till he told his father the good news. Pride wouldn't begin to do justice to how Palmer felt. He would be the last President of America. The Illuminati's plan would see to it. Not that he shall allow their plan to unfold.

Palmer had been seated, waiting patiently on The Lord of The High Table to grace him with his presence. Time was precious and Palmer had no intentions on wasting his. The intercom on Palmer's desk made a beeping sound.

A member of the secret service wishing to speak to him with urgent news. Palmer pressed a button to allow the agent to speak with him.

"Yes." Palmer asked, waiting for the response.

"Mr President, Lord Carlisle Dalton and Mr Syme to see you." The agent on the intercom informed him.

"Send them in." Palmer replied. He prepared for their imminent arrival. He placed out three glasses of scotch. The office door opened inward and Richard Syme entered followed by Lord Carlisle Dalton, looking like a million dollars as he always did. The arrogant asshole, Palmer thought. The hallway leading to the office was lined with secret service agents.

Palmer welcomed both men with his usual false smile which had won them over dozens of times.

"Gentlemen, welcome to Air Force One!" Palmer declared as he handed them a glass of scotch, they graciously accepted. Had Carlisle not been such a paranoid cunt, this would have been the perfect opportunity to poison him. The lunatic had an antidote which cured every known poison on his person at all the times.

Not that Palmer would ever use this such a thing. He always thought poison was a coward's weapon. When Dalton dies, it will be up close and personal with a blade between his ribs. Palmer enjoyed gazing into a man's eye, for in those last few seconds of life, you can witness it disappear from the face. It truly is a spectacular sight.

"Mr President…" Dalton attempted to speak with Palmer. He cut Dalton off. Palmer did enjoy hearing the title but not from his middle-aged Yorkshire mouth.

"No need for the "Mr President" formality. We are among friends." Palmer wanted Dalton to believe he held all the cards at least until the last moment when it all blew back at The Lord of The High Table's face.

"Steven, if I am not mistaken. I would detect the sound of victory in your voice. Quite right to, my friend. Have you done as I have asked?" Carlisle inquired. Palmer knew what he was getting at.

"Not yet, my lord. It shall be done upon my last visit to The White House." Palmer responded. He would do what Dalton wanted. The only difference would be. It was not intended towards The Illuminati agenda.

"Excellent!" Carlisle exclaimed before taking a large gulp of whisky. Alcoholic bastard, Palmer thought. The way he drank, Palmer could easily have forgotten this man grew up in an upper-class family. Greater than that. His family had been the head of the new world order for generations.

Yet this alcoholic was to be the lord of the world under Illuminati rule. Nothing noble about him with the exception of his name. Without his surname, he may as well be a hobo on the streets. After the drunkard devoured the contents of his glass, he spoke with a slur. He no doubt already had a few before boarding from the sound of it.

"I must say it is rather strange how you became President. They say your predecessor committed suicide. You wouldn't happen to know anything about that, would you?" Carlisle was merely curious as to how Palmer managed to make the death look like a suicide with zero suspicions.

"A magician never reveals his secrets." Palmer joked. Carlisle found it amusing as he smiled with intrigue. Syme remained silent as a ghost and had done so from the moment he entered. Palmer trusted Syme even less than he did Dalton. There was something off about Syme. He always thought of him as a snake in the grass, ready to bite when you least expected it.

"It hardly matters. Never liked the guy. There wouldn't have been a suitable place for him in the new world." Carlisle jested. He was mad on power. The bastard truly enjoyed the sound of his own voice. Palmer decided to shift the conversation back to more pressing matters of concern.

"Once I have returned to The White House. Where is the rendezvous point for the aftermath?" Palmer inquired. He needed the location of the other High Table members. It'll be like shooting fish in a barrel but with a nuclear bomb, he thought.

"You will receive instructions in due course. We will be far away from the affected zones. First, we will go public before the launch." Carlisle's words had finally gotten Richard's attention as the lurking snake finally decided to prove he possessed a voice.

"We are going public, Lord Dalton?" Syme asked with a surprised tone.

"How do you feel about the news?" Carlisle asked. Palmer was happy with this. The Illuminati revealing their existence to the world would ensure nobody was looking where it truly mattered. Palmer would meet his father and everything else would fall into place, exactly as planned.

"Are you serious, my lord?" Syme sounded scared at the very mention of the Illuminati coming out the closet. And so he should be.

"I am deadly serious, Mr Syme." Lord Dalton assured the snivelling little weasel. Palmer smiled for they had just signed their own death warrants.

THE 44th PRESIDENT OF THE UNITED STATES

THE OVAL OFFICE
THE WHITE HOUSE

WASHINGTON D.C.

THE UNITED STATES OF AMERICA

DECEMBER 23rd 2009

06:30pm

The President stood in front of the window of the oval office, his back to the rest of the room. He was alone, having asked his security team to not disturb him unless it was urgent. He was enjoying having some peace and quiet, a break from being the leader of the free world.

He looked upon The White House lawn, snow covered almost every inch of it. It was to fall heavily overnight. He held a glass of scotch in his hand, feeling at peace watching the snow fall from the winter sky.

Only a couple of days until Christmas. The President always enjoyed Christmas. All the more cause to celebrate. It was his first as The President of the United States of America, the first of many he thought. He exhaled with satisfaction as he enjoyed a mouthful of scotch.

He felt a second glass was well earned. The bottle was on his desk. He turned to reach for it. His heart nearly flew through his chest with fright.

Steven Palmer, The Speaker of The House of Representatives was standing on the other side of his desk.

"Jesus Christ!" The President exclaimed.

"Not quite." Palmer responded in a calm but sinister tone.

"What...I never heard the door open..." The President was confused to how or even why Palmer would enter the oval office in complete silence.

"The door never opened." Palmer smiled menacingly. The President felt uneasy. What was he doing here?

"I don't understand." The President stated in confusion.

"I wanted to inform you of my promotion." Palmer wasn't speaking any sense.

"Mr Palmer…" The President stammered, he felt stupid. He never stammered in his life and no doubt Palmer felt the terror in his voice. He seemed to marvel in The President's fear.

"It's nothing personal, Mr President. My lord, the one true lord commands it. Unfortunately, you have to be dead." Palmer coldly spoke to him. In the same moment, he felt something wrap itself around his neck, hoisting him up to the ceiling.

He was being hanged. How was this possible? The President clawed at his throat in a futile attempt to breathe. It was no use. Every passing second, he grew weaker.

"My lord thanks you. His name is Lucifer." Palmer chuckled whilst he watched the life drain from his body. The last thing The President saw was Palmer's face. What a menacing smile he had.

Everything went black as The President died from a lack of oxygen.

CHAPTER TWENTY-EIGHT

MICHAEL HARTNELL

Michael, Sarah and Nejuma hadn't slept in more than twenty-four hours. Caffeine had become Michael's new best friend. He'd probably ingested hundreds of cups of coffee as they researched Lucifer and The Whangie. Everything was pointing to The Gates of Hell.

The only hope of preventing Lucifer from returning depended on finding Connor Sullivan and his cult of followers. Nejuma had attempted to use his angelic abilities in the search for Connor Sullivan.

Nejuma had told Michael and Sarah that Connor had to be warded against angels. He was unable to sense The High Priest's location anywhere in the world.

Michael didn't know what he would do when they found Connor. What would it take to stop him from releasing Lucifer? Michael feared Sullivan wouldn't see sense and be forced to take his life if it were to go that far. He would bear the stain on his soul for the rest of his days if it meant Lucifer never set foot upon the Earth.

Sarah had been flicking through every news channel on their TV. Nejuma was reading from an old book on devil lore. Michael was sitting at the computer desk by the living room window, he was using his laptop. They had a close call with Wormwood. Michael would never leave Sarah alone.

The witch-demon Wormwood would have no second thought about taking a life, Michael thought. He dreaded to think what could have happened had Nejuma, the guardian angel not been present. One thing was certain. Wormwood would have murdered Sarah.

Michael felt like they were getting nowhere. He was angry, upset, conflicted and didn't know what to feel. Given the circumstances he was allowed to feel whatever emotion was on his mind, he thought. Michael shoved his laptop aside. He must have thrust it loud enough to acquire Sarah and Nejuma's full attention.

Nejuma closed the book he was reading and set it aside on the windowsill. He was next to impossible to know what his thoughts were. He showed pretty much nothing emotionally. Michael began to think of angels like "Vulcans" from his favourite TV show, "Star Trek". Completely emotionless.

Sarah turned her head to get a better view of Michael from the couch. He was behind her. Sarah stopped channel searching. The TV had been left on CNN, the news was currently airing.

"This is hopeless!" Michael exclaimed. There was silence in the room for a moment. Michael felt like this was a complete waste of their time. Sarah turned her attention away from her husband. He understood why. What could anyone say in a time like this?

If they failed, in less than twenty-four hours' time, Lucifer would be free to bring on the apocalypse.

All hell was about to break loose and Michael Hartnell felt powerless to prevent it.

"Oh, my God!" Sarah exclaimed whilst she reached for the television remote. She had the TV on mute as she searched for the world's news.

An American news host was speaking live to the world. What was going on in the States? Michael realised when he saw the news headline.

"It has officially been announced, The President of The United States is dead. The White House staff found him hanging from the ceiling earlier this evening. The cause of death is an apparent suicide." The news reporter stated. Michael couldn't understand it. What did the U.S. President have to do with Lucifer's followers? He wasn't buying his death as a suicide.

The news reporter delivered another terrible blow.

"In the same evening, the Vice President was killed at a political event in what is looking like an assassination. Our sources confirm the Vice President's body was found with a star-shaped mark on the back of his hand with his finger pointing to the east side of the stage. Many believe he caught sight of his shooter and may have been trying to point him out before dying.

The speaker for the House of Representatives, Steven Palmer has been sworn in as the nation's forty-fifth President."

"This is terrible!" Sarah shook her head in disbelief.

"It said the Vice President was pointing east." Nejuma stated in his usual cold tone manner.

"And?" Michael asked. He didn't see the relevance. He knew Lucifer had a hand in it but was unsure of what or why.

"If you travel far enough east from Washington D.C., you get Scotland, Glasgow and what is outside of the city?" Nejuma asked Michael. He understood every nightmarish occurrence in the last couple of days had been a part of some satanic ritual to free Lucifer from Hell.

"The Whangie…" Michael responded. He was stuck for words. This was happening. Every second brought it closer to becoming a reality.

"We won't be able to find Connor Sullivan. We know definitively, he and his followers will be there. That is our moment." Nejuma stated. Michael hoped it wouldn't have been cutting it so close. He was about to ask Nejuma something before he heard a familiar voice on the TV.

"My fellow Americans, people of the world. Words cannot begin to describe what has happened today." President Steven Palmer's American accent filled Michael with absolute terror.

Michael was so wrapped up in Lucifer. He hadn't stopped to consider thinking about him! Nejuma looked at Michael in curiosity. No doubt he registered how much he shook with fear at the TV. His eyes were glued to the screen, too frightened to look away.

"Michael, who is that man?" Nejuma asked with concern. The first bit of emotion he had seen from the guardian angel. Michael couldn't bring himself to speak the name, it was all becoming too real. Sarah had gotten up from the couch to comfort Michael. He held her close to him and spoke the name out loud through a tear filled, choked up throat.

"He is Mammon." Michael cried with fear. How could he have forgotten about that psychopath? He thought about if they did stop Lucifer. Mammon would still be running around. How could Michael stop the Antichrist? He was every bit as powerful as his father. But, he was nowhere near as crazy as Lucifer.

Mammon was crazier. A fuse ready to blow at any second.

"Who is Mammon?" Sarah asked in concern and confusion.

"The Antichrist." Nejuma calmly responded as he stared, he was transfixed on the television screen. Mammon continued to address the world as the United States President.

"Words cannot begin to describe it with the exception of one word. What happened to The President and Vice President is a blessing." Mammon chillingly spoke. He was insane. Michael shook his head from side to side, tears staining his cheeks.

"It is a blessing by my right hand. Yes, I killed them both. My father wished it to happen. By now many of you will be questioning who I am." Mammon leaned closer to the camera, he was in the oval office of The White House. Michael knew he was toying with the world, his new playthings.

"I will make life a hell of a lot easier. Allow me to introduce myself. My name is Mammon… The Antichrist." Mammon let out a sigh of relief after revealing his true identity to the world.

"Man, it feels good to say that… I was born from a follower on Christmas day last year… I know! I look like I have been around for a while… It's only my first birthday tomorrow… What better gift for me! My father, Lucifer, your lord and master will return tomorrow on the disgusting day you call Christmas." He hated the very mention of the word as if it left a foul taste in his mouth, Michael thought.

"Tomorrow, I will take my place by my father's side and change your pathetic little world for the better. For now, let me have some fun." Mammon's face was filled with a spine-chilling smile before the TV screen went to static. Michael was stunned. Mammon was already here and Lucifer was only a heartbeat away from breaking into this world.

"He isn't any younger." Michael said in puzzlement. Mammon was not any younger in the present day. He looked the exact same here as he did in the future.

"He will never age. Neither will Lucifer when he is freed." Nejuma explained Mammon's eternal youth.

"Lucifer won't escape… I cannot… I will not let it happen!" Michael was hellbent on altering history. He would never allow the world in the future to become a reality.

"What happens if he is freed? What happens if we can't stop the cult?" Sarah was panicked as she asked the angel for his wisdom.

"The beginning of the end." Nejuma responded without a hint of concern.

CHAPTER TWENTY-NINE

HIS EXCELLENCY CARLISLE DALTON

LOCATION: CLASSIFIED

DECEMBER 24th 2009

03:00pm

Carlisle Dalton sat impatiently waiting in front of a camera. He eagerly awaited for The Illuminati to interrupt the regular news and give his own live broadcast to the entire planet. The damn hackers were taking their sweet time to achieve his specifications.

He would rather have simply entered a news station, killed the reporter who was already broadcasting and get this over and done with. It would have been quicker, he thought.

"How much longer?" Carlisle asked the cameraman. His patience was wearing thin.

"You'll be live in thirty seconds, my lord." Dalton heard the quivering fear in the cameraman's voice. He need not worry, he was doing his job. It was the damn hackers who would receive a hole in the head.

"You are on in, five, four, three, two, one!" The cameraman gave Carlisle a thumbs up to confirm he was live on air. Carlisle sat staring into the camera with a pyramid symbol on a curtain behind him.

The Lord of The Illuminati addressed the people of the world.

"My name is Carlisle Dalton. I have been a member of the new world order since my birth. You may be wondering what the new world order is? We are often referred to as The Illuminati, the company or the shadow government."

Carlisle took in a breath before continuing. He wasn't used to making speeches this long.

"We are a secret society which exists in all world governments with only one goal, total control of this planet. I imagine if you were to search for us online. You would without a doubt discover we are one of the biggest conspiracy theories in the world." Carlisle chuckled at the thought of how deluded these sheep were.

"We are more than a theory. We are real! We have shaped your world into our image from behind the scenes. We are responsible for the assassination of JFK, we were the cause of the Chernobyl nuclear meltdown as part of our plan to destabilise the Soviet Union. We also destroyed the world trade centre on September 11th. We caused the global recession in 2008. We have been pulling the strings since the dawn of time... Alien life? Unfortunately, we are alone in the universe. Enough of the past." Carlisle momentarily paused to catch his breath before unveiling their ultimate plan to seize control of the world.

"The present is, we plan to launch nuclear attacks upon a capital city at random. Every hour on the hour until a global surrender has been reached. You have one hour to surrender, pledge fealty and allegiance to the new world order. If you don't. A capital city will be completely obliterated." Carlisle laughed. He knew the world was in the palm of his hand.

A few destroyed cities will make the world see sense. The policy of "no negotiating with terrorists" will be null and void.

"There is nowhere you can run or hide. We are everywhere. We are not only inside the governments of your world. We are in local law enforcements, hospitals and schools. Yes, you heard right. We teach your children. You will never see us coming. Oh, I almost forgot... Merry Christmas to one and all." Carlisle smiles before ending his hacked transmission.

CHAPTER THIRTY

THE SON OF PERDITION

MAMMON

THE OVAL OFFICE
THE WHITE HOUSE
WASHINGTON D.C.
DECEMBER 24th 2009
06:57pm

Mammon stared at his clock on the desk. He had been sworn in as President of The United States of America. Only a few minutes to midnight in The United Kingdom. In eighteen hours' time, Mammon would meet his father for the first time.

The Illuminati were far too caught up in their own self-indulgent bullshit. They hadn't seen Mammon's presidential broadcast. He knew where Dalton and Syme would be and will deal with them when the time came.

The intercom from his security team rang. Mammon answered with a click of a button.

"Yes." He spoke. Wondering what was so urgent. His secret service team were no more. Mammon replaced them with his followers and demons.

"Your mother is here to see you, Lord Mammon." The follower informed him.

"Send her in, brother." Mammon responded with excitement. He was happy to see his mother, Esther. She had been a loyal follower to his father. Lucifer would be grateful to her when they are reunited with each other tomorrow in Scotland. He would give her the world for her allegiance.

Esther entered the oval office. Mammon stood to attention. He was overjoyed by his mother paying him a visit. She is younger in appearance than Mammon, his alias, Steven Palmer had been in his early 30s since he looked the age.

Esther was a younger woman in her early 20s with long black.

She dressed for the cold winter's night, wearing a winter jacket.

"Mother!" Mammon greeted her as he approached her with welcome arms. Esther couldn't bring herself to look at her son. She flinched before he could wrap his arms around her for a hug.

"Are you all right, mother?" Mammon was concerned. What was wrong with his mother? She was shaking. She must be freezing from being outside, he figured.

"I saw… I saw your broadcast, Steven." Esther's voice trembled.

"A historical day, mother. Come, I will light a fire to warm you." Mammon gestured for her to sit by the fireplace across from the couch. With a wave of his hand, using his dark magic acquired from Hell, fires erupted in the fireplace, slowly filling the oval office with heat.

Esther still shook uncontrollably. She hadn't moved any closer to the fireplace.

"What is wrong, mother?" Mammon was concerned for her. What was on her mind?

"Steven, you don't…" She cried her eyes out. Esther was unable to speak her thoughts. Mammon moved to comfort her, she refused his attempt to console her.

"Mother, you are acting really strange. What's wrong?" Mammon demanded to know if she had some sort of issue with him. He wanted to know this instant.

"Don't go to him… Don't go to Lucifer…" Esther sobbed hysterically.

"He is my father… Why… Why would I not go to him? This is what you have been preparing me for." Mammon didn't understand. He spent the last year living and killing anyone who stood in his way to get to this point. Why had his mother changed her mind towards their cause?

"I made a mistake… I can't let you go to him." Esther cried.

Mammon felt anger towards his mother. She couldn't do this to him on the eve of his father's return.

"You can't keep me from my destiny!" Mammon shouted. Unbelievable, who did she think was?

"He can't take you away from me… It wasn't part of the deal… You are my son." She reached her hand out to touch him. Mammon recoiled to her touch in anger and sadness.

"The deal is whatever he wants it to be. He made me through you. I was born to rule beside my father, to exact his vengeance upon those who wronged him. I was created to help him teach the people of this world their rightful place... And I will!" Mammon spoke slowly. He thought to remind her of his purpose as the Antichrist.

"I can't let you go to him... You're a man, an extraordinary one. You are smart and strong... You are too precious to hand over to him... Six months ago, you were my baby... You will always be my son... I was wrong to make a deal with Lucifer... You don't have to be like him. You can be capable of so much good and one day, I hope you see it too..."

Mammon cut across her with a vicious strike to Esther's face. She was surprised by his slapping her and stood her ground whilst she held the stinging on her face.

"Don't ever speak of my father in such a manner." Mammon was filled with blind hatred towards her badmouthing of Lucifer.

"Steven, please don't go to him. He will kill you once he has what he needs..." Mammon begins to shout at the top of his lungs in fury. Esther ceased talking, she flinched and closed her eyes from fright of Mammon raising his voice.

"MY NAME IS NOT STEVEN!!!"

Esther looked upon her son's face and asked him who he thought he truly is.

"Who are you?"

"My name is Mammon." Esther sobbed uncontrollably. Her son was gone.

Mammon waves his hand, the fires from the fireplace flew out and engulfed Esther's entire body in flames. Esther's screams filled the office. She was consumed in fire.

The Antichrist smiled as he watched his mother burn to ash and dust.

CHAPTER THIRTY-ONE

BEN ARMSTRONG

SCOTTISH NATIONAL BLOOD TRANSFUSION SERVICE

GARTNAVEL HOSPITAL

GLASGOW

DECEMBER 22nd 2009

10:13am

Ben's thirst was quenched for the time being. He scrubbed his face in the sink of the gentlemen's toilets. It is difficult to wash his face. Vampires cannot see their own reflection in the mirror. No vampire could. It always proved to be problematic. He needed to ensure nobody was ever present. The reason for this was because there would be no explanation for why he didn't have a reflection.

Ben had to maintain he was human and occasionally went to the toilet to keep up the pretence despite the fact vampires do not require the use of the toilet. They don't need to relief themselves even though they are capable of ingesting food and drink alongside their sustenance of blood.

He felt a million times better. The contaminated blood bag would not sustain him for long. Hopefully by the time the lunch break came he could enjoy a proper drink from his thermos flask. He couldn't risk anyone seeing what he was actually consuming. Not that anyone ever questioned to the contents of his flask.

However, he could hear the thoughts of several of his colleagues around the lunch table over the years. Many thought Ben simply enjoyed a large flask of tea or coffee and a minority thought he was a secret alcoholic and couldn't for the life of them understand how he hid the smell of drink. Easy explanation he thought. He wasn't drinking alcohol. Not that it had an effect on any of his kind.

He did however always have with him some ham and cheese sandwiches to try and pass off as human. It obviously worked. Lunch time is the only time of any day that Ben actually ingests food. His diet was mostly of blood which he managed to acquire humanely. But it was highly illegal.

Ben finished washing his face in the sink before proceeding to dry himself with paper towels from one of the wall mounted dispensers in the bathroom. Time to head back to the lab for the next couple of hours before lunch.

Ben made his way out of the clinically clean bathroom. They were always clean. The perks of the National Health Service. But having white tiles was beyond ridiculous. Walking back along the corridor towards the lab, he hadn't been that long. He hardly thought any of his team had missed him.

Ben opened the lab doors and entered. To his surprise all the team were not at their workstations. All the staff were standing in a line with two security guards present along with Ben's boss, Diana Crichton, the head of the Scottish Transfusion Service.

She was a middle-aged woman in her forties, dressed in a business suit. She had short brown hair and wore spectacles. Ben knew immediately this was not an audit. This was something much worse.

"Nice of you to join us, Dr Armstrong." Diana greeted him. She held her hand out in a gesture for Ben to join his team. Ben, without saying a word joined his team. They all looked concerned.

"Now that we are all here. I am not going to beat about the bush. The reason we are here is to ascertain the truth. One or a group of you have stolen from the service." Diana announced to the team.

If Ben were capable of shitting himself. It would have been this moment. What else could they have discovered if not the blood bags he made disappear from the system?

"Stolen what?" Gillian asked defensively. She had every right to be angry. Not a single person in this room had anything to do with Ben's theft.

"Blood bags. So far, we have discovered over fifty have been registered for outpatient transfusion. Yet, not a single one of these patients exist." Ben really fucked it with this one. How could he have been so careless?

"You will all be individually interviewed. You have nothing to fear if you have nothing to hide. However, if it is discovered that you know who the culprit is and choose to remain silent. You will also be prosecuted for aiding them. The interviews will begin momentarily." Diana stated before making a hasty retreat from the lab.

No doubt an office had been set up for interviews.

What a farce! This had to be quick. Ben dread to think of what could occur if he didn't feed in the next few hours.

Gillian looked at Ben in disbelief.

"Who could have done this?" She asked him in shock. Ben remained silent. He wouldn't lie to his team. The thoughts of all his team members varied. Many didn't think anybody capable of such a crime, a small handful believed it to be a practical joke or some sort of extreme training exercise. Somewhere in the team, Ben heard the minds of those who were ready to point the finger at anyone they felt a grudge towards without a shred of evidence whatsoever.

Ben listened out for thoughts towards him. To his amazement, no-one was thinking about him. Ben began to wonder where he went wrong in covering his tracks. What moment led to the discovery? He obviously been incredibly careless for them to have discovered over fifty bags to have disappeared. That was only fifty they knew of. Maybe add a couple more zeroes on the end and it would be the rough figure of blood bags he stole for sustenance.

This wasn't going to die away any time soon. They would find the culprit or keep searching till they did. This could last for years. The only way out of this would be if he were caught. This would create a whole new set of problems to become known.

They would question his motive. Why had he stolen these blood donations? Sooner or later the truth would emerge.

Ben Armstrong is a vampire. The world was not ready for this knowledge. Not that the vampire law would allow that to be revealed.

There is another option to get out of this. Give them a patsy. Ben couldn't do that. To ruin an innocent person's life was a diabolical thought. This employee, whoever it was wouldn't only lose their job but their freedom. An offence of this type carried a prison sentence. Ben wouldn't do this to anyone. Not even to save his own skin.

Ben is faced with a dilemma, ruin some other poor unsuspecting bastard's life or out the vampire race to the world bearing in mind the law makers would never allow their existence to become public knowledge.

Ben knew he could escape with ease, super-speed past the security guards and bypass all the security doors in the building. The flaws in this plan were a great many. His disappearance would raise questions. This may result in the entire team losing their livelihoods.

The building was presumably on lockdown and even it wasn't, the sun was still shining outside. Ben would burst into flames before he made it ten feet from the front entrance.

Every member of the team had been talking amongst themselves. All speculating the current situation. One of the security guards stepped forward with a clipboard in his grip. Ben didn't have to be a mind reader to work out it was a register with the team's names.

"Can I have your attention?" The security guard had to shout to be heard over the team of doctors and scientists. The room went quiet and the guard had everyone's attention.

"The interviews have been sorted alphabetically. First is, Armstrong. Dr Ben Armstrong." The guard announced. Everyone's eyes were on Ben.

Shit! Ben thought. He wanted to scream inside. As he made himself known to the security guards, the minds of all his colleagues raced towards conclusions. As far as he could tell not one thought had him pegged as a suspect. How wrong his team were!

For the first time in over a century, Ben Armstrong was lost. He had no idea for how he and his team would come out of this predicament. Someone had to go down for this and until Ben learned what the service knew, he wouldn't be able to repair the damage done.

Two things were certain, he was not prepared to frame an innocent man or woman and he couldn't risk the exposure of vampires. If push came to shove, Ben would surrender himself to the authorities at sundown. No jail or prison could hold him. The service would get their culprit who would then escape justice and it keeps the vampire law out of the equation.

He always knew what the reality was. His time here with the blood transfusion service would one day come to an end. He always thought it would be someone eventually noticing he wasn't getting any older, the curse of eternal youth and vampiric immortality.

Ben never in a million years would have thought if he left his job, he would be running for his life. The security guard was a large man in his early forties. The transfusion service had hired an external security team given the circumstances.

"If you'd like to follow me, Dr Armstrong." The guard led the way out of the lab. The thoughts of the team raced through Ben's mind. Everyone thought this was a waste of time and Ben was innocent.

Ben was taken to a small office a few doors down the corridor from the lab. The guard opened the door to the office, daylight blast into the hallway. There was a window inside the office. Fortunately, vampires only feel the affects of sunlight when they are directly exposed to it. A window, especially good old British double glazing prevented the dangerous effects of the sun from harming Ben. He would be safe for as long as the window remained closed.

Diana Crichton was seated at the office desk. She had cleared it to lay out dozens of files in front of her. There was a notepad and pen at the ready. By the looks of it, she had plenty of evidence on the case and would be conducting the interview herself.

"I'll be outside if you need me, Dr Crichton." The guard informed her before leaving Ben inside the office. He closed the office door as he made his exit.

"Please take a seat, Dr Armstrong." Diana gestured with her right hand to the chair across the desk from her. Ben was eager to know what she discovered and seated himself without having to be asked twice. Diana opened a file on the desk. From the photograph inside the folder, Ben knew this was his own employee file.

Ben is the head of the department. The transfusion service would ensure they all the facts to uncover any potential motives for a suspect. Diana would probably have a heart attack if she found out where the blood bags were actually going. No-one would be putting their finger on the idea of the blood being consumed for sustenance by a century old vampire.

The chances were the entire service would have concluded that an employee would no doubt be selling blood on the side to anonymous donors on the black market to the highest bidder. Ben felt this kind of scenario would be less complicated than the truth.

Ben only noticed now that Diana also possessed a tape recorder. This interview was going to go on record, every word he spoke would be recorded. Ben needed to be sure how to answer any questions. He had to be careful. What he said, one slight hesitation or discrepancy in his story and all hell would break loose.

"Dr Armstrong, before we begin. I have to make you aware that for the purposes of this investigation, our interview is being recorded. Do you understand?" Diana asked him in an official sounding tone. She was hard to read. Her thoughts jumped all over the place.

"Yes, I understand." Ben responded. He had no say in the use of the recording equipment. It was in his contract that should an investigation be conducted.

Any and all interviews shall be recorded and used wherever necessary as evidence in a court of law.

"You are legally entitled to have legal representation at this time if you desire." Diana asked Ben if he required the assistance of a lawyer. He heard her thoughts this time. She knew if he asked for legal help that he would have to be guilty of something.

Intelligent woman, Ben admired her. He thought exactly the same thing. Had he a lawyer, Ben would have requested their services. Not to defend him but merely to forestall the interview. Diana wouldn't be able to continue her interview until after the lawyer arrived. The only problem was, Ben had never needed a lawyer. He avoided them due to some having connections to the vampire race. Ben didn't want anything to do with his kind.

All Ben required was to keep this farce going until the sun set, leave the building and disappear then pray the vampires didn't feel the need to descend upon the blood bank to conduct their own investigation. A cover-up would sum it up precisely.

Ben made up his mind. He wasn't about to throw anyone else under the bus and would sooner stake his own heart than bring the vampires out of the coffin. Unleashing the truth about vampires to the world may as well be Pandora's box. Once opened and it's out. Nothing will ever be the same.

The world is not ready for such knowledge.

"No, I have nothing to hide, Dr Crichton." Ben responded with his best poker face. He had years to master it. His whole life was a lie. He endured a longer life than Diana. If he had to lie about his identity on a daily basis in order to survive. This interview was easy enough to bullshit his way out of.

"The interview will now commence." Diana stated to Ben, her thoughts shifted. She was unsure of whether or not Ben could be a suspect. If anything, Ben felt she would tell him he was incompetent to allow this level of theft to go unnoticed under his leadership. Normally, she would be right, Ben thought.

"How long have you worked for the service?" Diana asked, she knew fine well. The employee file would answer that. She was starting off small and working her way up to asking him the more serious questions that would no doubt make a guilty man sweat with fear.

"I joined the service in 1999. Ten years ago as a phlebotomist in a donor centre at Nelson Mandela Place in Glasgow." Ben answered with calm precision, sparing no missed details.

"Interesting. You became the head of the department, when?" Diana asked, already knowing from the file. Her mind was difficult to read, one thing was certain. She was suspicious of Ben's position. The head of the Gartnavel laboratory, surely he knew something or had a stake in whatever was going on. Nothing in this lab would occur without his knowledge, she thought.

Diana knew fine well when Ben assumed the role as·department head. She interviewed him for the position. Ben responded with the most accurate answer she would probably hear all day.

"Four years, seven months and five days." Diana was taken by surprise at Ben's track of the time since his promotion. Her thoughts were filled with amazement at Ben's response. She also thought it may be a ploy to throw her off balance in the interview. She would be right. Ben needed the cover of darkness, the longer he stalled his own interview, the longer it would be before the rest of the team were interviewed.

The investigation in all likelihood would last for months, the interviews would only last hours. Ben hoped whatever happened now in this office would buy him enough time for the sun to go down. He was fortunate it was winter, less than six hours and Scotland would be engulfed in darkness.

Diana shrugged off the feeling of being flustered and proceeded with her interview.

"Well, one can only assume you would know your team." She suggested, hinting for him to reveal any of his own suspicions. He had none, he is the culprit. He decided to answer in a manner which begged more questions from Diana.

"As well as one can." Ben responded. Her thoughts were filled with stress. He knew her cage was being rattled. She was becoming agitated with him.

"Do any of your team stand out, Dr Armstrong?" Diana inquired, clutching at straws to unveil the thief.

"My team perform their jobs to the standards expected within the Scottish blood transfusion service. There isn't a single person I could think capable of such an offence. Who are you treating as a suspect?" Ben decided to turn the interview on Diana.

"Currently your entire team, including yourself are all suspects until proven otherwise." Diana responded. Ben heard the determination in her voice. She would stop at nothing until she had found the culprit.

"Do you have anyone in particular who stands out?" Ben continued to quiz her. He needed to know if they were onto him or someone else. Nobody was about to take the blame for his fuck-up, that much was certain. He would run but was not prepared to let someone else take the blame for his mistakes.

"No-one as of yet. More or less every single member of your department has had a blood bag go missing. The only thing connecting them is you… Your signature is on the sign off for all these documents. Can you shed some light on this?" Diana stared Ben out. She was testing him.

A guilty person would struggle to explain their way out of this. Ben had been chilled the second he took his seat and did not jump to conclusions. He was very good at his job and came up with a suitable and perfectly legally response to convince her.

"That is to be expected. I am the head of the department. Any and all outpatient donations have to be approved by myself. Everything checked out. There was never any need to reject the release of the donation to an off-site patient." Ben had answered better than anyone else would have. He knew his job and was well acquainted with all procedures.

"You never had your suspicions about these non-existent patients?" Diana's suspicions grew.

"Like I said, there was never any reason to be suspicious. Everything checked out." Ben knew she had absolutely nothing on him. All she could prove was Ben did his job like any other department head. Diana remained silent before reaching across the table. She placed down in front of Ben, an evidence bag containing a medical cotton bud for a cheek swab DNA test.

This wasn't good. He knew what the service required from him but failed to understand why? Diana's mind was tricky to read, it was all jumbled up.

"The service requires a DNA sample from you and before you ask. We do have a court ordered warrant from a judge." Ben couldn't do as she asked. He needed to know why and what it would be used for.

"It seems a tad extreme. Might I ask why?" Ben inquired. His sample would do all the talking for him. It will bring the vampires down upon this building.

The last time such an incident occurred anywhere, the vampire law killed the implicated vampire. Before doing the same to all witnesses to the event. It was made to look like an accident and ensured the existence of vampire kind remained in the shadows.

His DNA being examined in any lab would send alarm bells ringing to somewhere with vampire law enforcements watching. It was several hours until sunset. Ben demanded to know what and see if there was any loophole to avoid submitted his sample for testing.

"Certainly, Dr Armstrong. Upon our discovery of blood bags being stolen. We did our own examinations of storage units in which the donations were stored. The last bag we are aware of went missing four days ago. The suspect must have injured themselves. We were able to recover a foreign blood sample. It was degraded. However, we were still able to obtain DNA from it for comparison... It is male DNA."

FUCK! FUCK! FUCK! Ben thought. How stupid had he been? He remembered a refrigeration unit door slamming against his hand. Had he been human, the weight of the door would have crushed the bones in his hand. His rapid healing kicked in. No permanent damage.

Ben tidied the area up. Not too well apparently. They had found blood. His degraded vampire blood. The sample would have been far too damaged to have discovered anything unusual. To them it would have merely registered as dying human blood. Just as well, a fresher sample would have brought the vampire law to their front door.

"If I refuse?" Ben calmly awaited Diana's response.

"Dr Armstrong, need I remind you? We have a warrant for all members of staff's DNA. Failure to comply could impact your case in court if you were to be found guilty." Diana couldn't exactly force him to supply her with his sample.

"I choose not to give my sample at this time." Ben stated. He knew his rights. It didn't matter how guilty it made him look. The moment the sun disappeared, he would become their prime suspect when he fled for his life.

"You do realise how this makes you look, Dr Armstrong?" Diana asked him, trying to understand the logic behind whatever game he was playing.

"You can't force me." Ben stated. He knew his rights.

"You are right. We can't. However, it does not sit well. I can have these guards currently on site arrest you and take you to the police station right now. There is another option. You can give me your DNA sample and avoid any unnecessary hassle." Diana held up the cotton swab, implying that Ben had no other choice but to obey.

She had him by the balls and Ben knew it. If he were to be escorted outside, anyone present would witness the first ever recorded case in history of spontaneous human combustion. It would be easier to explain than vampires.

Ben's death would draw unwanted attention and his surrendering a DNA sample would put him in an extremely difficult situation.

Ben Armstrong was between a rock and a hard place. Every scenario would result in the vampires coming to know his current whereabouts and risked the lives of every man and woman in the lab.

Vampires will come. It wouldn't be if. They would come today no matter what option he chose. Ben concluded it would be better to stand against the vampires upon their arrival, he couldn't do that as a pile of ashes and dust.

The only hope any human in this building had was if Ben submitted his DNA for testing, running away was no longer an option. He would have to stay and fight off however many vampires the law sent in to ascertain their truth.

Ben, without further protest reached for the medical swab. It had a plastic cap on top. He unclipped it before placing it inside his mouth. Ben swabbed the inside of his cheek. He removed the swab from his mouth then resealed the cap before handing it over to Diana Crichton.

She looked content with his co-operation. Her thoughts of him had changed. All respect had been lost and as far as she was concerned. Ben was already guilty.

"Thank you, Dr Armstrong. We will inform you if there are any changes in circumstances. For now, you are free to return to the lab until further notice. Please send in Mark Brown." Diana sat in silence as Ben left the interview room without saying a word.

The guard in the corridor returned Ben to his lab, the team did not say a word. His face must have spoke volumes. He could hardly hear individual thoughts from any member of the team. Ben's own mind raced. The vampire law would descend upon this laboratory and kill every human present whether they knew the existence of vampires or not.

235

In a few hours, Ben's DNA would be run through the system. The service would have their thief and discover the existence of vampires. Ben needed to be ready for what came next. Otherwise, a lot of people will be killed today.

What he had to do was simple. He would just have to kill whoever the law sent or die trying.

Hours went by. They felt like years. The sun was beginning to set and Ben's original plan of flight was no longer an option. His swab sample would be compared to the thief at this very moment and elsewhere without any human knowledge, the vampire law would have flagged the vampiric sample being tested.

They too would be biding their time. Awaiting for the cover of darkness to conduct their own investigation. If Ben weren't here, he would hate to see how they would spin it to ensure the humans did not come to learn about vampire kind.

Ben had watched all the members of his team be taken out of the lab for questioning. Not one of them had pointed the finger at any member of staff. Their thoughts were on Ben. He knew Diana had asked about him and if they ever suspected him. Nobody had or ever would think Ben capable of the crime.

Ben only ever done what he needed to do to survive.

There are things he done in his past that Ben was ashamed of. Horrified by. He was not like the rest of his kind. The vampire law or those who lived in nests preyed upon humans. What he done here ensured no human would ever have to die so he could feed.

He was careless in covering his tracks and the law would kill all these people who worked alongside him. He condemned them all. If he were to die here today at the hands of the vampire law, he would be sure to take as many of them down with him.

The police had been called in and were guarding the team in the lab. This only meant one thing. The service had found their thief and were ready to press charges. Ben knew they matched his DNA to the sample they had on file. He would be amazed and filled with tremendous guilt if they believed the culprit to be anyone else other than him.

Two policemen spoke quietly to each other to prevent the team from overhearing what was being said. With Ben's enhanced hearing, they may as well have spoken out loud. The service had found their suspect and wished to share their findings with the department head.

One of the officers stepped forward. He was looking in Ben's direction. He like many of his team was seated at his lab's workstation.

"Dr Armstrong?" The officer addressed Ben from across the lab.

"Yes?" Ben responded with the thought of his imminent arrest.

"Dr Crichton wishes to speak with you." Ben was informed by the police. The thoughts of the team raced. If vampires could experience headaches from mind reading. His head would surely explode from the agonising pain. Their thoughts were mixed. Some continued to believe this was a radical training course. Others didn't believe he was capable of stealing blood bags and a select few started to doubt their trust in Ben.

They were beginning to believe he did it. They were right.

Ben made his way to the lab entrance under police escort. He never said anything to his team. They were as silent as the grave when he was taken away. The police officers walked with Ben along the corridor and led him inside the same office he was interviewed in earlier.

The officers remained outside the office door which Ben found surprising. If the service truly had discovered him to be their suspect capable of stealing blood, why would they leave him alone with the head of the transfusion service? He dreaded to think. Diana was still seated at the desk. She smiled upon Ben's entry.

"Please take a seat, Dr Armstrong." She gestured with her hand to the vacant chair across from her desk.

"Need to locate the bags." Diana's thoughts spoke. That's all she was thinking about. Strange, Ben thought. She wasn't thinking he was guilty. Her only concern was for where the bags were. What was going on?

Ben seated himself on the chair and patiently waited to hear Diana's findings. It wasn't as light in the office. In the distance the sun was setting. It was still powerful enough to burn a vampire alive.

"Thank you for your co-operation with me earlier, Dr Armstrong." Diana stated with satisfaction. Ben read her mind. She still wanted to know where the missing blood bags had gone and questioned Ben's very existence. He knew she personally looked at his swab sample under a microscope.

"I didn't really have much of a choice but to cooperate or be handed over to the authorities." Ben responded with his eyes fixed on the daylight outside disappearing from the world.

It would soon be night and the law would no doubt send a lone agent or several to silence the discovery.

"Your assisting my investigation has shot yourself in the foot." Diana's words surprised Ben. She wanted to desperately try and understand what Ben was but yet her focus was on the investigation.

"I beg your pardon?" Ben stated with confusion in the hope she would open up with him.

"We matched your sample to the one we recovered from the cold storage." Her mind was practically screaming "What are you?" yet, she couldn't bring herself to ask Ben.

"Arrest me." Ben responded. The sun was still in the sky. Time was running short.

"The officers will. First, I have questions. Where is the blood you stole? What did you do with it?" Ben didn't know if it was how ridiculous Diana was reacting or the fear of the vampire law's imminent arrival which made him laugh.

"Care to share what you find amusing, Dr Armstrong?" Her patience had worn out.

"Are those really the best questions you could be asking me?" Ben asked her, knowing full well she thought he was some kind of medical anomaly, in her eyes Ben had to be or else he wouldn't be sat in front of her.

"I don't..." Diana was flustered. She couldn't string two words together. She was at a loss for words. She kept thinking about what Ben could have possibly done to his DNA, if he had some sort of disease and if so, it was unlike anything she ever seen before.

Clever woman, he thought. She possessed the right mind. Diana had no intentions on releasing her discovery. The threat of vampire agents looming left Ben with no option but to share with her. If they were to survive. He would need her on his side and fully aware of the situation.

"My DNA is dead. That's what you really want to ask me?" Ben asked her. He was ready to tell her everything, the whole truth.

"Yes... I want... I want to know how such a thing is possible. Given you are quite clearly alive." She looked relieved to finally ask him and bewildered. She was disturbed by his condition. It was stressing Diana out. She wanted answers.

Ben had never seen his boss like this before. She had every right to be confused, stressed or angry. Ben was about to turn her whole world upside down.

238

Everything she knew about science would change faster than the snap of his fingers. Ben gathered his own thoughts for a second. He hadn't revealed his true nature to anyone for what felt like a lifetime. He didn't beat about the bush. Time was his enemy. It was better to get it said and be done.

"I am a vampire." Diana's face stared at Ben with more questions. He didn't have to be telepathic to realise she did not believe him. She laughed at him in disbelief. It was a lot to process. Diana Crichton could not wrap her mind around it.

"You cannot be serious?! A vampire?!" She tried her best to compose herself. It was absolute nonsense to her. She wiped the tears of laughter away from her face. Ben himself hardly believed it when he met his first vampire almost two centuries ago on the night he was turned.

"Do you really expect me to believe such garbage?" Diana mocked him. It was easier to laugh than to accept. Ben needed to make her a believer in this moment or never.

"Not really. However, I am able to prove it. I require a tissue or a wet wipe." Ben stated, fully aware she carried some in her handbag, human minds always wandered off, no matter the situation.

"Whatever for?" Diana suspiciously demanded to know what kind of trickery he was planning.

"Give me one." Ben ordered her. He had no time for twenty questions or show any manners.

Diana huffed as she exhaled from annoyance. She reached under the office desk for her handbag. She quickly opened it on her lap and rummaged for her packet of wet wipes. Upon find them she swiftly shoved the packet across the desk towards Ben. She thought he was lying in an attempt to plead insanity with the revelation of being a vampire.

Ben was not lying. He was able to show her the truth. He gripped the packet and opened it up. Ben pulled one wet wipe and began rubbing his face. It was extremely difficult to apply make-up without a reflection in any mirror. It was just as difficult to remove. He pulled the wipe away from his face to examine the amount of make-up on the wipe. He recognised enough would be wiped clean for Diana to see how pale his complexion is.

She did seem fascinated by how pale Ben was. It was as if his face had been drained of all its blood. Vampires did have blood. Not enough to show in their skin.

"Is that your proof? You have pale skin and cover it with foundation?" Diana wasn't impressed. Ben was not an idiot. He knew it would take a lot more to convince anyone. The fangs in upper jaw would prove it. However, the effect on most humans was never good. His fangs were a measure of last resort.

Ben knew what to do next. He doubted she would have encountered anyone with eyes like his. Ben reached for his eyes to remove the contact lenses he used to appear human. Diana did become uneasy at the sight of his eyes. How many people in the world had yellow eyes? No-one, Ben thought.

Before she spoke, Ben read her thoughts. She remained unconvinced to his true nature.

"Your eyes… An interesting colour. If anything all you have done is convince me you are an extremely ill man. Not a vampire." Diana stated in an unsatisfied tone. She wanted him to be honest. Thinking it didn't matter what he did. Ben Armstrong had committed a crime. He was going to prison, she thought.

Ben saw the sunshine outside the office window. It wouldn't be long till it was set. The rays of light were still capable of harming him. He needed to go all the way to make her believe him. Ben stood up from his chair without saying why.

"What are you doing, Dr Armstrong?" Diana felt threatened by his sudden movement and silence. Ben walked past her to the window. He opened it inward. He exhaled. This was not going to be pleasant. The burn in the back of his throat was fierce. He needed to consume blood. With what he was preparing to do. He would need to feed more. The damage from sunlight would take its toll.

Ben removed then threw his white lab coat to the floor and rolled the sleeve of his shirt up to his elbow. Diana believed this to be the most pathetic thing she had ever witnessed. She seen a lot of excuses to escape the ramifications of employees' mistakes or crimes. Ben Armstrong's won the prize for being the most ridiculous.

Ben heard ever snidey comment that raced through her brain. Ben stuck his bare arm out into what remained of the daylight. He winced in pain, watching his arm instantly become redder than the worst sunburn imaginable. He needed to keep his arm out.

Unfortunately, for his sake there were a few conditions around for humans whose skin blistered in sunlight. She would be unconvinced if he pulled his arm in this moment. Ben's skin blistered, he was close to screaming in agony. Diana smiled smugly. She believed him to be a liar and in the same second, the smile was wiped off her face.

Ben's arm burst into flames. He brought it back inside the office. His whole arm was on fire. His screams filled the small office. Diana panicked, there was no fire blanket or sink in the room. She grabbed her mug of coffee from the desk and threw the scalding hot liquid over Ben's arm to extinguish the flames.

Most of the fire had been put out. Ben extinguished what remained with his unburnt hand. Diana couldn't believe her eyes. How was that even possible? To burst into flames from being exposed to sunlight. It was not natural.

She gasped as Ben's burnt skin healed before her eyes. There were no burns or scars. His skin was completely healed within seconds. Diana looked at Ben's face and jumped with fright. Ben's fangs from his upper jaw had extended. They were longer than any tooth she had ever seen.

"Oh, my God!" Diana exclaimed. Ben knew she believed him completely. She didn't quite understand it but she believed him to be telling the truth, he is a vampire. Ben looked behind him to outside of the office. Darkness had engulfed the sky. The sun had set.

"Listen to me very carefully." Ben said. He knew he had her complete attention.

"How long ago was my sample run through the system?" Ben knew if she could tell him when precisely, he would have a better idea of how long before the vampire law had caught on to his DNA being tested.

"As soon... Only minutes after. It took some time to get a match. Your DNA isn't quite like anything I have ever encountered before." Diana answered with fascination.

"Shit!" Ben shouted. He kicked the desk with all his strength, knocking it over onto its side. Diana stared in awe of Ben's abnormal strength. Ben realised they probably didn't have very much time. His DNA would have been noticed somewhere on the vampire end.

The vampire law's system monitored everything to ensure their existence remained a secret.

"I don't have time to explain everything. My kind have a law, a government which monitors everything. Whilst you were testing my DNA. Without your knowledge, it would have been run through systems you didn't even know existed... Every single person in this building is in grave danger." Ben tried to stress the seriousness of the situation they were landed in.

"What danger? Who are we in danger from?" Diana was in a state of panic. She shook with fear.

"The vampire law will no doubt have someone on route to this lab as we speak. They will do anything to keep the knowledge of our existence a secret from the world. The only way to do so would be to kill everyone here. Before covering it up as some sort of catastrophe." Ben tried to make her see sense. She was seeing clearer than ever before.

"How long until they arrive?" Diana asked Ben. She was prepared to do her duty.

"I can't say. One thing is certain. They will be here tonight." He told her.

"Then we evacuate. Send the staff home..." Ben immediately cut her off.

"It won't make a damn bit of difference. The law will find them in their homes. By now they will know everyone who works here. They are extremely thorough at how they operate." It was true. The vampires would have done their research. They would know the names of all employees clocked in on today's shift and where they lived.

The vampires would find a way to silence them in their homes and kill others who would be present, spouses and children. This was a nightmare. Ben wouldn't allow any unnecessary casualties to be caught in the crossfires. Ben felt the lab was the safest place to be. It was where he could better protect his team from whoever the law sent as their agent.

Ben was suddenly hit with a terrifying realisation.

"Not possible." Ben spoke out loud.

"What's wrong?" Diana pleaded with him. She wanted to know what he came to understand.

"There were guards outside this office." Ben stated in horror. How could he have missed that?

"And? I don't see the relevance, Dr Armstrong." Diana didn't come to grips with what Ben was trying to break to her.

"When my arm was burning. No-one entered to see what all the commotion was about." Ben stared at the office door without blinking. Everyone on this floor would surely have heard his scream from when his flesh melted. Nobody had come to his aid. That was concerning.

"What do you mean?" She looked to the door in terror of the uncertainty of what may be behind it.

"The vampire law is already here!" Ben exclaimed. The office door flew open. It had been kicked in from the outside. The force from the kick had knocked it off its hinges. Ben stood in horror. He recognised who the law had sent to kill everyone.

The vampire outside the office was dressed from head to toe in a police uniform, her long blonde hair hung down to her shoulders. Ben couldn't believe his eyes. He knew her better than he cared to.

"You always had to be the centre of attention. Didn't you, lover?" Penelope winked at Ben with a sadistic smile.

"What have you done to them?!" Ben shouted at his wife in a blind rage.

"Them?" Penelope asked in a mock confusion. She had no regard for any human life.

"Oh, the police and the lab geeks! Sorry, I was feeling a bit peckish. Besides, they had to go. You know how strict the law is with regulations. All witnesses must be disposed of. No exceptions. I am a stickler for the rules, hubby." Penelope licked the fresh blood on her lips in a sick attempt to seduce Ben.

Penelope turned Ben's stomach. Whatever love he ever felt for her died two centuries ago. Ben heard Diana's thoughts. She wanted to run for her life.

"Don't!" Ben shouted to her. She looked confused as to how Ben knew what she was planning. Diana wouldn't make it out the office alive. The vampire law sent Penelope to do their dirty work. She killed the entire team and all the policemen.

Ben didn't understand. How did she get here so quickly? The sun had not long set.

"How did you get in here? It was daylight only a moment ago?" Ben was going to kill her.

"Oh, did I fail to mention? We have access to your underground tunnels. The ones you use in the summer months." Ben, from all the stresses of the day had completely forgotten about them. It had been months since he last used the tunnels. He was concerned. Penelope knew too much. How did she know his work schedule?

"Come on, husband of mine. You didn't really think the law wasn't keeping tabs on you? They have been watching you for years." Penelope laughed with joy. She was enjoying watching Ben squirm. He had never been free from the clutches of the vampire law.

243

They always knew his current whereabouts.

Penelope's attention turned to Diana.

"Ben, you shouldn't have brought me a snack. How thoughtful." Penelope sniggered as Diana hid behind Ben like a child hiding behind a sofa. He literally was a shield protecting her from the monster who wished to feast on her blood.

"You will not touch her!" Ben declared.

"I will rip your fucking head off!" Ben shouted at Penelope. He wasn't bluffing. He would kill Penelope without giving it a second thought. She smiled like a cat, toying with its food as she looked directly at Diana.

"Fuck off, love. I wish to speak to Ben alone." Penelope moved aside from the office doorway. Diana was unsure of Penelope's intentions and looked to Ben for reassurance. She was shivering from the adrenaline.

"Go. She will not harm you. I give you my word." Ben looked her in the eye and promised her. Diana nodded her head without speaking to Ben and slowly made her way through the office door and past Penelope without losing sight of the vampire assassin. As she exited the office, she ran for her life.

Both vampires listened to her footsteps run along the corridor away from them.

"Don't worry. They only sent me. Your little friend will be fine." Penelope spoke to Ben. Vampires unfortunately are unable to read the minds of other vampires. Who knew what really went on in Penelope's warped and demented brain? Not that he trusted a word coming out of her mouth.

Penelope pushed the fallen desk upright and threw herself into an office chair before putting both feet up on the desk. Ben prepared himself to jam a large wooden stake in her heart and end her once and for all. Penelope exhaled as she became settled in the chair with her feet up.

"How long has it been? Thirty years?" She asked Ben like they were long lost friends having a reunion. Ben lost it in an instant, unleashing his fury upon her.

"Are you mental?! You killed my entire team... You think you can come in here and talk as if we share some sort of connection." He was repulsed by her lack of humanity.

"Well, we do. We were married and you are my maker." Penelope sarcastically responded, infuriating Ben.

"What the fuck do you want?!" Ben snapped.

"A lot. Most importantly. We need to speak about the next few days." Penelope spoke with fear in her voice.

Something scared her and Ben Armstrong knew his wife did not scare easily.

CHAPTER THIRTY-TWO

NEJUMA

12 CROWWOOD STREET

GLASGOW

DECEMBER 25ᵀᴴ 2009

12:30pm

The Hartnell's were able to get a night's sleep. They would need all the energy they could for what was to follow. Nejuma had stood guard by their window all night as Michael and Sarah slept. What was supposed to be a day of peace for the Hartnell's became a day of stress, worry and dread of what may come to be.

If they were to fail, The Ruler of Hell would be free to walk the Earth for the first time since the dawn of creation. Nejuma had his orders and would protect Michael and Sarah with his life. He already died protecting Michael. He felt blessed to have been resurrected by his father, The Almighty God.

The Hartnell's were outside in the cold Christmas morning, shivering from the icy cold breeze and ankle deep snow.

All three of them were preparing for their long journey north to the Whangie with the hope of preventing Connor Sullivan from releasing Lucifer from Hell.

Michael managed to convince a neighbour for a loan of their car. Nejuma found the human race extraordinary. They were incapable of his angelic abilities which he never took for granted. Despite their not possessing powers, their technology enabled them to do as they required.

Nejuma truly did find them fascinating even though he never directly expressed his feelings about humanity.

"Nejuma, why do I need a car? Can't you... You know just beam us there or something?" Michael asked the angel in confusion.

He did not understand the reference of "beam" but he understood Michael was implying to his teleportation abilities and why they couldn't do so to transport themselves to the Whangie.

"There is angel warding. It suppresses my ability to teleport. We will have to drive or walk and given the time we possess. Driving there is our best option." Nejuma responded with his usual emotionless tone.

The demons were on high alert. Their part in the ritual to free their master prevented any angel from teleporting. Unfortunately, it also meant no angel could return to Heaven or enter the country. Nejuma could neither flee nor reach out for assistance from Heaven's army.

The three of them were the only hope of preventing billions of deaths. Lucifer would kill any human he could get his hands on. Sarah was already seated inside the small vehicle. Corsa, Nejuma read the words on the car. He was unfamiliar with types of cars. He didn't know if this was an expensive car or not.

Nejuma's attention was drawn to Michael. He was shaking but not from the cold.

"What is wrong, Michael?" Nejuma asked with concern. Michael recognised Nejuma's emotional reaction. It took him by surprise to see emotion from the angel.

"I'm... I don't know if can do this... What happens if we fail?" Michael was close to tears. He was scared. Nejuma would have thought him to have a lack of judgement if he weren't. Not that Nejuma would own up to it. He was scared of Lucifer too.

They had history in Heaven.

Every angel knew how dangerous Lucifer is and why Michael Hartnell would be able to stop him once and for all.

"I understand, Michael. Remember this, he will never know what it means to be human, to feel joy or love. You will stop him. It is known. Every angel in Heaven knows it. You will defeat The Devil." Nejuma explained to Michael, telling him exactly what he needed to hear without divulging everything to him.

"Why am I so special, Nejuma?" He desperately wanted to know but the time was not right and as much as Nejuma, his guardian angel wanted to tell him. He was forbidden to divulge that knowledge. The angel had sworn a vow before Jesus Christ. He could not break it.

"In time, you will learn for yourself." Nejuma rested the palm of his hand upon Michael's shoulder and smiled.

CHAPTER THIRTY-THREE

THE WITCH-DEMON WORMWOOD

THE WHANGIE

SCOTLAND

DECEMBER 25TH 2009

05:53pm

The demon Wormwood stood in a circle with the cult members around an enormous pentagram. It was made with blood. It stained the white snowy ground in front of the rock face of the Whangie, The Gates of Hell.

In less than ten minutes, her master would be free from his prison, she lived for this day and wasn't about to let that filthy angel stop her from reaching her goal. As soon as Lucifer was free of Hell, she could be rid of the buffoon who called himself, The High Priest of The Fallen God.

Connor Sullivan disgusted Wormwood, his touch on her skin made her want to retch. She would no longer have to maintain the pretence of being the human he came to know and love, Nicola Wood.

The stupid arse was standing in the centre of the pentagram. A huge smile stretched across his pathetic face, Wormwood knew Connor was loving every second of his fifteen minutes of fame. That was all it was ever going to be. She would make sure of it.

Everyone present wore long black hooded robes with pentagrams stitched onto the front of the material. Connor had a golden pentagram on his cloak. Pretentious arse, Wormwood thought. He was preparing to address his followers.

The only reason he was still breathing was because Wormwood required a human believer to perform the spell to free Lucifer. In other words, the ritual required the human race to consent to Lucifer's entry into their world.

"Welcome to The Gates of Hell!" Connor declared with opened arms. The cult members cheered with excitement, fucking sheep, Wormwood thought of them.

"Before we begin. I would like to take the time to thank all of you for coming." He smiled with pride, over a hundred people came to witness Lucifer's return. A select few were chosen for the circle around the bloody pentagram.

"Our God will be so thankful. The pentagram you see before you has been made with virgins blood." A small handful of worshippers actually gasped in shock upon hearing this news. Connor raised his hands up to bring assurance to the stunned followers.

"Don't worry. We didn't kill anyone. We were able to acquire blood from a donation centre." Connor smiled to calm his cult. Stupid idiot, the ritual required multiple lives, he was unknowingly murdering hundreds of virgins, the power in this spell would kill anyone whose blood had been unwillingly used.

"Now it is time to allow our God, our father, and our master to return to the world. To reshape it in his image." The cult cheered and applauded The High Priest. He raised his hands out in mid-air and aimed his palm towards the rock face of The Whangie.

He began chanting the spell to open a portal to Hell. The words were in Latin. Wormwood taught Connor well. His pronunciation was incredible for a human. The rough translation in English was "Lucifer, the one who was cast out from Heaven. You shall return to us today." This was repeated for several verses.

Connor felt the energy of the curse flowing through him. The entire pentagram lit up with a glowing red light. The energy travelled up through his body and he emitted a red beam from his palm onto the rock wall. The lights ceased and Connor collapsed to his knees from exhaustion.

The strength of the spell was overwhelming to humans. He was lucky to survive and had sacrificed fifty years of his life, not that Wormwood told him. She needed him to perform the spell willingly. Not that he would have lived to see the next fifty years. Wormwood would take great pleasure in ensuring it. For a brief moment, she was concerned nothing was going to happen, then to her amazement, The Whangie burst into flames as a circle shaped portal appeared on the rock face.

The Gates of Hell were open. Wormwood gasped in disbelief. She was overwhelmed by what her eyes saw inside the portal, a black figure slowly began to emerge. The figure was humanoid in shape, she knew they finally had succeeded. The person walking towards her and the cult stretched his angelic wings, they were deformed from the time in hell.

This was her lord and master, Lucifer.

Lucifer, for the first time since the fall, walked free of his fiery prison and set foot upon the human's world. Wormwood was deeply saddened by his appearance. Hell had inflicted pain upon his body which nobody should ever experience. His skin was without colour, his once brown hair was as black as tar.

He was half naked, the everlasting fires had ruined his robes, his face was almost unrecognisable. He was skin and bone, almost like a skeleton. Wormwood remembered the colour of his eyes from before the fall. They were beautiful. His eyes were now red as blood.

Wormwood still loved him no matter the tortures he endured. He was magnificent and she knew he was back with a vengeance, ready to finish what he started so long ago. Wormwood wanted to kill God for what he done to Lucifer. How could a father treat his son in such a horrendous and brutal manner?

Wormwood would never deprive Lucifer of the justice he so deserved and no doubt desired. The tool, Connor Sullivan was like the child who had been given the keys to the candy store. He was twitching with excitement and was making a theatre performance out of Lucifer's return like the showman he believed himself to be.

Connor Sullivan was an afront to the worship of Lucifer, Wormwood thought.

"Bow before Satan! God of the Demons and Hell!" He declared to his followers. Every man and woman knelt before Lucifer. They were ready to pledge to him their allegiance. The fools would not live to see the lord's reign. None would survive. Wormwood never felt so determined, the Earth would fall and then, Lucifer without a doubt would turn his attention towards Heaven.

The cult rose to their feet, one by one as their High Priest made his approach towards Lucifer. Their God was taking a moment to rejoice in the fresh air, his skin was burnt. The rapid healing swiftly kicked in and his burns were healed by the time Connor reached him.

The High Priest bowed before Lucifer and without looking upon his lord's face, he pledged his fealty to The Ruler of Hell.

"My Lord Satan. It is an honour to not only be in your presence but to be the one to release you from your eternal prison. I pledge myself to you for all eternity as your faithful servant to do as you ask of me." Sullivan vowed his services. Lucifer remained silent, an uneasy Connor looked up from where he was kneeling to gaze upon Lucifer's pale face.

Connor obviously felt like an insect in the presence of such a giant. He trembled with fear to even look his lord in the eye. Lucifer's face slowly filled with rage as he looked down at Connor Sullivan. The lord grit his teeth in fury and with the back of his hand, he struck Connor across the face. Connor fell flat on his backside, taken aback by Lucifer's response.

"Boy, you will never address me by that horrendous name. My name is not Satan! I am Lucifer." He declared before all present. His accent reminded Wormwood of American Southern, Alabama if she were to guess. A magnificent voice.

Connor held his face in pain. It stung like a bitch, Wormwood guessed. She enjoyed a good slap from Lucifer. Connor shook with fear of Lucifer.

"Apologies, Lord Lucifer." Connor's voice trembled as he address the dark lord. Lucifer belittled him in front of his entire following. Wormwood knew he would never recover his reputation after this. Not that it mattered to her. Connor Sullivan was yesterday's news.

Lucifer chuckled at how pathetic the young high priest reacted. He hated humans and would not rest until all of them were eradicated like the vermin they were. Lucifer gazed upon the blood soaked snow which formed the five-point star.

"Nice work with the pentagram." He complimented Connor, his gaze caught Wormwood's face. He smiled with happiness upon discovering his friend amongst the crowd.

"Wormwood, how long has it been? It is good to see you once more." Lucifer took her in his arms for a hug. Wormwood was honoured to be with him. She wished it could have been sooner. Circumstances prevented his freedom until today.

"The pleasure is all mine, Father Lucifer." Wormwood addressed him as she bowed before her lord. Connor looked flabbergasted. He was lost and confused by how she and Lucifer could have possibly been acquainted with each other.

"Nicola, how do you know him? What did…" He was interrupted by Wormwood. She had grown sick and tired of his Irish accent.

"My name is not Nicola, stupid!" She felt good to finally cut the little dimwit loose. Connor was stunned. He didn't know how to speak in response to Wormwood's harshness.

"She's a demon, Connor. One of the first to be cast out." Lucifer revealed the truth. Wormwood saw Connor's little heart break when the revelation shattered his entire world. He was close to tears.

Wormwood had gained his trust, pretended to be human to ensure he would do what was required when the time came. She had to appreciate he surpassed himself in the role he played. Unfortunately, for him. It was time to part ways.

"I thought you loved me..." Tears filled Connor's eyes.

"Oh, sweetie. I do..." Wormwood mocked him, not that the fool realised as she walked over to Connor. The witch-demon placed her hands on either side of his face.

"I do..." She smiled at Connor. His face brightened up. He smiled and cried with joy. Without a lot of strength, she broke his neck, like snapping a twig. She held onto him to watch the life drain from his eyes.

"I do... not." Wormwood coldly whispered before loosening her grip on his lifeless body. He slumped into the snow.

Connor Sullivan was dead.

The followers covered their faces in horror and screamed at the sight of their leader's corpse. Lucifer chuckled with amusement before turning his head to look upon the cult of satanic worshippers.

"What was it you expected? When you thought of releasing me? I, Lucifer, the fallen leader of the archangels, The Devil, the monster at the end of the book?" Every ear had his full attention, soaking up his words as if he were about to preach to them.

"Did you honestly believe I would thank you in ways beyond your wildest dreams?" Lucifer toyed with them. Wormwood knew it. She understood Lucifer all too well. He was like a cat playing with a live mouse, not that these foolish cult members understood.

A bunch of them actually nodded their heads in agreement to Lucifer's question. He found this highly amusing. He snorted through his nose when he sniggered at their naivety.

"Well, if you believed so. You do not know me... Humanity is a disease. I am the cure. I am not sorry for what has to come next." Lucifer smiled and chuckled before closing his eyes. Several of the cult members began to panic. They tried to escape whatever fate Lucifer was about to inflict.

It was no use. Demons had been amongst the crowd. They were here to prevent any attempt to flee Lucifer's wrath. Wormwood looked at him, his eyes closed. He was preparing to summon someone.

There was only one person who sprung to mind.

"Mammon, come to your father's calling." Lucifer summoned his son to their location. Lucifer's eyes opened to witness flames appear from nowhere. The fires formed the shape of a man and when they died, there stood Lucifer's son, Steven Palmer, who from this day forth would be addressed by the name bestowed upon him by Lucifer... Mammon.

Lucifer smiled at the sight of his son. This was the first time that father and son had met. Mammon was surprised and for a moment he stared upon his father's face in shock. He like Wormwood couldn't believe this day had finally come to be.

"Father? Is it truly you?" Mammon asked with such desperation, terrified this moment was a dream which he could be snatched away from him.

"Yes, my son. Come give your father a hug." Lucifer stretched his arms out. He was eager to meet his son. Mammon approached his lord and father. Lucifer wrapped his arms around his son. The Antichrist couldn't help but stare upon the permanent damage Hell inflicted upon his father.

"Father... What has he done to you?" Mammon asked Lucifer in horror. He was a shadow of the archangel he had once been. He was still beautiful in the eyes of the witch-demon.

"You need not worry about my appearance, Mammon. What matters is, I am free and we are finally together." The lord was over the moon to be free and rid of Hell. Wormwood would ensure Lucifer shall never return to Hell. She would sacrifice her life for his if it came to it. Wormwood would trade her life for his.

"It's good to see you, my son. I have a gift for you." Lucifer's eyes shifted towards the members of Connor Sullivan's cult. Mammon's face was filled with mischief.

"You know what to do." Lucifer chuckled as Mammon stood before all the black cloaked followers. They were shaking with fear. Too frightened to look at Mammon or Lucifer. The young Antichrist stared them all out and in the blink of an eye. He used his dark magic.

Every man and woman burst into flames. Mammon laughed hysterically, watching all the fanatics burn to death.

CHAPTER THIRTY-FOUR

MICHAEL HARTNELL

THE WHANGIE

SCOTLAND

DECEMBER 25TH 2009

06:01pm

The roads throughout the Scottish countryside were treacherous. Snow was falling heavily, slowing Michael down drastically, the little Corsa was not built for these extreme weather conditions.

There had been moments where Michael, Sarah and Nejuma had driven almost the entire journey without speaking a single word. Michael prayed they would not be late. He would not be late. Michael had to prevent Connor Sullivan from freeing Lucifer.

If they failed. Everything would be for nothing. The destruction and horrors he witnessed in the future would all come to exist. Michael brought the car off the country road and into the small carpark situated at the footpath to The Whangie.

The whole area was white with snow and there were dozens of parked cars. Connor Sullivan's cult, he figured. Michael's eyes squinted from the snow blinding him. He, Sarah and Nejuma parked the car and all of them got out. Michael frantically looked at his wristwatch, "18:01".

He knew if he ran, the chances were he could stop Connor before the ritual began. As Michael prepared himself to run down the path, the sky slowly became darker. What was strange was it only appeared to affect this area. The skyline in the distance was still daylight.

Michael jumped with fright, half a mile along the path, flames erupted up into the sky from behind a large rock. It burned rocks from where it had appeared. Something was wrong.

"Nejuma… What is going on here?" Michael feared the worst.

"He is here." Nejuma calmly replied. No, it couldn't be, Michael thought.

"No... We can't be... We didn't fail... We are here!" Michael cried. All of it was for nothing. Lucifer was free to bring on the apocalypse. Sarah held her husband in his despair.

Billions of people would die and it was all his fault.

"It's all still going to happen... The apocalypse, The Four Horsemen... Everything!" Michael furiously kicked the car door, leaving a dent in its side.

"Lucifer is not a full power." Nejuma responded.

"What does that mean, Nejuma?" He asked in frustration. Would it kill the angel to give him a straight answer? Michael thought.

"Lucifer has not been restored to his archangel form. He can be killed." Nejuma spoke in his calm manner. Michael didn't understand how he was capable of killing The Devil. His attempt to kill him with an archangel blade had been to no avail. Lucifer was impervious to bullets and knives.

How was Michael Hartnell supposed to kill what couldn't be killed?

"I've already tried to kill Lucifer. I used an archangel blade on him. If you happen to have all seven, feel free to cough them up." Michael was being out of line with Nejuma. He could no longer stand his attitude and answering questions which always begged more questions.

Their time was up, Michael wanted answers this minute. No more games or riddles.

"Michael, do not speak to me like I am foolish..." Nejuma's face was momentarily angry. He had not seen this side to the angel before. He didn't think him capable of such emotion from his previous lack of. He dared not speak against the guardian.

"When Lucifer was cast out. Most of his angelic abilities were stripped from his body." Nejuma told Michael without batting an eyelid.

"Lucifer is powerless?" Sarah asked with a sound of relief.

"Not completely. He still possesses some of his abilities. Whilst he is out of Hell. He does not possess his angelic immortality." Nejuma's words gave Michael an idea. He still had the gangster's gun in his possession. It was inside his leather jacket interior pocket.

Michael thought of everything he witnessed in the future, the world under Lucifer's rule and how the last of humanity struggled to survive. That was no future any human should ever have to bear.

Thou shalt not kill.

It was one of the ten commandments. Michael understood it was Lucifer's life or the world. He knew what must be done.

Michael Hartnell was going to kill The Devil.

"I can kill him?" Michael asked his guardian angel. He wondered if it was true and if it were, did he have that right?

"Yes." Nejuma nodded his head in agreement.

"You can't kill him, Michael. You don't have to... He isn't a threat." Sarah pleaded with Michael, begging him to not go through with his insane plan of murdering Lucifer. That's what it was, murder.

"Unfortunately, there is a way for Lucifer to restore his eternal life and his other angelic powers." Nejuma told them. Michael refused to accept this. There was still time to alter the future.

"How?" Michael needed to know how Lucifer was capable of becoming immortal.

"Lucifer will regain his eternal life with a ritual sacrifice and the drinking of The Antichrist's blood." Nejuma's words filled Michael with horror.

"If he kills someone and drinks Mammon's blood... He will... He will be here forever..." Michael couldn't bear the thought of it. An eternity with The Devil ruling over the human race.

Lucifer would rule this world with humans in hiding and struggling to be free of his sinister grip.

"Yes, Michael. You must stop him or billions will die." Nejuma's tone changed. He couldn't stress anymore how serious this is. Michael knew what must be done. He would kill Lucifer even if it cost him his own life. Sarah continued to plead with her husband.

"You don't have to kill him!" Michael saw the desperation in her eyes. She did not want him to kill anyone for the sake of his soul.

"Sarah, it's not only our lives at stake... It's the whole world... The people in the future need my help... Our grandson needs our help." Michael only realised he hadn't told Sarah about Tom.

Her face was filled with surprise by his revelation. There was a lot she did not know.

"What?" Sarah was stunned. Michael understood why. Children born in a world under Lucifer's rule. What kind of life it was for any child and for them as husband and wife to bring a child into the apocalypse?

"I am going to face Lucifer... I am ending this before it has a chance to begin." Michael declared, he was terrified and on edge. Adrenaline kept him clear which was good. He would use the energy from it to overcome his feelings and shoot Lucifer dead.

"I will be close by to guard you, Michael." Nejuma said with confidence. Michael knew despite the angel's lack of humanity, he would not fail to uphold his vow as a guardian.

"Sarah, I need you to stay here at the car. Should we not return. I want you to leave and get as far away from the city as you can..." Sarah then cut across Michael before could finish. He knew she wouldn't abandon him. Michael needed her to understand without question why he was telling her to do as he asked. It wasn't a request. It was a demand.

"Michael, I won't." Sarah was close to tears.

"If we don't come back... Lucifer has killed us. I need you to survive. Do not go back to Glasgow." Michael held his wife in his arms and kissed her forehead. He took in her scent, he was preparing to say goodbye. He knew if they failed to kill Lucifer, he and Nejuma would be killed and even if they succeeded, Mammon and any demons present would surely wish to have their vengeance for The Lord of Hell.

"I love you, Sarah Hartnell." Michael felt tears build up in his eyes. He let go of his wife and turned to begin his journey to The Gates of Hell. He heard Sarah's tears but would not allow himself to look at her. Michael knew if he did, he couldn't leave.

Nejuma's wings flew out from the neck of his trench coat he wore as he leapt up into the dark winter's sky. The light from The Whangie enlightened the entire surrounding area. Michael knew he was staring into the pits of the inferno, Hell.

It was a mortal sin to kill. He didn't seem to care. Lucifer may as well be baby Hitler. He would kill Lucifer without a moment's hesitation. Michael began his walk through the deep snow along the country path towards The Whangie and Lucifer. He pray to God he was not too late.

CHAPTER THIRTY-FIVE

THE DARK LORD OF HELL

THE WHANGIE

SCOTLAND

DECEMBER 25TH 2009

06:10pm

Lucifer clapped his hands at the sight of Mammon's handiwork. All members of Connor Sullivan's cult had been incinerated alive. Burnt to a crisp, Lucifer thought. He applauded Mammon's decision to burn them. Great minds think alike.

"You truly are my son... How does it feel?" Lucifer inquired. Mammon was part human, not that it matter. With time he would lose that side completely and become far greater than any human.

"I feel extraordinary, father. We will rule this world...I have prepared for your return. I became the President of the United States. With our combined powers and my presidency. We will rule this world till the end of time." Mammon without a shred of doubt was Lucifer's trueborn son. He possessed all the great thinking's of Lucifer and all the potential. He did feel Mammon still had much to learn. He would get there in time.

"President? You truly have exceeded yourself. We shall not require it. When I restore my immortality along with the rest of my abilities. I will be a God amongst the humans." Lucifer's power would be far greater than God's. All he needed was Mammon's blood.

He prepared for this moment for an eternity.

"How do you restore to full power, father?" Mammon sounded eager to help his father.

"With a ritual. You have already performed the first part." Lucifer chuckled at the sight of the black burnt corpses at their feet.

"And the next part, father?" Mammon was desperate to know.

"He drinks your blood as I cast a spell upon him, sealing the power inside him forever." Wormwood stepped forward to further explain the ritual to the young Antichrist. Mammon suddenly looked worried. His face filled with fright and confusion.

"Do I have to… die?" Mammon feared he would die so Lucifer could return to his former glory.

"No, of course not." Lucifer would never ask for Mammon's life. He was concerned that his son felt so.

"Tell me I won't die, father. I will give you as you command." Mammon declared with his brave face and loyalty to his father and lord. Lucifer wrapped his arms around his son before resting his palms upon Mammon's shoulders to look him in the eye as his equal.

"What kind of father would kill his own son?" Lucifer stated with love for his boy.

"God sent his son to die on a cross!" Mammon reminded Lucifer. He always found the story of the crucifixion hilarious. He laughed with amusement as he pictured Jesus Christ nailed to the cross.

"The Son of God, Jesus Christ… Never existed, a fairy tale to keep people in line. I promise you, all I require is less than a pint of your blood. You will heal as quickly as it is lost. Can you do that for me, son?" Lucifer politely asked of him. Mammon nodded his head in agreement before he rolled up his shirt sleeve.

"For you, father. I will do anything." Mammon declared. He dug his fingernail into his wrist, drawing blood from his veins. He held out the blood soaked wrist to his father, offering it up to Lucifer, who smiled before putting his lips to the wound. He began drinking the blood of The Antichrist.

Mammon winced in pain, the son of the fallen archangel had never endured pain of the flesh. He never would again, Lucifer thought. He was sorry for having to be in this situation to drink the blood of his own kin. It filled Lucifer with rage. Not toward Mammon but with God himself. It was he who had cast Lucifer to Hell and stripped him of his power.

Lucifer cursed the very thought of The Almighty for reducing him to this horrendous vile state. Lucifer pulled away from Mammon's wrist. He drank all he needed. Mammon's wrist injury healed by itself in a split second.

"How do you feel, my lord?" Wormwood asked Lucifer.

She looked concerned for his wellbeing. She need not worry. He felt a surge of energy pulse through his body. It worked, the sick and disgusting blood ritual was a success.

Lucifer, The Devil had been restored to his eternal life.

He wiped the excess blood from his lips with the back of his hand.

"I feel spectacular!" Lucifer declared as he pulled Wormwood closer to him, forcing a kiss upon her mouth. He had literally taken the witch-demon's breath away. She was stuck for words after he stopped kissing her.

"My lord... That..." Wormwood was speechless. Many would sell their souls for a kiss from The Devil.

"That was only a kiss, my dear Wormwood. Wait till later." He winked his eye in her direction. She smiled and giggled like a nervous college virgin, Lucifer thought. His own smile disappeared as he watched a young man emerge from the other side of The Whangie rock face.

The boy was white-skinned, wearing blue denim jeans, a white shirt with a black leather jacket. He held a gun in his right hand. Lucifer smiled with amusement. The boy's hand shook from the adrenaline. He obviously hadn't held a gun before, let alone pull the trigger.

The boy looked as if he saw a ghost when his eyes met Lucifer.

The portal from The Whangie was slowly closing. The boy looked horrified as he caught a glimpse into the pits of Hell. The raw power of eternal damnation. It was enough to drive anyone mad. The boy turned back to look upon Lucifer. It were as if he couldn't grasp reality of what was before him, Lucifer thought.

Tears stained his cold face, he had been crying and Lucifer knew if he pressed the right buttons. The young man would certainly cry once more.

"Lucifer!" He spoke the fallen archangel's name.

"Hello, Michael." Lucifer responded with a sinister grin. Lightning struck the top of The Whangie, creating a loud thunderous rumble. The portal closed completely, sealing the breaches between worlds. Michael was confused, it was written all over his stupid human face.

"How do you know my name?" Michael sounded worried as he made a demand of the dark lord.

"Wormwood told me you were coming. Michael Hartnell, the Christian set out to kill The Devil! Sounds like a great idea for a film." Lucifer mocked the young Christian. Mammon, Wormwood, and every demon present laughed at Michael.

The young foolish boy stood his ground in silence. This was not the first time he had been the laughingstock. He'd probably been bullied most of his pathetic little life.

"That was funny... Not as funny as this!" Michael had moves, Lucifer thought. He was a natural born gunslinger, he swiftly aimed the pistol and fired a perfect headshot at Lucifer. He applauded Michael's precision but it was all for nothing. The bullet flattened upon the impact with Lucifer's head before ricocheting into the rock wall.

Before Lucifer could further admire such skill and the audacity of Michael, Mammon flew for him and proceeded to beat the living shit out of him. Mammon stopped after a sharp blow to Michael's head. That would definitely be a concussion, Lucifer thought.

Michael was ever defiant. He stood to his feet but only barely. His left eye was sealed shut from a fist to the face, his nose was broken and blood ran from his lips. Michael seemed surprised by his shot at The Devil.

"How dare you try to hurt my father, you disgusting little maggot!" Mammon spat at Michael's face. He didn't flinch or wipe the saliva from his face.

"I don't understand... You are mortal." He shouted in despair at Lucifer.

"And who told you that?" Lucifer chuckled at Michael.

"I was. The funny thing about rituals, throw in a few burnt to a crisp cult corpses, blood drinking and voila, I am restored to my former glory!" Lucifer smiled menacingly at Michael. He didn't follow who Michael was. How did he come to learn of his return and most importantly why he thought he had the balls to try and prevent Lucifer's return!

Michael stood his ground and with all his strength and determination, with a struggle to breathe, he finally spoke.

"Jesus Christ, I summon you." Michael with all his energy shouted The Son of God's name in a futile attempt to summon him to The Whangie. Lucifer allowed for a moment of silence to further embarrass Michael. He laughed hysterically, Michael looked puzzled and concerned as to why the Nazarene failed to appear.

Lucifer turned to look at Mammon.

"You see, Mammon. Jesus Christ doesn't exist... A fairy tale!" Michael stared at Lucifer in horror. He seen the look upon Michael's stupid human face before on the faces of others who attempted to kill him. Michael had entered his presence with what he believed was an exceptional plan to kill The Devil, like so many had tried before him, only for it to all blow up in his face.

"Face it, Michael. You cannot defeat me. Stronger and better men than you have tried and failed horrendously!" Lucifer laughed. He was going to enjoy killing the young Christian, he was going to take it nice and slow to savour every moment before Michael died.

"Why?" Michael asked, confusing Lucifer.

"Why what?" Lucifer asked with a belittling snigger. He found Michael Hartnell pathetic. So much, he could barely contain himself.

"Why now?" Michael asked Lucifer, infuriating him for Michael was not being clear with the dark lord. Lucifer forgotten how slow and brainless humans were.

"Now what?" Lucifer hissed in fury, he was becoming impatient and almost ready to kill Michael with the snap of his fingers for trying his patience.

"You have had all of eternity... Why come back now?" Michael asked with desperation. Lucifer and Mammon laughed hysterically at his last question. Every demon at The Whangie burst into fits of laughter with their lord and prince.

"Is he serious?" Wormwood asked sarcastically.

"Oh, Michael... You've got some good knee-slappers. I'll give you that, boy." Lucifer snorted, this was the best joke he had heard for an eternity. Lucifer contained his hysterics and looked the fool in the face.

"Do you really think this was the first time anyone tried?" Lucifer said in a smug satisfaction. Michael didn't fully understand.

"Humans are so small minded. This wasn't the first time. That was actually in Pompeii in 79AD. You see, Michael. There are weak points in the world where the walls of reality are thin between dimensions. My demons failed to free me that day. However, they did unleash Hell upon the city of Pompeii."

Michael was horrified, Lucifer recognised he understood the significance of the location and the date in which he spoke of.

Lucifer's demons created the volcanic eruption from Mount Vesuvius, destroying Pompeii and killing thousands of people. A loss for Hell but a win at the same time, Lucifer thought. He despised humans. Lucifer felt like a James Bond villain telling Michael his devious plan. Unlike those idiots, Lucifer wouldn't fail to kill his adversary.

"Where they failed to release me. They couldn't attempt a second time. They attempted again to free me. This time in the North Atlantic Ocean. They were successful in creating a stable portal to Hell. Unfortunately, it only allowed entry to Hell, not out. Lots of people on your world found themselves stuck in Hell for eternity…. I believe sailors and pirates came to call this particular region of ocean as The Bermuda Triangle." Lucifer emphasised it to Michael to see its effect on his apelike face.

Michael looked stunned. He couldn't believe this wasn't the first attempt. Lucifer thought of the other attempts which Wormwood had filled him in on.

"Everything you know about the world and its history is a lie, Michael. My demons thought the third time would be the charm. It almost was. They found another weak spot and opened a portal in London in the year of 1666. It wasn't stable and unleashed hellfire upon the city, notoriously difficult to extinguish but not impossible." Lucifer chuckled, he heard that the government only recorded nine deaths from "The Great Fire of London". The good people of the world called him evil.

They didn't consider the lower class or people living in absolute poverty as casualties. Lucifer was right, the humans had no need of a God or a Devil for they were capable of their own wickedness.

Michael was repulsed by Lucifer. He was doing his best to conceal how he truly felt towards The Lord of Hell.

"Shall I continue with my little story down memory lane?" Lucifer laughed as Michael stood as still as a statue in horror at the truth.

"The fourth time was a little over a century ago. A very loud bang got everybody's attention in Siberia. The scientists and officials of your world were left baffled. There was nothing to explain what created such an explosive noise. A portal had opened then closed as fast as it had appeared. The end result… The Tunguska Explosion." Lucifer applauded and turned to his demons.

"Good work by the way. Fuck with the hairless apes' minds." Wormwood smiled and bowed her head as Lucifer complimented their work.

"In 1986, that Illuminati shower of fucktards were trying to destabilise the Soviet Union from the inside. My demons infiltrated them. They had tried magic and rituals. Wormwood was becoming impatient and decided to think outside the box." Lucifer pulled Wormwood in for a kiss, feeling her breasts with his free hand.

She drove Lucifer crazy, he would enjoy her company many times tonight. He chuckled before letting her go. She didn't get flustered as easily but the witch-demon enjoyed his touch.

Lucifer turned back to Michael, his face was a mess from Mammon's beating. His whole body trembled. He didn't know if Michael was cold or terrified.

"Wormwood decided to tackle it with a different perspective... Nuclear power! She tried to harness the power of opening a portal at Chernobyl... Let's just say it was extremely unstable and they blew up the reactor core, creating the disaster eventually leading to the end of the Soviet Union. The Dalton's could never have dreamt that idea up in a million years." Lucifer laughed as he saw how white Michael's face became.

A single tear ran down the boy's face. Lucifer enjoyed seeing him suffer and would put this pathetic little cunt out of his misery... Well, at least on Earth. An eternity in Hell would be extremely unpleasant to the little Christian, he thought.

"There was only one other attempt... Unfortunately, how can I put this delicately... There were two buildings in the way and they needed to be destroyed." Lucifer and his demons all laughed in unison as Michael retched the entire contents of his stomach.

"You killed... Thousands of people... You are a monster!" Michael spat on Lucifer's face, he merely wiped it away, sniggering at the petty human reactions and their feelings.

"I look forward to laughing at the footage later. Man... It's not every day you get to watch planes fly into the world trade centre." Lucifer laughed with amusement.

"Wormwood wasn't able to free me. It was successful. My Knights of Hell escaped and began to help her find... here."

Michael was pale from the cold of winter's bite and from vomiting his entire stomach. Yet, he still stood in Lucifer's presence with such hatred and defiance. He didn't make sense to Lucifer.

"I won't let you win!" Michael shouted with sheer hatred and terror at Lucifer.

"Michael, it's time to face reality and accept the hand you have been dealt... You cannot win against an enemy like me." Lucifer grinned with delight.

Suddenly an angel swooped down from the winter sky and knocked Wormwood off her feet. The trench coat wearing angel thrust his hand upon the witch-demon's face, a bright light emitted from the angel's hand.

Wormwood screamed in horror as the light consumed her entire body, catching fire, her screams were silenced as she is reduced to ashes. Lucifer's Knights of Hell prepared to retaliate. He held his hand up to delay their attack, he wanted to know the angel's identity.

Who would be so bold to kill The Devil's spell maker?

The angel stood up from the snow and faced The Lord of Hell. Lucifer was filled with a fiery fury upon seeing the face of Wormwood's killer.

"You?!" He spoke with surprise and disgust.

"You say we cannot win. It does not mean we cannot try." Nejuma spoke in defiance of Lucifer.

"My knights, bring me his fucking head!" Lucifer barked orders at his cloaked demons. All of Lucifer's demons flew towards Nejuma. He was stronger than Lucifer remembered. He knew his knights had no chance of survival against Nejuma, his strength was that of a guardian... He became a guardian angel?! They will give the position to any angel, Lucifer thought.

No matter, the knights would keep Nejuma busy for the time he needed to do what came next. Lucifer would reclaim the rest of his archangel abilities with Mammon's assistance. He turned and faced his son in a flash.

"You have to perform Wormwood's spell, my son. Chant it for me now!" Lucifer shouted with fear, in his current state, he himself would be incapable of taking on Nejuma.

Mammon gripped both sides of Lucifer's head before chanting the final part of the ritual. Lucifer felt it, the feeling of absolute and unlimited power flowing into his weakened body.

Michael watched in terror, Lucifer winked at him. His way of saying "I win.". The boy sobbed hysterically, knowing nothing would stop Lucifer now or ever. Nejuma had manage to kill all the demons who called themselves, The Knights of Hell. He attempted to reach Lucifer, kill him before the spell was completed.

Too late, Lucifer thought. He smiled like the Cheshire cat, his entire body became engulfed in flames. Mammon was thrown to the snow from the sudden blast wave from Lucifer's restoration to the height of his power.

The flames died as fast as they had engulfed The Lord of Hell. The ground around Lucifer was damp. The fires melted the snow. He felt as high as a kite. It was truly good to be back.

"Father…" Mammon was left speechless, he could obviously feel the power before him, which flowed through Lucifer, The Lord of the Earth. He became the most powerful being to ever walk this planet and all of creation. Lucifer was more powerful than The Almighty God.

"I am back!" He chuckled with satisfaction. He looked upon Michael's stupid face. He became accustomed to watching him squirm and would hope to continue it if he is to survive what happens today. He came with an angel. Not just any angel.

Michael Hartnell came here with Nejuma… Lucifer's sworn enemy!

Lucifer looked forward to his and Michael's next encounter. Whenever that may be.

"See you around, Michael." Lucifer laughed hysterically before he and Mammon used the powers of Hell to teleport away. Their bodies burst into flames and Lucifer briefly heard Michael's anguish before departing The Whangie.

It was time for his first target.

The city of Glasgow would fall… Then the world.

CHAPTER THIRTY-SIX

GRUPPENFUHRER DIETER SCHMIDT

BERLIN, GERMANY
NOVEMBER 11TH 1944
11:39pm

THE HEIGHT OF THE SECOND WORLD WAR

War had torn the world apart. Dieter Schmidt walked with his fellow officer through the deserted streets of Berlin. They spent the evening celebrating his promotion to Gruppenfuhrer. The streets were soaked from a downpour of rain throughout the day. Better it to be rain falling from the sky than the alternative: British bombs.

Schmidt truly enjoyed his evening. They drank their fill and were enjoying a cigarette on their walk through the city. Berlin was once an extraordinary city. It still was, despite its being at the centre of the whole world's attention.

He loved his country and the work they were doing, the filth had to be exterminated like the vermin they were. The British and the Americans were on the losing side of history, he thought.

The Nazi had yet to occupy Great Britain and hadn't so much as set foot in the United States like they had done with all of Europe. One day soon, the whole world shall be the Fatherland and Gruppenfuhrer Schmidt would stand side by side with the Fuhrer, Adolf Hitler, when he became the leader of an empire greater than the Romans could ever have hoped or dreamt to comprehend.

The streets were dimly lit as they continued walking downhill where homes and local businesses had once housed the filth… Jews! Wicked creatures, he cursed the thought of them.

The young officer, Klaus spoke to Schmidt of their night as they walked at a brisk pace to try and ignore how cold they felt. Schmidt laughed as Klaus spoke when he recalled a memory of their night of drinking.

His breath could be seen in the cold frosty air. Winters were harsh.

Their laughing ceases, faster than the beat of their hearts, the streetlights behind them suddenly go out, descending the entire street into darkness. The Nazi officers see no-one. They are unable to see their own hands in the pitch black. Schmidt feels something brush past him, his eyes slowly adjusted to the dark.

The young officer, Klaus. He was nowhere to be seen.

"Klaus?!" Dieter Schmidt exclaimed in panic. Where had his officer disappeared to? The sound of something heavy being dropped from the rooftops made Schmidt jump from fright. He felt his heartbeat in the back of his head as he approached what had fallen from above.

Whatever it was, it lay in the middle of the street. As he and the object became closer, Schmidt realised it was a body... Klaus' body!

Klaus' face was lifeless, he was pale. The Gruppenfuhrer didn't understand how someone could have killed him in such a manner, there hadn't been a sound or any sign of another person on the street besides from the two Nazi. Schmidt knelt beside the corpse to try and understand how Klaus had been murdered.

That's when he saw it, two small puncture wounds to the throat. Schmidt jumped to his feet in horror and prepared to flee. It was too late. The moment he turned to run back up the street, he stared into the eyes of Klaus' killer, a creature from the depths of Hell.

The murderer's face was soaked in blood.

"Hello." The vampire calmly greeted him before plunging his fangs into the Gruppenfuhrer's neck. The vampire was strong, he held onto Schmidt whilst he gorged on his blood.

Dieter Schmidt was in such agony, it was almost too painful to make any sound or call for help. From his sudden blood loss, he lost consciousness and the newly promoted Gruppenfuhrer Dieter Schmidt was dead.

CHAPTER THIRTY-SEVEN

BEN ARMSTRONG

BERLIN, GERMANY
NOVEMBER 11TH 1944
11:46pm

THE HEIGHT OF THE SECOND WORLD WAR

Ben Armstrong loosened his grip on the Nazi Gruppenfuhrer he killed. Ben was on the verge of starvation. The second world war had made it extremely difficult to consume what he required to survive. Blood was scarce. He acquired what he needed from the blood of wild animals and with the state of his home country from this war, animal blood was hard to come by.

Ben made the decision to go after a different kind of animal… The Nazi! And where better to find them than the rat's nest itself, Berlin.

"Bastards!" Ben cursed them whilst he stared upon the corpses of the Nazi officers he killed. The despicable acts these monsters had committed upon human beings in the camps, lost them any right to be human. They were fair game to Ben. They were the only humans he fed from. He would never take an innocent life.

So long as they occupy Europe, Ben would continue to feed off them and drink them dry. Ben Armstrong had witnessed many horrific things over the last century, but this war was the very worst of humanity to ever come into existence. Many believed it was only the Jews that these bigots were killing.

They were killing men, women, and children all for the colour of their skin too. Many black people as well as homosexual people were also being murdered in the camps. The Nazi were far worse than anything the vampires ever done.

Ben learnt all the history of his own kind after he lost Penelope, he never found her after that fateful night. The reason why he couldn't step through into his home was due to vampires having to be invited into a human home with their permission.

269

Penelope had indeed invited him in when she barked at him so she could give him a scolding for being drunk. Ben replayed that night in his head over and over every day. He doubted he would ever clap eyes upon his wife for as long as he walked this world.

Ben was brought back to reality as someone behind him, clapped their hands together, slowly. Like they were mocking what he done. Ben prepared himself to kill whoever stood behind him. If he allowed whoever it may be to speak, it could prove fatal for him.

The Nazi Gruppenfuhrer knew what Ben was, almost as if he'd seen vampires before tonight. Ben turned and prepared to throw a concealed blade at his applauder, he was taken by surprise to the man's identity. It was a face he would never forget. He had dyed his hair and was dressed in the S.S. uniform.

That didn't change anything. Ben still knew him and the officer knew him. Ben froze as he was taken aback. Never in a million years did he think their paths would cross.

"Nick?!" Ben spoke his maker's name in shock.

"Surprised? I always knew we'd meet again. Over a century though. Astonishing! How do you do?" Nick greeted him with the charm act he always seemed to possess whenever he spoke.

"What do you want?" Ben demanded.

"Isn't it obvious? I am a Nazi!" Nick responded, as if his answer made sense, Ben thought.

"I gathered that!" Ben stated, it didn't take a genius to figure that out. Nick had made his way out to Europe, where for all Ben knew had been living in for decades before joining the Nazi.

"More to the point. I am vampire with connections. Look at me. Do I look like I am starving?" Nick pointed out a fact, vampires do begin to show signs of deterioration from lack of blood. Where was he acquiring blood? Did Ben truly want to know?

"You should join us?" Nick suggested an alliance, if Ben were capable of vomiting, he surely would have. The thought of joining the Nazi made him feel sick in his gut.

"I won't join those crackpot fanatic fascists!" Ben cursed the very thought and the Nazi for everything they stood for.

"No, not them… Join us." Nick spoke as he turned to his side to look behind him, down the dark street. Out of the shadows, two female Nazi officers emerged dressed in uniform. Ben immediately recognised one of them as Anna. The other filled him with horror. She had long blonde hair, he longed to see her again but not like this.

"Penelope?" Ben asked in confusion. It was a trick. She couldn't be real!

"Long time no see, lover." Penelope spoke, she bit her lip seductively as she stared at Ben.

"You are with them?!" He asked in disgust. Why would she join them and however did she cross paths with these abominations?

"I found them on that fateful night. The night you turned me… They are real vampires! They know how to have fun and take what they want, whenever they want." Penelope spoke, mad with power. He'd seen this before in men with less strength than her.

Her being a vampire didn't mix well. She was still his wife. Penelope was still in there somewhere. He wanted to believe it so badly.

"Look at the state of you. A God among the humans, reduced to drinking the blood of filth, animals, and Nazi. What a disappointment!" Penelope looked down at Ben. He was like shit on the sole of her shoe.

"I will not end an innocent life. Not even at the cost of sustaining my own." Ben defended his actions. No human had to die so he could live. The Nazi were different. They would enslave the world if they were to win this horrendous war. All three of the Nazi uniformed vampires laughed at Ben's justifications. Nick shook off his humour and became serious.

"Come with us, my friend. You don't want to be drinking that blood. We have plenty to share with you. Join us, Ben." Nick extended his hand in the hopes of cutting a deal with Ben. He was not for having it. They were not shy in admitting to gorging on human blood.

The second world war was at its height, Ben had to wonder what they could possibly be consuming if they were not surviving on animal or Nazi blood.

"I struggle to get by. I've had to resort to drinking these bastards dry to survive. It begs the question. What exactly have you been drinking?" Ben knew this was probably best left unanswered. They were monsters.

"We drink those they capture." Anna spoke with delight. Capture? Who did she mean? Ben realised. It explained a bit, why Gruppenfuhrer Schmidt knew what Ben was. The Nazi knew about the existence of vampires.

"They know what you are?!" Ben exclaimed in horror. He dreaded to think what Hitler would do with such knowledge. Vampire soldiers, assassins, the horrific possibilities were endless to do what The Third Reich were capable of. The world would fall with vampires fighting on Hitler's side.

"Know?! God! Course they know! That isn't the half of it!" Penelope blurted out, speaking to Ben like a naïve child.

What was happening behind the scenes of this war?

Ben clearly had stumbled upon the tip of the iceberg, something bigger was at play. His main concern was whatever it may be could have ramifications for the vampires. Ben didn't want Penelope mixed up in this madness. He had to get his wife away from these monsters.

"Penelope Gallagher Armstrong." Ben addressed his wife by her full legal and married name. It got her attention. She no longer had a smile on her face and her laughing ceased.

"I know you may not feel like it or you are trying to rid yourself of it… I know, deep down you are still the same woman I fell in love with. You are the woman I wanted to grow old and have children with… I know you remember that. These acts you speak of are evil… The woman I know, she would never do such vile acts." Ben held out his hand to her. He had everyone's attention.

Penelope looked visibly stunned by his words, he was begging her to see reason and it appeared to be working. For the first time in over a century, he saw his wife, not the vampire she became, his beautiful wife who he loved more than anything in the world.

"Come with me, please… You can change and we can still be together." Ben pleaded with Penelope, his hand still hanging, praying she would reach for him. Nick and Anna looked to Penelope, concerned for where her true loyalties lay, Ben thought.

Penelope burst into hysterical laughter. Ben let his hand drop to his side. Nick stepped forward, shaking his head from side to side with a smirk on his face. He stood his ground by Penelope's side and looked directly at Ben.

"Sorry, mate. She's my wife now." Nick spoke with pride.

"Second wife!" Anna interrupted, she sounded envious.

"Yes, dear." Nick said in a sarcastic tone to keep peace with Anna. Nick pulls Penelope towards him by her waist. Ben watches with disgust as they begin to passionately kiss in front of him. Penelope keeps her eyes on Ben as she kisses Nick.

Ben felt uneasy and filled with rage as his maker kissed his wife, Ben's worst nightmare. The woman he loved in the arms of the man he hated most. He can no longer stand to witness it any further, he reaches inside his jacket for his wooden stake and with a tight grip, Ben screamed and charged towards his maker and Penelope.

They see him coming and narrowly avoid him, jumping aside to escape his wrath. Anna, who had been standing behind them was less fortunate. Ben plunged the stake into her chest, blood spurted from her mouth, the stake hadn't gone all the way in.

Ben released his grip on the sharp stake before taking his fist to the exposed wood, forcing the stake into Anna's heart. She screamed as her entire body burst into flames, incinerating every inch of her. All that remained of her was dust.

"NO! I WILL FUCKING KILL YOU!!!" Nick screamed at Ben with fury. He looked like a man on a warpath and close to tears. No tears would come for him. The curse of being a vampire. Crying was for the living. Penelope held Nick back, Ben was ready to kill them both.

Penelope was no longer the woman he married. Ben Armstrong's wife was dead.

"You bastard!" Penelope cursed Ben. He points the stake towards them, Ben had to kill them for what he felt.

"You're next!" Ben declared in a cold tone, he would relish in their deaths. Nick looked behind him, he was planning to flee. He knew there was no fight between him and Ben in which he would come out victorious.

"We will meet again... Don't know where." Nick winked at Ben before he and his vampire Nazi bride sped off on foot into the darkness of Berlin. Ben did not pursue them. The problem lay within The Third Reich. The Nazi were supplying vampires with an unlimited supply of blood from Jewish citizens they had rounded up and thrown into the concentration camps.

273

The only way this horror was ever going to end would be for this war to reach an ally victory. Ben knew what he had to accomplish. He planned to cut the head off the serpent.

Ben Armstrong was going to hunt down and kill Adolf Hitler.

CHAPTER THIRTY-EIGHT

THE MASTER OF THE DARK ARTS
SECOND IN COMMAND OF THE ILLUMINATI

RICHARD SYME

AURORA AIRCRAFT LOUNGE
DECEMBER 25TH 2009
LOCATION: CLASSIFIED
TIME: UNKNOWN

Richard Syme was seated in a luxurious private aircraft lounge. The floor was carpeted with the finest materials from Carlisle's favourite countries. The chairs they sat in were made from genuine leather. He had always been a snob when it came to travelling by air. He liked his comforts.

Lord Carlisle Dalton would be doing as he pleased come the day's end. He would become the conqueror who seized control of the planet in a single day. Richard felt uneasy and unable to relax. He couldn't understand how or why his brother was so calm.

They were already in the air, the other side of the globe. The aircraft they were travelling in was experimental and faster than any other plane in the world. If Carlisle's plan crashed and burned, no-one would ever be able to catch them. Lord Dalton was seated, slurping a glass of scotch, not a care in the world. He probably felt it was well earned after his broadcast to the people he would soon rule over as an emperor.

Richard kept his thoughts to himself. Other members of The Illuminati were no doubt nearby in other rooms within the plane. Richard sat in silence and had done so since they boarded.

"Not long, little brother." Carlisle spoke in between sips of his drink. Richard jumped with fright and filled with fear for his own life from being addressed in such a manner.

Richard had a rapid glance over his shoulder, praying nobody heard Carlisle call him "brother".

"Relax, Richard. You should see the look on your face. The room is soundproof." Carlisle shrugged it off, gulping the rest of his glass before getting to his feet. He walked towards the built in bar in the corner of the lounge. Carlisle poured himself and Richard a glass of scotch.

He spoke as he poured the drinks, the whole time without turning to look upon his brother.

"Why so quiet, Richard?" Lord Dalton asked with concern. Had Richard been so obvious for Carlisle to pick up on his behaviour?

"No reason." Richard responded in his best attempt to hide his fear. Carlisle walked back over to their seats and handed Richard his glass. Carlisle looked him in the eye from where he stood, looking down at his brother. Lord Carlisle Dalton had not believed a word he said.

"Speak freely, Richard. I always know when you are lying." Carlisle spoke sternly before seating himself in his own leather chair. He took a drink from his scotch without blinking. Carlisle kept his eyes on Richard.

"It's... just." Richard stammered before drinking some of his own scotch.

"I can't believe this aircraft exists." Richard said with false appreciation to avoid his true feelings.

"Oh, yeah. I understand." Carlisle said as he enjoyed a swirl of scotch.

"I wanted it to be a surprise. This jet is the experimental aircraft, Project Aurora. Capable of speeds of up to eight thousand miles per hour." Carlisle stated the facts with a raised eyebrow to show how impressive the aircraft was. He enjoyed explaining what made this plane special.

"We are travelling so fast that by the time the first capital city is obliterated. We will be half-way around the globe. Safe and sound in here." Carlisle paused as he had another mouthful of whisky from his crystal glass.

"We'll keep dropping nukes until the rest of the world gets the message. Once they see what will happen in an hours-time. They will have no choice but to surrender their governments to us, out of fear they themselves will burn in a nuclear fire. We will have our order before the day is done." Carlisle sounded so sure, completely confident that this extreme and insane plan would actually succeed.

Richard spoke his mind before Carlisle decided to have any more whisky.

"Suppose they don't surrender?" Richard asked, this was clearly a factor which Carlisle, no doubt had never ever thought to consider as a possibility.

"What are you saying, Richard?" Carlisle asked for an explanation to what he deemed an absurd question.

"We are planning to drop a weapon of mass destruction upon a random capital city… Realistically, the world is not going to welcome us with opened arms from a single attack… If we do this, lots of cities are going to be destroyed, countless lives will be lost before they even consider a global surrender… There will be no-one left to rule over… You are giving them the motivation to hunt us down!" Richard implored his brother to see reason. There had to be another way.

Anything but the horrors which were yet to come. Carlisle laughed at Richard's pleas.

"Little brother, you forget we have moles inside every government and military. We outnumber them. Should the rest of the world refuse to surrender and pledge fealty to me. I will take this world by fucking force if I have to!" Carlisle downed the rest of his drink in one gulp before jumping out of his chair and proceeding towards the bar.

He slammed his glass down on the counter so hard, Richard thought it might shatter. Carlisle was angry and impatient. He was drinking too much. His thoughts were not good, he swiftly grabbed a bottle of scotch from his stocked up liquor cabinet.

Carlisle poured himself another glass and without looking at Richard, he drank the contents of the crystal glass in one go. Carlisle turned to face his brother. Richard had never seen him this way before. He felt more scared now than he ever did in his entire life.

"Besides, if they don't surrender after the first attack, I would be amazed… The first target is Washington D.C."

RICHARD SYME

LOCATION: CLASSIFIED

DECEMBER 25th 2006

06:00pm

Richard sat with his brother, Lord Carlisle Dalton in the candlelit room of the Illuminati vault. He and his lord and brother were seated at the head of The High Table. They sat at the enormous black marble table.

The meeting had not long since adjourned. Carlisle had brought out a bottle of the "good stuff", always a rare scotch.

"Another year already, Richard." Carlisle said, no doubt feeling his age.

"It's a good plan. Unfortunately, it will be five years before we can implement The Armageddon Protocols. It's a lot of work to take on even for us." Richard tried to stress to Lord Dalton. This plan was one not to be taken for granted. One slip and it was over.

Time would have to be on their side. If this were to be rushed it would all come crashing down like a house of cards.

"We'll get there in half the time if all goes well. Can it be done in two years? Three at the max?" Carlisle was an impatient leader, he always had been. Time was precious to him. Richard respected his leadership but not at the cost of setting in motion a premature operation, which could have severe consequences for the entire new world order if it backfired.

"Lord Dalton, I cannot stress the timing of an operation this size, that being said, I will do my best to see what can be done in the next three years… But, I need you to promise me something… Is this room secure?" Richard asked to ensure their survival before he uttered another word.

"Is the Pope a catholic?" Carlisle jokingly responded.

Richard pulled a face of disapproval.

"Course he isn't. He is one of us… Yes, all joking aside. This is the most secure room on the planet. Speak freely." Carlisle patiently waited to hear what Richard deemed so dangerous.

"When we implement these protocols. If it gets out of hand, no matter what damage has been done… We stop whatever we are doing and walk away from all of this." Richard wanted his brother to accept, putting aside his pride and if the day where they were faced with the possibility of going into hiding or choosing death. He hoped his brother would agree.

"You want to stop if we go too far?!" Carlisle was outraged at the thought. Richard knew how much the new world order meant to Carlisle, as long as he heard him out it would be better than nothing.

"Would you care to elaborate as to why I would choose to walk away from all this?" Carlisle was finding Richard's thoughts amusing and waited to hear whatever ridiculous ideas came out of his mouth next.

"In the unlikely event, if we were in a situation where neither of us will rule…" Richard feared for his brother's life, all he ever wanted was to see Carlisle as the head of a new world. The last thing he wished to endure was to witness Carlisle's death in pursuit of this dream.

"Ah! I see. In the event we die in the process." Carlisle wasn't taking this seriously. Richard's patience was wearing thin. He contained his frustrations towards his brother, he was after all, The Lord of The High Table and was due the respect which came with it.

"I am serious, Carlisle!" Richard could no longer hide how he felt about Carlisle mocking him.

"Remember the title when you address me… So I am clear. You are asking me to assume a different identity and live, what kind of life?" Carlisle seemed genuine to Richard's request and wanted to know everything on his mind.

"One where we shall live." Richard knew if any other members of The Illuminati heard a word of this conversation, neither of them would see the light of day. Carlisle was different, he was Richard's brother, despite him being an illegitimate bastard of the previous Lord Dalton and Carlisle being a trueborn son. They were still brothers.

"You have my promise, Richard. Should the day come, we will walk away from The Illuminati." Carlisle's word was not sufficient.

Richard required something stronger. Words were meaningless. Actions spoke volumes. Richard reached inside his suit jacket and placed a dagger on the marble table. The dagger was razor sharp and the name "Illuminati" is engraved on the blade, the hilt was decorated and had a pyramid with an eye in its centre, the symbol of the new world order.

"Swear it in the blood of House Dalton." Richard demanded. This was an oath which no member could refuse to act on. Not one single member would dare violate it and no-one is exempt, not even The Lord of The Illuminati. Lord Carlisle Dalton chuckled in disbelief, a move so bold would forfeit the life of most men.

Carlisle reached across the table for the knife with his right hand, he used the blade to cut a small wound in the palm of his left hand. Carlisle grunted as he slashed his palm open. He turned the blade to allow Richard to take hold of the hilt. Richard grasped it before proceeding to the same as his brother.

Lord Dalton held his blood soaked hand out to Richard, the master of the dark arts, the brothers shook with bloody palms.

"I, Lord Carlisle Dalton, swear upon the blood of House Dalton and the new world order." Carlisle let his grip of Richard's hand loosen and the deal was made.

The brothers sealed the oath in blood to walk away from The Illuminati if the day shall come to pass.

CHAPTER THIRTY-NINE

MICHAEL HARTNELL

THE WHANGIE

SCOTLAND

DECEMBER 25TH 2009

06:31pm

Michael Hartnell fell to his knees in the deep snow, his sight was poorly from the severe beaten he had taken from the hands of Mammon. His head throbbed from the pain. He couldn't focus on that. It was not his highest concern. He felt horrendous from what happened.

Everything was for nothing. Lucifer was free and restored to the height of his power. The apocalyptic horrors of the future were all going to come true. He had failed to alter the course of history, dooming countless lives to a fate worse than death.

Sarah knelt beside Michael in his despair, whatever words she said in an attempt to console him, he heard none of them. His mind was everywhere else but in the present moment. He thought about everything he endured and what the world would soon come to bear.

Michael couldn't have said if he knelt in the snow for a minute, an hour, a day, or a year. Time was slowly passing by as he stared directly in the direction of his hometown of Glasgow.

He couldn't help how he felt, tears stained his face. The thought of the streets being overrun with demons, hell hounds, and infected filled Michael with grief. He would be responsible for all the suffering and deaths of billions under Lucifer's rule.

Michael Hartnell had been given the gift of a second chance and he wasted it.

It was the present he affected but with Lucifer's manipulation in the future, he allowed The Four Horsemen to be free. Michael got an idea, a dangerous idea. He no longer cared about his own life, not if he could stop Lucifer, once and for all.

The angel stood over Michael. Nejuma was as still as a statue and silent as always. He was an angel of few words, Michael thought.

"We need to find somewhere safe, Michael." Nejuma calmly informed him. Michael would never be safe for as long as Lucifer lived.

It was time to ask a favour of his guardian angel.

"Nejuma, you are sworn to protect me and my family at all costs?" Michael inquired, he needed to fully understand the extent of Nejuma's role as a guardian.

"Yes, Michael. I swore an oath before The Lord Jesus Christ, in the name of Heaven, God and all his angels, to protect and follow your commands even at the cost of my own life." Nejuma spoke with emotion. He sounded proud to be a guardian angel.

"And if I were to ask you a favour, you would be bound by your oath to honour it?" Michael knew it was wrong to deceive the angel, tricking him into revealing his duties, especially for what he required the angel to do.

"I am obligated to follow your commands or risk being stripped of my position and cast into the eternal fires of Hell." Nejuma responded. He didn't sound proud this time. He seemed suspicious of Michael's intentions.

"Back when we first met, I recall you saying, God sent you to return me to my own time period." Michael immediately saw the fear appear on Nejuma's face. He realised the angel did feel scared after all. He would have to be stupid if he were not afraid of what Michael was about to command of him.

"Michael, I know what it is you will ask of me. I am sorry. I cannot do that. Your life is of the upmost importance. Do not command it of me!" Nejuma pleaded in terror. Michael inhaled, once he spoke it, he will reach the point of no return. He would need to see it through till the end.

"Nejuma, I command you to take me back to 2059." Michael gave the guardian angel the command to return him to the horrors of the future.

TO BE CONTINUED

MICHAEL HARTNELL WILL RETURN

THE END CONTINUES…

An excerpt from

THE END: THE LAST DAY

By ROBERT T.C. ROONEY

THE FALLEN GOD

THE ROOFTOP
CITY CHAMBERS
GLASGOW, SCOTLAND
DECEMBER 25TH 2009
07:00pm

Lucifer's flames scorched the rooftop surface as he materialised. He scrubbed up well, he thought. Lucifer enjoyed freshening up, he was finished with Hell and scrubbed his skin raw to rid himself of its foul stench of sulphur and brimstone. He cut his hair short, his light brown hair had become dark as tar. He treated himself to a suit, his measurements had been arranged on his behalf. He acquired a tailor to make him new suits. A different one for each day, he thought.

He liked the Italian silks and had his suit made to conceal his damaged angelic wings. He also had it designed for compartments to store knives. Nothing better than up close and personal with a blade between the ribs, he smiled at the fun he was having.

Most of his wounds from Hell had healed all but the exception of his wings. He was curious as to why. Why they remained burnt and featherless. Hell's damage to his body deformed him. Already he silenced demons for making a mockery of his image. He allowed only one of those demons to live, in order for the rest of his army to know, Lucifer would take no prisoners if his appearance were to be joked of. It would spread like wildfire. They will soon remember their places. He hated his face, so thin and almost skeletal. He needed to do something about that in time. Perhaps a beard, he thought.

Today, marked the beginning of a new era and it was time to address his cattle. Lucifer felt his body fill with energy as he prepared to address every single pathetic human upon the Earth.

"People of the world. Do you believe in me?" Lucifer's voice was incredibly loud, he knew every living creature heard him speak, lambs to the slaughter, he thought. Lucifer smiled like the Cheshire cat. Nothing could stop him now. He thought of God, the old man. He hoped God would have shown himself, preventing Lucifer from reaching this stage of power... The coward failed to show his face, confirming what Lucifer believed all along.

God did not care, now or ever.

"If you do not believe I exist. You should! I am Lucifer. I now walk amongst you." Lucifer declared to the world. Below him, on Glasgow's George Square, people were fleeing in a futile attempt to save their own worthless hides.

"God will not save you… He does not care about any of you!" Lucifer spread his toxic pestilence throughout the world.

"I am running things now! By the power invested in me by… Me! I declare myself, The Lord of The Earth!" Lucifer shouted across the entire planet, he felt the fear of the hairless apes and he liked it. He liked it a lot.

"If you wish to declare fealty to me and live… Kill a Christian! Those who hunt the Christians and slaughter them! You will be welcomed with open arms into my new dominion." Lucifer sniggered from the power he felt. He controlled the world, the most powerful creature in existence.

He is The Lord of Hell and The Earth.

One day, he would seize control of Heaven from his father. One day at a time, he thought. Screams filled the air. The city was being purged of its filth, his father's favourites, the children of God.

Christianity would become a distant memory come the day's end. Lucifer would be the only God worshipped from this day forth. He liked the thought of it. He deemed himself better than The Almighty and it was time to exact his revenge for the years he spent burning in the pits of Hell's eternal flames.

"My father or God. He once said, "Let there be light.". I say, let there be darkness!" Lucifer screamed, reaching out with one hand into the sky, his eyes turned red as blood, he strained himself with all his might.

A light blasted from the sky directly into his hand. It flew towards him like a shooting star. The beam of light ceased. His whole body shuddered as he felt its energy. He stared into his hand with a smile so sinister.

"The power of the sun in the palm of my hand." Lucifer chuckled with delight. He held the solar system's sun in his grip. The Devil blew his breath onto the miniature ball of light, extinguishing it forever. Lucifer had taken away the sun, he watched as the sky erupted into flames, raining down fire upon the world.

LUCIFER WILL RETURN

ACKNOWLEDGEMENTS

I wish to thank you for taking the time to read this story and I hope to see you for:

"THE END: THE LAST DAY"

I wish to thank my amazing wife, Gillian, for always being there and supporting me throughout my entire writing process. You and Pip are everything to me. I would be lost without you.

I wish to thank my father, Robert Rooney snr. You have always told me great stories and I feel without your being there, this story wouldn't have come to be.

Scott Webster, I thank you. You were the first person to ever read about these characters and their story. Thank you for entertaining my madness. It encouraged me to keep on writing. Scott is also a successful writer, please look out for his novel "Dancing With Devils", it is a terrific read.

Leanne White, I thank you and hope you'll have the time to enjoy this book on your next flight to wherever they send you. You were the first reader to cry and shout at me for killing characters. Thank you.

Deborah Carmichael, my mentor in all things drama and creative writing. I thank you for your advice and I remember these words now and will till my last day

"This story is remarkable. A lot of people are going to wish it were theirs. It has the potential to transport you from an ordinary life to an extraordinary one." Thank you, Debbie.

I wish to express my gratitude to my aunt whose name I will not disclose because I strongly believe her to be a spy for one of the intelligence agencies. I thank you as you coined the name "Good Vs Evil" for the title of this series.

I want to thank my friend, David Clark, for his reading of my scripts and listening to the ravings of his mad friend as I conjured up the outlines for this novel series.

I doubt he will see this but I wish to thank "Prison Break" actor, Robert Knepper. You are the inspiration behind the creation of Lucifer. If this series were ever to be adapted for film or TV, I want you to play the part. I cannot picture anyone else in the role.

I thank, God, for blessing me with an extraordinary imagination and I know he wants us all to do well in life. I would encourage everyone at some stage in their life to have a shot at writing.

Till next time…

Robert T.C. Rooney

Other Works By The Author

Novels

The End: Hell on Earth

The End: The Last Day (Coming 2022)

Plays

Eat It N Beat It: The Worst Café in Scotland (Lulu Publishing)

Service With A Smile: The Sleaziest Café in Scotland (Lulu Publishing)

Charlie: The Tail of a Stupid Dog (Lulu Publishing)

Penny (Lulu Publishing)

A Walk Along The Canal (Coming August 2020)

Newhouse (Coming November 2020)

Short Stories

Good Vs Evil: The Complete Collection (Lulu Publishing)

Desire (Lulu Publishing)

Saving The World (Coming Soon)

Printed in Dunstable, United Kingdom

76661093R00168